The Petty Demon

FYODOR SOLOGUB

The Petty Demon

TRANSLATED FROM THE RUSSIAN, WITH A PREFACE
AND NOTES, BY *Andrew Field*

INTRODUCTION BY *Ernest J. Simmons*

INDIANA UNIVERSITY PRESS
Bloomington and London

"I wished to burn her, the wicked witch."

Introduction

By the 1890's, the great age of realism in Russian literature had run its course. Dostoevsky died in 1881, Turgenev two years later, and though the giant Tolstoy
continued to live on to 1910, he had long since turned
his back on art. The many writers that followed seemed
to represent an exhausted strain, and among them only
Chekhov stood out as a figure of major dimensions. In
short, the times were ripe for a revolt against the realistic trend which had dominated literature for some
fifty years and had encouraged readers to believe that
the purpose of poetry, fiction, and drama was not only
to create beauty and to entertain, but also to instruct
and make them conscious of social and political problems.

The new movement that arose in the 1890's to chal-
lenge realism transformed the cultural pattern of Russia, for it brought about significant changes not only in
literature and criticism, but also in the theater, ballet,
and in the plastic arts. In its initial stages the movement
was labeled "decadent" and later "symbolist," but what-
ever the designation, its adherents seemed determined
to formulate an entirely new aesthetic credo. Though
the Russian writers were admirers of Western symbolism, and somewhat influenced by it, they went their
own way in revolting against realism. They developed
aestheticism and encouraged an antisocial posture in the
arts that often took the form of extreme impressionism.
Combining great talent with conscious craftsmanship,

they stressed the emotional value of the form and sound of words instead of their exact meaning.

In the first generation of symbolists ("decadent" is more generically descriptive than defining in terms of the literary qualities of the members of this movement), which included such celebrated authors as Merezhkovsky, Balmont, Bryusov, and Rozanov, the most talented was unquestionably Fyodor Sologub. In fact, except for Alexander Blok, who belonged to the younger generation of symbolists, Sologub may be regarded as the greatest and most refined poet in a movement that contained a veritable nest of singing birds who rescued Russian verse from a hopeless state of mediocrity and elevated it once again to the lofty level of the Golden Age of Russian poetry of some sixty years earlier. In addition, Sologub was the only one of the symbolists poets to succeed supremely well in the novel, although several of these writers attempted fiction.

Unlike his fellow-symbolists, Sologub, who was born Fyodor Kuz'mich Teternikov in Petersburg in 1863, came from a working-class family. His father died when the son was quite young and his mother was compelled to hire herself out as a chambermaid. Her master, however, took an interest in her precocious boy and made it possible for him to receive an education up through the level of a pedagogical institute. After graduation he obtained a position as a teacher in a small provincial town. For a man with his interests, tastes, and talents, this poor and dull life as a provincial schoolmaster was an unhappy one and left its scars on him. Yet, unlike that other provincial schoolmaster, Peredonov, the central figure in *The Petty Demon*, Sologub succeeded well enough to win the post of district inspector of schools. By 1892 he was transferred to Petersburg, where for years he continued to work in the school system, both as a teacher and as an administrator.

Although Sologub began writing in the early eighties,

not until 1896 did any of his efforts appear in book form. In that year, however, he published three volumes: *Poems, Shadows,* a collection of short stories, and a novel, *Bad Dreams,* at which he had worked for some ten years. Another volume, *Collected Poems,* came out in 1904, and the next year his satirical prose, *Political Fables.* At first he was unable to find a publisher for his great novel, *The Petty Demon,* which had occupied him from 1892 to 1902. In 1905 it began to come out in a magazine in serialized form, but the magazine failed before the last installments could appear. When Sologub finally succeeded in securing a publisher in 1907, the novel immediately won widespread recognition for him and has ever remained a classic of Russian literature.

This success of the now balding, bespectacled, self-effacing school official persuaded him to give up his pedagogical career and rely entirely upon literature for an income. In 1908 he married Anastasiya Chebotarevskaya, a cultured lady and minor writer to whose collaboration in his future literary endeavors Sologub pays generous tribute. None of the works he published after *The Petty Demon* ever won the enthusiastic reception accorded that novel, although they rarely failed to possess the originality of content and the exquisite sense of form which are the hallmarks of his art. Among them are a number of short stories; perhaps his two best volumes of poetry, *The Circle of Fire* (1908) and *Pearly Stars* (1913); his most ambitious attempt at fiction, a trilogy, *The Created Legend* (1908-1912); two other novels, *Sweeter than Poison* (1912) and *The Snake-charmer* (1921); and a series of plays of which perhaps the best known are *The Victory of Death* and *Vanka the Steward and the Page Jean.*

Like most of the symbolists, Sologub evinced little interest in the political upheavals that agitated Russia during the latter part of his life. Although he displayed mild liberal sympathies in organizational work among writers at the time of the 1905 revolt and later, he remained coldly aloof during the bitter fratricidal strife of the 1917 Revolution. Like so many writers in revolution-torn Petersburg in those days, Sologub and his wife suffered much from hunger and cold. The usual outlets for publishing were denied him or had been closed up by the new government. Marxist critics scathingly denounced this artist of proletarian origins as an adherent of the outmoded literary degeneracy of the nobility. For two years he and his wife vainly sought permission to go abroad. When the request was finally granted in 1921, it was then too late, for his wife suffered a nervous breakdown and committed suicide.

Isolated and unwanted, barely able to exist on a tiny pension which he supplemented by meager earnings from translating French novels, Sologub found himself a lonely, expendable relic of the past in an age of revolutionary turmoil. Though he wrote a considerable amount during the last few years of his life, little of it was ever allowed to be printed, and many unpublished manuscripts remain in the archives of a Leningrad library. Aware of his approaching end, he said to a friend a few days before his death on December 5, 1927: "Must I die? It is odious! I've just begun to understand what life is. Does man understand this before old age? And now one must go. Why? For what reason? How do they dare?"

Though Russian Symbolists, like those in Western Europe, often made a kind of fetish of unintelligibility in both form and content, Sologub, in his own words, subscribed to the belief that "Art, on its visible surface, must be transparent and understandable to all." Yet one is tempted to assert that the beauty, simplicity, and clarity of his expression, especially in verse, somehow derive from the completeness with which he had thought through his strange and perverse philosophy of life. He rejects the entire visible world as evil and finds only within himself a world of good, of calm, and beauty. Essentially his art represents an eternal conflict between matter and desire—the main expressions of evil in the real world—and the ideal beauty of his own private inner world. But in his distaste of reality, Sologub interprets its manifestations with a sensuality that is often shocking and even nihilistic. In his ideal world, which is ruled by Satan, because God is really the creator of evil, death is the symbol of peace and beauty.

This symbolic world finds varied expression in Sologub's poetry, which swarms with demonic creatures, obsessive images such as the bare feet of women, lithe naked boys, and slender virgins, and themes that reflect a morbid preoccupation with cruelty and the humiliation of beauty. The meters of these lyrics are conventional, and the symbolism, once the poet's imaginary world is identified, is easily discovered for it rarely goes beyond the secondary meaning of the images or the words he uses. But his words are employed with such precision, grace, and formal mastery that Sologub could claim, with some justice, that all his sins as a man and poet would be forgiven him because of the purity of his craft.

Although Sologub's poetry is undoubtedly his finest artistic achievement, his reputation abroad, and to a considerable extent in Russia, rests solidly upon his prose fiction. His first novel, *Bad Dreams*, a somewhat autobiographical treatment of a provincial schoolteacher, is a more humane but less perceptive and intensive treatment of the subject matter of *The Petty Demon*. For one thing the hero seems to possess the capacity of rising above the vulgarity and stupidity of his provincial surroundings, and of catching a glimpse at least of the ideal vision of life that haunts his creator.

No such possibility is reflected in the superbly characterized Peredonov of Sologub's masterpiece, *The Petty*

Demon. He is condemned to destruction from the out-
set, and as "Peredonovism" his very name has become
the embodiment in Russian life of everything that is
vile, hypocritical, mean, and slimy. The world of reality
in this provincial town where Peredonov teaches school
has its counterparts in earlier Russian literature. Certain
works of Gogol, Dostoevsky, Saltykov-Shchedrin, and
even Chekhov have contributed something to its de-
scription, its mores, and its inhabitants. However, this
world of reality takes on special Sologubian characteristics when seen through the eyes of the demon-ridden
Peredonov with his persecution mania. Further, the
realism is interpenetrated by an underlying symbolism
which suggests that this evil wasteland is only a micro-
cosm of the total evil creation of God. For just as
Sologub believes that there is something of Peredonov
in all of us, so he also insists on the universality of Peredonov's mad world. Indeed these symbolically sugges-
tive universal implications impart to the novel its
mysterious, dark evocative power and elevate it far beyond the level of ordinary fiction.

Perhaps as a counterpoise to the unrelieved tragic
gloom of Peredonov, and also as a fullfilment of the
author's own perverted vision of life, Sologub introduces
into the novel the extensive episode of the seduction of
the handsome young schoolboy Sasha by the erotic and
sadistically-minded *demi-vierge* Ludmila. It is a *Lolita*
situation in reverse, and the scenes are wantonly delightful and flecked with humor and not a little satire. But
the benignancy of the symbolism is adulterated by the
sensuality of the imagery. Satan rules over this idyllic
kingdom. Though Ludmila and Sasha are Sologubian
symbols of beauty, they are also morbidly devoted to
sex and death.

As though conscious of his failure in *The Petty
Demon*—a happy one as it turned out—to transcend
the conventional pattern of realism by introducing

supernatural and symbolic elements, Sologub obviously attempted to give his fanciful world of ideas fuller play in his third novel, *The Created Legend*. Blatantly he declares at the beginning of this trilogy: "Mayst thou rot in darkness, thou boring daily life, or be consumed in raging fires, for I the poet will erect above thee my created legend of the beautiful and enchanted." In keeping with this incantation, the Satanist hero Trirodov, who embodies the serenity of death, manifests his calm contempt for the existing order of things in the 1905 revolutionary struggle that surrounds him. The first volume, *Drops of Blood*,* is full of scenes of horror, torture, illicit love-making, and black magic. With his ghostly followers, the "pale boys," symbolizing the cool and calm realm of inner beauty and death, Trirodov eventually deserts Russia for an imaginary archipelago in the Mediterranean, to which the action shifts in the second and third volumes—*Queen Otruda* and *Smoke and Ashes*. Here ensues a complicated story of love, political intrigue, and conspiracy, constantly overshadowed by impending danger from a live volcano, a symbol of perdition and ruin. In the end the volcano erupts, but as though convinced of their erring ways by the disaster, the people of the archipelago elect the Satanist Trirodov as their king.

The powerful central drive and evocative spirit of *The Petty Demon* are lacking in this trilogy which, however, is perhaps a truer reflection of Sologub's escapist philosophy. But the work wallows in a welter of symbolism, fantastic visions, and erotic passages, and the Prospero-like Trirodov, with his magic power over nature and human beings, never fundamentally compels belief. Despite these drawbacks, it is a notable fact that the sheer story element of *The Created Legend* hardly ever fails

* This is the only one of the three parts of the trilogy that has appeared in English, under the title, *The Created Legend*, translated by John Cournos, Secker, London, 1916.

to sustain reader interest, an accomplishment which very few of the greatest Russian novelists can claim.

The remainder of Sologub's fiction deserves only brief comment. *Sweeter than Poison*, the tragedy of a lower-middle-class girl whose dreams of love are defiled by a knave from the gentry, emphasizes a persistent symbolic connotation that runs through much of Sologub's writing, namely, that life is a disgusting fat slut whose touch makes everything appear gross and ugly. His last novel, *The Snakecharmer*, represents a distinct decline in power, but his short stories, a number of which have been translated into English, are among his finest artistic efforts. The earlier ones, in theme and realistic treatment, recall the substance and manner of his first two novels, but many of the later tales are filled with the fantastic imaginings and symbolic meanings that so markedly characterized the development of Sologub's literary art in the second half of his career. Even the best of these short stories are too numerous to mention here by title. Thematically they often bear a close relation to his poetry, and like his verse they are cast in the same beautiful, precise, impeccable language, one of the highest accomplishments of modern Russian prose.

Sologub lacked a true dramatic talent and hence his plays tend to be rather academic exercises, in which the leading characters personify this or that aspect of his philosophy. One of the few exceptions is the play already mentioned, *Vanka the Steward and the Page Jean*, which is based on a popular Russian folk ballad of a servant who becomes the lover of a princess. Sologub amusingly employs the theme to satirize the crudities of his countrymen, while at the same time symbolically suggesting the universality of social evils by drawing a comparison between life in Russia and France.

One cannot review the bulk of Sologub's writings without observing the sure hand of an unusual literary genius constantly at work. He is a writer whom we ought to know better, for in some respects his artistic approach is peculiarly attuned to creative trends today. Though his failings are sometimes blamed upon the cultural decadence of the *fin de siècle*, in which he lived, one of his contemporaries perhaps correctly conjectured that Sologub would have been a decadent even if that movement had never existed. His morbid fear of reality and his preoccupation with death were no doubt caused by mental and emotional abnormalities, but these in turn, as is so often the case with artistic genius, contributed to and directed his creative impulses. Thus, it is impossible to imagine any literary artist other than Fyodor Sologub writing that strangely brilliant masterpiece of fiction, *The Petty Demon*, perhaps the most memorable novel to emerge from Russia since Dostoevsky's *Brothers Karamazov*.

ERNEST J. SIMMONS

Translator's Preface

Literary reputation is, all too often, a conspiracy either of taste or of dogma. Time, fortunately, debilitates critical judgment as it does not great art. The silver age of Russian literature—the symbolist period—has been too long ignored by Russians and non-Russians alike. Recently the Soviet Union reprinted *The Petty Demon* for the first time in twenty-five years: granted, it was an extremely small printing (immediately sold out!) and in a special series of "writers hostile to the nation," but still, it is an encouraging indication of the growing maturity of contemporary Soviet society. Russia will, in time, see that it has reason to be proud of this "decadent" chapter in its literature, and the Western reader of Russian literature certainly ought, for his part, to acquaint himself with the Russian Poes, Baudelaires, and Rilkes.

Symbolism is the most demanding and difficult of all literary devices. For if it is too well defined by the narrative, symbolism degenerates into allegory which may only be understood intellectually. Symbolism is a result, not a device in art, and it is not to be equated with allegory, satire, or social criticism—although it may involve all of these factors. There are, strictly speaking, relatively few "symbolist" novels. *The Petty Demon*, in its extraordinary ambiguity of symbolism and realism, is clearly one of this small number. It is the most brilliant example of Russian symbolist prose and also—in spite of its present obscurity—a classic of twentieth century literature. *The Petty Demon* is serious and challenging in a manner which is, for some reason, peculiar to the great Russian novel.

Peredonov, the novel's protagonist, is a paranoiac schoolteacher who destroys himself in his quest to become a school inspector, and *The Petty Demon* is, ostensibly at least, the record of that downfall. Peredonov, according to Sologub, was modeled upon a schoolteacher whom he had actually observed in the provinces. From this real person he created a symbolic archetype of literature representing all of man's pathetic weakness and his potentiality for pettiness. As one Russian critic aptly quipped: "If there were no Peredonov, he would have to be created."

And the other characters are only slightly inferior to Peredonov himself. The entire town that is Sologub's novel exists only within its book, and it can be said (as it was said of Gogol's *Inspector General*) that no such town ever existed in Russia. It is Sologub's intent, however, to induce the reader to acknowledge a relationship to this petty world. In the conclusion to Chapter 22 he says of Peredonov:

> Blinded by illusions of personality and separate existence, he could not understand the spontaneous Dionysian ecstasies triumphantly calling in nature. He was blind and pitiful—like many of us.

The implication is clear. Peredonov is not himself the petty demon, but only the first among many, and the novel is simply the logical extension of an illogical reality.

In his hopeless struggle with life and the hostile society that surrounds him, Peredonov is a "decadent Don Quixote." *Don Quixote* was from Sologub's early childhood his favorite book, and motifs from it constantly occur throughout his work. Peredonov's relationship to Don Quixote is shown by his very name, Pere-don-ov —"the Don done over." Like Don Quixote, Peredonov is also searching for a better life. His misfortune is that he has no ideals save the meager values of the society in which he lives. Whereas Don Quixote aspired towards knighthood, Peredonov's knighthood has been reduced to the badge of an inspector's position. And where Don Quixote had his books of knight errantry, Peredonov early in the novel burns his own books with the help of his Sancho Panza, the sheeplike Volodin. Thus in Peredonov everything is reversed: his greatest good is evil.

The knight of La Mancha worships a coarse maiden from afar and calls her the beautiful Dulcinea, but it is Peredonov's lot to live with Aldonsa herself in the person of his vulgar mistress, Varvara. Sologub was intrigued by the symbolic implications in the images of Aldonsa and Dulcinea. "The Don," he once wrote, "recognized the potentialities of us all." Sologub even sees beauty in Varvara:

> . . . her body was beautiful, the body of a gentle nymph. It was as if the head of a faded harlot had been attached to it by some evil spell . . . And so it often is—truly in our age it is the lot of beauty to be violated and tainted.

For him beauty, symbolized by Dulcinea, is the only salvation from banal reality, represented by Aldonsa. But Dulcinea is only the cruel dream of a madman or a poet. Peredonov's Dulcinea is the Princess Volchanskaya, who, Varvara has led him to believe, will procure an inspectorship for him. He writes to her and says:

> "I love you because you are cold and distant. Varvara sweats, and it is uncomfortable to sleep with her. She's like an oven. I want to have a cold and distant lover. Come to me and fulfill my need."

The irony, of course, is that Peredonov's Dulcinea is none other than Varvara herself who forges the letters which supposedly come from the Princess.

Don Quixote sets out in pursuit of a lofty ideal, but Sologub's "Don done over," logically enough, is himself pursued by the phantasm which is in him and around him: the absurdity, the vulgarity, and the pettiness that, in Russian, is called *poshlost*. *Poshlost*, the demon's comic mask, follows Peredonov everywhere and assumes many different guises. It is present in the ashtray shaped like a peasant's sandal in one of the houses Peredonov visits, and it is unmistakable in the doctor who is always preparing to lead a simple life and so watches peasants to see how they blow their noses and scratch their necks. It reaches grand heights in Peredonov's dream in which a headmaster holds a golden wreath over him and (ecstasy of *poshlost!*) sings alleluias. The *poshlost* is only somewhat more refined in Peredonov's headmaster who lives *comme il faut* and publishes erudite and useless scholarly articles pieced together from foreign books. Each of these characters has his own role, his own "inspectorship" to obtain or to maintain in life, and in each of them there is, instead of a soul, "a skillful and busy inanimate mechanism."

Sologub's ability to derive humor from the demonic world of pettiness he has created is a mark of his kinship to the great master of *poshlost*, Gogol. It is interesting to note that Gogol too originally conceived of his *Dead Souls* as a kind of Russian *Don Quixote*. Both Gogol and Sologub have the ability to reduce life to its most elemental and ludicrous components. Peredonov's visits to the town officials may be said to retrace precisely the spiritual itinerary of Gogol's Chichikov. Chichikov busies himself with the purchase of nonexistent serfs from improbable sellers; and Peredonov is concerned with defending himself from imaginary slander so that he will not lose an equally imaginary appointment. Gogol and Sologub each give their characters comic, revealing names. Beside Gogol's Sobakevich (Mr. Dog) whose heavy furniture is a reflection of himself stands Sologub's Skuchaev (Mr. Boring) whose furniture is quiet and depressing. The dead souls of both authors cannot be separated from their mock-surroundings:

> "There once lived a pig who had no enemies," replied Avinovitsky, "but he was slaughtered too. Taste this. It was a good pig."
> Peredonov took a piece of ham and said . . .

This piece of ham reflects the symbolic movement of the novel. Peredonov will continue to sate himself on ham, raisins, tarts, vodka, and mutton (Volodin) until finally he has devoured himself and—in the end—melts away like one of the caramels he so loved to suck. In *The Petty Demon* a person *is* what he eats: madeira is reserved for the headmaster, and Peredonov is upset at one house when he is not offered a new jar "with better jam" than another guest. His vision of supreme happiness consists of "doing nothing and, shut off from the world, satisfying his belly." Taste is the lowest of the senses, and man seen in terms of and at a level with his food is *poshlost'* (im)pure and simple.

Unlike Gogol, however, Sologub presents an alternative to the repugnant spirit that pervades his novel. This alternative is the poignant affair between Ludmila Rutilova and a young boy, Sasha Pyl'nikov. Her passionate and arch dalliance with Peredonov's still immature pupil is beautiful in its intensity, perverse in its potentiality, and tragic in its impossibility. Sologub posits Ludmila's—and his own—worship of beauty as the only escape from Peredonovism. Ludmila is truly, in Nietzsche's term, beyond good and evil:

I love beauty. I am a pagan, a sinner. I ought to have been born in ancient Athens. I love flowers, perfumes, bright clothes, the naked body. They say there is a soul. I don't know, I haven't seen it. But why do I need one? Let me die completely like a water nymph, let me melt away like a cloud under the sun. I love the body, strong, agile, naked, and capable of enjoyment.

Ludmila, alive with color, fragrant with perfume, exists in an entirely different dimension than Peredonov. She is the light from a window thrown open during a shadow show and, in terms of the novel, the only acceptable reality. It is of little import that her relationship with Sasha is cut short—what is important is the moment in her existence in which she separates herself from the coarseness and baseness of life around her. It is, as F. D. Reeve has remarked, the "physical and spiritual Eden in the book's general moral structure." * Ludmila has triumphed over life . . . at least as much as a person is able to do that.

But even Ludmila is not immune to Peredonovism. In sending Sasha to the town masquerade dressed as a girl she realizes the perverse desire, foretold in one of her dreams, to see him tormented. The masquerade is the means by which Sologub concentrates society into a palpable unit and fully reveals its chaotic face. This is the petty demon, a spirit as ominous in Sologub's time as it was in Gogol's and one which, I think, still flourishes today, not only in Russia.

ANDREW FIELD

* F. D. Reeve, "Art as Solution: Sologub's Devil" (*Modern Fiction Studies,* Summer, 1957).

A Note on the Translation

Sologub has been justly called one of the foremost stylists of the Russian language. His prose with its finely wrought verbal effects, puns, and subtleties is difficult to translate. I have endeavored to remain close to the tone and pace of the original, seeking equivalent expressions wherever direct translation was not possible. The notes in the text and at the back of the book contain literal explanations of these passages as well as comments on other points of interest. The author's introductions to the various editions can also be found at the back of the book.

The transcription used is a slight variation of the Library of Congress system. The Russian soft sign, designated by an apostrophe, which is not pronounced but which softens a preceding consonant or separates two letters has been preserved in all names except those already having fixed spellings such as Olga. Similarly, established forms of other names are used, e.g., Ludmila instead of Liudmila.

A.F.

Cambridge, Mass.
1962

The Petty Demon

The Principal Characters

ARDAL'ON (ARDASHA, ARDAL'OSHA, ARDAL'OSHKA) BORISYCH
    PEREDONOV—*a provincial schoolteacher*

VARVARA (VARYA, VAR'KA) DMITRIEVNA MALOSHINA—
    Peredonov's mistress and, later, his wife

PAVEL (PAVLUSHA, PAVLUSHKA) VASIL'EVICH VOLODIN—
    Peredonov's best friend

LUDMILA (LUDMILOCHKA, LUDMILKA) PLATONOVNA RUTI-
    LOVA—*an unmarried young lady*

LARISA, DAR'YA (DASHEN'KA), AND VALERIYA (VALEROCHKA)
    —*Ludmila's sisters; she also has a brother*

ALEXANDR (SASHA, SASHEN'KA) PYL'NIKOV—*Ludmila's*
    young friend

EKATERINA IVANOVNA PYL'NIKOVA—*Sasha's aunt and*
    guardian

OLGA VASIL'EVNA KOKOVKINA—*Sasha's landlady*

NIKOLAI VLAS'EVICH KHRIPACH—*the headmaster of the*
    local gymnasium

VARVARA NIKOLAEVNA—*his wife*

MAR'YA OSIPOVNA GRUSHINA—*Varvara's crony*

SOF'YA EFIMOVNA PREPOLOVENSKAYA *and her husband*
    KONSTANTIN PETROVICH—*friends of the Peredonovs*

NATAL'YA AFANAS'EVNA VERSHINA—*a bewitching neighbor*

MARTA (MARFA, MARFUSHKA) STANISLAVOVNA NARTAN-
    OVICHA *and her brother* VLADISLAV (VLADYA)—*Ver-*
    shina's wards

CHEREPNIN—*Vershina's rejected suitor*

VLADIMIR IVANOVICH MURIN—*a small landowner;*
    Marta's suitor

YAKOV ANIKIEVICH SKUCHAEV—*the mayor*

SERGEI POTAPYCH BOGDANOV—*the district inspector of schools*

SEMYON GRIGOR'EVICH MIN'CHUKOV—*the chief of police*

NIKOLAI VADIMOVICH RUBOVSKY—*a police lieutenant*

ALEKSANDR MIKHAILOVICH VERIGA—*the marshal of the nobility*

ALEKSANDR ALEKSEEVICH AVINOVITSKY—*the district attorney*

NIKOLAI (NIKA) MIKHAILOVICH GUDAEVSKY—*the town notary*

IULIYA PETROVNA—*his wife*

IVAN STEPANOVICH KIRILLOV—*president of the local land-owners' association*

TISHKOV—*the rhyming merchant*

EVGENY IVANOVICH SUROVTSEV—*the gymnasium physician*

GEORGI SEMYONOVICH TREPETOV—*a doctor with Tolstoyan pretensions*

NADEZHDA (NADYA) VASIL'EVNA ADAMENKO—*a progressive young lady*

MISHA (MISHKA, MISHEN'KA)—*her little brother*

IRINYA (IRISHKA) STEPANOVNA ERSHOVA (ERSHIKHA)—*Peredonov's first landlady*

KLAVDIYA (KLASHKA, KLAVDIUSHKA, DIUSHKA)—*the Peredonovs' maid*

FALASTOV—*a gymnasium teacher*

MACHIGIN *and* SKOBOCHKINA—*country schoolteachers*

NIL *and* IL'YA AVDEEV—*local ruffians*

IOSIF KRAMARENKO, VOLODYA BUL'TYAKOV, ANTOSHA GUDAEVSKY, VITKEVICH—*gymnasium students*

1 : ᘓᕽᘓᕽ

After the holiday Mass, the parishioners drifted apart
to their homes. Some lingered under the old lindens
and maples by the fence behind the white stone walls
and chatted. All were attired in festive fashion and
looked at each other with good humor, and it seemed
that in this town people lived peacefully and amiably. And even happily. But all this was only an appearance.

The gymnasium* instructor, Peredonov, standing in
a circle of his friends and looking at them morosely with
his small, bloated eyes from behind gold-rimmed glasses,
said to them, "Princess Volchanskaya herself has promised Varya, that's quite certain. 'As soon as you marry
him,' she says, 'then I will at once manage to get an
inspector's appointment for him.' "

* The Russian *gimnaziya* is a private academic secondary school
intended for the children of noblemen and officials. I have used
the more familiar German spelling, gymnasium.

"Yes, but how are you going to marry Varvara Dmitrievna?" asked the red-faced Falastov. "Why, she's your first cousin! Has there been a new law passed which allows one to be married to first cousins?"

Everyone began to laugh. The ruddy and usually indifferently somnulent face of Peredonov became ferocious.

"She's a second cousin," he growled, angrily looking away from them.

"But did the Princess promise you personally?" asked the tall, pale, foppishly dressed Rutilov.

"No, not me but Varya," replied Peredonov.

"And you really believe that?" said Rutilov with animation. "You can *say* anything. Now why didn't you go see the Princess yourself?"

"It was this way—I did go with Varya, but we didn't catch the Princess in. We missed her by only five minutes," explained Peredonov. "She had gone off to the country and was going to return in three weeks, but, since I had to be here for the examinations, it was impossible for me to wait."

"There's something shady in that," said Rutilov, and he began to laugh, exposing his yellowed teeth.

Peredonov became pensive. His friends drifted off, leaving him alone with Rutilov.

"Of course, I can have anyone I want," said Peredonov. "I don't just have Varvara."

"It goes without saying, any girl would go for you, Ardal'on Borisych," affirmed Rutilov.

They went out through the gate and slowly walked along the dusty, unpaved square.

"Only what about the Princess?" said Peredonov. "She'll get angry if I throw Varvara over."

"Well what of the Princess!" Rutilov said. "You needn't pussyfoot on her account, you know.* Let her

* Rutilov's expression, "You're not christening kittens with her," means "You needn't spare her anything."

get you the position first—you'll manage to get hitched. Why go into it needlessly and blindly!"

"That's true," thoughtfully agreed Peredonov.

"And you tell that to Varvara," declared Rutilov. "First the position, you say, otherwise I'm not so sure! And when you get the job, well then marry whomever you want. Now you'd be better off to take one of my sisters—there are three, choose whichever you like. They're educated and intelligent young ladies, and that's no exaggeration. There's no comparing them to Varvara. She simply doesn't stand up to them."

"Umm," reflected Peredonov in a low voice.

"That's right. What's your Varvara? Here, smell this."

Rutilov bent down, tore off the fleecy stem of henbane and crumpled it up together with its leaves and dingy-colored flowers. He rubbed it all together in his fingers and thrust it under Peredonov's nose. Peredonov screwed up his face from the very heavy, unpleasant odor.

"To crumple up and throw away—there is your Varvara," said Rutilov. "She and my sisters? Listen here, brother, there is a great difference between them. They are lively young ladies, full of pep. Take whichever you like. She'll keep you on your toes! And they are young, why, the very oldest is three times younger than your Varvara."

All this Rutilov said in his usual rapid manner, smiling gaily. But, being a tall and narrow-chested person, he appeared delicate and frail. Short-cut, sparse, light hairs stuck out pitifully from under his fashionable new hat.

"Well, not quite three times," commented Peredonov dully as he took off his gold glasses and wiped them.

"It's really true!" exclaimed Rutilov. "Be smart, and don't get caught napping, for, as sure as I live, they have their pride, and, if you want one afterwards, it may be too late. But any one of them will have you with great pleasure now."

"Yes, they're all in love with me around here," said Peredonov with sullen boastfulness.

"Well there you are, and you should take advantage of it," pressed Rutilov.

"The main thing as far as I'm concerned is that she not be scrawny," said Peredonov with apprehension in his voice. "I'd rather have a chubby one!"

"Well, don't worry yourself on that account," said Rutilov enthusiastically. "They're plump young ladies even now, and they haven't at all reached their full growth yet—it's only a matter of time. When they get married they'll put it on like the oldest one, Larisa, who, as you yourself know, has become a regular meat-pie."

"I'd marry one of them," said Peredonov, "except that I'm afraid Varya would make a big scandal."

"You're afraid of a scandal. Now here's what you do," said Rutilov with a sly smile. "Just get married today or, if not, then tomorrow. When you come home with a young bride, there'll no longer be any problem. Would you like me to fix it up for you for tomorrow evening? Which one do you want?"

Peredonov suddenly broke into loud, abrupt laughter.

"Well, is it a deal? It's all fixed up, right?" asked Rutilov.

But Peredonov just as abruptly stopped laughing and said, gravely, quietly, almost in a whisper, "She'll inform on me, the loathsome shrew."

"She won't inform anything, there's nothing to inform," said Rutilov persuasively.

"Or she'll poison me," whispered Peredonov fearfully.

"You just leave everything to me," Rutilov insisted strongly. "I'll take care of everything for you just so. . . ."

"I won't marry without a dowry," Peredonov shot out angrily.

Rutilov wasn't at all taken aback by the new twist in the thoughts of his gloomy companion. With the same warmth he answered, "What a fool, do you think *they* don't have a dowry! Well now, it's a deal, all right? I'll run ahead and fix everything up. Only, mind you, keep mum, not a word to anyone, do you hear, not to anyone!"

He gripped Peredonov's hand and then ran off. Peredonov looked after him in silence. He recalled the young Rutilov girls, gay, laughing. An immodest thought brought out the vile semblance of a smile on his lips—it appeared for an instant and vanished. A vague uneasiness was aroused in him.

"But how will the Princess like it?" he thought. "You'll get no favor and not half a kopeck from it, but with Varvara you'll fall into an inspector's position and later they'll make you a headmaster."

He looked after Rutilov hastily bustling off and thought maliciously, "Let him run."

And this thought gave him a dull and insipid pleasure. Bored by his solitude, he pulled his hat over his brow, wrinkled his light eyebrows, and hurriedly set out for home along the unpaved, deserted streets, which were overgrown with white cowbells, marsh tea, and grass tramped down into the mud.

Someone called to him in a quiet and hurried voice, "Ardal'on Borisych, stop in at our house."

Peredonov raised his gloomy eyes and angrily looked across the fence. In her garden behind a gate, stood Natalya Afanas'evna Vershina, a small, slim, dark-skinned woman with black brows and dark eyes. She was dressed entirely in black and was smoking a cigarette in a dark cherrywood cigarette holder. She smiled slightly as if she knew something which is smiled at, but not talked about. Not so much with words as with her smooth, quick movements, she drew Peredonov into her garden. She opened the gate and, stepping aside, smiled imploringly and, at the same time, confidently motioned him in with her hands.

"Come in, why are you standing there?" they seemed to say.

And Peredonov did come in, submitting to her as if he had been hypnotized by her silent movements. But then he stopped on the sandy path, where pieces of dry twigs caught his eye, and glanced at his watch.

"It's lunchtime," he grumbled.

Although the watch had served him for a long time, he even now glanced at its large gold case with pleasure in the presence of others. It was eleven forty, and Peredonov decided that he would stay for a little while. Sullenly he walked behind Vershina along the path past neglected bushes of black and red currants, raspberries, and gooseberries.

The garden was yellow and gay with fruit and late flowers. There were many fruit trees, ordinary trees, and bushes—small spread-out apple trees, round-leafed pear trees, lindens, cherry trees with bright shiny leaves, a plum tree, honeysuckle. There were red berries on the elderberry shrubs and along the fence tiny pale pink flowers with purple veins—Siberian geraniums—bloomed densely. They thrust their vivid purple, thorny heads out from under the bushes. To the side stood a small, gray, wooden, one-story house with a broad terrace opening onto the garden. It seemed charming and cozy. Behind it could be seen a portion of the vegetable garden. There poppy pods were swaying, along with large cream-colored caps of camomile, and yellow sunflower blossoms were beginning to droop before withering. Among the edible herbs, arose the white umbrellas of hemlock and the pale purple ones of hemlock geranium. Bright yellow buttercups and small ladyslippers also flourished.

"Were you at Mass?" asked Vershina.

"I was," gloomily answered Peredonov.

"Marta has just returned too," said Vershina. "She often goes to our church. I really tease her about it. 'On whose account,' I say, 'do you go to our church, Marta?' She blushes and doesn't say anything. Let's go and sit awhile in the summerhouse," she said quickly and without any transition from what she had just been saying.

In the garden under the shade of the spreading maples stood the old gray summerhouse. Three steps led up to it. It had a moss-covered platform, low walls, six chiseled, potbellied columns, and a six-edged roof.

Marta, still dressed from Mass, was sitting in the summerhouse. She had on a light-colored dress with bows, but it wasn't becoming on her. Its short sleeves laid bare her protruding red elbows and her large, strong arms. Still, Marta was not at all bad-looking. Her freckles did not spoil her, and she even passed for pretty, especially among her own people, the Poles, quite a few of whom lived in the area.

Marta was rolling cigarettes for Vershina. She was impatiently longing for Peredonov to look at her and admire her. This wish was betrayed by the look of anxious friendliness on her naïve face. It did not, however, arise from the fact that Marta was in love with Peredonov: it was only that Vershina wished to get her married—her family was large—and Marta wanted to please Vershina, in whose home she had been living for several months since the funeral of Vershina's old husband. And not only for her, but also for her brother, a student at the gymnasium, who was also staying there.

Vershina and Peredonov came into the summerhouse. Peredonov morosely said hello to Marta and sat down. He chose his seat so that a column protected his back from the wind and his ears from drafts. He looked at Marta's yellow shoes with pink pom-poms and it occurred to him that they were trying to make a husband out of him. He always thought this whenever he encountered young ladies who were pleasant to him. He noticed only Marta's imperfections—her many freckles and her large, coarse hands. He knew that her father, who belonged to the Polish gentry, was leasing a small estate about six versts from the town. His income was small; his children, many. Marta had graduated from the pro-gymnasium, and the son was studying in the gymnasium. The other children were even smaller.

"Will you let me give you some beer?" quickly asked Vershina.

On a table stood some glasses, two bottles of beer, powdered sugar in a tin box, and a teaspoon made of German silver which had been dipped in the beer.

"I'll have a drink," said Peredonov curtly.

Vershina glanced at Marta. Marta poured out a glass, handed it to Peredonov, and, while doing this, a strange smile glimmered on her face . . . it was not happy and yet not frightened.

"Put some sugar in your beer," Vershina said in a hurried way, and the words seemed to spill from her mouth.

Marta handed Peredonov the tin box with the sugar, but he said spitefully, "No. It's abominable with sugar."

"What do you mean, it's delicious," Vershina let slip in her rapid, monotonous manner.

"Very delicious," said Marta.

"Abominable," repeated Peredonov, and he angrily glared at the sugar.

"As you like," said Vershina, and in the same tone, without a halt or transition, she began to talk about something else. "Cherepnin has been pestering me," she said and began to laugh.

Marta also began laughing. Peredonov looked on indifferently: he took no interest in other people's affairs.

He disliked people and did not think about them except in connection with his own benefit and pleasures.

"He thinks I'm going to marry him," Vershina said smiling contentedly.

"He's terribly bold," said Marta, not because she really thought so, but because she wanted to please and flatter Vershina.

"Yesterday he was peeping in the window," said Vershina. "He got into the garden while we were having supper. There was a barrel that we had put under the drain standing by the window. It had filled up and was covered with a board so that you couldn't see the water. He climbed onto the barrel and was looking in the window. A lamp was on inside—he saw us, but we couldn't see him. Suddenly we heard a noise. We were frightened at first and ran outside. As it turned out, he had fallen through into the water. However, he climbed out before we got there and ran away all dripping, leaving wet tracks along the path. We recognized him by his back."

Marta laughed lightly and happily in the way that well-behaved children laugh. Vershina related all this quickly and flatly, the words slipping out—just as she always spoke—and then all at once she became silent. She sat and smiled with the corners of her mouth, which wrinkled her dark, dry face and partly revealed her teeth, blackened from smoking. Peredonov became pensive and suddenly roared with laughter. He never immediately reacted to what struck him as funny—his responses were sluggish and dull.

Vershina was smoking cigarette after cigarette. She was unable to live without tobacco smoke under her nose.

"We'll soon be neighbors," observed Peredonov.

Vershina cast a quick glance at Marta, who blushed, looked at Peredonov with anxious expectation, and then at once turned her eyes away into the garden.

"You're moving?" asked Vershina. "But why?"

"It's a long way from the gymnasium," explained Peredonov.

Vershina smiled incredulously. She thought that it was more likely that he wanted to be a little nearer to Marta.

"Yes, but you've already been living there a long time, it's been several years," she said.

"Yes, and the landlady's a bitch," said Peredonov angrily.

"Really?" asked Vershina sarcastically, and she smiled crookedly.

Peredonov became somewhat enlivened.

"She put up new wallpaper, but it was done rottenly," he confided. "The pieces don't match up. All at once there's a completely different pattern over the door in the dining room. The whole room has patterns and little flowers, but over the door there are stripes and polka dots. Even the color isn't the same. We wouldn't have noticed it, but Falastov came and laughed at it. Now everyone's laughing at it."

"Why that's really terrible," agreed Vershina.

"Only we aren't telling her that we're leaving," said Peredonov, and at this point he lowered his voice. "We'll find an apartment and leave without telling her."

"That goes without saying," said Vershina.

"Otherwise, perhaps, there'll be a row," said Peredonov, and a fearful anxiety was reflected in his eyes. "The idea of paying her an extra month's rent for such a disgusting place!"

Peredonov burst out laughing with glee at the thought of leaving and not paying the rent for the apartment.

"She'll demand it," observed Vershina.

"Let her demand, I won't pay," said Peredonov

angrily. "We made a trip to Peter* and didn't use the apartment for that time."

"But, you see, the apartment was kept for you," said Vershina.

"So what of it! She should give us a discount. Why should we have to pay for the time when we weren't living there? And the main thing is, she's terribly insolent."

"Well, your landlady is insolent because your, uh, cousin is also quite a quarrelsome person," said Vershina with a slight hesitation on the word "cousin."

Peredonov frowned and dully looked straight ahead with his somnolent eyes. Vershina started to talk about something else. Peredonov took a caramel out of his pocket, peeled off its wrapping, and began to chew. By chance he glanced at Marta and thought that she looked envious and wanted caramels too.

"Should I give her one or not?" thought Peredonov. "She isn't worth it, but I'd better give her one so that they don't think I'm miserly. I have a lot. My pockets are full of them." And he pulled out a handful of caramels.

"Here—take one," he said, and he held out the sweets first to Vershina and then to Marta. "It's good candy, expensive too—I paid thirty kopecks a pound."

They each took one. "But take some more," he said, "I have a lot, and they're good caramels. I wouldn't eat bad ones."

"No thank you, I don't want any more," said Vershina quickly and without expression.

Marta repeated those same words after her, but with some hesitation. Peredonov looked at her incredulously and said, "What do you mean, you don't want any! Here, take some."

Then he took one caramel from the handful for him-

* St. Petersburg.

self and placed the remaining ones in front of Marta. Marta smiled silently and lowered her head.

"Boor!" thought Peredonov. "She doesn't even know how to say 'thank you' properly."

He didn't know what to talk about with Marta. She was uninteresting to him, like all things and people with which he did not have some sort of established relationship, whether good or bad.

The remaining beer was poured into Peredonov's glass. Vershina glanced at Marta.

"I'll get some," said Marta. She always guessed what Vershina wanted without words.

"Send Vladya, he's in the garden," said Vershina.

"Vladislav!" shouted Marta.

"Here I am," replied the boy so quickly and so nearby that it seemed as if he had been eavesdropping.

"Bring some beer, two bottles," said Marta. "It's in the chest in the hallway."

Soon Vladislav came silently running up to the summerhouse. He handed Marta the beer through the window, and greeted Peredonov.

"Hello," said Peredonov sullenly. "How many bottles of beer have you chiseled today?"

"I don't drink beer," said Vladislav, with a forced smile.

The boy was about fourteen years old, and his face was covered with freckles just like Marta's. And like his sister, he was also uneasy and clumsy in his movements. He had on a blouse of coarse brown holland.

Marta began to talk to her brother in whispers. They both laughed. Peredonov looked at them suspiciously. Whenever people laughed in front of him, and he didn't know what they were laughing about, he always assumed they were laughing at him. Vershina became uneasy and was about to say something to Marta. But Peredonov himself asked in a cross voice, "What are you laughing at?"

Marta turned to him, quivering, and did not know what to say. Vladislav, looking at Peredonov, smiled and blushed slightly.

"That sort of behavior is boorish in the presence of guests," reprimanded Peredonov. "Are you laughing at me?" he asked.

Marta blushed. Vladislav became frightened.

"Pardon us," said Marta. "We aren't laughing at you at all. We were talking about our own doings."

"A secret," said Peredonov angrily. "It's boorish to discuss secrets in front of guests."

"It's not a secret," said Marta. "We were laughing because Vladya is barefoot and can't come in here— he's bashful."

Peredonov was mollified and began to invent jokes about Vladya. Finally he treated him to a caramel.

"Marta, bring my black shawl," said Vershina. "Oh yes, and look into the kitchen for a minute to see how the pie is coming."

Marta went out obediently. She understood that Vershina wanted to speak with Peredonov and was glad there was no hurry about her return.

"And you run off a ways," said Vershina to Vladya. "There's no reason why you should hang around here."

Vladya ran off, and one could hear the noise of the sand under his feet. Vershina cast a cautious and rapid sideways glance at Peredonov through her never-ending cloud of smoke. Peredonov was sitting in silence, looking straight ahead with a vague expression, chewing a caramel. He was pleased that Marta and Vladya had left—otherwise they might have laughed again. Although he was certain that they had not been laughing at him, he nevertheless remained vexed, just as after a brush with stinging nettles the pain increases and lingers for a long time even though the nettles are far away.

"Why don't you get married?" Vershina suddenly

shot out. "What are you waiting for, Ardal'on Borisych? Pardon me, but I tell you right to your face that your Varvara just isn't a match for you."

Peredonov brushed his hand through his slightly ruffled chestnut-colored hair and said with sullen conceit, "No one's a match for me here."

"Don't say that," retorted Vershina, and she smiled sarcastically. "There are many better than she here, and any one of them would marry you."

She shook the ash from her cigarette with an abrupt movement as though she were placing an exclamation point upon something.

"I don't need just any kind of girl," answered Peredonov.

"And we're not talking about just any kind of girl," said Vershina quickly. "Now if the girl were a good one, you aren't the type to run after someone for a dowry. You, thank God, earn enough by yourself."

"No," retorted Peredonov, "it's to my advantage to marry Varvara. The Princess has promised her protection. She'll get me a very good position," said Peredonov with morose enthusiasm.

Vershina smiled slightly. Her face, all wrinkled and dark as if it had been cured in tobacco smoke, expressed condescending incredulity.

"But did this Princess herself say this to you?" Her emphasis was on the word "you."

"Not to me, but to Varvara," acknowledged Peredonov. "But it's all the same."

"You're relying too much on your cousin's word," said Vershina maliciously. "But tell me, is she much older than you? About fifteen years? Or is it more? She's under fifty, isn't she?"

"Nothing of the kind," said Peredonov with annoyance. "She isn't thirty yet."

Vershina smiled.

"You don't say," she said with unconcealed derision in her voice. "But she looks much older than you. Of course it's none of my business, but it just seems a pity to me, that such a fine young man doesn't live in the manner he deserves in view of his good looks and inner qualities."

Peredonov contentedly glanced down at himself. But there was no smile on his ruddy face, and it seemed that he was offended that not everyone understood him as Vershina did.

"Even without patronage you'll go far," continued Vershina. "Surely the authorities will see your value. So why hang on to Varvara! And none of the Rutilov girls is good enough for you. They're too light-headed, while you need a serious wife. You could marry my Marta, for example."

Peredonov glanced at his watch.

"It's time for me to go home," he said and stood up to say good-bye.

Vershina was convinced that Peredonov was leaving because she had hit his soft spot, and that it was only because of his shyness that he didn't want to talk about Marta now.

2 : ᐸᐊᐸᐊ

Varvara Dmitrievna Maloshina, Peredonov's mistress, was waiting for him, sloppily dressed, but carefully powdered and rouged.

Jam tarts were cooking for lunch—Peredonov loved them. Varvara ran around the kitchen from one place to another in high heels hurrying to prepare everything for his return. She was afraid that Natalya the maid— a stout, pockmarked girl—would sneak some tarts, and possibly more than a few. Therefore, Varvara did not leave the kitchen and, as usual, scolded the maid. A perpetually grumbling and spiteful expression lay on her wrinkled face which preserved the remnants of past beauty.

As always, displeasure and melancholy took hold of Peredonov upon returning home. He stamped into the dining room, flipped his hat onto the windowsill, sat down at the table, and yelled, "Varya, give me dinner!"

Varvara brought in the food from the kitchen, swiftly hobbling in her gaudy, tight shoes and served Peredonov herself. When she brought out the coffee, Peredonov bent over the steaming cup and sniffed at it. Varvara took alarm and asked him fearfully, "What're you doing, Ardal'on Borisych? Do you smell something in the coffee?"

Peredonov looked at her sullenly and said angrily, "I'm checking to make sure you haven't put poison in it."

"What's wrong with you, Ardal'on Borisych?" asked Varvara with fright. "God help you, what gave you such an idea?"

"You might have mixed poison hemlock with it!" he muttered.

"What would I gain by killing you," insisted Varvara. "Enough of your foolishness!"

Peredonov kept sniffing for a long time. Finally he calmed down and said, "If it really were poison, you could certainly detect it from the heavy odor, but you have to put your nose very close, right into the steam."

He became silent for a little while, and then suddenly he said spitefully and derisively, "The Princess!"

Varvara became agitated, "The Princess? What Princess?"

"Without the Princess I won't do anything," said Peredonov. "Let her first get me the position, and then I'll marry you. You write and tell her that."

"But you know, Ardal'on Borisych," Varvara began with a persuasive voice, "that the Princess has promised that only when I get married, otherwise it would be awkward for her to ask for you."

"Write her that we've already been married," said Peredonov quickly, happy with his inspiration.

Varvara was taken aback, but quickly recovered and said, "Why lie—suppose the Princess looks into it? No, you'd better set the day for our marriage. But leave time to have the dress sewn."

"What dress?" gloomily asked Peredonov.

"And would you want me to get married in this house dress?" cried Varvara. "Give me some money for a dress, Ardal'on Borisych."

"One would think you were being buried!" said Peredonov crossly.

"You're a beast, Ardal'on Borisych!" exclaimed Varvara reproachfully.

All at once Peredonov felt an impulse to tease Varvara. "Varvara," he asked, "do you know where I was?"

"Well, where?" asked Varvara uneasily.

"At Vershina's," he said and burst out laughing.

"You've found fitting company. There's nothing more to say!" Varvara flashed out angrily.

"I saw Marta," continued Peredonov.

"She's all freckles," retorted Varvara with mounting anger, "and her mouth stretches from ear to ear just like a frog's."

"Well even so, she's more beautiful than you are," said Peredonov. "Perhaps I'll take her and get married."

"Just you marry her," screamed Varvara, red and trembling from anger. "I'll burn out her eyes with acid!"

"I'd like to spit on you," Peredonov said calmly.

"Just you try it!" cried Varvara.

"I think I will," said Peredonov.

He stood up and, with a dull and indifferent expression, spat right in her face.

"Swine!" said Varvara rather calmly, as if the spit had refreshed her, and she began to wipe herself off with a napkin.

Peredonov was silent. Of late he had become cruder than usual with Varvara . . . and even before he had treated her coarsely. Encouraged by his silence, she began to speak louder. "A real swine. That's precisely what you are."

A bleating sound like a sheep's voice was heard in the hall.

"Keep quiet," said Peredonov, "we have company."

"Why it's only Pavlushka," answered Varvara with a smirk.

Pavel Vasil'evich Volodin came in laughing loudly and gaily. He was a young man who was surprisingly similar in face and manners to a sheep. He was curly-headed like a sheep, and his eyes were bulging and vacant. In short, he was like a lively sheep—a stupid young man. He was a carpenter, having learned in a manual arts school, and now he taught the trade in the town school.

"Ardal'on Borisych, old friend!" he called out gaily. "You're at home drinking coffee, and here am I—so we're together again."

"Natasha, bring a third spoon," called out Varvara.

The noise of Natal'ya jangling the sole remaining teaspoon—the rest had been lost—could be heard from the kitchen.

"Eat, Pavlushka," said Peredonov, and it was evident

that he wanted to be hospitable to Volodin. "And I, brother, am soon going to worm my way into an inspectorship—the Princess has promised Varya."

Volodin was pleased and burst into laughter.

"And the future inspector is drinking coffee!" he cried, slapping Peredonov on the shoulder.

"But do you think that it's easy when you climb into an inspectorship? They denounce you—and that's the end of you."

"But what could they denounce you for?" asked Volodin with a smirk.

"What difference does it make? They'll say I've been reading Pisarev* . . . and ftt!"

"Well you had better hide your Pisarev behind the bookcase," advised Volodin with a titter.

Peredonov glanced cautiously at Volodin and said, "Perhaps I never have had any Pisarev. Do you want a drink, Pavlushka?"

Volodin stuck out his lower lip and assumed the significant appearance of a man conscious of his own worth. Nodding his head, he said in a bleating voice, "I'm always prepared to drink if I'm in company, and you can bet your life on it."

Peredonov was also always ready for a drink. They drank some vodka and ate sweet tarts.

Suddenly Peredonov splashed the remains of his cup of coffee onto the wallpaper. Volodin stared with his sheeplike eyes and looked around in wonder. The wallpaper was soiled and torn. "What are you doing to your wallpaper?" asked Volodin.

Peredonov and Varvara burst out laughing. "It's to spite our landlady," said Varvara. "We're going to leave soon . . . only don't you blab."

---

* D. I. Pisarev was a leading nineteenth-century radical who challenged all established institutions including the family and the church. He died in 1868.

"That's wonderful!" cried Volodin, and he broke into joyous laughter.

Peredonov went up to the wall and began to kick it with the soles of his boots. Following his example, Volodin also kicked at the wall. "When we leave a place, we always soil the walls to give them something to remember us by," said Peredonov.

"What a mess you've caused!" exclaimed Volodin with ecstasy.

"Irishka will be beside herself," said Varvara with a mean, dry laugh.

And all three of them stood before the wall—they spat on it, tore at the wallpaper, and pummeled it with their shoes. Afterwards, exhausted and happy, they stopped.

Peredonov stooped down and picked up the tomcat. The cat was fat, white, and ugly. Peredonov tormented it, pulling its tail and its ears and shaking it by the neck. All the while, Volodin was roaring gleefully and encouraging Peredonov to do still more.

"Ardal'on Borisych, blow in his eyes!" he said. "Rub his fur the wrong way!"

The cat snorted and tried to work its way free, but didn't dare show its claws—it always got whipped terribly for that. The game finally began to bore Peredonov, and he threw down the cat.

"Listen to what I want to say to you, Ardal'on Borisych," began Volodin. "I kept reminding myself not to forget all the way here, and still I came close to forgetting."

"Well?" asked Peredonov sullenly.

"You love sweet things," said Volodin gaily, "and I know of a dish that'll make you lick your chops."

"I know all the good-tasting dishes myself," said Peredonov.

Volodin looked hurt. "Perhaps, Ardal'on Borisych,"

he said, "you do know all the good-tasting things which they make in your village, but how could you know all of the delicious foods that are made in my village, if you've never been there?"

And satisfied with the logic of his retort, Volodin laughed and made a bleating sound.

"In your village they guzzle dead cats," said Peredonov angrily.

"Excuse me, Ardal'on Borisych," said Volodin in a laughing, piercing voice, "it might be that they eat dead cats in your village, but we aren't discussing that. All I say is that you've never eaten *erly*."

"No, I've never eaten that," admitted Peredonov.

"What sort of a dish is it?" asked Varvara.

"Well, it's like this," Volodin began to explain, "do you know *kut'ya?*" *

"Of course, who doesn't know what a funeral pudding is like?" answered Varvara with a grin.

"Well, that's it—ground up *kut'ya* with raisins, sugar, and almonds. That's just what *erly* is."

And Volodin related in detail how they cooked *erly* in his village. Peredonov listened dejectedly. "Funeral pudding," he thought. "Can it be that Pavlushka wishes to do away with me?"

"If you want, just so that it's done right," continued Volodin, "you can give me the ingredients, and I'll make some for you."

"That would be like letting a goat into a vegetable garden," said Peredonov sullenly, and he thought to himself, "He might put something in it."

Again, Volodin was offended.

"If you think that I'll steal some of your sugar, Ardal'on Borisych, then you're mistaken. I have no need of your sugar."

* *Kut'ya* is a baked pudding of corn or rice with spices and honey which is served at Russian funeral dinners.

"Don't be a fool," interrupted Varvara. "You know how particular he is about everything. You'd best come here and make it."

"But you'll eat it by yourself," said Peredonov.

"Why is that?" asked Volodin with an injured and offended air.

"Because it'll taste like trash."

"As you wish, Ardal'on Borisych," said Volodin, shrugging his shoulders, "I only wanted to please you, but if you don't want it, that's your choice."

"But what about the tongue-lashing that the general gave you?" asked Peredonov.

"What general?" replied Volodin in a puzzled manner, and he blushed and stuck out his lower lip in offense.

"Oh, we've heard about it, we've heard about it," said Peredonov. Varvara smirked.

"Pardon me, Ardal'on Borisych," said Volodin excitedly, "you've heard about it, yes, but perhaps you didn't hear the whole story. I'll tell you what really happened."

"Well then, let's hear it," said Peredonov.

"It all took place the day before yesterday," said Volodin, "at just about this time. As you know, there are repairs going on in the workshop at my school. And Veriga, if you please, comes in together with our inspector to have a look around. We were working in the back room. That's fine—I'm not concerned with why Veriga came, that's his business and none of my affairs. I realize, of course, that he is the marshal of the nobility, but he has no business in our school . . . But I won't get into that. He came, so let him stay. We didn't interfere with him, we were doing our own work. Suddenly they came into our room, and Veriga, if you please, has his hat on."

"That shows that he has no respect for you," said Peredonov sullenly.

"And, if you please," said Volodin with pleasure, "there was an icon hanging in the room, and we ourselves had our hats off when he suddenly appeared just like some sort of Mohammedan. Well I told him quietly and graciously, 'Your Excellency,' I said, 'please take the trouble to remove your hat because,' I said, 'there is an icon here.' Wasn't that the right thing to say?" asked Volodin, and he stared inquisitively.

"You were smart, Pavlushka," cried Peredonov. "He got just what he deserved."

"Of course, why should they get away with it," affirmed Varvara. "You're a good fellow, Pavel Vasil'evich."

Volodin, with the air of a man unjustly accused, continued, "But he suddenly turned to me and said, 'Don't meddle in what doesn't concern you!'* Then he turned around and walked out. That's all that happened and nothing more."

Volodin felt that he had been a sort of hero. Peredonov gave him a caramel to console him.

Still another guest arrived, Sof'ya Efimovna Prepolovenskaya. She was a forester's wife, stout and with a cunning, good-natured face and smooth movements. They invited her for lunch.

"Why is it that you've been visiting Varvara Dmitrievna so often, Pavel Vasil'evich?" she shyly asked Volodin.

"It's not Varvara Dmitrievna, but Ardal'on Borisych that I come to visit," answered Volodin bashfully.

"And you haven't fallen in love with anyone?" asked Prepolovenskaya laughingly.

It was well known to everyone that Volodin had been trying to find a bride with a dowry, and that he had proposed to many and been refused. Prepolovenskaya's joke seemed in bad taste to him. In a trembling

---

* "Every cricket should stick to his own place under the stove"— a folk saying.

voice suggesting an injured sheep, he said, "If I were to fall in love, Sof'ya Efimova, it would be nobody's business except hers and mine, and, thus, it would have nothing to do with you."

But Prepolovenskaya didn't stop there.

"Just suppose," she said, "that you yourself were in love with Varvara Dmitrievna. Then who would bake sweet tarts for Ardal'on Borisych?"

Volodin stuck out his lips and raised his eyebrows. He didn't know what to say.

"But don't be timid, Pavel Vasil'evich," continued Prepolovenskaya. "Why aren't you married? You're young and handsome too."

"Perhaps Varvara Dmitrievna wouldn't want to marry me," said Volodin giggling.

"Why, how could she not want to," Prepolovenskaya answered. "You're overly modest."

"And, perhaps I don't want to marry her," said Volodin coyly. "It just might be that I don't want to marry other people's cousins. Maybe I have a niece of my own growing up in my village."

He had already begun to think that Varvara wouldn't mind marrying him. Varvara was angry. She considered Volodin a fool, and, moveover, his salary was only three quarters that of Peredonov's. Prepolovenskaya wanted to marry Peredonov to her own cousin, the plump daughter of a priest, and that was why she was trying to make Peredonov quarrel with Varvara.

"What are you trying to marry me for?" said Varvara, with annoyance. "You'd do better to match your little fool cousin up with Pavel Vasil'evich!"

"Why should I take him away from you!" she retorted playfully.

Prepolovenskaya's jokes were giving a new turn to Peredonov's sluggish thoughts—this and the *erly* had been firmly planted in his head. Why had Volodin recommended such a dish? Peredonov did not like to have to mull things over, and he always believed what anyone told him at once. So naturally, he believed that Volodin was in love with Varvara. "I'd marry Varvara," he thought, "but then when I went off to my inspector's job, I would be poisoned along the way with *erly*, and Volodin would take my place—I'd be buried as Volodin and he would be the inspector. Very clever!"

Suddenly a noise was heard in the hall. Peredonov and Varvara became frightened. Peredonov fixed his squinting eyes on the door while Varvara sneaked up to the hall door, opened it a little, glanced around, and then, just as quietly, she returned to the table on tiptoe with her arms held out for balance. She smiled awkwardly.

Shrill cries and noises were coming from the hallway as if there was an argument going on. Varvara whispered, "It's Ershikha, drunk as drunk can be. Natashka won't let her in, but she's charging into the hall."

"What'll we do?" asked Peredonov fearfully.

"We'll have to go into the hall so that she doesn't get in here," decided Varvara.

They went into the hall, closing the door tightly behind them. Varvara went out into the entrance hall in the faint hope of detaining the landlady or sitting her down in the kitchen. But the impudent old woman had already forced her way into the hall. She halted in the doorway with her hands on her hips, and, as a sort of greeting, she poured out abusive language. Peredonov and Varvara were fussing around her trying to seat her on a chair nearer the hall and farther from the dining room. Varvara brought her some vodka, beer, and tarts on a tray from the kitchen. But the landlady would not sit down, or take anything, and kept forcing her way towards the dining room. Somehow, however, she was unable to locate the door. She was flushed, dirty, disheveled, and vodka could be smelled on her breath from quite a distance.

"No," she cried out, "you must invite me to your table. What's this tray, I want a tablecloth! I am the mistress of this house and so you must show me respect. And don't you think that I'm drunk either, for I'm an honorable woman and my husband's wife."

Varvara, smirking with both apprehensiveness and insolence, said, "Yes, we already know all that."

Ershova winked at Varvara, burst into raucous laughter, and suddenly snapped her fingers. She was becoming more and more bold.

"Cousin!" she cried. "We know that you're his cousin. And why is it that the headmaster's wife has never paid you a visit? Eh? Why?"

"Just don't shout so," said Varvara.

But Ershova began shouting even louder, "How dare you order me about! I'm in my own house, and I'll do what I want. If I want, I'll turn you right out so that not even your smell will be left. It's just that I'm too kind to you. You can live here, all right, as long as you don't ruin the place."

All this time Volodin and Prepolovenskaya sat timidly near the window and were silent. Prepolovenskaya was smiling slightly and pretending to look into the street, but she was really sneaking glances at the furious landlady. Volodin sat with an expression of injured importance on his face.

In time Ershova worked herself into a good mood, and, drunkenly smiling and gaily slapping her on the shoulder, she said to Varvara in a friendly manner, "Now you do what I tell you—seat me at your table, and let's have a little high-sounding chitchat. Yes, give your landlady something nice to eat and show her some respect, my little dearie."

"Here are some tarts," said Varvara.

"I don't want any of your meat pies, I want fancy stuff," exclaimed Ershova waving her arms and smiling blissfully.

"The swells sure do stuff themselves on tasty food! It's scrumptious!"

"No, I don't have any of that stuff for you," answered Varvara growing bolder as her landlady became gayer. "Here are some tarts, gorge yourself on these."

Suddenly Ershova made out the door to the dining room and let out a violent roar, "Make way, you viper!"

She pushed Varvara out of the way and rushed towards the door before they could grab her. With her head down and her fists clenched, she burst into the dining room, flinging back the door with a bang. She stopped on the threshold, looked at the soiled wallpaper, and let out a piercing whistle. She put her hands on her hips, stamped furiously, and screamed violently, "Aha! So you really are going to move!"

"Why what do you mean, Irin'ya Stepanovna," said Varvara with a quivering voice, "we aren't even considering it. Someone's been fooling you."

"We're not going anywhere," affirmed Peredonov, "everything is fine for us here."

The landlady was not listening. She marched up to the panic-stricken Varvara and waved her fists about in her face. Peredonov stayed behind Varvara. He would have run away but he was curious to see what happened between the landlady and Varvara.

"I'll stand on your one leg and tear you in half with the other," screamed Ershova fiercely.

"What's the matter with you, Irin'ya Stepanovna," said Varvara. "Stop this. We have guests."

"Bring your guests here," cried Ershova. "I should like to get a hold of your guests too!"

Ershova dashed staggering into the hall and suddenly she completely changed her speech and her whole manner and said calmly to Prepolovenskaya with a low bow in which she scarcely kept from falling on the floor, "Dear Madam Sof'ya Efimovna, please forgive me, a drunken old woman. But kindly listen to what I have to say. You often visit them, but do you know what she says about your cousin? And to whom? To me, that's who, a drunken shoemaker's wife. Why? So that I'll tell everybody, that's why!"

Varvara turned crimson and said, "I haven't told you anything."

"You didn't eh? Why you vile creature!" cried Ershova, advancing toward Varvara with clenched fists.

"Just be quiet," muttered Varvara in confusion.

"No, I won't be quiet," shouted Ershova maliciously, and she again turned to Prepolovenskaya, "Here is what the little beast told me. She said that your cousin is making time with your husband!"

Sof'ya turned on Varvara with angry and cunning eyes. She stood up and said with a sarcastic smile, "Thank you ever so much. I didn't expect that."

"You lie!" screeched Varvara spitefully at Ershova.

Ershova cried out in anger, stamped her foot, and shook her hand at Varvara. Then she turned to Prepolovenskaya for still another time.

"And what he says about you . . . dear madam, what he says! That you went the rounds before you got married! That's what they are, the most loathsome kind of people! You should spit in their mugs, my good woman, and have nothing to do with such base people."

Prepolovenskaya flushed and walked in silence to the entrance hall. Peredonov ran after her trying to justify himself, "She's a liar, don't believe her. Only once I told her that you're a fool, and that was just in anger. But I swear to God I never said any more—she's made all this up herself."

"Of course, Ardal'on Borisych," answered Prepolovenskaya calmly, "I can see that she's drunk and that she herself doesn't know what she's babbling. Only why do you allow all this in your house?"

"But what can one do with her!" answered Peredonov.

Prepolovenskaya, upset and angry, put on her jacket. Peredonov didn't offer to help her. He was still mumbling something, but she didn't even hear him. Then Peredonov came back into the hall. Ershova had begun to reproach him loudly. Varvara ran out onto the porch to mollify Prepolovenskaya.

"You yourself know what a fool he is," she said. "He doesn't even know what he's talking about himself."

"Absolutely. Don't get upset," answered Prepolovenskaya. "It makes no difference what a drunken woman babbles."

Tall, dense nettles grew around the house where the porch stuck out. Prepolovenskaya smiled slightly, and the last trace of displeasure vanished from her pale, stout face. She began to be friendly and gracious with Varvara as before—she would gain vengeance for her mortification, and without a quarrel. They walked into the garden together to wait for the landlady's departure.

All the time Prepolovenskaya looked at the nettles which grew densely in the garden along the fence. Finally she said, "You have so many nettles here. Do you use them?"

Varvara laughed. "What use would I have for them!" she answered.

"If you don't mind terribly, I'd like to gather some of yours since we don't have any," said Prepolovenskaya.

"But what do you want with them?" asked Varvara with surprise.

"I just need them," said Prepolovenskaya smiling.

"Tell me, darling, for what?" inquired the curious Varvara.

Prepolovenskaya leaned over to Varvara's ear and whispered, "When you rub yourself with nettles, you don't lose weight. It's from nettles that my Genichka has grown so stout."

It was well known that Peredonov had a preference for plump women and disliked skinny ones. Varvara was distressed that she was so slender and was getting even scrawnier. One of her main problems was how she could put on some weight—she was always asking people if they knew a way. Prepolovenskaya was now convinced that Varvara would rub herself heartily with nettles according to her direction. Thus, she would punish herself.

3 : ༄༅༄༅

Peredonov and Ershova went outside. "Come here!" he muttered.

She was happy and shouting with all her might. They were going to dance. Varvara and Prepolovenskaya went through the kitchen into another room, where they sat by the window to see what would happen outside.

Peredonov and Ershova embraced and went into a dance on the grass around the pear tree. Peredonov's face remained dull and expressionless as before. His gold eyeglasses bounced upon his nose, and his short hair flopped around on his head mechanically, as though he were a lifeless puppet. Ershova screamed, shouted, and flung her arms about. All the while she was swaying.

"Hey you, snooty," she shouted to Varvara in the window, "come out and dance! Or don't you like our company?"

Varvara turned away.

"The devil with you! I'm tired out!" cried Ershova as she fell down heavily in the grass drawing Peredonov with her.

They sat there for a while still embracing, and then they began to dance again. And this was repeated several times—first the dance and then the rest under the pear tree, either on the bench, or right on the grass.

Volodin was genuinely happy as he looked at their dancing from the window. He burst out laughing, made weird faces, squirmed about, lifted his knees up, and exclaimed, "They're crazy! What fun!"

"The damn bitch!" said Varvara angrily.

"The bitch," agreed Volodin with a laugh. "Just wait, my darling landlady, and I'll show you something. Let's mess up the hall too. It's all the same now—she won't come back today. She'll tire herself out in the grass there and go home to sleep it off."

He laughed happily and pranced about, bleating like a ram. "Yes, mess everything up, Pavel Vasil'evich," Prepolovenskaya encouraged him, "and the hell with her. If she returns, we can say that she did it herself when she was so drunk that she didn't notice it."

Volodin, laughing and hopping up and down, ran into the hall and began to scrape his boots along the wallpaper.

"Varvara Dmitrievna, get me some rope," he cried.

Varvara, waddling like a duck, went through the hall into the bedroom, and from there she brought back a piece of knotted and shredded cord. Volodin made a noose, got up on a chair in the middle of the hall, and hung the noose from the lamp socket.

"This is for the landlady!" he exclaimed. "It's so that she'll have something to hang herself from in her fury when you leave."

Both women squealed with laughter.

"Now let me have a scrap of paper and a pencil," cried Volodin.

Varvara rummaged in the bedroom some more and brought back a scrap of paper and a pencil. Volodin wrote "For the landlady" on it and stuck it to the noose. He did all of this with absurd grimaces. Then he again began to jump furiously along the walls, scraping them with his heels and shaking with laughter all the while. The entire house was filled with his screeching and bleating laughter. The terrified white cat had its ears back and was looking out of the bedroom, evidently not knowing where to run.

Peredonov at last separated himself from Ershova and came back into the house alone. Ershova was tired and went home to sleep, just as had been predicted. Volodin met Peredonov with gay laughter and shouted, "Hurrah! We really made a mess in the hall!"

"Hurrah!" cried Peredonov, and he laughed loudly and jerkily as if he were hurling forth his laughter.

The women also cried, "Hurrah!" and a general celebration began. Peredonov shouted, "Pavlushka, let's dance!"

"Let's, Ardal'osha," answered Volodin with a silly snigger.

They danced under the noose and both kicked up their legs absurdly. The floor was quivering under Peredonov's heavy stamps.

"Ardal'on Borisych is dancing for all he's worth," remarked Prepolovenskaya with a slight smile.

"Don't even talk about it. He does all sorts of foolish

things," answered Varvara angrily, but she was admiring Peredonov.

She sincerely thought that he was handsome and a fine fellow. His most foolish actions seemed proper to her. To her he was neither foolish nor offensive.

"Let's perform a funeral service for the landlady," cried Volodin. "Let's have a pillow!"

"What they won't think up," said Varvara laughing.

She threw a pillow with a dirty cotton cover out of the bedroom. They placed the pillow on the floor, in place of the landlady, and they began to perform a funeral service over her with savage and piercing voices. Then they called Natalya in and had her play the *ariston** while all four of them danced a quadrille, twisting absurdly and kicking up their legs.

After the dance Peredonov had a flash of generosity. Animation, dull and morose, shone on his bloated face. A decision had taken hold of him, an almost automatic decision, which was perhaps a consequence of his strenuous activity. He pulled out his wallet, counted out several bills, and, with a haughty and self-satisfied expression, threw them at Varvara.

"Take them, Varvara!" he exclaimed. "Get a wedding dress made for yourself."

The bills scattered about the floor. Varvara quickly snatched them up—she was not in the least offended by such a method of presentation. Prepolovenskaya thought spitefully, "Well, we'll see who's going to get him," and she smiled with malice. Volodin, of course, didn't offer to help Varvara pick up the money.

Prepolovenskaya soon left. In the hall she met a new visitor, Grushina.

Mar'ya Osipovna Grushina was a young widow with a prematurely faded appearance. She was slightly built,

* The *ariston* is a hand organ somewhat similar to our hurdy-gurdy.

and her dry skin was covered with wrinkles which almost seemed to be filled with dust. Her face, though, was not unpleasant, but her teeth were dirty and black. Her hands were thin, and her fingernails were long and clawlike. Under her fingernails there was dirt. At first glance she not only appeared very dirty, but also gave the impression that she never washed and was inseparable from the clothes she wore. One would think that if she were struck several times with a carpet-beater, a column of dust would rise to the very heavens. Her clothing hung on her with rumpled creases as though it had just been taken from a bound packet where it had been overlooked for a long time. Grushina lived on a pension, small sales, and the interest from money which she loaned on security of property. Her conversation was generally immodest, and she habitually bothered males in the hope of finding a husband. There was always some sort of unmarried official occupying a room in her house.

Varvara was happy to see Grushina: she had a job for her to do. They at once began to talk about the servant in whispers. The curious Volodin sat near them and listened, while Peredonov was sullenly sitting alone at the table and kneading the edge of the tablecloth with his hands.

Varvara was complaining to Grushina about her Natalya. Grushina suggested and praised a new servant named Klavdiya to her. They decided to go after her at once to the Samorodina region where she was living for the time being at the house of an excise official who had been transferred to another town a few days ago. It was only the name that troubled Varvara, and she asked in perplexity, "Klavdiya? What can I call her— Klashka?"

"You can call her Klavdiushka," suggested Grushina.

This pleased Varvara. "Klavdiushka—*diushka*," she

repeated with a screeching laugh. It should be pointed out that in our town pigs are called *diushkas*. Volodin grunted, and everyone guffawed.

"Darling Diushka," prattled Volodin between bursts of laughter, screwing up his stupid face and protruding his lips.

And he continued to grunt and make a fool of himself until they told him that he was being tiresome. Then he left his seat with an injured expression on his face and sat down near Peredonov. He lowered his wide forehead like a ram and stared at the soiled, spotted tablecloth.

Varvara decided to buy the material for her wedding dress at the same time that she was on the way to Samorodina. She always went shopping with Grushina who helped her to make the selections and bargain.

Concealing it from Peredonov, Varvara crammed various cookies, sweet tarts, and favors for her children down into Grushina's pockets. Grushina surmised that Varvara wanted her to do something for her today.

Her tight shoes and high heels did not let Varvara walk much. She soon tired and that was why she very often went by cab although the distances in our town were not great. Lately she had been visiting Grushina's frequently. The cab drivers were aware of this—there were about a score of them. When they were seating Varvara, they no longer even asked where she was going.

They got into the cab and went to see the people at whose house Klavdiya was living, to find out about her. Everywhere there was dirt in the streets even though it had just rained the night before. The cab would no sooner rumble onto stone pavement, than it would return again to the sticky mud on unpaved streets. Varvara's voice, in contrast, jarred on unchangingly, often fortified with Grushina's sympathetic prattling.

"My goose went visiting Marfushka again," said Varvara.

"That's how they're trying to catch him," answered Grushina with sympathetic maliciousness. "He'd be a good husband for anyone and especially for Marfushka. She hasn't even dreamt of getting someone like him."

"I really don't know what to do," complained Varvara. "He has become so restless that it's simply dreadful. Believe me, my head's in a whirl. He'll marry, and I'll have to take to the street."

"What's wrong with you, Varvara Dmitrievna, old girl," consoled Grushina, "don't think such things. He would never marry anyone but you. He's accustomed to you."

"Sometimes he goes away at night, and I can't sleep," said Varvara. "Who knows but that he might, perhaps be getting married somewhere. Sometimes I toss the whole night. They're all after him. The stout Zhenka and even those three Rutilov mares . . . but they'll chase after anyone."

And Varvara continued to complain for a long time, and from all that was said, Grushina saw that she still had some sort of request to ask of her, and she looked forward with pleasure to a reward.

Klavdiya was pleasing, and the wife of the excise official recommended her. They hired her and instructed her to come that very evening inasmuch as the excise official was leaving that day.

Finally they arrived at Grushina's. Grushina lived in a rather slovenly fashion in her own house with her three small children. They were shabby, dirty, stupid, and angry like scalded puppies. Only now did Varvara and Grushina get down to business.

"My fool, Ardal'oshka," began Varvara, "is demanding that I write to the Princess again. But it would be stupid to write her! She would either not answer or give

me an answer I don't want. Our acquaintance is not
terribly close."

The Princess Volchanskaya, with whom Varvara had
once lived as a domestic seamstress for simple tasks,
could have been able to render patronage to Peredonov: her daughter was married to Shchepkin, an important government official in the Ministry of Education. She had already written to Varvara, in response to
a request she had made last year, that she could not
seek favor for Varvara's intended, but it would be a
different matter for her husband, and she could ask if an
opening occurred. That letter hadn't satisfied Peredonov, for only a nebulous hope was given, and it had
not been definitely stated that the Princess would manage to get an inspector's position for Varvara's husband. In order to settle this dissatisfaction, they had
gone to Petersburg recently. Varvara saw the Princess
and later brought Peredonov to her, but purposely
delayed their arrival so that they would not run into the
Princess. Varvara realized that, at best, the Princess
would advise them to get married quickly and make several indefinite promises to help them in the event of an
opening—promises which would be quite inadequate
for Peredonov. Thus, Varvara decided not to have
Peredonov meet the Princess.

"I'm counting on you to give me solid support,"
said Varvara. "Help me, Mar'ya Osipovna, old friend."

"How can I help you, Varvara Dmitrievna, darling?"
asked Grushina. "You must know that I'm ready to do
anything for you. Would you like me to tell your fortune?"

"Well, I know your ability at sorcery," said Varvara
with a smile. "No, you must help me in another way."

"What is that?" asked Grushina with restless and
pleasant anticipation.

"It's very simple," said Varvara with a smirk. "You

write a letter as though it were coming from the Princess, in her handwriting, and I'll show it to Ardal'on Borisych."

"Oi, dearest, how could you think that I could do that!" said Grushina with mock fear. "What would become of me if they found out about this business?"

Varvara was not at all troubled by her reply. She drew a crumpled letter out of her pocket saying, "Here, I've brought the letter from the Princess to you for a model."

For a long time Grushina refused. Varvara clearly saw that Grushina would agree, but wanted to get more for the job. Varvara, of course, wanted to give less. She cautiously increased the reward and promised various little gifts, including an old silk dress, until Grushina finally saw that Varvara would not give any more. Words of entreaty poured from Varvara's mouth. Grushina consented and took the letter, but she acted as though she were only doing it from pity.

4 : ⁊⯊⁊⯊

The billiard hall was smoke-filled. Peredonov, Rutilov, Falastov, Volodin, and Murin—a robust landowner with a stupid appearance who owned a small estate and was a resourceful and well-to-do person—all five of them had finished their game and were preparing to leave.

Evening was approaching. Many emptied beer bottles were stacked on the dirty plank table. The players had had a lot to drink during the game—their faces were red and they were getting boisterous. Only Rutilov retained his usual sickly paleness. True, he had drunk less than the others, but even after hearty drinking he would only have been still more pale.

Coarse words flew back and forth, but no one was hurt by this—it was all among friends.

As almost always, Peredonov had lost. He played billiards poorly, but he maintained an unperturbed gloomy expression on his face and, reluctantly, paid his debts.

"Fire!" Murin shouted loudly, and he aimed his cue at Peredonov.

Peredonov cried out from fright and cowered away. The foolish thought that Murin wished to shoot him flashed through his mind. Everyone burst out laughing.

"I can't stand such jokes," grumbled Peredonov with vexation.

Murin was already remorseful of having frightened Peredonov. His son was a student in the gymnasium, and therefore he considered it his duty to please the instructors at the gymnasium in every way possible. Now he began to apologize to Peredonov and treated him to wine and tonic.

"My nerves are shot," said Peredonov gloomily. "I'm dissatisfied with our headmaster."

"The future inspector has lost," exclaimed Volodin in a bleating voice. "He's feeling sorry for his lost money!"

"Unlucky at play, lucky in love," said Rutilov, smiling and showing his somewhat decayed teeth.

Even without this, Peredonov was not in a good mood because of his loss and his scare. When, on top of that, they began to tease him about Varvara, he cried, "I'll get married, and Var'ka can clear out!"

His companions laughed heartily and egged him on. "You wouldn't dare," they said.

"But I do dare. Tomorrow I'll go and find someone to marry," he answered.

"That's a bet! All right?" said Falastov. "I'll wager ten rubles."

But Peredonov began to worry about the money. Perhaps he might lose and then have to pay . . . he turned away and was sullenly silent.

At the garden gate they split up and went their separate ways. Peredonov and Rutilov walked off together. Rutilov began persuading Peredonov that he should marry one of his sisters immediately. "Don't worry, I've set things up," he assured him.

"There has been no marriage announcement," objected Peredonov.

"I've taken care of it all, I tell you," Rutilov ran on. "I've found a good priest who knows that you're not related to our family."

"There are no ushers," said Peredonov.

"You think not. We can get them right away. I'll send for them, and they'll come straight to the church, or I'll go for them myself. But it couldn't have been done earlier or your cousin would have found out and interfered."

Peredonov was silent and gloomily looked about him at the small, dark, silent houses behind drowsy gardens and uneven hedges.

"You just wait here by the gate," said Rutilov persuasively, "and I'll bring out whichever one you like. Listen, I'll prove it to you . . . twice two is four, is that so or not?"*

"That's true," answered Peredonov.

"Well, since twice two is four, it follows that you should marry a sister of mine."

* This is a reference to a well-known passage in Dostoevsky's *Notes from the Underground* in which the underground man claims that "twice two is four" is a statement that hinders and mocks man. While Peredonov himself is hardly an "underground man," the influence of Dostoevsky in regard to other aspects of Sologub's novel is quite clear—see note on p. 165.

Peredonov was at a loss. "Yes, that's true," he thought, "twice two is four." And he glanced with respect at the sober-looking Rutilov. "You can't argue with him, I'll have to marry one of them!"

The two friends just then came up to the Rutilov house and stood by the gate.

"It can't be done so suddenly," said Peredonov angrily.

"Fool! Why they simply can't wait," exclaimed Rutilov.

"But perhaps I don't want to."

"What do you mean, you don't want to, you fool! Do you want to be lonely all your life?" retorted Rutilov with conviction. "Or will you go into a monastery? Or aren't you sick of Varya yet? Why just think what faces she'll make if you bring a young wife home."

Peredonov burst into short, jerky laughter, but suddenly he again became gloomy and said, "But, perhaps they don't want to."

"How could they not want to, you idiot!" answered Rutilov. "I have already given you my word."

"They're haughty," reflected Peredonov.

"So what's that to you, it's all the better."

"They're laughers."

"But not at you," declared Rutilov.

"How do I know?"

"Just believe me, I wouldn't deceive you. They hold you in esteem. You aren't some sort of Pavlushka so that they would laugh at you."

"According to you, yes," said Peredonov distrustfully. "No, I want to convince myself that they don't laugh at me."

"What a fool," said Rutilov with surprise. "How could they dare laugh at you? Well, just how would you like to assure yourself of it?"

Peredonov thought awhile and said, "Let them come out into the street right now."

"Well all right, that's easy enough," agreed Rutilov.

"All three," continued Peredonov.

"Fine."

"And let each one tell me how she would please me."

"What for?" asked Rutilov with astonishment.

"Then I can find out what they want. Otherwise, you'll lead me by the nose," explained Peredonov.

"No one is going to lead you by the nose."

"They might want to laugh at me," reasoned Peredonov, "but let them come out here, and then if they want to laugh, I'll be the one who'll laugh at them."

Rutilov thought a bit, moving his hat to the back of his head and then to his forehead again. Finally he said, "Well wait a minute, I'll go and tell them. What an odd one you are! Only you'd best step into the yard for a while, otherwise the devil will bring someone along the street and you'll be seen."

"I would spit on them," said Peredonov, but all the same he followed Rutilov through the gate. Rutilov went into the house for his sisters, while Peredonov waited outside.

In the living room, which faced out towards the gate, sat all four sisters. They all looked alike, and they all resembled their brother. They were all attractive, rosy, and gay. There was the married Larisa, calm, pleasant, and stout; the frivolous and clever Dar'ya, who was the tallest and most slender of the sisters; the quick to laugh Ludmila; and the small, tender, delicate-looking Valeriya. They were munching on walnuts and raisins and, evidently, were waiting for something. For this reason they were in a state of excitement and laughed more than usual, recounting the latest town gossip and lampooning their friends as well as strangers.

Ever since morning they had been prepared to be married. It only remained for one of them to put on a presentable wedding dress, and pin on a veil and some flowers. The sisters did not mention Varvara in their conversation, as if there were no such person in the world. But the very fact that these relentless gossips, who picked everyone to pieces, did not mention a single word about Varvara the whole day, this alone, showed that the unpleasant thought of her was sitting like a nail in each sister's head.

"I've brought him," exclaimed Rutilov as he entered the living room. "He's standing by the gate."

The sisters got up excitedly and began to talk and laugh all at the same time.

"There's only one problem," said Rutilov smiling.

"Well, what's that?" asked Dar'ya.

Valeriya knitted her beautiful dark brows in annoyance.

"Well now, let's see, how should I put it?" pondered Rutilov.

"Well hurry up and be quick about it," pressed Dar'ya.

With a little embarrassment, Rutilov explained what Peredonov wanted. The young girls raised a cry and began to abuse Peredonov, but little by little their displeased exclamations turned to jokes and laughter. Dar'ya made a face of grim expectation and said, "This is how he is standing by the gate."

Her imitation was a good one and very funny.

The girls began to look out of the window toward the gate. Dar'ya opened the window slightly and shouted, "Ardal'on Borisych, can we say it from the window?"

A morose voice was heard—"You cannot."

Dar'ya hurriedly banged the window shut. The sisters went into loud and uncontrolled laughter and ran out of the living room into the dining room so that Peredonov wouldn't hear them. In this merry family they knew how to pass from a very angry disposition to laughter and jokes, and a cheerful word most often settled the matter.

Peredonov stood and waited. He felt depressed and afraid. He considered running off, but he couldn't make up his mind to do it. From somewhere very far off the sound of music reached him: most likely it was Veriga's daughter playing the piano. The frail and tender notes floated in the quiet and dark evening air, producing melancholy and giving birth to sweet fantasies.

At first Peredonov's fantasies had an erotic tendency. He imagined the Rutilov girls in the most seductive positions. But the longer his waiting was prolonged, the more irritated Peredonov became at being forced to wait. Even the music, which had slightly aroused his deadened and coarse feelings, no longer affected him.

Night was falling around him, quietly rustling with its sinister footsteps and whispers. And it seemed even darker all around because Peredonov stood in a spot illumined by the living room lamp; the light fell in two bands outside, broadening as they reached the fence, beyond which could be seen the dark wooden walls of the neighboring house. The trees at the back of the Rutilov garden were turning suspiciously dark and whispering about something. Along the sidewalks nearby someone's slow heavy steps were heard for a long time. Peredonov was by now beginning to be afraid that, while he was standing there, he would be fallen upon and robbed or even killed. He pressed right up against the wall in the shadows so that he would not be seen and waited timidly.

But suddenly long shadows shot along the strips of light outside, doors banged, and voices could be heard behind the porch door. Peredonov stirred. "They're coming," he thought happily, and pleasant fantasies about the beautiful sisters again slowly began to stir in his mind, the foul offspring of his meager imagination.

The sisters were standing in the hall. Rutilov went outside to the gate and looked about to see whether there was anyone coming along the street. No one was to be seen or heard.

"There's no one here," he said to his sisters in a loud whisper through cupped hands. He remained there to keep watch in the street, and Peredonov joined him on the street.

"Well now, they'll soon tell you what you want to know," said Rutilov.

Peredonov was standing very near the gate and was looking through the crack between the gate and the gatepost. His face was gloomy and almost fearful. All the fantasies and thoughts in his mind faded away and were replaced by a ponderous, vague longing.

Dar'ya was the first to come up to the half-open gate. "Well, what can I do for you?" she asked.

Peredonov was sullenly silent.

"I'll make the most delicious pancakes for you, hot ones," said Dar'ya, "only don't choke on them."

From over her shoulder, Ludmila called, "But I shall go around the town every morning and gather all the gossip to tell you later. It will be jolly fun."

The capricious and delicate face of Valeriya appeared for a moment between the gay faces of her sisters, and in her slight voice she said, "I won't say what I'll do for you for anything—you'll have to guess that yourself."

The sisters ran away engulfed in laughter. Their voices and laughter were cut off by the door. Peredonov turned away from the gate. He was not quite satisfied. "They babbled something and left," he thought. "It would have been better if they'd written it out. But it's already getting late to be standing here waiting."

"Well, have you seen what you want?" asked Rutilov. "Which one do you want?"

Peredonov became lost in thought. "Of course," he finally reasoned, "I should choose the youngest. Why should I marry an older one!"

"Bring out Valeriya," he said decisively.

Rutilov returned to the house, and Peredonov again entered the garden.

Ludmila had been peeping out of the window trying to hear what was being said, but she had heard nothing. Now steps sounded on the walk outside. The sisters became quiet and sat in nervous embarrassment.

Rutilov entered, declaring, "He has chosen Valeriya. He's standing near the gate waiting."

The other three sisters began to make noise and laugh, but Valeriya grew slightly pale.

"Well, well," she repeated. "That's just what I want, just what I need." Her hands were trembling.

They began to array her, and all three sisters bustled around her. As always, she was slow and particular, but her sisters were hurrying her. Although they congratulated Valeriya, they were envious of her. The happy and excited Rutilov chattered endlessly—he was pleased that he had carried off the job so easily.

"But do you have the cab drivers at hand?" asked Dar'ya with concern.

"How could I?" Rutilov answered with annoyance. "The whole town would have come running, and Varvara would have dragged him home by his hair."

"But what are we going to do?"

"Just this—we'll go to the village square in pairs and hire the cabs there. It's very simple. First you with the bride, then Larisa with the groom . . . but not all at once, otherwise someone in town will still notice it. Ludmila and I will stop off at Falastov's, and they'll go together while I go to get Volodin."

That the other sisters did envy Valeriya was involuntarily shown in the way they laughed at her as well as the manner in which they scolded her and gave her light shoves for her sluggishness and fastidiousness. "What's wrong with all of you?" she finally said. "He's no great catch, and if you want to know, I still don't want to marry him." And she burst into tears.

The sisters exchanged glances and rushed to console her with kisses and fondling.

"Don't be upset, my little fool!" said Darya. "We were only teasing."

"If you'll only get married, you'll have him in your hands," said Larisa soothingly and gently.

Little by little Valeriya was comforted.*

Peredonov, who had been left alone, was buried in sweet dreams. Valeriya appeared to him in the allure of their wedding night, naked and ashamed, but happy— all slenderness and subtlety.

As he was dreaming, he took out some caramels which had stuck in his pocket and sucked them.

Then he recalled that Valeriya was a coquette. That means she'll demand fine clothes and trappings, he thought. Then, perhaps, he would not be able to put away money each month, and she might even squander his savings. She'd be a haughty wife and not even look into the kitchen. And on top of that, his food would get poisoned, for Varya would bribe the cook out of spite.

"And besides," thought Peredonov, "Valeriya is too much of a dainty little thing. You don't know how to act with a girl like that. How could I curse at her? How could I push her around? How could I spit on her? She would run out in tears and put me to shame before the whole town. No, it would be awful to be tied to her. Ludmila, now, is simpler. Why shouldn't I take her instead?"

He went up to the window and banged on the windowsill with his walking stick. In a few moments Rutilov stuck his head out of the window.

"What do you want?" he asked uneasily.

* The dialogue from "What's wrong with all . . ." to ". . . Valeriya was comforted" is deleted from a later edition, perhaps in order not to raise any doubts about Peredonov's eligibility in the eyes of the Rutilov girls.

"I've changed my mind," growled Peredonov.

"And?" exclaimed Rutilov fearfully.

"Bring me Ludmila," said Peredonov.

Rutilov left the window. "He's a devil in eyeglasses," he grumbled and went to his sisters.

Valeriya was pleased. "It's your good fortune, Ludmila," she said gaily.

Ludmila began to laugh loudly. She fell into a chair, threw herself back, and laughed and laughed.

"What shall I tell him?" inquired Rutilov. "Is it all right or not?" Ludmila was laughing so hard that she couldn't say a word and only waved her hands.

"Yes, of course she agrees," said Dar'ya for her. "Tell him quickly, or the fool will run off and not wait."

Rutilov went out into the living room and said in a whisper through the window, "Just wait a minute, she'll be ready presently."

"Well, be quick about it," said Peredonov angrily. "Why are they dawdling there?"

They dressed Ludmila quickly, and she was completely ready in about five minutes.

Peredonov was thinking about her. She was gay and plump. The only thing was that she liked to laugh a lot. Perhaps she would laugh at him. That would be terrifying. Dar'ya, although lively, was stouter and quieter. And beautiful too. It would be better to take her. He again knocked at the window.

"He's knocking again," said Larisa. "Do you think he wants you, Dar'ya?"

"The devil!" railed Rutilov, and he ran to the window.

"What now?" he asked in an angry whisper. "Have you changed your mind again or what?"

"Bring me Dar'ya," answered Peredonov.

"Well, wait," whispered Rutilov savagely.

Peredonov stood and thought about Dar'ya—and again his short erotic vision of her was replaced by fear.

Already she seemed very quick-tempered and sharp-tongued. She would harass him. "And why stand and wait here?" he thought. "I might catch cold. In the ditch by the road or in the weeds by the fence, there may be someone hiding who'll suddenly leap out and kill me." Peredonov became depressed. "And they are without dowries," he thought. They have no patronage in the Ministry of Education. Varvara will complain to the Princess." As it was, the headmaster had a grudge against Peredonov.

Peredonov began to get annoyed with himself. Why had he gotten entangled with Rutilov? It was as though Rutilov had charmed him. Yes, maybe he really had charmed him! He must recite a counter charm immediately.

Peredonov turned himself around in place, spat on all sides, and mumbled: "*Chur-churashki, churki-balvashki, buki-bukashki, vedi-tarakashki. Chur menya. Chur menya. Chur, chur, chur. Chur! Perechur! Raschur!*" *

A stern expression appeared on his face as if he were performing a very solemn ritual. After having performed this all-important act he felt himself out of danger of Rutilov's hex. He banged his stick against the window with force, angrily mumbling, "I could denounce them—they're setting a trap for me. No, I don't want to get married today," he declared to Rutilov whose head was sticking out of the window.

"What is the matter with you. Ardal'on Borisych? Everything is all ready," Rutilov attempted to persuade him.

"I don't want to," said Peredonov firmly. "Let's go to my house and play cards."

"What a devil!" stormed Rutilov. "He's backed out

---

* Peredonov's own version of a common superstitious chant against evil spirits and hexes. *Chur* signifies a magic line or boundary, hence *Chur menya* has the approximate meaning of "Don't touch me!"

—he doesn't want to get married," he declared to his sisters. "But I'll still talk the fool into it. He's asked me to his house to play cards."

The sisters cried out in unison berating Peredonov. "And you're going to that scoundrel's house?" asked Valeriya with vexation.

"Yes, I'm going, but I'll make him pay. And he still won't get away from us," said Rutilov, trying to preserve an assured appearance, but feeling very uneasy.

The girls' anger at Peredonov quickly changed to laughter. Rutilov left. The sisters ran to the window. "Ardal'on Borisych," cried Dar'ya, "why can't you make up your mind? One mustn't do things like that!"

"Sourpuss!" shouted Ludmila with laughter.

Peredonov was vexed. In his opinion the sisters ought to have wept with sorrow that he had rejected them. "They're just pretending!" he thought as he silently left the yard. The girls ran over to the windows facing the street, shouting and jeering after Peredonov until he had disappeared into the darkness.

5 : ੬✿੬✿

Peredonov was feeling weary and depressed. He had no more caramels in his pocket, and this saddened and annoyed him. Almost the whole way only Rutilov talked, continuing to extoll his sisters. Only once did Peredonov enter into the conversation when he angrily asked, "Does a bull have horns?"

"Yes, but what of it?" asked Rutilov at a loss.

"Well, I don't want to be a bull," declared Peredonov.

"You, Ardal'on Borisych, will never be a bull, because you are a downright pig," said the thoroughly annoyed Rutilov.

"You lie!" said Peredonov sullenly.

"No, I'm not lying, and I can prove it," said Rutilov maliciously.

"Prove it," demanded Peredonov.

"Just you wait a minute, and I will," answered Rutilov with the same spitefulness in his voice.

Both became silent. Peredonov was fearfully waiting, and his anger at Rutilov was tormenting him. Suddenly Rutilov asked, "Ardal'on Borisych, do you have any piggy-bank feed in your pockets, say, a five-kopeck piece?"

"Yes, I have, but I won't give it to you," Peredonov replied crossly.

Rutilov burst into laughter.

"If you have pig food, then you must be a pig!"* he cried out gleefully.

Peredonov grabbed his nose in terror and grumbled, "You're lying, I haven't got a pig's nose, I've got a human snout."

Rutilov laughed loudly. Peredonov looked at Rutilov with anger and apprehension and said, "You purposely led me past a bewitching *durman*† plant today and *durman*ized me so that you could marry me to your sisters. One witch would be bad enough, but to marry three at once!"

"Fool, then how was it that I didn't get bewitched?" asked Rutilov.

"You know of some way," said Peredonov. "Perhaps

* Rutilov's pun here is on the word *pyatachok* which means both a five-kopeck piece and a pig's snout.
† *Durman* is a kind of datura which is supposed to have bewitching powers.

you breathed through your mouth and didn't allow any of it in your nose, or you may have said some words—I don't know what one must do against witchcraft. I'm not a sorcerer. Until I recited a counter charm, I was thoroughly *durmanized*."

Rutilov laughed loudly. "How did you do it?" he asked. But Peredonov was silent.

"Why are you so stuck on running after Varvara?" said Rutilov. "Do you think that life will be good for you if you get a position through her? She'll really ride you then."

This was incomprehensible to Peredonov.

"After all," he thought, "she's doing this for her own sake. It will be better for her when I become an important bureaucrat and receive more money. That means she should be thankful to me and not I to her." And in any case, he was more at ease with her than he could be with anyone else.

Peredonov was used to Varvara. He was drawn to her, perhaps, as a result of his habit of bullying her, which was very pleasant for him. One couldn't find another one like her in the whole world.

It was already late. The lights were on in Peredonov's apartment. The bright windows stood out in the darkness of the street. Guests were sitting around the tea table. There was Grushina, who now was at Varvara's every day, Volodin, Prepolovenskaya, and her husband, Konstantin Petrovich, a tall man of under forty with an ashen face and black hair. He was an extraordinarily silent person. Varvara was all primped up and had on a white dress. They were drinking tea and chatting. As always, Varvara was upset that Peredonov had stayed away so long. With his gay, bleating laughter, Volodin said that Peredonov had gone somewhere with Rutilov. This greatly increased Varvara's uneasiness.

Finally Peredonov appeared with Rutilov. They were

met with shouting, laughter, and stupid, coarse jokes.

"Where is the vodka, Varvara?" Peredonov cried angrily.

Varvara jumped up from the table, smirking guiltily, and soon brought back the vodka in a coarsely cut crystal decanter.

"Let's drink," proposed Peredonov in a surly voice.

"Wait," said Varvara. "Klavdiushka will bring the *zakuska*.* Hurry up, you dolt!" she yelled into the kitchen.

But Peredonov was already filling the glasses. "Why wait?" he growled. "Time doesn't wait."

They downed their drinks and then ate blackberry jam tarts. Peredonov had only two stock entertainments for his guests—vodka and cards. Inasmuch as they had to wait for the tea to be served before sitting down to cards, there remained the vodka.

At the same time the *zakuska* was brought in so that they could drink some more. Klavdiya did not close the door as she went out, and Peredonov became upset. "The doors are always wide open," he grumbled.

He was afraid of drafts—he might catch cold—and, therefore, it was always stuffy and smelly in his apartment.

Prepolovenskaya picked up a hard-boiled egg. "They're good eggs," she said. "Where do you get them?"

"They're nothing special," said Peredonov. "Why on my father's estate there was a hen which laid two large eggs every day all year round."

"What of it?" replied Prepolovenskaya. "What a rarity—that's nothing to boast of! At our house in the country, there was a hen which laid two eggs and a spoon of butter every day."

"Yes, yes, we also had one of those," said Peredonov

* *Zakuska* is the Russian hors d'oeuvres consisting of tarts, small meat pies, jams, and various pickled and salted foods.

not noticing the mockery. "If other hens laid that, ours did it too. We had an extraordinary hen."

Varvara laughed. "You're making a fool of yourself," she said.

"Listening to your foolishness is enough to make one's ears droop,"* said Grushina.

Peredonov looked at her savagely and replied with ferociousness, "If your ears are drooping, they should be yanked off."

"You always say something like that, Ardal'on Borisych!" Grushina complained, taken aback.

The others laughed sympathetically. Volodin shook his head and smilingly explained with screwed-up eyes, "If one's ears droop, then one must pull them off, otherwise they'll wither up completely and start to swing to and fro, to and fro." And Volodin showed with his fingers how limp ears would dangle.

"That's the way you are," Grushina snapped at him, "you don't know how to make up anything yourself, but you ape other people's jokes!"

Volodin was hurt and said with dignity, "I have a sense of humor myself, Mar'ya Osipovna, but when we are having a pleasant social gathering, why not keep up someone else's joke! But if it displeases you, well, so be it. To each his own."

"That's reasonable, Pavel Vasil'evich," approved the smiling Rutilov.

"Pavel Vasil'evich is able to stand up for his rights," said Prepolovenskaya with a sly smile.

Varvara was slicing a piece of bread, and, absorbed with Volodin's ingenious talk, was holding the knife in her hand. Its edge glistened. Peredonov was frightened that she would suddenly slash him with it.

"Varvara, put down the knife!" he cried.

Varvara started. "Why are you shouting, you fright-

---

* "It makes my ears droop" is a way of saying "It hurts me to listen to you" or "You give me an earache."

ened me!" she said as she put down the knife. "He's squeamish about all sorts of things, you know," she explained to the taciturn Prepolovensky seeing that he was stroking his beard and preparing to say something.

"That happens," said Prepolovensky in a sorrowfully sweet tone. "I had one acquaintance who was very fearful of needles. He was always afraid that someone would jab him with one and it would enter his insides. And whenever he saw a needle, you can imagine how terrified he was. . . ."

And, having once begun to speak, he was unable to stop and told the same story over and over with different variations, until someone interrupted him and began to talk about something else. Then he again lapsed into silence.

Grushina shifted the conversation to erotic subjects. She related how her deceased husband had been jealous of her, and how she had deceived him. Afterwards, she told a story which she had heard from a Petersburg acquaintance about the mistress of a certain high-ranking personage who met her benefactor while she was walking along the street.

" 'Hello there, Zhanchik!' she shouts to him. And this was on the street, mind you!" related Grushina.

"Why I ought to denounce you to the authorities," said Peredonov angrily. "How can you babble nonsense about such important people?"

"But I haven't done anything, you see. This is just what was told to me," said the frightened Grushina quickly. "I pass on what they give me."

Peredonov maintained an angry silence while he drank his tea from a saucer, leaning on the table with his elbows. He thought that in the home of a future inspector it was improper to speak disrespectfully about important personages. He was angry with Grushina. Volodin, who was calling Peredonov the future inspector much too often, also annoyed him and made him suspicious. Once Peredonov even said to Volodin, "Say, brother, you're jealous, I bet! It's not you who'll be the inspector but I."

To this, Volodin, with a dignified expression on his face, replied, "To each his own, Ardal'on Borisych. You're a specialist in your business and I in mine."

"Our Natashka," announced Varvara, "went straight from us and got a job with the police lieutenant."

Peredonov trembled. There was an expression of terror on his face. "Are you lying?" he asked.

"And why should I lie?" retorted Varvara. "Go ask him yourself if you want."

This unpleasant news was confirmed by Grushina. Peredonov was stunned. She might say a lot of things, true and untrue, which the police lieutenant might take note of and, perhaps, report to the ministry. It promised to be a nasty business.

At that very moment Peredonov's eyes came to rest on the bookshelf over the dresser. There stood several bound books. The thin ones were Pisarev; the thicker ones, *Annals of the Fatherland*.* Peredonov blanched and said, "These books must be hidden, otherwise I'll be denounced."

Earlier Peredonov had displayed these books openly to show that he had liberal ideas, although, in reality, he did not have any opinions or even the desire to form them. He kept these books just to show, not to read. For a long time now he had not read a single book— he said he had no time—and he did not even subscribe to a newspaper, but found out all his news from con-

---

* *Otechestvennye zapiski*—a journal, founded in 1839, which changed hands several times in the course of years and represented many shades of progressive thought. Among its contributors were Belinsky, Lermontov, Turgenev, Chernyshevsky, Dobroliubov, Pisemsky, and Dostoevsky. After 1868 when the poet Nekrasov became its editor, the journal experienced severe difficulties with the censorship and, in April, 1884, was forced to close.

versation. Actually, there was nothing for him to know, for nothing in the outside world interested him. He even made fun of those who did subscribe to newspapers, saying that they were wasting time and money. One would have thought that his time was very valuable!

He went up to the bookshelf, grumbling, "That's the sort of town we have, they'll denounce you any moment. Give me a hand here, Pavel Vasil'evich," he said to Volodin.

Volodin walked up to him with a serious and understanding face and carefully took the books which Peredonov handed to him. Peredonov took a small pile of books and went into the hall followed by Volodin, to whom he had given the larger pile.

"Where are you going to hide them, Ardal'on Borisych?" he asked.

"You'll soon see," answered Peredonov with his customary gruffness.

"What are you taking out there, Ardal'on Borisych?" asked Prepolovenskaya.

"Strictly forbidden books," answered Peredonov without stopping. "I'll be denounced if they are seen."

In the hall Peredonov squatted in front of the stove and threw the books onto the iron grating. Volodin did the same thing. Then Peredonov began to cram book after book forcibly into the small opening. Volodin, squatting not quite beside him, handed him the books, preserving an air of foolish comprehension upon his sheeplike face, his protruding lips and wrinkled forehead expressing his feeling of importance.

Varvara glanced at them through the door and said with a laugh, "It looks as if they're making fools of themselves again."

"Oh no, Varvara, my dear, you mustn't say things like that," Grushina interrupted her. "There could be great difficulties if they found out about it. Especially in the case of a teacher. The authorities are dreadfully afraid that the instructors will teach the boys to rebel."

They finished drinking their tea and sat down to gamble at cards. All seven of them sat around a single card table in the hall. Peredonov played intensely, but poorly. After each twenty points, he had to pay what he had lost to the other players, especially to Prepolovensky, who collected for both himself and his wife. The Prepolovenskys won most often. They had special signs—taps and little coughs—by means of which they exchanged information about their cards. Peredonov was having no luck at all today. He was in a hurry to win his money back, but Volodin was slow to deal and shuffled the cards painstakingly.

"Deal, Pavlushka," exclaimed Peredonov impatiently.

Volodin, since he felt that he was especially important to the game and was socially equal to all the others, asked with dignity, "Just what do you mean by this Pavlushka? Is it in friendship or what?"

"In friendship, in friendship," answered Peredonov without concern. "Only deal faster."

"Well, if it was in friendship, then I am glad, very glad," said Volodin with a happy and stupid laugh, as he dealt the cards. "You're a good fellow, Ardasha, and I even like you very much. But if it had not been in friendship, then it would have been an entirely different matter. But if it was in friendship, I'm glad. I've dealt you an ace for it," said Volodin, and he turned up trumps.

Peredonov really did get an ace, but it was not the right one, and he had to discard it. "You dealt me an ace, but not the right one!" said Peredonov angrily. "There's something underhanded here," he grumbled. "I needed the trump, but what did you deal me? Why did I need that pot-bellied spade?"*

* Peredonov has exchanged the initial letters of *pikovy tuz* (ace of spades) making *tikovy puz* (teak belly).

Rutilov picked up the phrase with a laugh, "You got the pot-bellied spade because your own tummy is getting stout."

Volodin bleated and sniggered, "The future inspector is mumbling. His pot-bellied sounds like tot-bellied." *

Rutilov was incessantly chattering, gossiping, and telling anecdotes, sometimes highly off-color. In order to irritate Peredonov, he began to assure him that the gymnasium students were behaving very poorly, especially those who lived in apartments. He claimed that they smoked, drank vodka, and were chasing after girls. Grushina affirmed it, and Peredonov believed them. These tales gave Grushina special satisfaction. She herself, after the death of her husband, had wanted to board about three or four gymnasium students at her house, but the headmaster would not permit it, in spite of Peredonov's recommendation. She had a bad reputation in the town. Now she began to abuse the mistresses of those houses where students were living.

"They bribe the headmaster," she announced.

"Those landladies are all bitches," said Volodin with conviction. "Take mine for instance. We had an understanding when I took the room that she would give me three glasses of milk in the evening. Well, everything went fine for a month or two."

"And you didn't get drunk?" asked Peredonov with a laugh.

"Why should I get drunk!" replied the offended Volodin. "Milk is a useful product, and I'm used to having three glasses a night. Suddenly I see that they are only bringing two glasses. 'What is the meaning of this?' I ask, and the servant says, 'Anna Mikhailovna says to beg your pardon and tell you that their cow don't give much milk now.' But what business is that of

---

* Volodin's pun, fully as inane as Peredonov's, is *puz, puz, karapuz. Karapuz* is a word for a small child.

mine, an agreement is worth even more than money. Suppose their cow gave no milk at all, does that mean I wouldn't get any? I finally told him that if there wasn't any milk to tell Anna Mikhailovna that I want her to give me a glass of water. I'm used to drinking three glasses, and two glasses aren't enough for me."

"Our Pavlushka is a hero," said Peredonov. "Tell them how you tangled with the general, old boy."

Volodin repeated the story willingly, but this time they laughed at him, and he stuck out an offended lower lip.

Before dinner was over they all got drunk, even the women. Volodin suggested that they mess up the walls some more. Everyone was delighted, and, although they had not finished eating, they started the job and amused themselves thoroughly. They spat on the wallpaper, poured beer over it, threw paper gliders with butter-smeared tips at the walls and ceiling, and flipped pieces of chewed-on bread onto the ceiling. Afterwards, they thought of tearing off strips from the wallpaper and betting to see who could get the longest. In this game the Prepolovenskys won a ruble and a half more.

Volodin lost, and, because of this as well as his drinking, he suddenly became depressed and began to complain about his mother. He put on a reproachful expression and, for some reason rapping his hand down, said, "Why did she give birth to me? What was she thinking of at the time? What a life I now lead! She was not a mother to me, she was only the person who bore me. A real mother worries about her child, but mine only gave birth to me and gave me away to be brought up as a public ward when I was still extremely young."

"On the other hand you've learned from it and have made something of yourself," said Prepolovenskaya.

Volodin lowered his head and shook it back and

forth. "No," he said, "what sort of life do I lead—the lowest sort. Why did she give birth to me? What could she have been thinking of?"

Peredonov again thought of yesterday's *erly*. "Since he complains about his mother and why he was ever born," thought Peredonov about Volodin, "he obviously does not wish to be Pavlushka. It's quite evident that he does envy me. Perhaps he's even thinking of marrying Varvara and crawling into my skin," he thought as he looked apprehensively at Volodin.

He would have to get him married to someone.

That night, in their bedroom, Varvara said to Peredonov, "Do you think that all those wenches who're chasing you are as pretty as they are young? They're all rubbish, and I'm prettier than all of them."

She quickly undressed, and smirking insolently, she showed Peredonov her body—slightly varied in hue, slender, beautiful, and supple.

Although Varvara was staggering from drunkenness and her face would have repelled any decent person with its flabby, lewd expression, her body was exceedingly beautiful, like the body of a gentle nymph. It was as if the head of a faded harlot had been attached to it by some evil spell. And this superb body was nothing more than the source of the basest temptation for these two drunken and dirty creatures. And so it often is—truly in our age it is the lot of beauty to be violated and tainted.

Peredonov's gloomy laughter resounded as he looked as his naked companion.

All that night he dreamed of all sorts of women, naked and hideous.

Varvara believed that the nettle rubbing, which she had administered according to Prepolovenskaya's advice, was helping her. It seemed to her that she had immediately begun to get plumper. She asked all her friends, "It is true that I've filled out a little, isn't it?"

And she thought that Peredonov would certainly marry her now, when he saw how she was gaining weight and when he received the forged letter.

Peredonov's own prospects were not quite so pleasant. He had been convinced for a long time that the headmaster was hostile towards him. And the headmaster of the gymnasium did, in fact, consider Peredonov a lazy, incompetent instructor. Peredonov thought that the headmaster ordered the boys not to respect him, which was obviously one of Peredonov's own foolish imaginings. Nevertheless, there was lodged within Peredonov the conviction that he must defend himself from the headmaster. Several times he had begun to speak disparagingly of the headmaster before his older classes. Such talk pleased many of the gymnasium students.

Now, when Peredonov was hoping to become an inspector, the headmaster's unfriendly attitude towards him seemed especially unpleasant. Although it was true that, if the Princess so desired, her protection would override the headmaster's intrigues, they were still not without danger for him.

And there were other people in town, as Peredonov had noticed of late, who were hostile towards him and wanted to interfere with his appointment to an inspector's position. Take Volodin—it was not for nothing that he continually repeated the words "future inspector." It had happened before that a person assumed someone else's name and lived happily off it. It would, of course, be a little difficult for Volodin to take the place of Peredonov himself, but an imbecile like Volodin might have the most ridiculous notions. Clearly, one should always be wary of an evil man. In addition there were the Rutilovs, Vershina and her Marta, not to mention his envious fellow teachers—all of whom would be happy to harm him. How would they do this?

It would be easy enough to discredit him in the eyes of the authorities and make him out to be a disreputable person.

Thus, Peredonov had two worries: one, to prove his own trustworthiness and, two, to rid himself of the danger of Volodin by marrying him to a rich woman.

"Are you still longing for Marta?" Peredonov once asked Volodin. "Isn't a whole month enough time to be consoled? If you want, I'll get you matched up with the Adamenko girl."

"Why should I pine for Marta!" replied Volodin. "My proposal was a great honor for her, but if she didn't want me, what's that to me! Do you think I can't find myself other young girls? I can get as many as I want."

"True, but Marta has tweaked your nose for you," chided Peredonov.

"I don't know what sort of husband they're after," said the offended Volodin. "If there were at least a dowry, but they're giving peanuts. She's chasing after you, Ardal'on Borisych."

"If I were in your place, I would smear her gates with tar," * advised Peredonov.

Volodin sniggered, but he became serious at once and said, "It would be a nasty business if they caught me."

"Why do it yourself? Find someone else for the job," said Peredonov.

"It ought to be done, by God, it ought to be done!" said Volodin with animation. "A girl, who doesn't want to get married lawfully, but lets young fellows come into her house through the window, has it coming. It just shows that people have no shame or conscience!"

---

* A great public humiliation—when the gates of a house are painted with tar it signifies that a young girl in the household has lost her virginity.

6 : ⠦⠢⠦

On the next day Peredonov and Volodin set out to see
the Adamenko girl. Volodin was all decked out. He
had on his new tight-fitting frock coat, a freshly
starched shirt, and a gaudy neckerchief. He had pasted
down his hair with pomade and scented himself. He
was in excellent spirits.

Nadezhda Vasil'evna Adamenko lived in town with
her brother in a brick-red home that belonged to her.
Not far from town was an estate which she leased out.
Two years before she had graduated from the local
gymnasium and now she spent her time lying on a
couch and reading books of every sort. She also disciplined her brother, an eleven-year-old gymnasium
student, who protected himself from her strict demands
by saying, "It was much better with mama. The only
thing she used to stand in the corner was the umbrella."

With Nadezhda Vasil'evna lived an aunt, a character-
less and decrepit creature, having no voice in the running of the house. Nadezhda Vasil'evna was very cir-
cumspect in all her relations. Peredonov seldom visited
her house and was only slightly acquainted with her. It
was for that reason alone that he was able to imagine
that he could marry the young woman to Volodin.

She was surprised at this unexpected visit, but she
welcomed her uninvited guests graciously. The visitors
had to be amused, and it seemed to Nadezhda Vasi-
l'evna that the most pleasant and suitable conversation

for a Russian teacher would be about educational conditions, gymnasium reforms, raising children, literature, symbolism, and Russian literary periodicals. She touched upon all of these matters but did not receive anything but perplexing replies which revealed to her that her guests were not interested in these questions. She perceived that there was only one possible topic of conversation—town gossip. Nevertheless, Nadezhda Vasil'evna made one more attempt.

"Have you read Chekhov's 'Man in a Shell'?" she asked. "Isn't it a fine piece of work?"

She had directed this question to Volodin. He smiled pleasantly and asked, "Is it an article or a novel?"

"It's a short story," explained Nadezhda Vasil'evna.

"A Mister Chekhov, did you say?" inquired Volodin.

"Yes, Chekhov," said Nadezhda Vasil'evna with a smile.

"And where did it appear?" continued Volodin with curiosity.

"In *Russian Thought*," * she answered graciously.

"What issue?" pressed Volodin.

"I don't quite recall, perhaps it was one of the summer numbers," answered Nadezhda Vasil'evna with the same cordiality but some astonishment.

A young gymnasium student appeared from behind a door. "It was in the May issue," he said with his hands on the door, looking at his sister and the visitors with cheerful blue eyes.

"You're still too young to read novels," said Peredonov angrily. "You should study instead of reading lecherous stories."

Nadezhda Vasil'evna looked at her brother sternly.

* *Russkaya mysl'* was one of the leading "thick journals" of the period. (Chekhov's story appeared not in the May but in the July, 1898, number.) Sologub's reference to this particular story is interesting because Belikov, the man in a shell, could well have a place in *The Petty Demon*.

"How sweet! Eavesdropping behind doors!" she said, and she made a right angle by touching the ends of her little fingers to each other.

The young student frowned and left. He went to his room and stood in the corner glancing at the clock. A right angle with her little fingers was a sign that he had to stand in the corner for ten minutes. "No," he thought with vexation, "it was better with mama. The only thing mama used to stand in the corner was the umbrella."

Meanwhile, in the living room, Volodin was assuring his hostess that he would without fail get a copy of the May *Russian Thought* and read the story by Mister Chekhov. Peredonov was listening to all this with an expression of unconcealed boredom on his face.

Finally he said, "I also haven't read it. I don't read such nonsense. They are writing all kinds of nonsense in novels and stories nowadays."

Nadezhda Vasil'evna smiled warmly and said, "You regard contemporary literature very severely. But good books are being written even now."

"I read all the good books a long time ago," announced Peredonov. "I'm not about to read the things they're writing now."

Volodin looked at Peredonov with respect. Nadezhda Vasil'evna sighed slightly and—there was no alternative—served up small talk and gossip as best she could. Although such conversation was displeasing to her, she kept it up with the deftness and vivacity of a well-mannered young girl. The guests began to perk up. She was intolerably bored, but they thought she was being particularly gracious with them and ascribed it to Volodin's fascinating personality.

When they went out in the street, Peredonov congratulated Volodin upon his success. Volodin gaily laughed and hopped about. He had already forgotten all the girls who had rejected him.

"Don't kick so," Peredonov told him. "You're skipping about like a young sheep. Just wait, or you'll get your nose tweaked yet."

But he said this in jest, and he himself was firmly convinced of the success of this match which he had thought up.

Scarcely a day went by that Grushina didn't run to see Varvara, and Varvara was at Grushina's even more often, so that they were almost never separated. Varvara was very anxious, but Grushina was in no rush. She assured her that it was very difficult to forge the letters precisely.

Peredonov still didn't want to set the wedding date. He was again demanding that he be given the inspector's position first. Recalling how many girls were ready to marry him he more than once, as he had during the last winter, said threateningly to Varvara, "I'm going out to get married now. I'll return in the morning with a wife, and out you go. This is your last night here."

And with these words he would go out—to play billiards. From there he would sometimes come home, but more often, he would go on a spree in some dirty haunt with Rutilov and Volodin. On such nights, Varvara was unable to fall asleep, and because of this she suffered from migraines. It was all right if he returned at one or two at night—then she could breathe freely. If, however, he did not appear until morning, Varvara greeted the day quite ill.

Finally, Grushina got the letter finished and showed it to Varvara. They looked it over for a long time and compared it with the Princess's letter of the past year. Grushina swore that it was so similar that the Princess herself would be unable to detect the forgery. Although there was, in reality, little similarity, Varvara believed her. And she also knew that Peredonov would not be able to recall the unfamiliar handwriting enough to detect a forgery.

"Well," she said happily, "Here it is at last! I've been waiting and waiting and had almost lost patience. But there is still the matter of the envelope. What'll I say if he asks about it?"

"One can't forge the envelope, there is the post-mark," said Grushina with a smile, looking at Varvara with her cunning unequal eyes—the right one being slightly larger than the left.

"What shall I do?"

"Just tell him that you threw the envelope into the stove, dearest Varvara Dmitrievna," she replied. "What would you have wanted to keep the envelope for?"

Varvara's hopes were revived. "Once he marries me," she said to Grushina, "I won't run for him. No, I shall sit and he can do the running for me."

On Saturday, after dinner, Peredonov went to play billiards. His thoughts were heavy and sad. "It's awful to live among envious and hostile people. But what can be done? They can't all be inspectors!" he thought. "It's the struggle for existence!"

At an intersection of two streets he met the police lieutenant. An unpleasant encounter!

Lieutenant Colonel Nikolai Vadimovich Rubovsky, a stocky man of average height with bushy eyebrows, cheerful gray eyes, and a limping gait which caused his spurs to jingle loudly and irregularly, was an extremely pleasant person and, therefore, well liked in society. He knew all the people in the town, all their affairs and relations, and loved to listen to gossip, although he himself was as withdrawn and quiet as the grave, causing no one any unnecessary unpleasantness.

They stopped, greeted each other, and began to talk. Peredonov scowled, looked about, and said cautiously, "I've heard that our Natasha is living at your house. Don't believe what she says about me, she's lying."

"I never listen to a servant's gossip," said Rubovsky with dignity.

"She is a bad one herself," continued Peredonov, not paying any attention to Rubovsky's remark. "She has a Polish lover, and perhaps she has come to you on purpose in order to filch some secret document."

"Please don't be disturbed on that account," retorted the lieutenant colonel drily, "I have no fortress plans in my possession."

The mention of fortresses puzzled Peredonov. It seemed to him that Rubovsky was hinting at something. Perhaps he wanted to put Peredonov in prison.

"What has it to do with a fortress?" he growled. "It's an entirely different matter, namely, that all sorts of stupid things are being said about me, mainly from envy. Don't you believe any of them. They are informing on me in order to cast the suspicion from themselves, but I can do some denouncing myself."

Rubovsky was at a loss.

"I can assure you," he said, shrugging his shoulders and jingling his spurs, "that I have received denunciations about you from no one. Someone has evidently been playing a joke on you, but it hardly matters what people say sometimes."

Peredonov didn't believe him. He imagined that the police officer was hiding something, and he became frightened.

Each time that Peredonov walked past Vershina's garden, Vershina would stop him, and, with her bewitching movements and words draw him into the garden. Against his will, he would enter, submitting to her gentle witchcraft. Perhaps she had a better chance to gain her end than the Rutilovs. Peredonov was equally unrelated to them all, and what reason was there why he shouldn't get married to Marta? But it was clear that the marsh into which Peredonov was falling was so tenacious, that not even sorcery could succeed in getting him out of it and into another.

Just then, as Peredonov was walking past after the encounter with Rubovsky, Vershina, dressed as always in black, lured him into her garden.

"Marta and Vladya are going home for the day," she said, looking sweetly at Peredonov through the smoke of her cigarette with her brownish eyes. "You ought to go visit with them in the country. A workman has come after them with a cart."

"The cart would be crowded," said Peredonov sullenly.

"So it would be crowded," answered Vershina. "You'll manage all right. You might be a little squeezed but that's no disaster. After all, it's not far, only six versts.

At that moment Marta ran out of the house to ask Vershina something. The excitement of the trip had reduced her laziness, and her face was more lively and gay than usual. They both again began to invite Peredonov to the country.

"You'll manage quite well," Vershina assured him. "You and Marta can sit in the back, and Vladya and Ignaty in the front. Look over there, the cart is in the yard."

Peredonov followed Vershina and Marta into the back yard where the cart was standing. Vladya was busying himself around it stacking things in it. The cart was quite roomy, but Peredonov looked it over and said sullenly, "I'm not going, it would be too crowded. There are four of us plus all those things."

"Well, if you think it will be too crowded," said Vershina, "Vladya can go on foot."

"Of course," said Vladya with a pleasant but restrained smile. "I'll go on foot and get there easily in an hour and a half. I'll start walking now and be there before you."

Then Peredonov said that it would be bumpy, and he didn't like bumps. They returned to the summer-house. Everything was all in place, but the driver, Ignaty, was still eating in the kitchen, slowly but solidly gorging himself.

"How are Vladya's studies?" asked Marta.

She could not think up anything else to talk about with Peredonov, and Vershina had more than once reproached her for not knowing how to entertain him.

"Poor," said Peredonov. "He's lazy and doesn't pay attention."

Vershina loved to grumble, and she began to scold Vladya. Vladya turned red and smiled, shrinking his shoulders as though he were cold and lifting one shoulder higher than the other, as was his custom.

"But the year has only begun," he said. "I still have plenty of time to do well."

"You must study from the very beginning," said Marta with grown-up severity, which made her blush slightly.

"Yes, and he acts badly," complained Peredonov. "Yesterday he was fooling around with some other boys as though they were guttersnipes. He's ill-mannered too. On Thursday he spoke impudently to me."

Vladya suddenly flared up and began talking, although he still kept his smile. "I wasn't impudent, I only told the truth," he said. "You missed about five mistakes in each of the other notebooks, but you marked all of mine and gave me a two, even though mine was better written than those to which you gave threes." *

"And you are still being impudent to me," insisted Peredonov.

* The Russian marking system is based on the numbers one through five, a five being an "A."

"It wasn't impudence," said Vladya vehemently. "I only said that I was going to tell the inspector that my two was unjustly . . ."

"Vladya, you forget yourself!" said Vershina angrily. "Instead of excusing yourself, you are only repeating what you said."

Vladya suddenly remembered that he must not provoke Peredonov since he might marry Marta. He blushed even more deeply and, in his consternation, tightened the waistband of his blouse.

"I'm sorry," he said timidly. "I only meant to ask you to make the correction."

"Quiet, quiet, please," Vershina interrupted him. "I can't stand such arguing, I can't stand it," she repeated, and her frail body trembled imperceptibly. "You be quiet when you're spoken to!"

And Vershina poured abuse upon Vladya while smoking a cigarette and smiling wryly, as she always smiled no matter what she was talking about. "I'm going to tell your father so that he'll punish you," she concluded.

"He should be whipped," decided Peredonov, and he looked angrily at Vladya, who had offended him.

"Certainly," agreed Vershina. "He should be whipped."

"He should be whipped," said Marta, and she reddened.

"I'm going with you to your father's today," said Peredonov, "and I'll see to it that you get a darn good birching."

Vladya looked silently at his tormentors, shrugged his shoulders, and smiled through his tears. He had a harsh father. Vladya tried to console himself, thinking that these were only threats. Surely, he thought, they did not really want to spoil his holiday. For a holiday was a day of special significance and happiness, and

everything about a holiday was incongruous with weekday and school matters.

But Peredonov was pleased when little boys cried
and especially if he arranged it so that they cried and
apologized at the same time. Vladya's confusion, the
tears he was holding back in his eyes, and his timid,
guilty smile, all these made Peredonov very happy. He
decided to go with Marta and Vladya.

"Well, all right, I'll go with you," he said to Marta.

Marta was glad, but somehow she was frightened too.
Naturally, she wanted Peredonov to come with them,
or, more correctly, Vershina wanted it for her, and had
instilled the desire in her with her subtle power of
domination. But now that Peredonov had said that he
was going, Marta became uneasy for Vladya. She felt
sorry for him.

Vladya too became alarmed. Could Peredonov be
going because of him? He wanted to mollify Peredonov
and said, "If you think that it will be crowded Ardal'on
Borisych, I'll go ahead on foot."

Peredonov looked at him suspiciously and said, "But
if you are left alone, you'll run off somewhere. No, we
had better take you to your father, and let him take
care of you."

Vladya blushed and sighed. He was becoming ill at
ease, unhappy, and vexed at this cruel and morose man.
He decided to make Peredonov a more comfortable
seat in the cart in order to tame him down.

"Well," he said, "I'll fix it so that you will be comfortably seated," and he hurriedly ran off towards the
cart.

Vershina, smoking a cigarette with her wry smile,
looked after him and quietly said to Peredonov, "They
are fearful of their father. He is very strict with them."

Marta blushed.

Vladya would have liked to take his new English fishing rod, which he had bought with his savings, to the country with him. And there was something else he wanted to take—but all this would have occupied a good deal of room in the cart, so Vladya carried his belongings back into the house.

The sun was going down, and it was not hot. The road, damp from the morning rain, was not dusty. The cart rolled evenly over the small cobblestones carrying its four passengers out of the town. The well-fed gray pony trotted along as though she did not notice their weight, and the lazy and taciturn driver, Ignaty, directed her with movements of the reins perceptible only to an experienced eye.

Peredonov was sitting beside Marta. Such a wide seat had been made for him that Marta's was very uncomfortable. But he did not notice this. And even if he had noticed it, he would have thought it perfectly proper—he was the guest.

Peredonov was in a good mood. He decided to make pleasant conversation with Marta, to joke with her, and to entertain her. He began in the following manner:

"Tell me, are you going to rebel soon?"

"What do you mean rebel?" asked Marta.

"You Poles are always preparing to rebel, but it's all in vain."

"I'm thinking of no such thing," said Marta, "and there's no one among us who wants to rebel."

"Well, that's only what you say, but you hate the Russians."

"Not at all," said Vladya turning to Peredonov from the front seat where he was sitting with Ignaty.

"Oh, we know how you people think," said Peredonov. "Only we aren't going to give you back your Poland. We conquered you. We have given you countless benefits, but it's evident that however much you feed a wolf, it still looks towards the forest."

Marta did not reply. Peredonov became silent for a while and then said, "The Poles are idiots."

Marta blushed.

"There are all sorts among both Russians and Poles," she said.

"No, I'm right," insisted Peredonov. "The Poles are stupid. The only thing they can be made to understand is force. Now the Jews, they're clever."

"The Jews are cheats and aren't at all clever," said Vladya.

"No, the Jews are a very clever people. A Jew always gets the best of a Russian, but a Russian never gets the best of a Jew."

"But it isn't necessary to swindle," said Vladya. "Is mind only to be used for fraud and cheating?"

Peredonov looked angrily at Vladya. "Mind is for studying, and you don't study," he said.

Vladya sighed and turned back to watch the horse's even trotting.

"Jews are clever in all things, including learning," said Peredonov. "If Jews were allowed to become professors, all professors would be Jews. But the Poles are all slobs."

He looked at Marta, noticing with pleasure that she was blushing violently. "But don't think I'm talking about you," he said out of kindness. "I know that you'll make a good housekeeper."

"All Poles are good housekeepers," answered Marta.

"Well, yes, on the surface they're clean housekeepers, but their petticoats are dirty. But then again, you did have your poet Mickiewicz.* He is better than our Pushkin. I have his picture hanging on my wall. Push-

---

* Mickiewicz (1798-1855), the Polish national poet, is considered the Polish equivalent of Pushkin—the terms of the comparison frequently depending upon the nationality of the critic.

kin used to hang there, but I've moved him to the bath-room. He was a court flunky."

"But you're a Russian," said Vladya, "so what is our Mickiewicz to you? Mickiewicz is good, and Pushkin is good."

"Mickiewicz is greater," repeated Peredonov. "The Russians are fools. They have invented only the samovar and nothing else."

Peredonov screwed up his eyes and looked at Marta. "You have a lot of freckles," he said. "They're un-attractive."

"What can I do?" asked Marta smiling.

"I also have freckles," said Vladya turning around in his narrow seat and brushing against the taciturn Ig-naty.

"You're a boy," said Peredonov, "and it doesn't mat-ter if a man isn't good-looking. But it isn't becoming on you," he continued turning to Marta. "No one will marry you because of it. You should bathe your face in cucumber brine."

Marta thanked him for the advice.

Vladya looked at Peredonov and smiled.

"What are you grinning at?" said Peredonov. "Just wait till we get there, you'll get what's coming to you."

Vladya turned around in his place and looked at-tentively at Peredonov, trying to decide whether he was joking or in earnest. But Peredonov could not stand to have anyone stare at him.

"What are you looking at me like that for?" he asked harshly. "I don't have any designs on me. Or do you wish to give me an evil eye?"

Vladya was frightened and turned away his eyes.

"Pardon me," he said timidly, "I didn't do it in-tentionally."

"Do you really believe in the evil eye?" asked Marta.

"One can't give an evil eye, that's superstition," said Peredonov angrily. "But it's still horribly rude to stare."

There was an awkward silence for several minutes.

"And you're also poor," said Peredonov suddenly.

"Well, we're not rich," answered Marta, "but still we aren't poor. Each of us has something put aside."

Peredonov looked at her with disbelief and said, "Well, it happens I know that you're poor. You go barefoot at home all the time."

"We don't do it because we're poor," exclaimed Vladya.

"What then, do you do it because you're rich?" asked Peredonov, and he broke into laughter.

"It's not at all from poverty," said Vladya, growing red. "It's very beneficial to the health, it toughens one up, and it's pleasant in the summer."

"You lie," said Peredonov gruffly. "Rich people don't go barefoot. Your father has many children, but he doesn't earn half a kopeck. He can't afford to keep you all in shoes."

7 : 🐦🐦

Varvara did not know anything about where Peredonov had gone. She spent a terribly distressing night.

But, even when Peredonov returned to town in the morning, he did not go home, but asked to be driven to church, where Mass was just beginning. He felt that it was now dangerous for him not to be in church often. He might still be denounced.

Peredonov encountered a pleasant-looking young schoolboy with a rosy, simple face and clear blue eyes in the church gateway. "Ah, hi there, Mashen'ka, sweetie pie," he said.

Misha Kudryavtsev blushed violently. Peredonov had already teased him by calling him Mashen'ka several times before. Kudryavtsev could not understand why, and he had not brought himself to complain. Several of his companions, stupid boys, standing clustered together, began to laugh at Peredonov's words. They too enjoyed teasing Misha.

The church, named for the prophet Iliya, was an old one, having been built under Tsar Mikhail.* It stood in the square opposite the gymnasium. For this reason, on church holidays and at Masses and Vespers, the gymnasium students were obliged to gather there and stand in rows by the left wall of the chapel of St. Catherine the Martyr, while behind them stood one of the school proctors to keep order. Also in a row, nearer the center of the church, stood the gymnasium instructors, the inspector, and the headmaster together with their families. It was customary for almost all the Orthodox schoolboys to gather there, except for a few who had been granted permission to go to their own churches with their families.

The schoolboy choir sang well, and therefore the church was attended by well-to-do merchants, officials, and families of the landed gentry. There were not many common people there, primarily because the Mass was performed later than in the other churches in accordance with the headmaster's wish.

Peredonov stood in his customary place from where he could see the whole choir. Wrinkling up his eyes, he looked at them and thought that they were standing in a disorderly fashion and that he would tighten up on them if he were the inspector of the gymnasium.

* The church is indeed old. Mikhail Fyodorovich was the first of the Romanovs and the only tsar named Mikhail. He ruled from 1613 to 1645.

There was the swarthy Kramarenko, small, frail, and fidgety, who was always turning this way and that, whispering something, smiling. And no one did anything about it, as though it were nobody's business.

"Disgraceful!" thought Peredonov. "These choirboys are always good-for-nothings. That swarthy boy has a fine, clear soprano voice, so he thinks that he can whisper and laugh in church." And Peredonov frowned.

Beside him stood a latecomer, the inspector of public schools, Sergei Potapovich Bogdanov, an old man with a brownish, stupid face on which there was a never changing expression which made it seem as if he wanted to explain something to someone which he couldn't quite understand himself. No one could be so easily astonished or frightened as Bogdanov. He would no sooner hear something new or alarming than his forehead would wrinkle from his painful internal agitation and from his mouth would fly a volley of incoherent and confused exclamations.

Peredonov bent towards him and said in a whisper, "One of your women instructors goes about wearing a red blouse."

Bogdanov was frightened. His white Adam's apple bobbed up and down with fear under his chin.

"What, what are you saying?" he whispered hoarsely. "Who, who is this person?"

"It's the loud-mouthed, fat one, but I don't know her name," whispered Peredonov.

"Loud-mouthed, loud-mouthed," repeated Bogdanov in perplexity. "That would be Skobochkina."

"Yes, that's the one," affirmed Peredonov.

"Well, who would have thought it, who would have thought it!" exclaimed Bogdanov in a whisper. "Skobochkina in a red blouse! But have you seen this yourself?"

"Yes, I've seen her, and they say she parades around in school like that. And, even worse, she goes about dressed in a *sarafan* as though she were a peasant girl."

"You don't say! I must find out about this. I must find out about this. This cannot, cannot be. She'll have to be reprimanded, reprimanded for this," murmured Bogdanov. "She's always been like that."

The Mass was over and everyone went out of the church. Peredonov said to the Kramarenko boy, "Why were you laughing in church, you dark little devil? You just wait until I tell your father."

Peredonov sometimes addressed the gymnasium students familiarly as he had just done, but he never did it to those who were of noble families. These he always addressed in the formal manner. He found out who the upper-class students were in the office, and these distinctions were fixed firmly in his memory.

Kramarenko looked at Peredonov in surprise and ran past him without saying anything. He belonged to that group of students which looked upon Peredonov as being crude, stupid, and unjust and, therefore, disliked and despised him. The students who held these views were in the majority. Peredonov imagined that the headmaster had prejudiced these boys against him, if not personally, then through his sons.

Volodin approached Peredonov from behind the fence with a happy chortle. His blissful face made it seem as though it were his birthday. A derby was perched on the back of his head, and he brandished a walking stick.

"I've got something to tell you, Ardal'on Borisych," he whispered gaily. "I've persuaded Cherepnin, and, in a few days, he'll smear Marta's gate with tar."

Peredonov remained silent, considering something, and then he suddenly broke into morose laughter. Volodin at once ceased grinning and assumed a somber expression. He fixed his hat and glanced at the sky. "The weather is good now," he said waving his cane, "but it may rain this evening. Well, let it rain, we'll spend the evening at the future inspector's house."

"I won't be able to sit at home," said Peredonov, "I have important business to take care of in town."

Volodin made a comprehending face, although he did not, of course, have any notion of what business Peredonov had suddenly come across. Peredonov felt that he must, without fail, make several visits. Yesterday's chance meeting with the police officer gave him a thought which seemed to him extremely good, namely, to go around to all the important people in town and assure them of his trustworthiness. If this worked out, then, should the need arise, Peredonov could find supporters in the town, who would testify to the correct attitude of his thoughts.

"Where are you off to, Ardal'on Borisych?" asked Volodin, seeing that Peredonov was turning off from the way he usually returned home. "Aren't you going home?"

"Yes, I am going home, but I'm afraid to go along that street now."

"Why is that?"

"There's lot of *durman* growing there, and the odor is powerful. It affects me strongly and leaves me stupified. My nerves are weak now. There've been all sorts of unpleasant things happening."

Volodin again formed a comprehending and sympathetic expression on his face.

Along the way, Peredonov pulled off some thistles and put them in his pocket. "What did you pick those for?" asked Volodin grinning.

"For the cat," answered Peredonov sullenly.

"Are you going to rub them into its fur?" asked Volodin in a matter-of-fact way.

"Yes."

Volodin giggled, "Don't begin without me," he said. "It should be amusing."

Peredonov invited him to come at once, but Volodin said that he had business: he suddenly felt that it was not right for him not to have business too. Peredonov's words about his own affairs had set him going, and he imagined that it would be a good time for him to drop in on the Adamenko girl by himself to tell her that he had some new and very fine etchings that he was going to frame and ask if she would like to look at them. "Anyway," thought Volodin, "Nadezhda Vasil'evna will treat me to a cup of coffee."

And Volodin did just that. He even thought up another intricate scheme—he suggested to Nadezhda Vasil'evna that he should teach her brother to do woodwork. Nadezhda Vasil'evna, imagining that Volodin was in need of work, immediately consented. They arranged for him to work for two hours, three times a week, for thirty rubles a month. Volodin was in ecstasy—here was both pin money and the opportunity to meet Nadhezda Vasil'evna more often.

Peredonov returned home gloomy as usual. Varvara, pale from her restless night, grumbled, "You might have told me in the evening that you weren't coming home."

Peredonov, taunting her, told her that he had gone to Marta's home in the country. Varvara said nothing. She had the Princess's letter in her hands. True, it was forged, but still . . .

At lunch, she said with a smirk, "While you were running around with Marfushka, I accepted a letter for you from the Princess."

"You mean you really wrote to her?" said Peredonov, and his face lit up with a dull gleam of expectation.

"Well, aren't you the fool," answered Varvara with a laugh. "You yourself told me to write it."

"Well, what does she write?" asked Peredonov excitedly.

"Here is the letter. Read it yourself."

Varvara rummaged for a while in her pockets as though she were trying to find where she had put the letter, then found it, and gave it to Peredonov. He stopped eating and lunged at the letter eagerly. He read it through and was delighted. Here, at last, was a clear and definite promise. He had no doubts about its authenticity. Quickly finishing lunch, he went to show the letter to his acquaintances and friends.

With sullen excitement he quickly entered Vershina's garden. Vershina, as almost always, was standing by the gate smoking. She was overjoyed, for formerly she had had to lure him in, but now he came in by himself.

"That comes of having gone with her. He spent some time with her, and he comes running! I wonder whether he means to propose?" thought Vershina with happy anticipation.

Peredonov immediately disillusioned her by showing her the letter.

"You have always doubted it," he said, "but here the Princess herself has written. You read it and see for yourself."

Vershina looked at the letter with disbelief and quickly blew tobacco smoke on it several times, smiling wryly. "But where is the envelope?" she all at once quietly asked.

Peredonov suddenly became frightened. He began to think that Varvara might have deceived him with this letter, might have written it herself. He must demand that she produce the envelope as soon as possible.

"I don't know," he said. "I'll have to ask about it."

He hurriedly said good-bye to Vershina and set out quickly towards home. It was imperative for him to assure himself of the source of this letter as soon as possible. The sudden doubt was tormenting him.

Vershina, standing at the gate, looked after him with

her wry smile, hurriedly puffing her cigarette as though hastening to finish a tiresome daily lesson on time.

Peredonov ran home with a disturbed and frightened face, and, while still in the hall, he cried out in a voice tense with agitation, "Varvara, where is the envelope?"

"What envelope?" asked Varvara in a trembling voice. Although she looked at Peredonov insolently, she would have blushed, had she not been thoroughly rouged.

"The envelope that the letter from the Princess came in today," explained Peredonov, looking at Varvara fearfully and malevolently.

Varvara gave a strained laugh. "I burnt it, what did I want to save it for?" she said. "Do you think I'm making a collection of envelopes? They don't pay money for envelopes. You only get money back for empty bottles at the tavern."

Peredonov gloomily paced around the rooms and growled, "There are all sorts of Princesses, you know. Perhaps this Princess lives here."

Varvara pretended not to understand his suspicions, but she was trembling violently.

When Peredonov walked past her garden that evening, Vershina stopped him. "Did you get the envelope?" she asked.

"Varya says that she burnt it," answered Peredonov.

Vershina laughed, and fine, white clouds of tobacco smoke hung in front of her in the cool, quiet air.

"It's strange," she said, "that your cousin is so careless—an important letter and suddenly, no envelope! You would have been able to tell from the postmark when the letter was sent, and from where."

Peredonov was extremely vexed. In vain, Vershina invited him to come into the garden, and, in vain, she promised to tell his fortune with cards. Peredonov went away.

Nevertheless, he showed the letter to his friends and boasted, and they believed it.

But Peredonov did not know whether to believe it or not. In any case, he decided to begin visiting important people in the town on Tuesday to strengthen his position. One couldn't start on a Monday, it was an unlucky day.

8

As soon as Peredonov left to play billiards, Varvara went to Grushina's. They quarreled for a long time, and, finally, they determined to correct their mistake with a second letter. Varvara knew that Grushina had acquaintances in Petersburg. With their help, it would not be difficult to have a letter which they prepared here sent back from Petersburg.

As on the first occasion, Grushina for a long time feigned reluctance. "Oh, Varvara Dmitrievna, my darling," she said, "I'm all atremble from the first letter. I'm so afraid. Whenever I see a policeman near the house, I become terrified, and I think that they are coming to put me in prison."

Varvara worked on her for a full hour, promising her gifts and even a little advance money. At last Grushina agreed. They decided upon this course of action: first Varvara would say that she had written the Princess a note of thanks. Then the letter would come in several days as if the Princess had written again. In this letter it would be even more definitely stated that there were going to be positions open, and that, if they married quickly, she could now manage to obtain one of them for Peredonov. Grushina would, as before, write the letter, seal it, and put a seven-kopeck stamp on it. Then she would enclose it in a letter to her friend who would drop the letter into a mailbox in Petersburg.

And so Varvara and Grushina went to a shop on the very outskirts of town, and there they bought a package of narrow envelopes with a flowered border and some flowered paper. They chose paper and envelopes which were the last of that sort in the store—a precaution suggested by Grushina to conceal the forgery. Narrow envelopes were selected so that the forged letter could be easily enclosed inside the other one.

When they returned to Grushina's house, they composed the letter from the Princess. When, in two days, the letter was ready, they scented it with sweetbriar and burnt the remaining envelopes and paper so that no trace would be left.

Grushina wrote to her friend explaining the exact day on which the letter was to be mailed. They calculated that the letter would arrive on Sunday and then the postman would give it to Peredonov—additional proof that the letter was not forged.

On Tuesday Peredonov was trying to get home from the gymnasium early. Luck was with him—his last lesson was in a classroom the door of which opened onto the corridor near where the clock was hanging, and where the watchman, an alert retired battalion officer, rang a bell at fixed intervals. Peredonov sent the watchman to the office for the attendance book during which time he moved the clock a quarter of an hour ahead. No one noticed the change.

At home Peredonov refused lunch and asked that supper be served late. He had some business to attend to.

"They're always scheming, and I must untangle their schemes," he said angrily, thinking of the intrigues which his enemies were constructing against him.

He put on a little-used frock coat which was tight and uncomfortable on him. His body had grown stouter with the years; but the coat had stayed the same. He was annoyed that he had no medals. Others had them—even Falastov at the public school had some—but he had none. It was all the headmaster's fault. Not once had he nominated him. His advancement in rank was assured, the headmaster could not take that away, but what good were ranks if they could not be seen. Well, anyway, it would show on his new uniform. It was pleasant that the epaulettes would show his rank, not the position he held. * That would be impressive—the epaulettes were like a general's and had a single star. Everyone in the street would at once be able to see that a state councilor was walking by.

"I shall have to order my new uniform soon," thought Peredonov.

He went out into the street and only then began to wonder with whom he should begin.

It seemed to him that the most important people for him were the chief of police and the district attorney. It was obvious that he ought to begin with them or with the marshal of the nobility. But Peredonov was afraid to start out with them. Marshal Veriga was a general aiming for a governorship; and the district attorney and the chief of police were the fearful representatives of law and order.

"At first," thought Peredonov, "I should choose a lesser official and then sniff around and investigate to find out how they regard me and what they are saying

---

* The Russian civil service had fourteen classes. The better positions were designated by military ranks. *Statsky sovetnik* or state councilor is the fifth-class rank.

about me." Therefore, Peredonov decided it was wisest to begin with the mayor. Although he was a merchant and had received his education in a country school, he went everywhere and received everyone at his house. He enjoyed respect in the town as well as in other towns and even had some rather important acquaintances in the capital.

Peredonov set out resolutely for the mayor's house.

The weather had become gloomy. Leaves were falling from the trees wearily and submissively. Peredonov felt somewhat apprehensive.

In the mayor's house the smell of the freshly waxed floors mingled with the barely perceptible, yet pleasant smell of food. Everything was quiet and dull. The mayor's children, a son in the gymnasium and a young girl—"She's under the care of a governess," the father often said—spent their time, as they were supposed to, in their own rooms. It was cozy, peaceful, and pleasant there; the windows looked onto a garden; the furniture was well arranged; there were all sorts of games both in the rooms and the garden; and the children's voices could be heard.

In the first-floor rooms where guests were received, everything was pretentious and austere. The red, wood furniture was like toy furniture magnified many times, and it was quite uncomfortable for ordinary people to sit on. When you sat on it, you felt as if you had dropped onto a stone. The heavy host, however, seemed to sit quite comfortably on it. The archimandrite of the near-by monastery, who often visited him, called these chairs and sofas "soul-saving," to which the master of the house would answer, "Yes, I don't like those dainty feminine things that one finds in other houses. You sit on springs and tremble. You shake, and the furniture shakes—what is there good in that? And besides, the doctors don't approve of soft furniture."

The mayor, Yakov Anikievich Skuchaev, met Peredonov at the entrance to his living room. He was a tall, stout man with closely cut black hair. He carried himself with dignity and courtesy, although he was not altogether free from contemptousness toward people of small means.

Peredonov sat heavily in a wide chair, and, in reply to his host's first polite questions, he said, "I've come to see you on business."

"With pleasure. How may I serve you?" inquired his host politely.

A spark of contempt gleamed in his crafty, black eyes. He thought that Peredonov had come to borrow money and decided that he would not give him more than a hundred and fifty rubles. Many officials in the town were in debt to Skuchaev for more or less sizable amounts. He never asked for repayment of the loans, but he never gave further credit to delinquent debtors. He gave willingly the first time according to the standing and position of the borrower.

"You, Yakov Anikievich, as the mayor, are the first person in the town, and so it is necessary for me to talk with you," said Peredonov.

Skuchaev assumed a dignified position, bowed slightly and seated himself in an armchair.

"They're spreading all sorts of nonsense about me in the town," said Peredonov sullenly, "and they make up things that never happened."

"You can't stop people from talking," said the host, "and besides, it is well known that the scandalmongers in our provincial Palestines have nothing to do but wag their tongues."

"They say that I don't go to church, and that's not true," continued Peredonov. "I go regularly. Granted I wasn't there on Iliya's Day, but that was because I was down with a stomach ache. Otherwise, I always go."

"I am able to affirm that," said the host, "as I happened to see you, although I do not always go to your church. I usually drive out to the monastery. It's a custom in our family."

"They spread all sorts of nonsense," said Peredonov. "They make out that I tell dirty stories to my gymnasium students. But that's nonsense. Of course, sometimes you say something amusing to liven up a lesson. Your own son is a gymnasium student, and he hasn't said anything bad about me, has he?"

"That's true," agreed Skuchaev, "there has been nothing of that sort said. On the other hand small children are cunning. They don't say what they know they mustn't. Mine, of course, is still young and could blurt out something stupid. He has, however, said nothing."

"Yes, and in the older classes they know everything by themselves," said Peredonov. "But I still never say anything improper there."

"The fact is," answered Skuchaev, "that a gymnasium is not a market place."

"But we have people who make up things that never happened," complained Peredonov. "That is why I have come to you, as you are the mayor of the town."

Skuchaev was extremely flattered that Peredonov had come to him. He did not completely understand what it was all about, but he had sense enough not to show that.

"And they say even worse things," continued Peredonov. "They say that I am living with Varvara and that she is not my cousin but my mistress. But I swear to God that she is my cousin. Only she is far removed— a third cousin—so that I could marry her; and I am going to marry her."

"Ah, of course!" said Skuchaev. "Anyway, a marriage will settle the matter."

"And I could not do it earlier," said Peredonov. "I had important reasons. It could not have been done, otherwise I would have married long ago, believe me."

Skuchaev assumed a dignified air, frowned, and tapped on the dark tablecloth with his plump white fingers.

"I believe you," he said. "If that is so, then it is an entirely different matter. Now I believe you. If you will permit me to say so, I must confess that it was somewhat questionable for you to be living with your companion since you were not married. It was in bad taste, you know, because youngsters are keen-minded and are apt to develop bad habits. It's difficult to teach them the good, but the bad comes of itself. That's why it was questionable. But whose business is it anyway—that's how I look at it. I'm flattered that you've come to complain to me, because, although I am only one of the common fold, never having gone farther than district school, I still enjoy the respect of society. And this is my third term as mayor, so my word counts for something among the townspeople."

Skuchaev talked on and his ideas became all the more confused, and it seemed to him that he would never end his long, drawn-out speech. He abruptly cut short his talk and thought with annoyance, "But why fill the air with this empty talk. The trouble with these scholars is that you can't find out what they want. Everything is clear to him in books, but when the scholar takes his nose out of his books, he gets entangled and gets other people entangled."

His keen eyes, fixed on Peredonov with annoyed perplexity, began to grow dull, his corpulent body sank back in the chair, and he no longer seemed a bold administrator, but simply a foolish old man.

Peredonov also became silent for a while as though he had been hypnotized by his host's words. Then, screwing up his eyes with an indefinite and vague expression, he said, "As the mayor, you are able to say that all this is nonsense."

"That is, as regards what?" inquired Skuchaev guardedly.

"For instance," explained Peredonov, "if they should denounce me in the district and say that I don't go to church or something, and if they should come and ask you."

"We can do that," said the mayor. "In any case, you may rest assured. If that happens, we shall stand behind you—why shouldn't we put in a word for a good man! If it's advisable, we shall present you with a testimonial from the town council. We can do all of that. Or a recommendation of a prominent citizen might be advisable, and if it's necessary, we can do all of this."

"So I shall rely upon you," said Peredonov sullenly, as if he were answering something not altogether pleasant to him. "The headmaster is always persecuting me."

"You don't say!" exclaimed Skuchaev, shaking his head sympathetically. "I don't see how that could come from anything besides slander. Nikolai Vlas'evich, it seems to me, is a fine man who wouldn't harm anyone for nothing. I can tell that from his son. He is a serious and strict man who gives no favors and makes no discriminations. In a word, he is a just man, so it could not be from anything else but slander. Why are you at odds with him?"

"We don't see things the same way," exclaimed Peredonov. "And there are those in the gymnasium who are jealous of me. They want to become inspectors, and, since Princess Volchanskaya has promised to obtain an inspector's post for me, they're beside themselves with jealousy."

"So-o-o! So-o-o!" said Skuchaev cautiously. "But at any rate, why make dry conversation? Let's have a bite and something to drink."

Skuchaev pressed the button of an electric buzzer near the hanging lamp.

"A useful gadget," he said to Peredonov. "Now I think it would be good for you to get into another official position. Dashen'ka," he said to the pleasant-looking maid of muscular build who came in answer to the bell, "bring us some sort of *zakuska* and coffee, hot, understand?"

"I'll get it," answered Dashen'ka with a smile, and she went away treading surprisingly lightly considering her weight.

Skuchaev again turned to Peredonov. "Go into some other field," he said. "You might try the ecclesiastical life, for example. If you took the holy vows, you would make a serious and reliable priest. I could help you into it, as I have some good friends in the church."

Skuchaev named off several diocesan and suffragan bishops.

"No, I am not going into the priesthood," answered Peredonov. "I'm afraid of the incense. It makes me nauseous and gives me a headache."

"In that case, the police would be good," advised Skuchaev. "You might become an officer. Do you mind telling me what your rank is?"

"I am a state councilor," said Peredonov impressively.

"Well now!" exclaimed Skuchaev. "I must say that they have given you an important ranking. And is this all because you teach our children? It just shows what knowledge is worth! And, even though there are people nowadays who attack scholarship, still we can't live without it. Even though I only went to a country school, I am sending my son to a university. Everyone knows that you almost have to lead them through gymnasium by force, but they're ready enough to go on to a university all by themselves. But I never whip him, you know, and, if he is lazy or gets into mischief, I just take him by the shoulders and lead him to the window from where you can see the birches in our garden. I point to the birches. 'Do you see those?' I say. 'I see them, Papa, I see,' he says. 'I won't do it again.' And it really helps—he mends his ways just as though he had really been birched. Akh, children, children!" sighed Skuchaev in conclusion.

Peredonov stayed at Skuchaev's for about two hours. When the official business was over, abundant hospitality followed.

Skuchaev entertained him—in the way he did everything—with great decorum as though he were engaged in an important affair. At the same time he tried to bring in some clever conversation pieces. They brought in mulled wine in large glasses, just like coffee, and he called it his own kind of coffee. The vodka glasses that were brought in had their stems broken off and sharpened so that they could not be stood on a table.

"I call these, 'Fill and Empty,'" explained the host.

Then the merchant Tishkov arrived, a small, gray-haired, gay, and cheerful man in a long frock coat and oversized boots. He drank a great deal of vodka, said all sorts of nonsense in rhyme very quickly and gaily, and was evidently very satisfied with himself.

At last Peredonov decided that it was time to go home, and he began to say good-bye.

"Don't hurry off," said his host. "Sit awhile."

"For company's sake, your seat do take," said Tishkov.

"No, it's time for me to leave," said Peredonov with an anxious air.

"He mustn't be lating, his cousin is waiting," said Tishkov, and he winked at Skuchaev.

"I have something to do," said Peredonov.

"Who has something to do, gets praised through and through," Tishkov quickly replied.

Skuchaev escorted Peredonov into the hall. As they parted, they embraced and kissed. Peredonov was very well satisfied with this visit.

"The mayor is with me," he thought assuredly.

"They've been gossiping about him," said Skuchaev as he returned to Tishkov.

"Gossip they may, but the truth will stay," Tishkov caught up at once, gaily pouring himself a glass of English bitters.

It was evident that he did not think about what was said and only caught up the words for his rhymes.

"He's not bad—a good mind, and he doesn't drink foolishly," continued Skuchaev, pouring himself a drink and paying no attention to Tishkov's rhymes.

"If he can hold his drink, it means he can think," cried Tishkov boisterously as he poured down his glass.

"And what difference does it make if he does play around with a mistress!" said Skuchaev.

"With girls like that come bedbugs fat," replied Tishkov.

"The czar doesn't punish those who have not sinned against God!"

"We all want to love, so we've all sinned above."

"But he wants to cover up his sin with a wedding."

"Though they hide their sin fast, they'll carouse to the last."

Tishkov always talked in this manner so long as the conversation did not concern him. He would have bored everyone frightfully except that they got accustomed to him and did not notice his rapid production of couplets. Every once in awhile, however, they would dump him on a newcomer. But it was all the same to Tishkov whether they listened to him or not, he just could not stop catching words for rhymes and acted with the infallibility of a shrewdly devised boredom machine. Looking at his quick, precise movements for a long time, one would have thought that he was not a living man, but that he was already dead, or that he had never lived and did not see or hear anything in the living world except his dead-sounding words.

9 : ॄॖॄॖ

On the following day, Peredonov went to see District Attorney Avinovitsky.

The weather was again gloomy. The wind was coming in gusts and stirring up whirlwinds of dust in the streets. Evening was approaching, and everything was permeated with a cloudy, sorrowful mist as if there were no sunlight. A depressing silence reigned in the streets, and it seemed as if all these pitiful houses had sprung up to no purpose, as if their hopelessly decrepit shapes hinted at the poor, tedious, and boring life within their walls. A few people were out, and they walked slowly and with no purpose, as if they had barely escaped submission to restful slumber. Only the children, tireless and eternal representatives of God's happiness on earth, were lively and ran and played. But sluggishness descended even upon them, and some sort of faceless and invisible monster nestling behind their shoulders looked out now and then with its menacing eyes on their suddenly dulled faces.

In the midst of this weariness in streets and in homes, on an earth alienated from the heavens, an unclean and impotent earth, walked Peredonov, tormented with vague fears—there was no consolation for him in the heavens, no joy on earth, because now, as always, he looked on the world with the eyes of the dead, like some demon tormented in gloomy solitude by fear and sadness.

His senses were dull, and his consciousness was a corrupt and deadening mechanism. Everything that penetrated into it was transformed into vileness and filth. His eyes found the imperfections in everything, and he found pleasure in them. When he walked past an erect and clean column, he had a desire to make it lopsided or to spatter it with dirt, and he laughed joyously when something was being dirtied in his presence. He detested and persecuted his cleanly scrubbed students and called them "the sweet little scrubbers." He could understand the slovenly ones more easily. For him there were neither beloved objects nor beloved people, and, therefore, nature could only act in a one-sided fashion upon his feelings and was able only to oppress them. The same was true of his contact with people, especially with strangers and new acquaintances to whom he could not say rude things. Happiness for him was doing nothing and, shut off from the world, satisfying his belly.

"And now, against my will, I must go and explain things," he thought. "How tiresome! What a bore!" If he could only mess up the place where he was going, but he could not even have this consolation.

The district attorney's home strengthened and confirmed Peredonov's feelings of grim apprehension. And truly, this house did have an angry, evil look. The high roof gloomily sloped down upon the windows, which touched the ground. Both the wooden trim on the house and the roof itself had once been painted brightly and gaily, but time and the rains had made the color gloomy and gray. The huge and ponderous gates, higher than the house itself, as if their purpose was to repel enemy attacks, were always bolted. Behind them rattled a chain, and a dog growled deeply at every passer-by.

Bare spots, vegetable gardens, and hovels were scattered all about. There was a long, hexagonal plot in front of the district attorney's house, the center of which was somewhat deeper than the rest, all unpaved and overgrown with weeds. By the house itself stood a lantern post, the only one in the whole square.

Peredonov slowly and unwillingly ascended the four steep steps to the porch, which was covered with a double-pitched roof. He pulled the blackened copper handle of the bell. It sounded with a sharp and continuous tinkle somewhere close by. Soon stealthy footsteps could be heard. Someone had come up to the door on tiptoes and was standing ever so quietly. Very likely, someone was looking at him through some invisible crack. Then a metal key rattled, and the door was opened. A dark-haired, gloomy and pock-marked girl stood in the doorway, sizing him up with suspicion.

"Whom do you want?" she asked.

Peredonov said that he had come to see Aleksandr Alekseevich on business. The girl let him in. As he came inside, Peredonov pronounced a charm over himself. And it was well that he had done it in a hurry, for he had not had time to remove his coat before the sharp, angry voice of Avinovitsky was heard in the living room. The district attorney's voice was always terrifying—he never spoke in any other way. And so it was that now he shouted in an angry, abusive voice from the living room a greeting of welcome and happiness that Peredonov had finally made up his mind to visit him.

Aleksandr Alekseevich Avinovitsky was a man of gloomy appearance, as though he had been fitted by nature to scold and dress down others. He was a man in perfect health—he went from ice bath to ice bath.

Nevertheless, his thick black beard with a tinge of blue in it was so large that it made him appear thin. He brought an uneasy feeling, if not fear, upon everyone because he was always shouting at someone or threatening someone with penal servitude in Siberia.

"I have come on business," said Peredonov in confusion.

"Do you have a confession? Have you killed someone? Did you set fire to something? Have you pilfered the mail?" Avinovitsky angrily exclaimed as he admitted Peredonov into the drawing room. "Or have you yourself been the victim of some terrible crime—which is more than possible in our town? Our town is rotten, but its police force is even worse. I'm astonished that dead bodies don't turn up lying in the market place every morning. Well, sit down. What is your business? Are you a criminal or a victim?"

"No, I haven't done anything," said Peredonov. "The headmaster would be happy to have me in prison, but I haven't done anything."

"So you haven't brought a confession?" asked Avinovitsky.

"No, I have nothing of that sort," mumbled Peredonov fearfully.

"Well, if that's the case," said Avinovitsky with violent stress on his words, "let me offer you something."

He took a small bell from the table and rang it. No one came. Avinovitsky grasped the bell in both hands, raised a violent racket, then threw the bell on the floor, stamped his feet, and screamed in a savage voice, "Malan'ya! Malan'ya! Devils! Demons! Beasts!"

Unhurried steps were heard, and Avinovitsky's son, a thick-set, black-haired gymnasium student of about thirteen years with a strong air of confidence and self-assurance, entered. He bowed to Peredonov, picked up the bell, placed it on the table, and then said calmly, "Malan'ya has gone out to the garden."

Avinovitsky calmed down for the moment and looked at his son with a tenderness which did not quite suit his overgrown and angry face. "Well, run along and fetch her, son, and tell her to bring us *zakuska* and something to drink," he said.

The boy calmly walked out of the room. His father looked after him with a pleased and happy smile. But, while he was still in the doorway, Avinovitsky suddenly frowned fiercely and shouted in a terrifying voice, which made Peredonov jump: "Step lively!"

The boy began to run, and the doors could be heard as they were noisily opened and shut. The father smiled with his thick red lips as he listened. Then he again began to speak in an angry voice, "My heir, pretty good, eh? What do you think will become of him? He may be a fool, but villain, coward or spineless—never."

"Yes—uh—" mumbled Peredonov.

"People nowadays are trivial, a parody on man," thundered Avinovitsky. "They consider health to be absurd. A German invented undershirts. I would have sentenced that German to penal servitude. Imagine my Vladimir in an undershirt! My boy was in the country all summer and never once wore boots—and for him to wear an undershirt! Why my boy gets out of his bath to run stark naked in the cold and roll in the snow— and for him to wear an undershirt! A hundred lashes for that damned German!"

Avinovitsky passed from the German who invented undershirts to other criminals.

"Capital punishment, my dear sir, is not barbarism!" he roared. "Science recognizes that criminals are born. Since this is so, my friend, there is nothing more to be said. They should be exterminated and not fed at the state's expense. A man is a scoundrel, but he is given the assurance of a warm corner in prison for his whole life. He may be a murderer, an arsonist, or a seducer, but the taxpayer must support him out of his own pocket. No, it's much more just and cheaper to hang 'em."

There was a round table in the dining room covered with a white tablecloth with a red border, and on it were various plates with fat sausages and other pickled, salted, and smoked foods, as well as decanters and bottles of various sizes and shapes with all sorts of vodkas, brandies, and liqueurs. All this just suited Peredonov, and even the slight carelessness of arrangement pleased him.

His host continued to bellow. Apropos of the food he abused shopkeepers, and then, for some reason, he began to talk about ancestry.

"Ancestry is an important institution!" he shouted savagely. "For the *muzhik* to enter the aristocracy is stupid, foolish, impractical, and immoral. The soil is becoming poorer, the towns are filled with unemployed, the harvests are poor, there is idleness, suicide—does all that please you? You may teach the *muzhik* as much as you want, but don't give him rank, otherwise the peasantry will lose its best members and all that's left are rogues and cattle. The nobility also suffers from the influx of uncultured elements. In his own village he was better than all the others, but amongst the nobility he brings in something coarse, ungallant, and plebeian. His livelihood and his belly are his most important interests. No, my friend, castes were a wise institution!"

"Yes, and our headmaster lets all sorts of riff-raff into the gymnasium," said Peredonov angrily. "There are many children of the merchant class and even peasants."

"A fine mess I must say!" shouted his host.

"There's a circular telling him not to admit all sorts of scum, but he does as he pleases," complained Peredonov. "He refuses almost no one. He says that life in our town is poor, and there are too few gymnasium students anyway. What does he mean too few? It would be better if there were fewer still. As it is there's no time to correct their notebooks, and there's no time to read the books. And they purposely write strange words in their themes, so that one must correct them all with a dictionary."

"Have something to drink," suggested Avinovitsky. "Now what is your business with me?"

"I have enemies," grumbled Peredonov, first staring dejectedly into his yellowish vodka and then gulping it down.

"There once lived a pig who had no enemies," replied Avinovitsky, "but he was slaughtered too. Taste this. It was a good pig."

Peredonov took a piece of ham and said, "They're spreading all sorts of rot about me."

"Yes, I can say that there is no worse town for gossip!" screamed his host. "What a town! The minute you do something shady, all the swine begin to grunt about it."

"Princess Volchanskaya promised to obtain an inspector's position for me, and suddenly they've all begun to gossip. It might injure my chances, and it all comes from envy. Take the headmaster—he's corrupted the gymnasium. The students who live in apartments smoke, drink, and run after girls, and there are local boys who do the same thing. It's he who's corrupted them, but he's persecuting me. And it might go farther and reach the Princess."

Peredonov spoke long and incoherently about his apprehension. Avinovitsky listened angrily and, from time to time, exclaimed loudly, "Villains! Rogues! Children of Herod!"

"What sort of nihilist am I?" said Peredonov. "It's almost funny. I have an official cap with a badge, but I don't always wear it—sometimes I wear an ordinary hat. As for Mickiewicz hanging on my wall, it is for his poetry and not because he was a rebel. Why I've never even read *The Bell*."

"Well you got that from another opera," said Avino-vitsky without ceremony. "Herzen published *The Bell*, * not Mickiewicz."

"That's another one," said Peredonov. "Mickiewicz also published something called *The Bell*."

"I didn't know that. It's a scholarly discovery. You ought to publish it. You'll become celebrated."

"One is not allowed to publish it," said Peredonov angrily. "I'm not allowed to read forbidden books. I never read. I am a patriot."

After lengthy complaints in which Peredonov poured himself out, Avinovitsky concluded that some-one was attempting to blackmail Peredonov and with this purpose in mind was circulating rumors about him in order to frighten him, thus laying the groundwork for a sudden demand for money. Avinovitsky explained the fact that these rumors had not reached him by assuming that the blackmailer was shrewdly working in Peredonov's closest circle of friends since it was only necessary to frighten Peredonov.

"Whom do you suspect?" asked Avinovitsky.

Peredonov became pensive. By chance Grushina came to his mind, and he vaguely recalled his recent conversation with her when he had interrupted her story with the threat of denouncing her. That he had threatened to inform against Grushina was confused in his mind and became the notion of informing in gen-eral. Whether he was to inform or be informed on was unclear to him, and Peredonov had no wish to take the trouble to recall precisely. One thing was clear—Grushina was an enemy. And the worst of it was that

* *Kolokol* was a revolutionary paper published by Herzen in Lon-don between 1857 and 1867. It defended particularly the cause of Polish freedom.

she had seen where he had hidden Pisarev. He would have to reconceal the books.

"Grushina is one of them," said Peredonov.

"I know, she's a first-class rascal," snapped Avinovitsky.

"She is always coming to our house and sniffing around," complained Peredonov. "She is greedy and you always have to give her things. Perhaps she wants me to pay her money so that she won't denounce me for having owned Pisarev. Or maybe she wants to marry me. But I don't want to pay, and I'm already engaged. Let her denounce, I'm not guilty of anything. The only thing is that it's unpleasant for me to have these stories going about as they could interfere with my appointment."

"She is a well-known charlatan," said the District Attorney. "She used to tell fortunes with cards and defraud fools, but I told the police to have it stopped. On this occasion the police were sensible and did what I told them."

"She is still telling fortunes," said Peredonov. "She has spread out the cards for me, and she always sees a long trip and an official letter."

"She knows what to say to everyone. Just wait, she'll rig something up and then try to extort some money. Then you come straight to me, and I'll give her a hundred hot lashes," said Avinovitsky using his favorite expression, which was not to be taken literally but simply meant a good dressing down.

And so Avinovitsky promised his protection to Peredonov. Nevertheless, Peredonov left agitated with vague fears brought on by Avinovitsky's loud, menacing tirades.

Every day Peredonov made a single visit before dinner. He did not have time to make more than one, because everywhere he had to make sufficient explanations. In the evening, as usual, he went to play billiards.

As before Vershina drew him in with her witchlike movements, and as before Rutilov raved about his sisters. At home Varvara was pressing him to marry her at once—but he remained indecisive. Of course, sometimes he thought that getting married to Varvara would be the best thing he could do. But what if the Princess should suddenly deceive him? He would be laughed at all over town, he thought, and this possibility made him pause.

Being pursued by young women, envied by his comrades, suspecting all sorts of intrigues—more his imagination than reality—all these things made his life wearisome and dolorous, like the weather, which had been gloomy for several days and often turned into slow and sparse, but long and cold rains. Peredonov felt that life was becoming a loathsome thing, but soon, he thought, he would be made an inspector, and then things would change for the better.

10 : ࣷ࿇ࣷ࿇

On Thursday Peredonov set out to see the marshal of the nobility.

The marshal's house reminded one of a spacious summer cottage somewhere in Pavlovsk or Tsarskoe Selo, a cottage full of every convenience even for winter habitation. Although there was no striking luxuriousness, the newness of many things seemed unnecessarily excessive.

Aleksandr Mikhailovich Veriga was waiting for Peredonov in his study. He made it seem that he was hurrying to greet his guest and only his work had prevented him from coming sooner.

Veriga held himself unusually erect even for a retired cavalry officer. It was said that he wore a corset. His clean-shaven face was uniformly crimson as if it had been painted. His head was shaved with the closest cutting clippers—a convenient method of minimizing his bald spot. His gray eyes were amiable yet cold. Although his views were fixed and severe, his deportment was extremely affable towards everyone. In all his movements there was apparent strict military discipline, and slight indications of a future governor sometimes showed through.

Peredonov, sitting opposite him at a carved oak table, explained, "There are all sorts of rumors concerning me going about, and as a teacher, being therefore entitled to call myself a gentleman, I am turning to you. They are saying all sorts of nonsense about me, your excellency, and it's not true."

"I haven't heard anything," replied Veriga, smiling warmly and looking expectantly at Peredonov with his attentive gray eyes.

Peredonov stared into a corner and said, "I have never been a socialist, but, if sometimes one says things one shouldn't, remember that everyone gets easily excited in his youth. But now I never think such things."

"So you once were quite a liberal?" asked Veriga with a friendly smile. "You wanted a constitution, isn't that so? But then we all wanted constitutions when we were young. Would you like one of these?"

Veriga pushed a cigar box at Peredonov. Peredonov was afraid to take one and refused. Veriga lit one himself.

"Of course, your excellency," said Peredonov. "I was that way too at the university, but I alone wanted a kind of constitution different from all the others."

"In what respect?" asked Veriga with a hint of approaching displeasure in his voice.

"This was a constitution without a parliament," explained Peredonov. "All they do in a parliament is quarrel."

Veriga's gray eyes lit up with faint delight. "A constitution without a parliament!" he said pensively. "You know, that's an idea."

"But even that was a long time ago," said Peredonov, "and now I don't want anything." And he looked hopefully at Veriga.

Veriga blew a fine stream of smoke from his mouth, was silent awhile, and finally said, "Now you're a pedagogue, and my duties in the district have dealings with the schools. In your considered opinion which type of school do you give preference to, the parochial or the so-called secular school?"

Veriga flicked the ash from his cigar and fixed a friendly but too attentive stare upon Peredonov.

"The public schools ought to be overhauled," said Peredonov, frowning and staring from corner to corner.

"Overhauled?" repeated Veriga in a doubtful tone. "Hmm." And he let his eyes rest on his cigar as if preparing to hear a lengthy explanation.

"The instructors are nihilists," said Peredonov, "and the women teachers don't believe in God. They stand in church and blow their noses."

Veriga shot a look at Peredonov, smiled, and said, "Well, you know, it's necessary sometimes."

"Yes, but one blows her nose like a trumpet so that all the choirboys laugh," said Peredonov angrily. "She does it purposely—that's the sort of woman Skobochkina is."

"Yes, that's not good," said Veriga, "but in Skobochkina's case it is mostly lack of proper upbringing. She has no manners at all, but she's a diligent schoolmistress. But in any case, that's not good, and someone should speak to her."

"She walks about in a red blouse," continued Peredonov, "and sometimes she goes barefoot in a *sarafan*. And she plays games with the small boys. And there is no discipline—they have too much freedom in the schools. They don't want to punish them at all. And you can't treat the peasant children the way you treat the upper-class children. They must be whipped."

Veriga looked calmly at Peredonov; then, as if feeling ill-at-ease from hearing his tactless remarks, he dropped his eyes and said coldly, in an almost gubernatorial tone, "I must say that I have noticed many good qualities in the public-school pupils. Without doubt, in the great majority of cases, they do their work conscientiously. Of course, like all children, they commit offenses. As a consequence of poor upbringing and bad environment, these offenses of theirs can take a rather coarse form, especially since, among the rural population in general, the feelings of responsibility, honor, and respect towards the property of others are poorly developed. The school is obliged to pay strict attention to these offenses. When all means of persuasion fail, or if the offense is great, then, of course, in order to prevent the boy's expulsion, harsh measures are in order. And this, by the way, holds true for all children, even the nobility. But, generally speaking, I agree with you that in schools of this type the inculcation of gentlemanliness is inadequately organized. Madam Shteven, * by the way, in her extremely interesting book. . . . Have you read it?"

"No, your excellency," said Peredonov in confusion.

* A. Shteven, a teacher and journalist-crusader of populist sympathies. She combined reverence for the past with faith in "the people" and condemned the urban way of life, blaming it for all of Russia's ills.

"There's so much work in the gymnasium that I never have time. But I will read it."

"Well, it's not so vital," said Veriga with a friendly smile as though he were forbidding Peredonov to read that book. "Yes, this Madam Shteven relates with great indignation how two of her students, young men about seventeen years old, were sentenced in the rural court to be whipped. It turned out they were haughty young fellows, but, let me add, we all suffered while their shameful punishment was being carried out, and later this kind of thing was done away with. And I say to you that, in Madam Shteven's place, I too would want to tell all of Russia what happened. Just imagine, they were sentenced for taking some apples. I ask you to consider—for stealing! And she even writes that these were her best pupils, yet they still took the apples. Fine upbringing! It must be candidly stated that we don't recognize the right of private property."

Veriga got up from his seat in excitement, took about two steps, and then, recovering himself, sat down again.

"Well if I am made an inspector of public schools, I shall do things differently," said Peredonov.

"And do you have the job in view?" asked Veriga.

"Yes, the Princess Volchanskaya has promised it to me."

Veriga put on a pleased expression. "It will be my pleasure to congratulate you," he said. "I don't doubt that, in your hands, things will take a turn for the better."

"But the thing is, your excellency, that they are spreading all sorts of rumors about me in the town, and, perhaps someone may yet denounce me in the district and interfere with my appointment. But I haven't done anything."

"Whom do you suspect of spreading these untrue rumors?" asked Veriga.

Peredonov became confused and mumbled, "Whom should I suspect? I don't know. I only know they do talk about me, and I have come to you because this might injure my chances for the job."

Veriga thought that he did not have to know the particulars because he was not yet the governor. He again assumed his role of marshal and delivered a speech to which Peredonov listened with melancholy and fear.

"I am thankful for the confidence which you have shown in calling on my (Veriga wanted to say 'patronage' but held himself back) intervention between you and the society in which, according to your story, unpleasant rumors concerning you are going about. These rumors have not as yet reached my ears, and you may be sure that the slanders being spread about you would not dare to rise out of their origin in low, town society and, so to speak, will grovel in darkness and obscurity. But it is very pleasing to me that you, who hold your job by appointment, at the same time value the importance of public opinion and the dignity of your position as a teacher of young people so highly, you who are one of those to whose enlightened care we, as parents, entrust our greatest treasure, our children, the descendants of both our names and our fruits. As an official you have your chief in the person of your esteemed headmaster, but as a member of society and a gentleman, you always have the right to count upon the . . . co-operation of the marshal of nobility in questions concerning your honor and dignity as a man and a gentleman."

Continuing to speak, Veriga stood up and, spreading the fingers of his right hand out on the edge of the table, he looked at Peredonov with that impersonal and attentive expression with which orators look upon a crowd while delivering beneficent official speeches. Peredonov also got up and, folding his hands across his stomach, looked sullenly at the rug under his host's feet.

"I am very glad that you have turned to me," said Veriga, "because, in our time especially, it is important for the members of the highest class always to remember first of all that they are gentlemen and to value their membership in this class—not only their rights, but also their obligations and their honor as gentlemen. The gentlemen in Russia are, as you well know, predominantly in the civil service. Strictly speaking, all governmental responsibilities except for the very lowest, it goes without saying, should be in the hands of gentlemen. It is the presence of commoners in the civil service which, of course, constitutes one of the main causes of undesirable occurrences such as this one which has disturbed your peace of mind. Slander and intrigue—these are the tools of a lower breed of people not raised in the fine traditions of the gentleman. But I hope that public opinion will speak out loudly and clearly in your behalf, and you may count upon my full co-operation in this affair."

"I humbly thank you, your excellency," said Peredonov, "and I shall count upon you."

Veriga smiled warmly and did not sit down, thus making it clear that the conversation was ended. When he finished his speech, he suddenly felt that his whole speech had been out of place and that Peredonov was nothing more than a timorous office-seeker, haunting doorways in his search for patronage. He parted from Peredonov with the cold disdain that he actually felt towards him because of his disorderly life.

As he put on his coat in the hallway with the help of a lackey, he could hear the sounds of a piano from a far-off room. Peredonov thought that haughty and proud people, who thought highly of themselves, lived in this house. "He aspires to a governorship," thought Peredonov with respectful and envious wonder.

On the stairway he met the marshal's two small sons returning from a walk with their tutor. Peredonov looked at them with gloomy curiosity.

"They're so clean," he thought. "There isn't even any dirt in their ears. They're so alert and they probably are disciplined strictly. It's very likely," thought Peredonov, "that they've never even been whipped!"

Peredonov looked after them angrily as they quickly climbed the stairs talking gaily. He was astonished that their tutor treated them as equals and did not frown or shout at them.

When Peredonov returned home, he found Varvara with a book in her hands, a rare occurrence. She was reading a cookbook, the only book which she sometimes opened. The book, which was in a black binding, was old and worn. The black binding caught Peredonov's mind and made him depressed.

"What are you reading, Varvara?" he asked angrily.

"What? You know what it is—a cookbook," answered Varvara. "I have no time to read drivel."

"Why a cookbook?" asked Peredonov in terror.

"What do you mean, 'why?' I'm going to prepare some new dishes for you, you're always complaining so," explained Varvara with a sarcastic smile of self-satisfaction.

"I won't eat what's prepared from a black book!" announced Peredonov firmly, and he suddenly snatched the book from Varvara's hands and carried it into the bedroom.

"A black book! And even to prepare dinners from it!" he thought with fear. It had even come to this, that they were openly attempting to destroy him with black magic. "I must destroy this horrible book," he thought, not paying any attention to Varvara's grumbling.

.   .   .

On Friday Peredonov went to see the president of the local landowners' association.

Everything in this house said that here they wished to live simply and well, and to work for the public good. There were many things in view reminding one of simple rural life—an armchair with an arched back and arms made from ax handles, an inkstand shaped like a horseshoe, and an ashtray that looked like a peasant's sandal. There were many measures in the hall, on the windowsills, on tables, and on the floor with samples of various grains in them. Some of them contained pieces of the coarse bread used in famines—dirty lumps that resembled peat. In the living room were drawings and models of various farming machinery. The study was spilling over with cases of books on agriculture and education. On the table were papers, printed forms, and shoeboxes with assorted cards of various sizes. There was much dust and not a single picture.

The host, Ivan Stepanovich Kirillov, was very anxious on the one hand, to be cordial in the continental manner, and, on the other, not to compromise his position as a landowner in the district. He was a strange and contradictory person, as though he were two halves welded together. It was evident from his surroundings that he did a lot of work and did it well. But to look at him you would think that all this land business was only a temporary amusement for him which kept him busy, but that his real cares were somewhere in front of him where his alert eyes stared—eyes which, with their tinny gleam, were somehow not alive. It was as though someone had taken out of him his living soul and put it in a long box, replacing it with a skillful and busy inanimate mechanism.

Not at all a large man, he was slender and youngish —so youngish and red that every once in a while he looked like a small boy who had glued on a beard and adopted, rather successfully, adult manners. His movements were quick and precise. When greeting someone he would bow adroitly, shuffle his feet, and glide on the soles of his fancy boots. One had the impulse to call his clothing a costume—his little gray jacket, his unstarched batiste shirt with its turn-down collar, his blue string tie, his narrow trousers, gray socks. And his exceedingly polite conversation also had two sides. He would be speaking quite reservedly when suddenly a naïve smile, like a child's, would break out. But when you looked at him the next moment, he was again grave.

His wife, a quiet and sedate woman, who appeared older than her husband, came into the study several times while Peredonov was there and each time asked her husband for some detailed information concerning district affairs.

Their town house was always in confusion due to frequent visitors either on business or simply to drink tea. Peredonov had hardly seated himself when they brought him a glass of not very warm tea and some buns on a plate.

Another guest had come before Peredonov and sat opposite him. Peredonov knew him . . . but then who does not know everyone else in our town? Everyone knows everyone else, but some have quarreled and broken off the relationship.

The other guest was the physician of the district, Georgi Semyonovich Trepetov, a man even smaller than Kirillov. He had a pimply, sharp, and insignificant face, and he wore blue eyeglasses which he always looked under or to the side of, as if he were trying to see the person to whom he was speaking. He was unusually honorable and never gave a kopeck for anyone else's benefit. He was deeply contemptuous of anyone who he found was a bureaucrat—he would shake hands upon meeting but stubbornly refrained from conversation. For this he was considered to be intellectually bright, as was Kirillov, although he knew little and was an incompetent doctor. He was always preparing to lead a simple life, and with this goal in mind, he watched the peasants as they blew their noses, scratched the backs of their necks, and wiped off their lips with the backs of their hands. When he was by himself he sometimes imitated them, but he always put off his simplification for the next summer.

Peredonov here too repeated all the complaints about the town gossip which he had been making for the past several days concerning the envious ones who wished to interfere with his coming into an inspector's position. At first Kirillov felt flattered by the attention being paid him.

"Yes, now you can see what goes on in the provincial milieu!" he exclaimed. "I have always said that the only hope for thinking people is to unite, and I am glad that you have come to the same conviction."

Trepetov snorted angrily in offense. Kirillov looked at him fearfully.

"Thinking people!" said Trepetov with contempt and snorted again.

Then, after a short silence, he began to speak in a thin contemptuous voice, "I don't know how thinking people can behave with such musty classicism!"

"But you do not take into account that a person does not always have the power to choose his own position, Georgi Semyonovich," said Kirillov indecisively.

Trepetov snorted contemptuously, which quite stopped the polite Kirillov, and lapsed into deep silence.

Kirillov turned to Peredonov. When he heard him talk about an inspector's position, he had become worried. He thought that Peredonov wanted to be an inspector in our district. But in the local council a plan had been drawn up to establish a special inspector's job for their own schools to be chosen by the council and approved by the ministry of education.

Then the Inspector Bogdanov, who had charge of the schools in three districts, would be moved to one of the neighboring towns, and the schools of our district would be turned over to the new inspector. The council members had an instructor in a teachers' college in the nearby township of Safata in mind for the job.

"I have patronage there," said Peredonov, "but the headmaster, yes, and others too, are trying to pull me down here. They are spreading all sorts of nonsense. So, should there be any inquiries about me, I want you to say that all that is being said about me is nonsense. Don't believe these people."

"I have no time, Ardal'on Borisych," replied Kirillov hurriedly, "to get mixed up in town relations and gossip—I'm up to my neck in work. If I didn't have my wife to help me, I don't know what I should do. I never go anywhere, never see anyone, never hear anything. But I fully believe that all this that is being said about you—although I assure you that I have heard none of it—is nothing but gossip. I fully believe you. But this position you want does not depend upon me alone."

"They might question you," said Peredonov.

Kirillov looked at him with surprise and said, "Well they haven't asked yet, but, of course, they will. But the important thing that we must keep in mind . . ."

At this moment, Mrs. Kirillov appeared in the doorway and said, "May I see you a moment, Ivan Stepanovich." * Her husband went out to her.

* Kirillov is here referred to by his wife as Stepan Ivanych even though he is identified as Ivan Stepanovich on p. 115. The few

"I think that you had best not mention that we have Krasil'nikov in mind for the job," she whispered worriedly. "I don't trust that creature. He might do something to impede Krasil'nikov."

"Do you think so?" whispered Kirillov in reply. "Yes, yes, you might be right. This is a nasty business." He put his hands to his head.

His wife looked at him with the sympathy of a secretary and said, "You had better say nothing at all about this as if there were no position."

"Yes, yes, you're right," whispered Kirillov. "But I have to go back in—this is awkward."

He ran back into the study and began to say pleasant things to Peredonov.

"So you will if . . ." began Peredonov.

"Rest assured now, rest assured that I shall keep you in mind," said Kirillov quickly. "We still have not completely settled this matter."

Peredonov did not understand what matter Kirillov was talking about and felt apprehension and fear.

"We are making a school network," said Kirillov. "We hired specialists from Petersburg, and they've been working the whole summer. It's cost us nine hundred rubles. We're getting it ready for the meeting. It's an amazingly thorough piece of work—all the distances have been considered and all the school points marked out."

And for a long time Kirillov explained the school network in detail, that is, the dividing of the school district into small parts with a school in each in order that each village would have a school nearby. Peredonov understood nothing, and his dull thoughts became entangled in the wordy strands of this web which

---

such inconsistencies have been "normalized" in this translation. Another is the name of the eldest Rutilov sister which occurs both as Larisa and Larissa.

Kirillov was constructing so quickly and deftly before him.

Finally, Peredonov said good-bye and left, hopelessly depressed. "In this house," he thought, "they hadn't wanted to understand me or even listen to me. The host was babbling something incomprehensible. Trepetov was snorting angrily for some reason, and the hostess came in and out ungraciously. Strange people live in this house," thought Peredonov. "A wasted day!"

11 : ೭☙೭☙

On Saturday Peredonov prepared to visit the chief of police. "Although he isn't as important a bird as the marshal of the nobility," thought Peredonov, "he could still hurt me more than anyone else, and, on the other hand, he could help me with the authorities by his recommendation. The police are very important."

Peredonov took his official cap with the badge from its box. He decided that, from that time on, he would wear only it. It was all very well for the headmaster to wear any hat—he was in good standing with the authorities—but Peredonov still had to secure his inspector's position, he couldn't depend upon patronage alone. He had to do something himself to show his worth. Already, several days ago as he was about to begin his visits to the town powers he had thought of this, but his ordinary hat happened to be at hand. Now, however, Peredonov arranged things differently—he tossed this hat onto the stove so that he would surely not use it.

Varvara was not at home, and Klavdiya was washing all the floors. Peredonov went into the kitchen to wash his hands. On the kitchen table he saw some blue wrapping paper and some raisins which had fallen out. This was a pound of raisins which had been bought for the tea buns which were baked at home. He began to eat the raisins just as they were, unwashed and dirty, and he ate the whole pound quickly and greedily, standing near the table with one eye on the door so that Klavidya should not come in and surprise him. Then he carefully folded up the thick blue paper, carried it out under his coat into the hall, and there placed it in the pocket of his overcoat so that he could throw it away when he went out into the street and, in this way, destroy the evidence.

He went out. Soon Klavdiya noticed that the raisins were gone and she was frightened. She began to search but she could not find them. When Varvara returned and discovered the loss of the raisins, she began to abuse Klavdiya. Varvara was positive that Klavdiya had eaten the raisins.

In the street it was quiet and breezy. There were only a few little clouds passing overhead. The puddles were drying up. There was a pale, joyful glow in the sky, but Peredonov's soul was heavy.

Along the way he stopped in at the tailor's in order to speed up the new uniform which he had ordered two days ago.

As he walked past the church, Peredonov took off his hat and crossed himself three times, energetically and sweepingly, to let everyone see how correctly the future inspector walked past the church. He never used to do it, but now he had to be on his guard. Perhaps there was a spy walking quietly behind him or someone hiding and peeking from behind a corner or a tree.

The chief of police lived on a street at the out-skirts of town. At the gates, which were wide open, Peredonov encountered a policeman—a meeting which had of late put him in low spirits. Several *muzhiks* could be seen standing around outside, but not the usual kind one sees—these were unusually quiet and orderly. The yard was littered. Carts covered with matting were standing about.

In the dark hallway Peredonov met still another policeman, a small skinny man, evidently capable, but somehow depressing in appearance. He stood motion-less and held a book bound in black leather under his arm. A ragged barefoot girl ran out of a side door, took Peredonov's coat, and led him into the living room.

"Please wait, Semyon Grigor'evich will return at once," she said.

The living-room ceiling was low, and it depressed Peredonov. The furniture was pressed closely against the walls, and twine rugs were on the floor. To the right and to the left noises and whispers could be heard from behind the walls. Pale women and tuber-cular children, all with shiny, curious eyes, kept peeking in through the door. Sometimes some questions and answers which were spoken louder could be distin-guished among the whispers—

"I brought . . ."

"Where shall I take this?"

"Where do you want me to put this?"

"It comes from Ermoshkin, Sidor Petrovich."

The chief of police soon came in. He was buttoning up his coat and smiling pleasantly. "Pardon me for holding you up," he said, shaking Peredonov's hand in his two large, grasping hands. "Various people have been calling on business. Our work is such that it won't bear delay."

Semyon Grigor'evich Min'chukov was a tall, solid, black-haired man with a slight bald spot in the center of his head. He was slightly stooped over, and his hands with their rakelike fingers hung down. He frequently smiled in a way suggesting that he had eaten something forbidden but pleasant and was now licking his lips. His lips were bright red and thick; his nose was bulbous; and his face was eager, zealous and stupid.

Peredonov was confused by everything that he saw and heard here. He mumbled some incoherent words and, sitting in an armchair, tried to hold his cap so that his badge could be seen. Min'chukov sat opposite him on the other side of the table, very erect and smiling pleasantly all the while as his rakelike hands quietly opened and closed on his knees.

"They're saying all sorts of things that never happened about me," said Peredonov. "And I could do some informing myself, only I don't want to. I'm nothing they say, but I know what they are. They spread all sorts of scandal behind your back and then laugh in your face. You will agree youself that in my position this is a very delicate situation, for, although I have patronage, they keep slandering me. Their following me about is useless—they are only wasting time and annoying me. Wherever one goes, the whole town knows about it. I hope then that you will support me if anything happens."

"Of course, of course, my dear sir, with the greatest pleasure," said Min'chukov, gesticulating with his large hands. "But the police must know whether or not there is someone you suspect."

"Of course I don't give a fig personally," said Peredonov angrily. "Let them gossip. The only thing I'm afraid of is that they might injure me in my position. They're crafty. You can't see how they're all gossiping, like Rutilov, for example. How do you know that he's not defrauding the treasury? He's trying to turn attention from the guilty to the innocent."

At first it seemed to Min'chukov that Peredonov was drunk and babbling nonsense. Then, after he had listened awhile, he imagined that Peredonov was complaining about someone who was spreading slanders about him and asking him to take certain measures.

"They are young people, and they think highly of themselves," continued Peredonov, thinking about Volodin. "They are dishonest themselves, and they are plotting against others. It is well known how young people act. Some of them even work in the police department, and they also poke their noses into things there."

And he talked about young people for a long time, although for some reason, he did not want to name Volodin. At any rate, he talked about young people in connection with the police and let Min'chukov understand that there were some displeasing elements in the police under suspicion. Min'chukov decided that Peredonov was hinting at two young police officials in his department—young and frivolous chaps who were always chasing after girls. Min'chukov involuntarily took on some of Peredonov's confusion and obvious fear.

"I'll look into it," he said anxiously, and for a moment he was pensive. Then he again began to smile amiably. "Two of my young officers are still a little green. I swear to God that one of their mamas still stands him in the corner, would you believe it?"

Peredonov burst into cackling laughter.

During this time Varvara was at Grushina's, where she learned an astonishing piece of news.

"Darling Varvara Dmitrievna, I have some news for you that will simply make you gasp," said Grushina excitedly when Varvara had scarcely come through the door.

"Well, what is it?" asked Varvara with a smirk.

"You would not imagine that there could be such low people in the world! Why they'll go to any ends to attain their goal!"

"What's this all about?"

"Well just wait a minute, and I'll tell you."

But the crafty Grushina first gave Varvara coffee, and then she chased her children out into the street which made the oldest girl stubborn and unwilling to go.

"Akh, you worthless trash!" Grushina shouted at her.

"You're trash yourself," replied the sharp-tongued little girl, and she stamped her feet at her mother. Grushina grabbed the girl by the hair and threw her out the door, slamming it after her . . .

"Headstrong creature!" she complained to Varvara. "There's nothing but worry with these children. I'm alone with them, and there's no rest. They should have a father."

"Why don't you marry again so that they'll have a father," said Varvara.

"You never can tell how a man will turn out, Varvara Dmitrievna darling, he might begin to treat them badly."

Just then the girl ran back from the street and threw a handful of sand in the window which landed on her mother's head and dress. Grushina stuck her head out of the window and shouted, "I'll get hold of you, you trash! Just wait until you come home— I'll give you what's coming to you, you lousy trash!"

"You're trash yourself, you wicked fool," called the girl from the street, jumping on one leg and shaking her dirty little fists at her mother.

"Just you wait till I get hold of you," Grushina shouted at her daughter, and she closed the window.

Then she sat down calmly as if nothing had happened. "I have some news for you, but I don't know if I ought to tell," said Grushina. "Now don't you fear, Varvara Dmitrievna, my dear, they won't succeed."

"Well, what?" asked Varvara fearfully, and the saucer and cup of coffee trembled in her hands.

"You know that now there is a student, Pyl'nikov, who has entered the gymnasium right into the fifth form. They say he came from Ruban' because his aunt has purchased an estate in our district."

"Yes, I know," said Varvara. "I saw him just as he arrived with his aunt. He's as fetching as a little girl, and always blushing."

"My dearest Varvara Dmitrievna, why shouldn't he resemble a girl—you see, it's a disguised young lady!"

"You can't mean it!" exclaimed Varvara.

"They've thought it up on purpose in order to snare Ardal'on Borisych," said Grushina, speaking quickly and waving her hands. She was happy and excited because she had such important news to tell. "What happened is that this girl has a cousin who is an orphan, and he went to school in Ruban'. The mother of this young lady took him from the school and has sent her daughter here with his papers. And observe that they have placed him in a house where there are no other students. He is there alone where they thought everything could be kept under cover."

"But how did you find out about it?" asked Varvara skeptically.

"News flies quickly, dearest Varvara Dmitrievna. It seemed suspicious from the very beginning—all the other boys act like boys, but this quiet one is always tiptoeing about. Although to look at him he seems to be just a red-cheeked, chesty young fellow, his comrades say that he is so modest that if they say a word to him he blushes. They actually tease him for being a girl, only they think it's a joke and don't realize it's the truth. And just think, they've been so cunning that even the landlady doesn't know anything."

"But how did you find out?" repeated Varvara.

"Now what is there I don't know, my dearest Varvara Dmitrievna! I know everyone in the district. Besides, it is well known to everyone that they still have a small boy living at home who is just about as old as this one. Now why do you suppose they didn't enter them both in the gymnasium together? They say that he was sick during the summer and that he is resting a year, and then he will enter the gymnasium. But that's all nonsense—he is the real schoolboy, and it's also common knowledge that they had a young girl. They claim that she got married and went to the Caucasus, but that's just another lie—she never went away but is living here disguised as a schoolboy."

"But what are they doing it for?" asked Varvara.

"What indeed!" said Grushina excitedly. "They want to catch one of the instructors—there's a premium on bachelors—or someone else for that matter. As a schoolboy she can get into one of their apartments, and then anything can happen."

"She's a comely bitch," said Varvara fearfully.

"I should say so, a renowned beauty," agreed Grushina. "She's being careful now, but just you wait—she'll get used to things, loosen up a bit, and set the whole town spinning. So now you can imagine how clever they are. Just as soon as I found out all about this I tried to meet his landlady, or maybe I should say her landlady—who knows?"

"Phew, the girl's a regular werewolf—God help us!" said Varvara.

"The landlady's a devout one, and so I went to Vespers at the parish on St. Paneteleimon's Day. 'Olga Vasil'evna,' I says to her, 'why do you have just one student living with you now? Isn't one a little unprofit-

able for you?' I say. 'And tell me why I need any more,'
she says. 'They're nothing but fuss.' Then I says, 'But
you always used to keep two or three in past years.'
And then she says, imagine dearest Varvara Dmitrievna, 'They arranged to have Sashen'ka live with me
alone. They aren't poor people,' she says, 'and they
paid me a little more as though,' she says, 'they were
afraid that he would get corrupted being with the
other boys. Isn't that something?' "

"The lowlife!" said Varvara spitefully. "Well, did
you tell her that 'he' is a vixen?"

"I told her—be careful, I said, Olga Vasil'evna, that
they haven't dumped a girl instead of a boy on you."

"Well, and what did she say?"

"First she thought I was kidding and laughed. Then
I got more serious and said, 'My dearest Olga Vasil'evna,' I said, 'do you know that they are saying that
the boy is really a wench!' But she still wouldn't believe it. 'Nonsense,' she says, 'how could he be a girl,'
she says—'I'm not blind . . .' "

This story flabbergasted Varvara. She completely
believed that everything was just as Grushina said and
that an assault on her future husband was being prepared from still another side. Somehow she had to tear
the mask from this disguised girl as quickly as possible.
They discussed how they might do this for a long time,
but for the present could think of nothing.

At home Varvara was upset still more by the disap-
pearance of her raisins.

When Peredonov returned home, Varvara told him
hurriedly and excitedly that Klavdiya had hidden the
pound of raisins somewhere and wouldn't confess.

"And besides that," said Varvara angrily, "she lies
and says that perhaps the *barin* ate them. She said that
you came into the kitchen for something while she was

washing the floors and that you lingered around for a long time there."

"I wasn't there long at all," said Peredonov sullenly. "I only washed my hands, and I didn't see any raisins there."

"Klavdiushka, Klavdiushka!" cried Varvara. "The *barin* says that he didn't see any raisins, which means that you've hidden them somewhere."

Klavdiya showed her reddened, tear-streaked face from the kitchen.

"I didn't take your raisins," she exclaimed in a sobbing voice. "I'll pay you for them, but I still didn't take your raisins!"

"You'll pay! You'll pay!" shouted Varvara angrily. "I'm not obligated to fatten you up on raisins."

"Our little pig Diushka's filched a pound of raisins," exclaimed Peredonov laughing loudly.

"Scoundrels!" cried Klavdiya, and she slammed the door.

After dinner Varvara was unable to stop herself from telling what she had heard about Pyl'nikov. She did not consider whether this would be useful or harmful to her or how Peredonov might react—she simply spoke from spite.

Peredonov tried to recall Pyl'nikov, but somehow he couldn't quite remember him. Until this moment he had paid little attention to this student. He had looked with disdain upon him because of his attractiveness and cleanliness and because he conducted himself with reserve, studied well, and was the youngest of the fifth form students. But now Varvara's tale incited a lecherous curiosity in him. Immodest thoughts were slowly stirred up in his dark mind . . .

"I'll have to go to Vespers to have a look at this disguised wench," he thought.

Suddenly Klavdiya ran in triumphantly and threw

a piece of blue wrapping paper crumpled into a ball on the table. "You said that I ate up the raisins, but what is this?" she cried. "Much I need your raisins."

Peredonov guessed what she was talking about. He had forgotten to throw away the wrapping paper in the street, and now Klavdiya had found it in his coat pocket.

"Oh hell!" he exclaimed.

"Where did this come from?" screamed Varvara.

"I found it in Ardal'on Borisych's pocket," replied Klavdiya gloatingly. "He ate them himself and put the blame on me. It's no secret that Ardal'on Borisych has a big sweet tooth, but why should he blame others if he himself . . ."

"Now wait a minute," said Peredonov angrily. "You're always lying. I didn't take anything—you must have slipped it into my pocket."

"God forgive you, why should I put anything into your pocket?" said Klavdiya, taken aback.

"How dare you go through his pockets!" screamed Varvara. "Were you looking for money?"

"I wasn't going through his pockets," answered Klavdiya with anger. "I took the coat to clean it off, it was all muddy."

"But why did you go into his pocket?"

"It fell out of his pocket itself. I don't go searching pockets," said Klavdiya defending herself.

"You lie, Diushka," said Peredonov.

"What right have you to call me a pig, you tormentors!" exclaimed Klavdiya. "The hell with you—I'll pay you for your raisins but I hope they choke you—you guzzled them, and I have to pay. Yes I'll pay for them all right—evidently you have no conscience and there's no shame in your eyes, and still you call yourselves gentlefolk."

Klavdiya went into the kitchen crying and cursing at them.

Peredonov cackled loudly and said, "Look how huffed up she is."

"She certainly will pay," said Varvara. "If you let them, these ravenous devils are ready to devour anything."

And for a long time after that they both teased Klavdiya because she had eaten the pound of raisins. They took the money for it out of her salary, and they told all their guests about the raisins.

The cat, as if attracted by all the shouting, came out of the kitchen, made its way along the wall, and sat near Peredonov, looking at him with its avid and evil eyes. Peredonov bent down to catch hold of the animal, but the cat hissed violently, scratched Peredonov's hand, and then ran away, hiding under the cupboard. As it peeped out from there, its narrow green eyes glimmered.

"That cat's just like a werewolf," thought Peredonov fearfully.

Meanwhile, Varvara, still thinking about Pyl'nikov, said, "Why do you always play billiards every night—it would be better if you sometimes dropped in on your students at their lodgings. They know that the teachers seldom drop in to look around, and the inspector only comes once a year. The result is that all sorts of shocking things go on in their apartments including card-playing and drunkenness. Why don't you, for example, drop in on this disguised girl? Go later at bedtime; then you'll catch her off guard and confuse her."

Peredonov thought awhile and laughed loudly. "Varvara is a cunning rogue," he thought. "She can teach me a few tricks."

12 : ౕ౿ఀౕ౿ఀ

Peredonov set out to Vespers at the gymnasium church. There he stood behind the students and attentively watched how they were conducting themselves. It seemed to him that some of them were playing tricks, pushing one another, whispering, and laughing. He noted them and tried to remember their names, but there were many and he reproached himself for not having thought of bringing a paper and pencil to mark down names. He was upset that the students were behaving so poorly and no one was paying any attention to it, in spite of the fact that the headmaster and even the inspector were standing there in the church with their wives and children.

Actually, the students were standing quietly and decorously. Some were crossing themselves automatically while thinking of things far removed from church, while others prayed diligently. Very rarely someone would whisper something to his neighbor—two or three words almost without turning his head—and receive an answer in kind—short and quiet—or perhaps even nothing more than a quick movement, a glance, a shrug of the shoulders, or a smile. But these slight movements, unnoticed by the disciplinary proctor, produced the illusion of great disorder in Peredonov's dull but disturbed imagination. Even in a tranquil moment Peredonov, like all shallow people, was unable to appraise little incidents. He either did not notice them, or else he greatly exaggerated their significance. And so now, when he was agitated by expectations and fears, his senses served him even more poorly, and little by little all reality became clouded before him by a shroud of offensive and evil mirages.

And besides, what did the students mean to Peredonov? They were merely a cause of having to waste ink on paper with a pen and of having to retell by rote what had already been said in real language! In all his time as a teacher Peredonov very clearly did not understand or think that his students were real people too, just like grownups. Only those students who shaved and were beginning to be attracted to women suddenly became equal to himself in his eyes.

After he had stood in the back for a while and gathered a sufficient number of disturbing details, Peredonov moved forward a little to the center aisles. There at the very end of an aisle to the right stood Sasha Pyl'nikov. He was praying unpretentiously and often dropped to his knees. Peredonov looked him over, and he was especially pleased when Sasha dropped to his knees as if he were being punished and looked straight ahead at the gleaming altar doors with a worried and imploring expression on his face, with entreaty and sorrow in his black eyes, which were shaded by long blue-black lashes. Slender and dark, which was especially noticeable when he dropped on his knees quietly and simply as though he were being sternly watched, and with a high and broad chest, he seemed to Peredonov at that moment certainly to be a girl.

Now Peredonov firmly resolved to visit him that evening after Vespers.

People began to leave the church. It was noticed that Peredonov was not wearing a hat as he always had before, but a cap with a badge.

"How is it you're sporting a badge now, Ardal'on

Borisych?" asked Rutilov with a smile. "This must mean that a certain person has his eye on an inspectorship."

"Will soldiers have to salute you with respect now?" asked Valeriya with affected innocence.

"Akh, what nonsense!" said Peredonov angrily.

"You don't understand at all, Valerochka," said Dar'ya. "It has nothing to do with soldiers! It's just that Ardal'on Borisych will now get much more respect from his students than formerly."

Ludmila laughed loudly, and Peredonov was quick to say good-bye in order to get away from their laughter.

It was still too early to visit Pyl'nikov, and he didn't want to return home. Peredonov strolled along the dark streets trying to think where he could waste an hour. There were many houses, and lights were burning in many windows. Occasionally voices could be heard from opened windows. People returning from church walked along the streets, and gates and doors could be heard opening and closing. Everywhere lived people strange and hostile to Peredonov, perhaps some of them were even now drawing up evil plans against him. Perhaps someone was wondering why Peredonov was now walking alone at such a late hour and where he was going. It seemed to Peredonov that someone was following him and slinking after him. Anguish possessed him. He walked on hurriedly and aimlessly.

He thought about how each house has its dead and about how all those who had lived in these houses about fifty years ago were now dead. He even remembered some of them. "When a man dies," thought Peredonov sadly, "his house should be burnt—otherwise it's frightening."

Olga Vasil'evna Kokovkina, in whose house the schoolboy Sasha Pyl'nikov lived, was the widow of a paymaster. Her husband had left her a pension and a smallish house which was so constructed that she could rent out two or three rooms to boarders. She preferred gymnasium students. As it happened, the best-behaved boys, those who studied faithfully and completed the gymnasium were always placed with her. In the other student lodgings there were a large number of boys who wandered from one school to another and never finished their studies.

Olga Vasil'evna was a tall and erect but emaciated old woman with a kindly face upon which she nevertheless tried to maintain a strict expression. She and Sasha Pyl'nikov, a well-fed schoolboy, strictly brought up by his aunt, were having tea. Today it was Sasha's turn to supply the jam—which he had gotten in the village—and for that reason he felt that he was the host, and his black eyes shone as he treated Olga Vasil'evna ceremoniously.

The doorbell rang, and soon after that Peredonov appeared in the dining room. Kokovkina was quite amazed at this late visit.

"I have come to look at our gymnasium student and to see how he lives," he said.

Kokovkina offered Peredonov something to eat, but he refused. He wanted them to finish drinking their tea more quickly so that he might be alone with the student. When they had had their tea, they crossed over into Sasha's room, but Kokovkina did not leave them and was talking endlessly. Peredonov looked morosely at Sasha, who was timidly silent.

"Nothing will come from this visit," thought Peredonov with vexation.

The maid called Kokovkina for something. She went away. In misery Sasha watched her leave. Sasha's eyes, shaded by his lashes, grew dim, and it seemed as though these unusually long lashes threw a shadow over his entire dark but suddenly paler face. He felt ill at ease before this gloomy man. Peredonov sat down next to him and awkwardly put his arm around him.

"Has little Sashen'ka said her prayers well?" he asked without changing the fixed expression on his face.

Sasha glanced at Peredonov with fear and embarrassment. He blushed and was silent.

"Well? Did you say them well?" asked Peredonov.

"I did," said Sasha at last.

"Akh, what rosy cheeks you've got," said Peredonov. "Won't you confess that you're a girl? You're a wench, you rogue!"

"No, I'm not a girl," replied Sasha, and suddenly, angry with himself for his bashfulness, he asked in a high pitched voice, "How am I like a girl? Your students invented this to tease me because I dislike dirty words. I'm not used to saying them, and there's no reason why I should. Why should I say nasty things?"

"Would your Mamma punish you?" asked Peredonov.

"I don't have a mother," said Sasha. "Mama died a long time ago. I have an aunt."

"Well then, would your aunt punish you?"

"Of course she would punish me if I said nasty things. There's nothing good about it, is there?"

"But how would your aunt find out?"

"Besides, I myself don't want to speak like that," said Sasha quietly. "And there are several ways my aunt might find out. I might even give myself away."

"And which of your comrades say dirty words?" asked Peredonov.

Sasha again blushed and was silent.

"Come now, speak up," insisted Peredonov. "Don't conceal anything—you have to tell me."

"No one says them," said Sasha in confusion.

"You yourself were just complaining about it."

"I wasn't complaining."

"Do you deny it?" said Peredonov angrily.

Sasha felt as though he were caught in some sort of awful trap. "I was merely explaining to you why some of my comrades tease me for being a girl," he said. "But that doesn't mean I want to tattle on them."

"Aha! And why not?" asked Peredonov maliciously.

"It's not nice," said Sasha with an annoyed smile.

"In that case I'll tell the headmaster, and he'll force you to speak," said Peredonov, full of malicious joy.

Sasha, his eyes burning with anger, looked at Peredonov. "No, please, don't tell him, Ardal'on Borisych," he begged and from the cracking sounds in his voice it could be perceived that, while he was making a great effort to ask, he really wanted to shout strong and threatening words.

"No, I shall, and then you'll see if you can cover up nasty things. You yourself should have complained about them at once. Just wait and see what happens to you."

Sasha stood up and in his confusion adjusted his belt. Kokovkina came in.

"Your quiet one is a good boy, I must say," said Peredonov angrily.

Kokovkina became frightened. She quickly went up to Sasha and sat down beside him. When she was excited her legs always grew weak. "What are you talking about, Ardal'on Borisych?" she asked fearfully. "What has he done?"

"Why not ask him?" said Peredonov with sullen anger.

"Well Sashen'ka, what are you guilty of?" asked Kokovkina, touching Sasha's elbow.

"I don't know," said Sasha, and he began to weep.

"Now what's the matter with you? Why are you crying?" asked Kokovkina. She put her hands on the boy's shoulders and drew him to her, not noticing that this disturbed him. Sasha stood hunched over, covering his eyes with a handkerchief.

"He's learning dirty words in the gymnasium and he doesn't want to say who's teaching him," explained Peredonov. "He not only learns the dirty words himself, but he also covers up for the others. He mustn't shield them."

"Akh, Sashen'ka, Sashen'ka, how could you do such a thing! How could you? Aren't you ashamed!" said Kokovkina in confusion as she let go of Sasha.

"I didn't do anything," sobbed Sasha. "I didn't do anything wrong. They tease me because I won't say bad words."

"Who is it who says these bad words?" asked Peredonov again.

"No one says them," exclaimed Sasha in despair.

"You see how he lies," said Peredonov. "He needs a good punishment. He must reveal those who are saying nasty things, otherwise our gymnasium will get a bad reputation, and we won't be able to do anything about it."

"Forgive him, Ardal'on Borisych," said Kokovkina, "how could he tell on his comrades? They would make life miserable for him."

"He has to tell because it will be very useful," said Peredonov angrily. "We'll adopt measures to correct the situation."

"But won't they beat him up?" said Kokovkina hesitantly.

"They won't dare. If he is still afraid, let him tell in secret."

"Well, Sashen'ka, tell in secret. No one will know that you told."

Sasha wept silently. Kokovkina drew him to her, embraced him, and for a long time whispered something in his ear. He shook his head back and forth.

"He doesn't want to," said Kokovkina.

"If you birch him, he'll talk," said Peredonov fiercely. "Bring me a rod, and I'll make him tell."

"Olga Vasil'evna—what for?" cried Sasha.

Kokovkina stood up and embraced him. "Now that's enough crying," she said tenderly and strictly. "No one's going to touch you."

"As you wish," said Peredonov, "but in that case I'll have to tell the headmaster. I thought it would be better for him if it were at home. Perhaps your Sashen'ka is one of the rascals himself. We still don't know why they tease him as a little girl. Perhaps there's a completely different reason. Maybe he's not being taught but is corrupting others."

Peredonov left the room in anger, and Kokovkina came after him.

"Ardal'on Borisych, how could you embarrass a boy for nothing whatsoever!" she said reproachfully. "It's a good thing that he still doesn't understand what you're talking about."

"Well, good-bye," said Peredonov angrily. "I still am going to tell the headmaster. This matter must be followed through."

He left, and Kokovkina returned to comfort Sasha. Sasha was sitting gloomily by the window looking at the starry sky. His black eyes were now peaceful and strangely sad. Kokovkina silently stroked his head.

"It's my own fault," he said. "I let out the reason that they tease me, and he fixed onto it. He's an extremely crude man—not one of the students likes him."

On the next day Peredonov and Varvara finally moved to their new apartment. Ershova stood at the gate and exchanged abuses with Varvara. Peredonov hid from her behind the moving vans.

As soon as they were in their new quarters they had a prayer service performed. It was essential in Peredonov's eyes to show that he was a religious man. During the blessing, the odor of incense surrounding his head put him in an almost religious mood.

One strange thing troubled him. A surprising creature of nebulous features ran out from somewhere—a small, gray lively *nedotýkomka*.* It laughed, quivered, and whirled around Peredonov. When he stretched out his hand towards it, it quickly flashed by and hid behind the door or under the cupboard—only to reappear in a minute and quiver and tease—the gray, formless sprite.

When the service was finally over, Peredonov was apprehensive and recited a charm in a whisper. The *nedotýkomka* hissed ever so softly, contracted itself into a tiny ball, and rolled away behind the door. Peredonov gave a sigh of relief.

"It will be nice if it has rolled away for good, but maybe it lives in this apartment somewhere under the floor and will again come to tease me."

Peredonov became chilled and depressed.

"Why is there all this uncleanness in the world?" he thought.

After the blessing had been finished and the guests had departed, Peredonov for a long time considered where the *nedotýkomka* might be hidden. Varvara went to Grushina's, and Peredonov started to search and began to rummage in her things.

"I wonder if Varvara took it away in her pocket," thought Peredonov. "It doesn't need much space, and it could hide itself in a pocket and sit there until the right time comes."

---

* Peredonov's demon is something to be felt more than literally understood. *Nedotýkomka* is a term applied in folk *byliny* to an angry, sullen figure, a person whom "one can't touch." Sologub makes the *nedotýkomka* a symbol of all the ugliness, meanness, and chaos implicit in reality. A poem written in October, 1899, suggests similarities between the *nedotýkomka* and the figure of *gore* or "woe" in the seventeenth-century "Tale of Sorrow and Misfortune." A variant, *nedotyka*, used by Pushkin, was in Sologub's time, often applied to a haughty streetwalker, cf. the story, "The Creature," by Zinaida Gippius.

One of Varvara's dresses especially attracted his attention. It was all frilly with bows and ribbons as if specially made to hide something. Peredonov looked it over for a long time and then by force, with the help of a knife, he half ripped, half cut away the pocket, threw it into the stove, and then proceeded to rip and cut the whole dress into tiny pieces. Strange, vague thoughts whirled about in his head, and his soul was hopelessly depressed.

Varvara soon returned—Peredonov was still shredding up the dress. She thought that he was drunk and began to scold him. Peredonov listened for a long time and finally said, "What are you yapping at, fool! Perhaps you are carrying a devil in your pocket. I must look into this matter and see what's going on."

Varvara was taken aback. Satisfied by the effect he had produced, Peredonov hurried to look for his hat and go play billiards. Varvara ran out into the hall, and, while Peredonov was putting on his coat, she shouted, "I don't have any devil—maybe it's you who are carrying a devil in your pocket. Where could I get a devil for you? Perhaps I could order you one from Holland!" *

The young official Cherepnin—the same one about whom Vershina told how he had looked in her window—had begun to pay attention to Vershina when she first became a widow. Vershina would not have been averse to marrying a second time except that Cherepnin seemed too insignificant to her. Cherepnin was embittered and, consequently, accepted with gleeful spite Volodin's suggestion of smearing Vershina's gates with tar.

---

* "Dutch devil" is an expression which originated during the period of Peter's reforms—see note to the title. Peter had himself received training in Holland, and he imported many of his ideas from there.

He agreed but afterwards began to reconsider. Suppose they were to catch him? Being an official, it would be awkward for him. He decided to delegate the task to others and bribed two young fellows with twenty-five kopecks, promising them another fifteen kopecks each when they finished the job. And so one dark night the deed was done.

If someone at Vershina's house had opened a window after midnight, he would have heard the slight rustle of bare feet on the wooden sidewalk in the street, quiet whispering, and faint sounds as if the fence were being swept. Then there was a slight clinking, the rapid patter of feet going faster and faster, faraway laughter, and the troubled barking of dogs. But no one opened a window.

And in the morning . . . the gate and the fence around the garden and the front yard were streaked with brownish-yellow traces of tar. Dirty words were written on the gates with tar. People who walked by made exclamations and laughed—soon the news traveled, and the curious came.

Vershina walked about quickly in the garden smoking. Her smile was even more wry than usual, and she was mumbling angry words. Marta did not come out of the house and wept bitterly. Mar'ya, the maid, tried to wash away the tar and exchanged abuses with curious onlookers who were laughing uproariously.

On the same day Cherepnin told Volodin who had done it. Volodin was quick to communicate this information to Peredonov. Both knew these boys, who were renowned for their bold mischief.

Peredonov, on his way to play billiards, dropped in at Vershina's. It was gloomy. Vershina and Marta were sitting in the drawing room.

"Your gates have been painted with tar," said Peredonov.

Marta blushed. Vershina quickly told how they got up and saw that people were laughing at their fence and how Mar'ya had washed the fence.

"I know who did it," said Peredonov.

Vershina looked at Peredonov with disbelief. "How did you find out?" she asked.

"Oh, I found out."

"Tell us who it was," said Marta crossly. She was quite unattractive now because she had angry tear-stained eyes with reddened and swollen eyelids.

"Of course I'll tell you—that's what I came for," replied Peredonov. "These smart alecks should be taught a lesson. Only you must promise that you won't say who told you."

"And why is that, Ardal'on Borisych?" asked Vershina with surprise.

Peredonov maintained a significant silence and then explained, "They're the sort of people who might fracture my skull if they found out who told on them."

Vershina promised to remain silent.

"And don't you say that I told you either," said Peredonov turning to Marta.

"Very well, I won't say anything," agreed Marta hurriedly because she was anxious to find out the names of the guilty ones as quickly as possible.

It seemed to her that they should have to undergo cruel and shameful punishment.

"No, you had better swear," said Peredonov cautiously.

"All right— I swear to God I won't say anything," consented Marta, "just tell us quickly."

Vladya was eavesdropping behind the door. He was happy that he had had the sense not to go into the living room because he had not been forced to make any promises, and so he could tell whomever he pleased. He smiled with pleasure at this opportunity to get revenge on Peredonov.

"I was going home along your street at one o'clock last night," related Peredonov, "when all at once I heard someone fooling around near your gates. At first I thought it was thieves. I was thinking about what I should do, when suddenly I heard them running straight towards me. I pressed myself against the wall, and they didn't see me, but I recognized them. One had a brush and the other had a pail. They were Avdeev, the locksmith's sons, well-known hooligans. As they ran one said to the other, 'We haven't wasted the night. We've picked up fifty-five kopecks on the side.' I would like to have grabbed one of them but I was afraid they'd smear up my face, and I had my new coat on."

Peredonov had barely left when Vershina went to the chief of police with a complaint. Chief Min'chukov sent an officer after Avdeev and his sons.

The boys came boldly, thinking that they were merely under suspicion because of previous misdeeds. Avdeev, on the other hand, a gaunt and dejected old man, was absolutely convinced that his sons had again done something reprehensible. The chief told Avdeev what his sons were accused of doing.

"They are unmanageable," said Avdeev. "Do what you want with them, I've already injured my hands on them."

"This wasn't our job," declared Nil firmly. He was the older boy and had bristling red hair.

"They blame us no matter who does anything," said Il'ya the younger in a whining voice. He was also bristle-headed but with white hair. "We did wrong once, and now we have to answer for everything."

Min'chukov smiled pleasantly, shook his head, and said, "You'd best own up to it honestly."

"We have nothing to own up to," said Nil rudely.

"Oh? Then who gave you fifty-five kopecks for your

work, eh?" And, seeing by the momentary confusion of the boys that they were guilty, Min'chukov said to Vershina, "It's clear that these are the ones."

The boys began to deny it again. They were taken into the storeroom and whipped. Unable to endure the pain, they confessed. But even after they had confessed, they did not want to say who gave them the money for it.

"We did it ourselves," they said.

They whipped each in turn leisurely until they said that Cherepnin had bribed them, and then they turned the boys over to their father.

"Well, we've punished, I mean their father has punished them, and you know who did this to you," said the police chief to Vershina.

"I'm not going to let this Cherepnin get off," said Vershina. "I'll take him into court."

"I don't advise it, Natalya Afanas'evna," said Min'chukov abruptly. "It's best to let the whole thing drop."

"What! Let such villains go? Never!" cried Vershina.

"The important thing is that we have no evidence," said the police chief quietly.

"What do you mean 'no evidence' if the boys themselves confessed?"

"That makes no difference—they might deny it in court, and there'd be no one to whip them there."

"How could they deny it? The officers are witnesses," said Vershina with less confidence.

"Some witnesses! If you beat the hide off a man, he will confess to anything—even things that never happened. They're scoundrels of course, and they got what they deserved, but you won't get anything out of them in court." Min'chukov smiled sweetly and looked calmly at Vershina.

Vershina left the chief of police feeling very dissatisfied, but, after she had thought it over, she agreed that it would be difficult to prove Cherepnin's guilt and nothing but more publicity and scandal would come of it.

13 : ᠄᠊᠊᠊᠊

Towards evening Peredonov went to see the headmaster on business.

The headmaster, Nikolai Vlas'evich Khripach, possessed a certain number of rules which served him well in life and which were not too burdensome to maintain. In his job he quietly did everything that was demanded of him by the rules or by the orders of the authorities and also observed a moderate, "correct" liberalism. Therefore, the authorities, the parents, and the students were all equally satisfied with their headmaster. He did not know moments of doubt, indecision, or conflict—what was the use of them? One could always depend either upon the decision of the pedagogical council or on the instructions of the authorities. And he was just as reserved and correct in his personal relations. His very appearance gave the impression of eminent respectability—he was smallish, stocky, and active, with sharp eyes and a confident voice. He seemed like a man who got along not badly and intended to get along better yet. There were many books on the shelves in his library. He took excerpts from some of them and, when he had a sufficient number, he put them in order and paraphrased them in his own words—thus a textbook was written, printed, and circulated. They were not as widely used as the books by Ushinsky and Evtushev-sky* but still—they did well enough. Sometimes he gleaned his material mainly from foreign books, and the result—respectable and necessary to no one—was published in a journal also respectable and necessary to no one. He had many children, and all of them, both the boys and girls, already showed signs of various talents. One wrote poems, another drew, and another was making rapid success in music.

"You're always picking on me, Nikolai Vlas'evich," said Peredonov sullenly. "Perhaps someone has slandered me to you, but I've done nothing they say."

"Excuse me," interrupted the headmaster, "but I fail to understand what slanders you have in mind. In the matter of running the gymnasium, which has been entrusted to me, I am guided by my own observations, and I dare to hope that my service and experience are sufficient to evaluate what I see and hear with sufficient correctness, especially in view of my scrupulous attitude towards my job, which I have made an inflexible rule for myself," said Khripach quickly and distinctly, and his voice sounded dry and clear like the noise made by zinc rods when they are bent. "In regard to my personal opinion of you, I still continue to think that there are annoying lapses in the performance of your job."

"That's right," said the sullen Peredonov, "you've taken it into your head that I'm not good for anything, even though I am constantly concerned about the gymnasium."

Khripach raised his eyebrows in astonishment and looked at Peredonov questioningly.

"Little do you know," continued Peredonov, "that we have a scandal that might break out in the gym-

* K. Ushinsky was the author of a standard pedagogical textbook; V. Evtushevsky wrote several mathematics texts.

nasium that I alone spotted and that no one else has noticed."

"What sort of scandal?" asked Khripach with a dry laugh, and he nimbly paced up and down his study. "You intrigue me, although I will tell you frankly that I hardly believe in the possibility of a scandal in our gymnasium."

"Yes, but you don't know whom you have accepted," said Peredonov with such spiteful glee that Khripach paused and looked attentively at him.

"All the newly accepted students have been investigated," he said drily, "and, moreover, the new students in the first form were evidently not rejected by another gymnasium. The lone student who entered the fifth form came to us with such recommendations that the possibility of uncomplimentary assumptions is out of the question."

"Yes, but they should have sent him to another institution and not to ours," said Peredonov morosely, almost unwillingly.

"I must ask you to explain, Ardal'on Borisych," said Khripach. "I hope that you don't wish to say that Pyl'nikov ought to be sent to a reformatory."

"No, this scoundrel should be sent to a boarding school without ancient languages," * said Peredonov evilly, and his eyes gleamed with fury.

Khripach, who had thrust his hands into the pockets of his short house jacket, looked at Peredonov with extraordinary astonishment.

"What sort of boarding school?" he asked. "Do you know what sort of institution that signifies? And if you do know, why did you decide to use such an improper term?"

Khripach blushed deeply, and his voice sounded still drier and more decisive. At another time these hints of the headmaster's anger would have driven Peredonov

* The expression refers to a house of prostitution.

into confusion, but now he did not flinch. "You all think that this is a boy," he said derisively, screwing up his eyes, "but it's not a boy—it's a girl, and what a girl!"

Khripach laughed abruptly and drily—the same clear and resounding official laugh that he always laughed. "Ha, ha, ha!" he laughed crisply and, when he had finished laughing, sat down in his armchair and threw back his head as though he had dropped from laughter. "You have really surprised me, my most esteemed —ha, ha, ha!—Ardal'on Borisych! Tell me, if you will be so kind, upon what you base your supposition—if the premises which led you to this conclusion are not private secrets! Ha, ha, ha!"

Peredonov told him all that he had heard from Varvara and at the same time also enlarged upon Kokovkina's bad characteristics. Khripach listened, from time to time bursting into his dry, crisp laugh.

"Your imagination has outdone itself, Ardal'on Borisych," he said as he stood up and clapped Peredonov on the sleeve. "Many of my esteemed colleagues, just as I, have their own children, and we were not born yesterday. Do you suppose then that we could take a disguised girl for a boy?"

"That's what you say, but if something comes of it, then whose fault will it be?" asked Peredonov.

"Ha, ha, ha!" laughed Khripach. "What consequences are you afraid of?"

"Depravity will begin in the gymnasium," said Peredonov.

Khripach frowned. "You go too far," he said. "Nothing that you have said to me so far gives me the slightest cause to share your suspicions."

In the course of this evening Peredonov went around hurriedly to all his colleagues from the inspector to the disciplinary proctors and told them all that Pyl'nikov was a disguised girl. They all laughed and did not believe it, but many had their doubts after he left them. The teachers' wives, on the other hand, almost all believed him at once.

By the next morning many of them came to school with the thought that perhaps Peredonov was right. No one spoke of this openly, but they didn't quarrel with Peredonov, and they limited themselves to hesitant and ambiguous replies—each feared that he would be considered stupid if he started to argue, and it suddenly turned out to be true. Many were anxious to hear what the headmaster had to say—but the headmaster, contrary to custom, did not leave his home at all except when he went, rather late, to his sole lesson that day in the sixth form. He continued to sit there an extra five minutes when it was over and then went straight to his study without seeing anyone.

Finally, before the fourth lesson, the gray-headed religious instructor and two other teachers went into the headmaster's study under the pretext of some sort of business, and the parson cleverly got the subject around to Pyl'nikov. But the headmaster laughed so good-naturedly and sincerely that all three were at once firmly convinced that it was all foolishness. Then, the headmaster quickly turned back to other subjects, told some new town gossip, and then complained of a severe headache, saying that it looked as if he would call in the honorable Evgeny Ivanovich, the gymnasium physician. In an extremely amiable tone, he related how his lesson today had worsened his headache because it had happened that Peredonov was in the neighboring classroom, and for some reason the students there laughed often and unusually loudly. When he had laughed drily, Khripach said, "This year fate has been merciless to me—three times a week I have to teach in the class next to the one in which Ardal'on

Borisych is, and, if you can imagine it, the laughter is continuous and quite extraordinary. By all appearances Ardal'on Borisych is not an amusing man, and yet he continually awakens such gaiety!" Then, without giving anyone an opportunity to comment on this, Khripach quickly shifted once again to another subject.

Actually, there had been a good deal of laughter in Peredonov's classes of late—and it did not at all please him. On the contrary, children's laughter irritated Peredonov. Yet he was unable to refrain from saying something unnecessary or in bad taste. He would tell a stupid anecdote or he would begin to tease one of the good boys. Several students could always be found in the class who were happy at any chance to cause disorder, and at each of Peredonov's antics they would go into uproarious laughter.

Toward the end of the school day, Khripach sent for the doctor but took his hat and set out towards the orchard which lay between the gymnasium and the river bank. The orchard was spacious and shady. The small schoolboys loved it and ran about in it during recess. For this reason, the disciplinary proctors did not like the orchard. They were afraid that something might happen to the boys, but Khripach demanded that the boys be there during recess. This was necessary to him in order to make his reports appear more attractive.

Passing through the hall, Khripach paused by an open door leading to the gym, stood awhile, lowered his head, and entered. By his somber face and his slow gait, everyone at once knew that he had a headache.

The fifth form was assembled for gym. They were arranged in a single line, and the instructor, a lieutenant in the local reserve battalion, was preparing to command something until he saw the headmaster and went straight towards him. Khripach shook his hand, casually glanced at the students, and asked, "Are you satisfied with them? Do they make an effort? They don't get tired?"

In his heart the lieutenant deeply despised his students who, in his opinion, did not have military bearing. If they had been his cadets, he would have said straight out what he thought about them. But it was hardly worth-while to tell the unpleasant truth about these louts to the man upon whom his lessons depended. And so he said, pleasantly smiling with his thin lips and looking at the headmaster sweetly and gaily, "Oh yes, they're fine boys."

The headmaster took several steps along the line, turned to leave, and then suddenly stopped as if he had remembered something. "And are you satisfied with your new pupil? Does he make an effort? Does he tire easily?" he asked casually and gloomily, putting his hand across his forehead.

The lieutenant—just for variety's sake—and since, in fact, the student was a stranger, said, "Well he's a little delicate, and he tires easily."

But the headmaster had already left and did not even hear him.

A breath of air evidently refreshed Khripach a little, because in half an hour he returned, stood by the door for a moment, and again dropped in on the lesson. They were doing exercises on the gym apparatus. There were two or three idle students who did not notice the headmaster and who were leaning against the wall using the time when the lieutenant was not looking at them. Khripach went up to them.

"Ah, Pyl'nikov," he said, "why is it you're leaning against the wall?"

Sasha blushed deeply, straightened up, and was silent.

"If you get tired so easily, then don't you think gymnastics may be harmful to you?" asked Khripach sternly.

"It's my fault, I'm not tired," said Sasha fearfully.

"One of two things," continued Khripach. "Either you shouldn't attend gym classes, or . . . in any case, drop in to see me after your classes."

He hurriedly left, leaving Sasha frightened and embarrassed.

"You're in for it!" his comrades said to him. "He'll be lecturing you until evening."

Khripach loved to make prolonged speeches, and the students feared his "invitations" more than anything.

After classes Sasha timidly set out to see the headmaster. Khripach took him in at once. He quickly went up to Sasha, almost gliding on his short legs, got close to him, and looking him attentively in the eyes, asked, "Does gym really tire you, Pyl'nikov? You seem like a healthy enough lad, but, you know, appearances can be deceiving! Do you have any sort of illness? Perhaps gym is bad for you."

"No, Nikolai Vlas'evich, I'm healthy," replied Sasha, all red from confusion.

"Nevertheless," answered Khripach, "Aleksei Alekseevich has complained about your frailty and says that you tire easily, and I myself noticed today that you seemed exhausted, or am I perhaps mistaken?"

Sasha did not know where to hide his eyes from the penetrating glance of Khripach. "Pardon me, I won't do it again, I was simply standing still from laziness. I am really healthy. I'll do gymnastics faithfully," he mumbled confusedly.

Suddenly, quite unexpectedly for himself, he burst into tears.

"Well now," said Khripach, "you evidently are exhausted—you're crying as if I were giving you a severe reprimand. Calm down." He placed a hand on Sasha's shoulder and said, "I didn't call you in for a lecture, but to get things cleared up . . . now just you sit down, Pyl'nikov I can see that you're tired."

"I'm not at all tired," said Sasha as he hurriedly wiped his wet eyes with a handkerchief.

"Sit down, sit down," repeated Khripach, and he moved a chair over to Sasha.

"It's really true, Nikolai Vlas'evich—I'm not tired," declared Sasha.

Khripach took him by the shoulders, sat him down, and seated himself opposite him. "Let's talk calmly, Pyl'nikov," he said. "You yourself aren't capable of knowing the actual state of your health. You are, in all respects, a well-behaved and diligent boy, and therefore I completely understand why you didn't want to ask for exemption from gym classes. By the way, I have asked Evgeny Ivanovich to come see me today inasmuch as I myself have not been feeling well. He might as well look you over too. I hope that you don't have any objection to this?"

Khripach, without waiting for a reply, looked at his watch and began to talk with Sasha about how he had spent the summer.

Shortly Evgeny Ivanovich Surovtsev appeared. The gymnasium physician was a small, dark, active man who loved to talk about politics and news in general. He had no great training, but he cared for the sick attentively, preferred diet and hygiene to medication, and therefore was successful in making his patients well.

Sasha was ordered to take off his clothes, Surovtsev examined him carefully, and, although he could find no defect, Khripach was at last completely convinced that Sasha was not a girl. Even though he was convinced of it before, he considered this useful so that, if he had to fill out question forms for a district investigation, the school physician could affirm the matter without additional questions. As he was letting Sasha go, Khripach said to him in a kindly tone, "Now that we

know that you are healthy, I shall tell Aleksei Alekseevich not to show you any mercy."

Peredonov had no doubt that the discovery that one
of the gymnasium students was a girl would bring
him to the attention of the authorities, and that, besides a promotion, they would decorate him. This encouraged him to watch the conduct of the students
vigilantly. Moreover, since the weather for several days
running had been gloomy and cold and not many
showed up to play billiards, there remained nothing
for him to do but to go about the town and visit students' lodgings, even some of those students who lived
with their parents.

Peredonov chose those parents who were less refined:
he would come, complain about the boy, and the boy
would be whipped, thus satisfying Peredonov. First of
all he complained about Iosif Kramarenko to his father, the owner of a brewery in the town, and said that
Iosif had misbehaved in church. The father believed
him and punished his son. This same fate also befell
several others. Peredonov did not go to those who, in
his opinion, might stand up for their sons or complain
in the district court.

Each day he visited at least one student's lodgings,
and conducted himself there in an authoritarian
manner, scolding, ordering, and threatening. But at
home the students felt more independent, and occasionally some of them stood up to Peredonov. Nevertheless, Flavitskaya, a tall, energetic lady with a resounding voice, whipped her small lodger, Vladimir
Bul'tyakov, very severely at Peredonov's request.

In his classes on the following day, Peredonov
would relate his exploits. Although he did not name
any names, his victims would give themselves away by
their embarrassment.

14 : ও⇒ও⇒

Rumors that Pyl'nikov was a disguised girl spread quickly around the town. Among the first to hear of it were the Rutilovs. The inquisitive Ludmila always tried to see everything new with her own eyes. She was seized by a burning curiosity to see Pyl'nikov. Naturally, she had to have a look at the masquerading vixen. It happened that she was acquainted with Kokovkina, and so one evening she said to her sisters. "I'm going to see this young lady."

"Busybody!" cried Dar'ya angrily.

"She's all dressed up," observed Valeriya with a restrained smile.

They were vexed that they had not thought of it, but it would be awkward for three to go. Ludmila was dressed a good deal better than usual, but she herself did not know why. At any rate she loved to dress up and dressed more revealingly than her sisters. Her arms and shoulders were more exposed, her skirt was shorter, her shoes were daintier, and her stockings were sheerer and more transparent and flesh-colored. At home she liked to go about barefooted in only her skirt and to put her shoes on without stockings—her skirts and petticoats were also always quite fancy.

The weather was cold and windy, and fallen leaves drifted in speckled puddles. Ludmila walked quickly and under her light cape she almost didn't feel the cold.

Kokovkina was having tea with Sasha. Ludmila surveyed them attentively—they were doing nothing but sitting quietly, drinking tea with rolls and talking. Ludmila kissed her hostess and said, "I've come to you on business, Olga Vasil'evna, but that can come after you warm me up with some tea. Ai, what a young chap you have here!"

Sasha blushed and bowed awkwardly. Kokovina introduced him to her guest. Ludmila sat down at the table and began to relate gossip in a lively manner. The townsfolk loved to receive her because she knew everything and could tell it all clearly and pleasantly. Kokovkina, a stay-at-home, was sincerely overjoyed to see her and treated her cordially. Ludmila gaily chattered, laughed, and frequently jumped up from her place to mimic someone and brushed against Sasha.

"You must get bored, darling," she said. "Why should you always sit at home with this sour gymnasium student when you could peek in at our house sometimes?"

"Well, I'm already too old to go visiting," replied Kokovkina.

"What do you mean 'visiting!'" exclaimed Ludmila gaily. "You come and sit with us as if you were at home, and that's that. You needn't swaddle this young fellow."

Sasha looked injured and blushed.

"Such a prude!" said Ludmila full of mirth, and she began to nudge Sasha. "You ought to talk to your guest."

"He's still a little fellow," said Kokovkina. "He's my modest boy."

Ludmila glanced at her with a smile, "I'm modest too," she said.

Sasha laughed and innocently replied, "Come now, are you really modest?"

Ludmila burst into laughter. Her laughter was, as always, delightful and gay. As she laughed, she blushed deeply and her eyes became mischievous and guilty— they tried to avoid looking at her companions.

Sasha was confused, but he mastered himself and attempted to set things right.

"But what I meant to say is that you are lively and not modest, not that you are immodest." Then, feeling that this had not come out in words as clearly as it would have in a letter, he laughed and blushed.

"How impudently he talks!" cried Ludmila laughing and blushing. "This is simply too charming!"

"You have confused my Sashen'ka completely," said Kokovkina, but she looked sweetly at Ludmila and Sasha.

Ludmila, leaning forward with a catlike movement, stroked Sasha on the head. He laughed bashfully in a ringing voice and ducked out from under her hand and ran to his room.

"Get me married, darling," said Ludmila all at once without any transition.

"I'm some matchmaker!" replied Kokovkina with a smile, but it was evident from her face that she would take on the matchmaking with pleasure.

"Why aren't you a matchmaker?" answered Ludmila. "Aren't I an eligible girl? Certainly you wouldn't be ashamed to be my matchmaker."

Ludmila put her hands on her waist and skipped around in front of her hostess.

"Now look at you!" said Kokovkina. "You're just like a beautiful wildflower."

"Do it for me even if it's just for having nothing better to do," said Ludmila laughing.

"Just what sort of husband do you need?" asked Kokovkina with a smile.

"Let him be, let him be brown-haired, my dear, definitely let him be brown-haired—deep brown," said

Ludmila quickly. "Deep as a pit. Let your gymnasium student serve as an example, yes, just like him with the same black eyebrows and sad eyes, the same black hair with a bluish fringe, and the same ever-so-thick eyelashes, the blue-black eyelashes. Your young fellow is an attractive one, you know, he's really handsome! Get me just such a one."

Soon Ludmila prepared to leave. It had already grown dark. Sasha came to accompany her.

"Only to the cab!" requested Ludmila in a sweet voice, and she looked at Sasha with her gay eyes, blushing guiltily.

On the street Ludmila again livened up and began to question Sasha. "Well now, are you always working on your lessons? Do you read any books?"

"I read books too," answered Sasha. "I love to read."

"Andersen's fairy tales?"

"Not at all fairy tales, but all sorts of books. I love history, and poetry too."

"Oho—poetry. And who is your favorite poet?" asked Ludmila sternly.

"Nadson,* of course," answered Sasha with a deep conviction in the impossibility of any other answer.

"Mmm!" said Ludmila approvingly. "I also like Nadson, but only in the morning. In the evening, my little one, I like to dress myself up. And what do you like to do?"

Sasha looked at her with his cheerful black eyes, and they suddenly became moist as he said, "I like to cuddle."

---

* Semyon Yakovlevich Nadson was a poet of civic themes in the tradition of Nekrasov. Nadson died in 1887 from tuberculosis at the age of twenty-seven. His verse, now neglected, once had many intense partisans. Mellifluous, idealistic, and more forthright than profound, it is naturally suited to the tastes of an intelligent young boy.

"What a sweetheart," said Ludmila, and she put her arm around his shoulder. "You love to cuddle. And do you love to paddle in the tub?" *

Sasha tittered. "In warm water?" asked Ludmila.

"In both warm and cold," said the boy with embarrassment.

"And what sort of soap do you like?"

"Glycerine."

"And do you like green grapes?"

Sasha laughed. "You're a funny one! Glycerine and green grapes—they're completely different words, but you make them sound the same. Only you can't fool me."

"As if I had to fool you!" said Ludmila chuckling.

"Yes, I know that you're a tease."

"Where did you get that?"

"That's what everyone says," said Sasha.

"You don't say—what a gossip!" said Ludmila with pretended anger.

Sasha blushed.

"Well there's a cab. Cab!" cried Ludmila.

"Cab!" cried Sasha also.

The cabman rolled to a stop in his clumsy, rattling *drozhki*, and Ludmila told him where to go. He thought a little and demanded forty kopecks.

"Do you think it's that far, my good man?" said Ludmila. "Evidently you don't know the way."

"What'll you give?" asked the cabman.

"You can have whichever half of what you wanted that you like."

Sasha laughed.

"Add just five more kopecks, my gay miss," said the cabman with a grin.

"Thank you for accompanying me here, my little

* Ludmila is playing with the two similar verbs *laskat'sya* (to caress) and *poloskat'sya* (to paddle in the water).

one," said Ludmila. She squeezed Sasha's hand firmly
and sat down in the *drozhki*.

Sasha ran all the way home gaily thinking about the
gay young lady.

Ludmila returned home smiling and dreaming about
something amusing. Her sisters were waiting for her.
They were sitting in the dining room around a circular
table lit by a hanging lamp. On the white tablecloth
was a bright brown decanter of Copenhagen Cherry
Heering, and the tinsel on its neck shone brightly.
Surrounding it were plates with apples, nuts, and hal-
vah.

Dar'ya was a bit high. Flushed, disheveled, and half-
dressed, she was singing truculently. Ludmila heard her
singing the next to last verse of a popular ballad:

> *Where is her dress, where is her tune?*
> *Naked, he leads her along the dune.*
> *Shame prevents passion, passion drives away*
> *shame.*
> *The shepherdess sobs in tearful regret:*
> *'What you have seen, oh please forget!'*

Larisa, well dressed and serenely happy, was also
there. With a knife she was cutting an apple into
sections and eating it. "Well, what have you seen?"
she asked laughingly.

Dar'ya became quiet and looked at Ludmila. Valeriya
leaned on her elbow, held her little finger out, and, tilt-
ing her head, imitated Larisa's smile. But Valeriya was
slender and frail, and her smile was a nervous one.
Ludmila poured herself a glass of the cherry-red
liqueur and said, "It's nonsense! The lad is quite au-
thentic—and charming. He has dark brown hair, his
eyes glitter, and he is young and guiltless."

And suddenly she laughed in a high voice. Looking at her, her sisters also began to laugh.

"Well that means that this was all Peredonovian rubbish," said Darya. She waved her hand and then thought a moment with her elbows leaning on the table and her head bowed. "I might as well continue to sing," she said and began to sing with piercing loudness.

A strained and sullen liveliness resounded in her screeches. If a corpse were to be pulled out of the grave so that he could sing all the time, he would sing in just this manner. But the sisters had long since become used to Darya's tipsy bawling, and now and then they joined in singing with her with intentionally shrill voices.

"What howling," said Ludmila laughing. It was not that she did not like it, but that she was anxious to relate something and wanted her sisters to listen to her.

"What's wrong with you, I'm not bothering you!" cried Darya, breaking off her song in the middle of a word. She at once took up singing again from that very place, and Larisa said, "Let her sing."

> *I'm a wet young lass,*
> *And I can't find a place to stay,*

sang Darya shrilly, distorting sounds and inserting syllables as the folk singers do to make their songs more pathetic. The result was something like this:

> *I'm ah we-e-e-t yuhhhng la-a-ass.*

Those sounds upon which the stress did not fall were drawn out especially painfully.* It produced an ex-

---

* The Russian song, unlike its translation, has seventeen syllables of which eleven are unstressed.

traordinary effect—the song would have induced a fatal anguish in a new listener . . .

O, fatal anguish, resounding in the fields and in all places of our vast native expanse! An anguish personified in her wild fury, an anguish which devours the living word in hideous flame, reducing once living song to mad wailing! O fatal torment! O, dear, ancient Russian song—will you really die? . . .

Suddenly Darya jumped up, put her arms akimbo and began to shout out a gay *chastushka** and to dance, snapping her fingers:

> *Away with you, my lad*
> *For a robber is my dad.*
> *I don't care what looks you've got*
> *I'll plant a knife into your pot.*
> *I don't need a peasant man*
> *I love one of my father's clan.*

Darya sang and danced, and her eyes, not moving in her face, seemed as motionless as the dead moon in its orbit. Ludmila laughed loudly, and her heart lightly skipped a beat and she felt faint, partly from joy and partly from the powerful sweet-cherry liqueur. Valeriya laughed quietly, a laugh that tinkled like glass, and looked at her sisters enviously—she would have liked such happiness, but she was somehow unhappy. She thought she was the last, "the bottom of the pot," and that was why she was frail and unhappy. And she laughed as though she were just about to cry.

Larisa glanced at her and gave her a wink, and

---

* The *chastushka* is a form of folksong which originated scarcely more than a century ago. It uses simple rhymes, is only a few lines in length, and has a quick tempo, although the rhythm is not always clear. In form the *chastushka* has elements of the *skazka* or folktale as well as certain epic features. Sometimes it is sung to the accompaniment of a balalaika or concertina.

Valeriya suddenly became happy and full of fun. Larisa got up, swayed her shoulders to and fro, and in a minute all four sisters were circling around in rapturous joy, suddenly seized by a frenzied rhythm and shouting the stupid words of one *chastushka* after another after Dar'ya, each one louder and more senseless than the preceding one. The sisters were young and beautiful, and their voices rang out loudly and wildly—the witches on Bald Mountain* would have envied them their dance.

All that night Ludmila dreamt torrid African dreams!

She dreamt that she was lying in a stuffy, overheated room and that her quilt was slipping off her, laying bare her burning body—and then a scaly, ringed serpent slithered into her bedchamber and, lifting itself up, it crept onto the trunk of her body and along its branches, her naked, beautiful legs . . .

Next she dreamed of a lake on a hot summer evening under slowly moving, threatening clouds—and she was lying on the shore, naked, with a smooth golden crown on her forehead. There was a stale odor from the warm water and the slime and from the grass decaying because of the sultriness. And along the water, the dark and evilly still water, floated a white swan, strong and majestically sovereign. He beat the water fiercely with his wings and, hissing loudly, he approached her and embraced her—it was sweet, exhausting, and sinister . . .

Both the serpent and the swan as they bent over Ludmila had Sasha's pale, almost blue face with his dark dark, mysteriously sad eyes. His blue-black eye-

* Bald Mountain, according to folk tradition, is a spot near Kiev where witches are supposed to celebrate their Sabbath. It is known to non-Russians through Moussorgsky's fantasy composition *Night on Bald Mountain*.

lashes, jealously covering his enchanting gaze, descended heavily, fearfully.

Then Ludmila dreamt of a magnificent chamber with massive, low arches—and crowded into it were strong, handsome, naked boys—and the prettiest of all of them was Sasha. She was sitting on high, and the naked boys took turns in lashing one another. And when Sasha was placed on the floor with his head towards Ludmila and was whipped, and he laughed piercingly and wept, she laughed loudly as one sometimes laughs in sleep when the heart suddenly beats strongly—long and uncontrollably, the laugh of self-oblivion and death . . .*

In the morning after these dreams Ludmila felt that she was passionately in love with Sasha. An impatient desire to see him seized Ludmila, but it vexed her to think that she would have to see him dressed. How stupid that small boys don't go about naked! Or at least like the street urchins in the summer whom Ludmila loved to watch running barefoot and sometimes exposing their legs quite high.

"It must be truly shameful to have a body," thought Ludmila, "that even little boys hide it."

* The erotic swan dream has many sources both in poetry and in art, e.g., Correggio's painting "Leda and the Swan." Ludmila's last dream reflects a similar theme in *The Brothers Karamazov*: Liza's dream in which she imagines that she is eating pineapple compote while watching a child being crucified. Significantly, the title of this scene in Dostoevsky's novel (Part IV, Book XI, 3) is *Besyonok* which means "the little demon."

15 : ई●ई●

Volodin was going to the Adamenkos regularly to give lessons. His dreams that the young lady would ask him to coffee had not materialized. Each time they led him straight to the little room set aside as a workshop. Misha was usually already standing there in an apron by the workbench, having prepared everything that would be needed for the lesson. He did everything that Volodin directed obediently but without enjoyment. In order to lessen the amount of work, Misha tried to draw Volodin into conversation. Volodin wished to be conscientious and resisted his efforts.

"You work for two hours, Mishen'ka," he would say, "and then, if you like, we'll talk. Then you may talk as much as you want, but not now because your work comes first."

Misha would sigh lightly and set himself to work, but at the end of his lesson he never had a desire to talk, and he would say that he had no time because he had many things he had to do.

Sometimes during the lesson Nadezhda Vasil'evna came to look on while Misha worked. Misha observed —and made use of the fact—that in her presence Volodin could be more easily drawn into conversation. Nadhezda Vasil'evna, however, as soon as she saw that Misha was not working, would at once remark to him, "Misha don't be lazy!" And then she would leave, having said to Volodin, "Pardon me, I have interfered with you. My little one is the sort who becomes lazy if you give him his way."

At first Volodin was taken aback by such behavior on the part of Nadezhda Vasil'evna. Later, he reasoned that she was shy about inviting him to have coffee with her, fearing that gossip might come of it. He also considered that she might well not have visited him during the lessons at all, but she did, and what other reason could there be for that but that she enjoyed seeing Volodin? And Volodin interpreted in his favor the fact that Nadezhda Vasil'evna had at once willingly agreed to have him give the lessons and had not haggled with him. Peredonov and Varvara both confirmed these interpretations.

"It's clear that she's in love with you," said Peredonov.

"What better bridegroom could she want!" added Varvara.

Volodin looked modest and was happy with his success.

Once Peredonov said to him, "You're engaged, and yet you're wearing a worn-out necktie."

"I'm not engaged yet, Ardasha," replied Volodin soberly, although he was palpitating with joy, "but I can buy a new tie."

"You should buy yourself a patterned tie so that it can be seen that you're in love."

"A red tie," said Varvara, "and even more splendid, a tie pin. You can buy a tie pin with a stone in it very cheaply—it would be *chic*."

Peredonov thought that perhaps Volodin did not have enough money or that, to save money, he might buy a plain black tie. "That would be horrible," thought Peredonov. "Adamenko is a well-bred young lady, and, if he proposes to her in that sort of tie, she might be offended and refuse."

"Why buy a cheap one, Pavlusha?" said Peredonov.

"You've won enough from me for a tie. How much do I owe you—a ruble and forty kopecks?"

"You're right about the forty kopecks," said Volodin grinning and making a face, "only it wasn't a ruble but two rubles."

Peredonov himself knew that it was two rubles, but he preferred to pay only one. "You lie—two rubles indeed!" he said.

"Varvara Dmitrievna's my witness," declared Volodin.

"Pay up what you lost, Ardal'on Borisych—even I recall that it was two rubles," said Varvara with a smirk.

Peredonov thought that as Varvara was taking Volodin's part, it meant she was going over to his side. He frowned and dug the money out of his purse.

"Very well," he said, "let it be two and forty, I won't be ruined. You're a poor man, Pavlushka, so take it."

Volodin took the money, counted it, and then assumed an injured look, lowering his broad forehead, and sticking out his lower lip. "It happens, Ardal'on Borisych, that you are in debt to me and have to pay, and my being poor has nothing to do with it," he said in a bleating and jarring voice. "And I still don't beg my bread from anyone, and you know that the only man who is poor is the devil who doesn't have his bread to eat—and since I still have my daily bread, and even with butter, it means that I'm not poor."

And quite comforted, he blushed from joy that he had answered so satisfactorily and let his lips relax into a smile.

At last Peredonov and Volodin decided to go arrange the match. Both overdressed themselves and had a solemn and stupider than usual appearance. Peredonov wore a white neckerchief; Volodin, a motley red one with green stripes. Peredonov reasoned thus: "I am going to do the matchmaking and my role is the more sedate so that I have to wear a white necktie, but you are the bridegroom-to-be and so you have to show your ardent feelings."

Peredonov and Volodin sat tense and solemn in the Adamenko living room—Peredonov on the sofa, Volodin in an armchair. Nadezhda Vasil'evna looked at her guests with surprise. The guests chatted about the weather and gossip with the appearance of people who had come about delicate business and did not know how to begin. Finally Peredonov cleared his throat, frowned, and said, "We have come on business, Nadezhda Vasil'evna."

"On business," repeated Volodin. He put on an impressive appearance and stuck out his lips.

"It's about him," said Peredonov pointing with his thumb at Volodin.

"Yes, it's about me," affirmed Volodin, and he also pointed his own thumb at his chest.

Nadezhda Vasil'evna smiled. "Go on," she said.

"I will speak for him," said Peredonov. "He is modest and can't bring himself to do it. But he is a good and worthy man who doesn't drink. He doesn't earn much, but that doesn't matter—some need money, others need a man. Well, why are you silent?" he said turning to Volodin. "Say something."

Volodin lowered his head and, in a quivering voice, like a ram bleating, said, "It's true I don't receive a large salary, but I'll always have my piece of bread. It's true I was never in a university, but I live, as God grant everyone may, and don't find any fault with myself—and, anyway, let him who wishes judge me. In a word, I am satisfied with myself."

He spread his hands, bowed his forehead as if preparing to butt, and was silent.

"So then," said Peredonov, "he is a young man, and

he ought not to live as he does. He needs to get married. In any case, it's better to be hitched."

"If the wife reciprocates, all the better," declared Volodin.

"And you," continued Peredonov, "are a young girl —you also should get married."

A quiet rustle was heard behind the door, short muffled sounds as if someone was breathing hard or laughing and covering his mouth. Nadezhda Vasil'evna glanced sternly at the door and said coldly: "You are too thoughtful of me"—with annoyed emphasis on the word "too."

"You don't need a rich husband," said Peredonov, "you yourself are rich. You need someone to love you and please you in everything. And as you already know him, you have had the opportunity to judge him. He is not indifferent to you, and perhaps the same is true of you. In a manner of speaking, I have the buyer and you have the goods—that is, you yourself are the goods."

Nadezhda Vasil'evna blushed and bit her lip to keep from laughing. The same sounds continued to be heard behind the door. Volodin modestly lowered his eyes. It seemed to him that the affair was going well.

"What sort of goods?" asked Nadezhda Vasil'evna cautiously. "Pardon me, I don't understand."

. "What do you mean—don't understand!" said Peredonov incredulously. "Well, I'll speak plainly— Pavel Vasil'evich is seeking your hand and heart, and I have come to make the proposal for him."

Behind the door something dropped to the floor, and it seemed as though it were snorting and grunting. Nadezhda Vasil'evna, red from suppressed laughter, looked at her guests. Volodin's proposal seemed to her to be a piece of ludicrous insolence.

"Yes," said Volodin. "Nadezhda Vasil'evna, I ask your hand and heart."

He blushed, got up, scraped his foot heavily along the carpet, bowed, and quickly sat down. Then he again stood up, placed his hand on his heart, and said, looking sweetly at the young lady, "Nadezhda Vasil'evna, allow me to explain. Since I even love you very much, you will reciprocate, won't you?"

He dashed forward, dropped on his knee before Nadezhda Vasil'evna, and kissed her hand.

"Nadezhda Vasil'evna, believe in me! I swear to you!" he cried, and he lifted his hand upwards, waved it about, and struck himself on the chest so that a hollow sound reverberated quite far.

"Please get up!" said Nadezhda Vasil'evna in confusion. "What is all this for?"

Volodin stood up and returned to his place with an injured look. There he pressed both hands to his breast and again exclaimed, "Nadezhda Vasil'evna, believe me! I shall love you with all my heart until I die."

"Forgive me," said Nadezhda Vasil'evna, "but I really cannot. I must educate my brother—listen to him crying there behind the door."

"So what, educate your brother," said Volodin thrusting out his lips in offense. "I can't see how this will interfere."

"No, in any case this concerns him," said Nadezhda Vasil'evna hurriedly getting up, "and I shall have to ask him. Wait a moment."

She quickly ran out of the living room, her light yellow dress rustling, seized Misha by the shoulder from behind the door, and ran with him to his room. There, standing by the door and panting from running and from suppressed laughter, she said in an irregular voice, "It is utterly, utterly useless to ask you not to eavesdrop. Must I resort to the most strict measures?"

Misha embraced her by the waist and, pressing his head against her, laughed, shaking from the laughter and his effort to stifle it. His sister pushed Misha into the room, sat down on a chair by the door, and began to laugh.

"Did you hear what he has dreamed up, your Pavel Vasil'evich?" she asked. "Come with me into the living room, and don't you dare laugh. I shall ask your permission about this, and don't you dare consent. Understand?"

"Umph!" blurted out Misha, and he thrust the end of his handkerchief into his mouth in order to stop laughing—but to no avail.

"Cover your eyes with your handkerchief when you want to laugh," advised his sister, and she again took him by the shoulder into the living room.

There she sat him down in an armchair and seated herself next to him on a chair. Volodin, his head lowered, looked like an injured sheep.

"Look," said Nadezhda Vasil'evna pointing at her brother, "he can scarcely repress his tears, poor boy! I take the place of a mother to him, and suddenly he thinks that I shall leave him."

Misha covered his face with the handkerchief. His whole body was shaking, and, in order to hide his laughter, he moaned continually, "Ooooooo."

Nadezhda Vasil'evna hugged him and, unnoticed, pinched his hand. "Don't cry, darling, don't cry," she said. This caught Misha off guard and hurt him so, that tears appeared in his eyes. He dropped his handkerchief and angrily looked at his sister.

"The boy might suddenly go berserk and begin to bite," thought Peredonov. "They say human spit is poisonous."

He moved closer to Volodin so that, in the event of an attack, he could hide behind him.

"Pavel Vasil'evich asks my hand," said Nadezhda Vasil'evna to her brother.

"Hand and heart," corrected Peredonov.

"And heart," said Volodin modestly but with dignity.

Misha covered himself with the handkerchief and, sobbing from suppressed laughter, said, "No, don't marry him—what would become of me?"

Volodin spoke in a voice quivering from excitement and injury. "It surprises me, Nadezhda Vasil'evna," he said, "that you ask advice from your brother, who is really just a boy. Even if he were a grown-up youth, you might speak for yourself. But the way that you ask his advice at his age, Nadezhda Vasil'evna, surprises and even astounds me very much."

"I think it's absurd to ask advice of small boys," said Peredonov sullenly.

"Whom shall I ask then? His aunt is indifferent to him, and, since I must bring him up, how can I marry you? And perhaps you would treat him cruelly. Wouldn't you be afraid of his brutality, Mishka?"

"No, Nadya," said Misha peeping out from behind his handkerchief with one eye, "I wouldn't fear his brutality—why should I! But I am afraid that Pavel Vasil'evich will spoil me and not let you stand me in the corner."

"Believe me, Nadezhda Vasil'evna," said Volodin pressing his hands to his heart, "I won't spoil Mishen'ka. I too think that there's no reason to spoil a boy. They should be dressed, fed, and shod, but never spoiled. I am also able to stand him in the corner so that he doesn't get spoiled. In fact, I can do more. Because you're a girl, I mean a young lady, it's inconvenient for you, of course, but I could whip him."

"I will be stood in the corner and whipped too," said Misha tearfully, again covering himself with the handkerchief. "No, I don't like that. No. Don't you dare marry him, Nadya."

"Well, you hear," said Nadezhda Vasil'evna. "I positively cannot."

"It seems very strange to me that you act this way, Nadezhda Vasil'evna," said Volodin. "I've come to you with good intentions and, one could say, ardently, and, in spite of that, you refuse because of your brother. If you decline because of your brother, another refuses because of her cousin, a third because of her nephew, and still another because of some other of her relatives, then no one will get married, and the human race will come to a complete end."

"Don't worry about that, Pavel Vasil'evich," said Nadezhda Vasil'evna, "the world is not yet threatened by such a danger. I don't wish to get married without Misha's consent, and he, as you have heard, is unwilling. It's perfectly clear that you have promised to whip him from the first. Why you might also thrash me."

"Heaven forbid, Nadezhda Vasil'evna, how could you think that I could be so inconsiderate!" cried Volodin in confusion.

Nadezhda Vasil'evna smiled. "I myself do not feel the desire to get married," she said.

"Would you perhaps like to become a nun?" asked Volodin in an injured voice.

"Better yet—join the Tolstoyan sect* and dung the fields," corrected Peredonov.

"Why should I go anywhere?" asked Nadezhda Vasil'evna harshly, getting up from her place. "I'm fine right here."

Volodin also stood up and stuck out his lips in a hurt manner. "After this," he said, "since Mishen'ka has shown such feelings towards me, and you, as it turns out, ask him what to do, don't you think I ought to

---

* Beginning in 1881, various agricultural colonies were organized, unsuccessfully, by disciples of Tolstoy to put his teachings to practical application.

stop giving him lessons and leave, if Mishen'ka feels this way towards me?"

"No, why is that?" answered Nadezhda Vasil'evna. "That is an entirely different matter."

Peredonov thought that he still ought to attempt to persuade the young lady—perhaps she might yet agree. "You had best consider carefully, Nadezhda Vasil'-evna," he said gloomily. "Why are you acting this way without rhyme or reason? He is a good man. He's my friend."

"No," said Nadezhda Vasil'evna, "there's nothing to think about. I thank you very much, Pavel Vasil'evich, for the honor, but I cannot."

Peredonov glanced angrily at Volodin and stood up. He thought that Volodin was a fool because he did not know how to make the young lady fall in love with him.

Volodin, standing by his armchair, lowered his head. "So that means you've made up your mind definitely, Nadezhda Vasil'evna?" he asked reproachfully. "Ech! If that's the case," he said waving his hand, "well, God grant you all the good in the world, Nadezhda Vasil'evna. It simply means that such is my wretched fate. Ech! A fellow loves a girl, and she doesn't love him. God sees! Well, I'll cry, and that's that."

"You're scorning a good man, and you don't know what sort you might get," persisted Peredonov.

"Ech!" exclaimed Volodin once more, and he would have gone to the door. But suddenly, he decided to be magnanimous and returned to shake hands with the young lady and even with Misha, the offender.

On the street Peredonov muttered angrily, and Volodin complained the whole way in an offended, whining voice as though he were bleating.

"Why did you refuse the lessons?" growled Peredonov. "What a rich man!"

"I merely said, Ardal'on Borisych, that perhaps I ought to stop, but she was pleased to tell me that it wasn't necessary to stop, and, as I didn't make any answer, it turns out that she asked me. So now it depends on me—if I wish, I'll refuse, and, if I wish, I'll go."

"Why refuse?" said Peredonov. "Go as if nothing had happened." Peredonov was thinking: "Let him at least be of use there—he will be all the less envious of me."

Peredonov was depressed. Volodin was not yet settled, and, if he didn't watch him sharply, he might get to cooking something up with Varvara. Moreover, perhaps Adamenko was angry with him because he came to do the matchmaking for Volodin. She had family in Petersburg and she might write and do him harm.

Even the weather was unpleasant. The sky was overcast, and crows were flying about and cawing. They were cawing directly over Peredonov's head as though they were teasing him and predicting new and still worse troubles. Peredonov wrapped his scarf around his neck and thought that it was not difficult to catch cold in such weather.

"What sort of flowers are these Pavlusha?" he asked, showing Volodin some blossoms by a fence in someone's garden.

"Those are bleeding hearts, Ardasha," replied Volodin sadly.

Peredonov recalled that there were many such flowers in his garden. And what a terrible name they had!* Perhaps they were poisonous. Suppose Varvara took them, picked a whole bunch, brewed them up instead of tea, and poisoned him. Then, when the appointment came, they could substitute Volodin for him. Perhaps they

* The flowers in the Russian are buttercups. Peredonov's fear grows out of the connection he makes between the similar but unrelated words *liutiki* (buttercups) and *liutyi* (fierce).

have already arranged it. "It's not for nothing that he knows what the flower is called," thought Peredonov.

But Volodin said, "Let God judge her! Why did she offend me? She is waiting for an aristocrat, but she does not realize that there are all sorts of aristocrats too—with some she might weep; but a good, simple man would be able to give her happiness. And now I shall go to church and light a candle for her health and pray that God will give her a drunkard for a husband, and that he beats her, squanders her money, and abandons her in the world. Then she will remember me, but it will be too late. She will wipe away her tears with her hand and say, "I was a fool to refuse Pavel Vasil'evich—there was no one to make me listen to reason. He was a good man."

Moved by his own words, Volodin wept and wiped the tears away from his bulging, sheeplike eyes with his hands.

"You should break her windows during the night," advised Peredonov.

"Well, God be with her," said Volodin mournfully, "they might catch me. No—but what a boy! My God, what did I do to him that made him decide to injure me? I have done my best for him, but he, as you see, arranged such an intrigue against me. What do you think of such a thing for a child? Tell me, please, what do you think will come of him?"

"Yes," said Peredonov angrily, "one can't contend with a little boy. Ech, you bridegroom!"

"So what?" retorted Volodin. "Of course I'll be a bridegroom—I'll find another. She needn't think that I'm going to cry over her."

"Ech, you bridegroom!" Peredonov teased him. "You even put on a new tie. How did a rogue like you think he was going to get into society? Bridegroom!"

"That's right—I'm a bridegroom, and you, Ardasha,

are a matchmaker," said Volodin seriously. "You yourself dressed me up, but you didn't succeed in making
the match. Ech, you matchmaker!"

And they began to tease one another diligently,
squabbling at length as though they were discussing
business.

After she had seen her guests to the door, Nadezhda
Vasil'evna returned to the living room. Misha was
lying on the sofa laughing. His sister dragged him from
the sofa by the shoulder and said, "So you forgot that
you are not allowed to eavesdrop." She raised her
hands and wanted to cross her little fingers, but suddenly she began to laugh, and the fingers did not
cross. Misha rushed towards her, and they hugged and
laughed for a long time.

"All the same," she said, "into the corner for eavesdropping."

"Oh, you shouldn't," said Misha. "I rescued you
from your would-be bridegroom. You ought to be grateful to me."

"Who saved whom! You heard how he was going to
whip you. Get yourself to the corner."

"It would be better for me to stay here," said Misha,
and he knelt by his sister's legs and placed his head on
her knees. She caressed and tickled him, and Misha
laughed and crawled around the floor on his knees.
Suddenly his sister pushed him aside and changed
her seat to the sofa. Misha was left by himself, and he
stayed there a little while, looking questioningly at his
sister. She seated herself more comfortably and took a
book as if to read, but she really continued to watch
her brother.

"I'm tired of this," he said sorrowfully.

"I'm not holding you, you put yourself there," answered his sister smiling from behind her book.

"Well, I have already been punished—let me go," entreated Misha.

"Did I put you on your knees?" asked Nadezhda Vasil'evna with feigned indifference. "Then why are you bothering me!"

"I won't get up until you forgive me."

Nadezhda Vasil'evna laughed, put aside her book, and drew Misha to her by the shoulder. He squealed and rushed to embrace her, exclaiming, "Pavlusha's betrothed!"

16 : ❧❧

The dark-eyed boy filled all of Ludmila's thoughts. She often discussed him with her own family and with acquaintances, often quite inopportunely. Almost every night she saw him in her dreams, sometimes quiet and ordinary, but more often in wild and bewitching surroundings. Her accounts of these dreams became so habitual that her sisters soon began to ask her every morning how she had dreamt of Sasha that night. Daydreams about him occupied all her leisure moments.

On Sunday Ludmila persuaded her sisters to ask Kokovkina in after Mass and keep her there awhile. She wanted to catch Sasha alone. She herself did not go to church. "Tell her that I overslept," she instructed her sisters.

The sisters laughed at her undertaking but, of course, agreed. They lived very amiably. And why not give

Ludmila a hand in catching a boy—that would leave the real eligibles to them. Thus, they did as they promised and invited Kokovkina in after Mass.

In the meantime Ludmila was all prepared to go. She had dressed herself up gaily and prettily, scented herself with soft and light lilac mist, and put an unopened bottle of perfume into one pocket, and a small atomizer into the other. She concealed herself behind the curtain by the window in the living room in order to be able to lie in wait and see when Kokovkina was coming. She had thought of taking the perfumes with her earlier to scent the student in order that he might not smell of his nasty Latin, ink, and boyishness. Ludmila loved perfume and used it in great quantity. She ordered her perfume from Petersburg. She loved fragrant flowers, and her room always smelled sweetly of something whether it was flowers, perfume, pine, or, in the spring, fresh birch twigs.

The sisters were coming, and Kokovkina was with them. Ludmila ran happily through the kitchen, across the garden, through the gate, and down the alley in order not to meet Kokovkina. She smiled gaily as she walked quickly to Kokovina's house, playfully swinging her white parasol about. The warm autumn day cheered her, and it seemed as if she were carrying with her and spreading about her own peculiar perfume of happiness.

Kokovkina's servant told her that the *barynya* was not at home. Ludmila laughed loudly and joked with the red-cheeked girl who had opened the door. "Maybe you're fooling me," she said, "and maybe your mistress is hiding from me."

"Hee, hee, why should she hide!" answered the maid. "Come inside and look for yourself, if you don't believe me."

Ludmila looked into the living room and playfully called, "Is anyone living here? Ah, the student!"

Sasha peeped out of his room, spied Ludmila, and became cheerful—and Ludmila became even more happy because of his gladdened eyes. "But where is Olga Vasil'evna?" she asked.

"She's not at home," Sasha replied. "She went somewhere after church and hasn't come home yet. I've returned, but she isn't here yet."

Ludmila pretended that she was surprised. Waving her parasol, she said with annoyance, "How can that be? Everyone has already returned from church. She always sits at home, and now what do I find, not here. Is it you, my young classic, who carry on so, that the old girl won't stay at home?"

Sasha smiled silently. Ludmila's voice, her clear laughter made him happy. He was trying to think how he might volunteer to escort her in order to be with her at least a few more minutes, to look at her and to listen to her.

But Ludmila was not thinking of leaving. She looked at Sasha with a sly smile and said, "And why don't you ask me to sit down, my dear young man? I dare say I'm tired! You might at least let me rest a little."

She walked into the living room, smiling and caressing Sasha with her quick, tender eyes. Sasha became confused, reddened, and was happy—she was going to be with him!

"Would you like me to smother you?" asked Ludmila with animation. "Would you like that?"

"What a person you are!" said Sasha. "You come right in and want to smother me! What have I done to deserve such cruelty?"

Ludmila gave a ringing laugh and fell back against her chair. "You don't understand at all, stupid!" she exclaimed. "I want to smother you with perfume, not with my hands."*

* The verb *dushit'* means both "to scent" and "to suffocate."

"Ah, perfume!" said Sasha gaily. "Well, that's a different matter."

Ludmila took the atomizer out of her pocket and turned the attractive vessel of dark red glass with gold designs and a bronze top with a rubber bulb around in front of Sasha. "Look, I bought a new atomizer yesterday," she said, "but I forgot and left it in my pocket." Then she drew out of her other pocket the large perfume bottle with its dark, varicolored label— it was *Pao-Rosa* by Guerlain from Paris.

"What deep pockets you have!" said Sasha.

"Well, you needn't expect anything else," answered Ludmila gaily. "I haven't brought you any honeycakes."

"Honeycakes!" repeated Sasha laughingly. He watched with curiosity as Ludmila unstopped the bottle. "But how will you pour it out of there without a funnel?" he asked.

"You'll give me a funnel," said Ludmila brightly.

"But I don't have one," said Sasha in confusion.

"As you will—but give me a funnel," insisted Ludmila smiling.

"I could get one from Malan'ya, but she uses it for kerosene," said Sasha.

Ludmila laughed heartily. "Akh, you slow-witted young man. Give me a little piece of paper if you can spare it—and there is your funnel."

"Akh, that's right!" exclaimed Sasha happily. "You can twist one out of paper. I'll bring some right away." Sasha ran to his room.

"Is notebook paper all right?" he called from there.

"Yes, it doesn't matter," called back Ludmila gaily. "You can tear it out of one of your books, a Latin grammar—I don't mind."

Sasha laughed and shouted back, "No, I had better take it out of my notebook." He took out a clean notebook and ripped out a middle page. He was about to run back to the living room, but Ludmila was already standing in the doorway.

"May I come in, sir?" she asked playfully.

"Please! I would be very happy," cried Sasha merrily.

Ludmila sat down at his table, rolled a funnel out of the paper, and with a preoccupied, businesslike face began to transfer the perfume from the bottle to the atomizer. The paper funnel grew wet and dark at the bottom and to the side where the little stream flowed. The fragrant liquid accumulated in the funnel and trickled down slowly. A warm and sweet fragrance of rose mixed with the sharp odor of spirits was wafted about. Ludmila poured half of the perfume out of the bottle into the atomizer and said, "Now that should be enough."

She began to put together the atomizer. Then she crumpled up the damp paper and rubbed it between her palms. "Sniff," she said to Sasha and brought her palm up to his face.

Sasha leaned forward, half-closed his eyes, and sniffed. Ludmila smiled, gently clapped her palm onto his lips, and held her hand on his mouth. Sasha reddened and kissed her warm, fragrant palm with a light touch of his quivering lips. Ludmila sighed, and a soft expression fleeted across her pretty face before it again changed back to its usual look of happy mirthfulness.

"Now just hold still while I sprinkle you," she said and squeezed the bulb. A fragrant mist spurted out, spraying out and spreading in the air and on Sasha's blouse. Sasha laughed and turned about obediently as Ludmila shoved him.

"It smells good, eh?" she asked.

"It's very nice," answered Sasha happily. "And what do they call it?"

"What next, my little baby! Read the bottle, and you'll find out," she said in a teasing voice.

Sasha read it and said, "It smells sort of like oil of roses."

"Oil!" said Ludmila reproachfully, and she playfully slapped Sasha on the back. Sasha laughed, gave a yelp, and stuck out the tip of his tongue rolled into the shape of a tube.

Ludmila stood up and looked through Sasha's schoolbooks and notebooks. "Is it all right for me to look?" she asked.

"Go right ahead," said Sasha.

"Where are your ones and your zeros, show me."

"I haven't been that lucky yet," said Sasha with an injured look.

"Well, you're lying about that," said Ludmila resolutely. "You've undoubtedly been stuck a few times. You've probably hidden them."

Sasha smiled silently.

"Latin and Greek," said Ludmila. "They must bore you awfully.

"No, not at all," replied Sasha, but it was evident that even conversation about schoolbooks was bringing their usual boredom upon him. "It's tedious to grind away," he confessed, "but it's not so bad because I have a good memory. I love to solve problems though."

"Come to see me tomorrow after dinner," said Ludmila.

"Thank you. I'll come," said Sasha blushing. He was pleased that Ludmila had invited him.

"Do you know where I live?" asked Ludmila. "You will come?"

"I know. I'll come gladly," said Sasha with happiness.

"Yes, come without fail," repeated Ludmila sternly. "I shall be waiting for you, do you hear?"

"But what if I have a lot of homework?" said Sasha more from conscientiousness than from really thinking that he might not come because of his lessons.

"That's nonsense—come anyway," insisted Ludmila. "It won't hurt you."

"But why should I?" asked Sasha laughingly.

"Because you have to. Just come—I have something to tell you and to show you," said Ludmila, humming and skipping about, raising her skirt, and shaking her pink little fingers. "Come to me, sweet one, silver one, golden one."

Sasha laughed. "Tell me today," he asked.

"I can't today. Why should I tell you today? Then, you say, you won't have any reason to come tomorrow."

"Well, I'll come gladly and without fail if they'll let me."

"What do you mean? Of course 'they'll let you.' They aren't holding you in chains."

As she was leaving, Ludmila kissed Sasha on the forehead and raised her hand to his lips for him to kiss it. And Sasha would have liked to kiss the soft, white hand once more, but he was embarrassed. How he blushed!

And Ludmila, as she was walking away, turned around several times and smiled slyly and tenderly.

"How sweet she is!" thought Sasha.

He was left by himself. "How quickly she left," he thought. "She suddenly got ready and was gone before I had time to think about it. If she had only stayed a little longer!" thought Sasha, and he was ashamed that he had forgotten to volunteer to accompany her. "I could have spent a little more time with her!" dreamed Sasha. "How far has she gone? Could I still catch her? If I run quickly and with haste I can overtake her. But perhaps she will laugh at me," thought Sasha. "And maybe I will only be getting in her way."

And so he decided not to pursue her. He became depressed and ill at ease. The tender sensation of kissing her still remained on his lips, and her kiss burned on his forehead.

"How softly she kisses!" recalled Sasha dreamily. "Just like a dear sister."

Sasha's cheeks burned. He was both happy and embarrassed. Nebulous fantasies were born within him.

"If only she were my sister!" dreamed Sasha longingly, "and I could come to her, embrace her, and say something sweet. I could call her my dearest Ludmilochka! Or even by some sort of very special name —Tinkle or Dragonfly. And she would answer. What happiness that would be."

"Of course," thought Sasha sadly, "she is a stranger. Sweet, but a stranger. She came and went, and I'm sure she's already not even thinking about me. Only the sweet fragrance of lilac and rose is left, and the sensation of the two tender kisses—and a vague disturbance in my soul which is creating a sweet dream just as the waves gave birth to Aphrodite."

Soon Kokovkina returned.

"Phew, how strongly you smell!" she said.

Sasha blushed. "Ludmilochka was here," he said, "but she didn't find you in. She sat for awhile, sprayed me, and left."

"How sweet!" said the old woman with surprise. "You're already calling her Ludmilochka."

Sasha laughed confusedly and ran to his room. Kokovkina reflected that the Rutilov sisters were very gay and cheerful girls, and that they infected both young and old with their gaiety.

From the morning of the next day Sasha continually thought happily about his invitation, and at home he awaited dinner with impatience. After dinner, all red with embarrassment, he asked Kokovkina's permission to go to the Rutilovs' until seven o'clock. Kokovkina was surprised, but she let him go. The happy Sasha ran out, carefully combed and even pomaded. He was gay and slightly excited as if something important and pleasant was before him. And it was pleasant to think that he would arrive, kiss Ludmila's hand, and she would kiss his forehead—and afterwards, when he was leaving, they would again exchange these same kisses. He happily envisioned Ludmila's soft, white hand.

All three sisters met Sasha in the hallway. They all loved to sit by the window looking at the street, and, for that reason, they had seen him at a distance. Merry, dressed-up, and chattering in ringing voices, they surrounded him with an uproarious blizzard of gaiety— and he at once became happy and at ease with them.

"Here is my young, mysterious gentleman!" exclaimed Ludmila happily.

Sasha kissed her hand and did it deftly and with great pleasure. He also kissed in their turns the hands of Dar'ya and Valeriya—he could not get around them— and discovered that this also was exceedingly pleasant. Moreover, all three of them kissed him on the cheek— Dar'ya, loudly but indifferently as though he were a board; Valeriya tenderly dropped her eyes—her crafty little eyes—lightly giggled, and ever so gently touched him with her soft, smiling lips, as though a soft, fragrant apple blossom had fallen on his cheek; and Ludmila gave him a joyful, gay, smacking kiss.

"He is *my* guest," she declared firmly, and she took Sasha by the shoulders and led him to her room.

Dar'ya immediately became quite angry. "So go ahead and kiss him!" she crossly cried out. "You've found a treasure! No one will take him away."

Valeriya did not say anything but only smiled—it was hardly worth-while to talk with a little boy! What could he understand?

It was spacious, pleasant, and light in Ludmila's room because of two large windows, barely covered with light yellow lace, which looked out onto the garden. There was a pleasant odor in the room, and everything was neat and fresh. The chairs and armchairs were upholstered in a yellow-gold material with a scarcely discernable white pattern. Various bottles with perfume and cologne, small glass vessels, little boxes, fans, and several Russian and French books could be seen.

"I saw you in my dreams last night," said Ludmila laughing. "It seemed that you were swimming near the town bridge, and I was sitting on the bridge and caught you with a fishing rod."

"And put me into a bottle?" asked Sasha with a smile.

"Why into a bottle?"

"Where else?"

"Where? I pulled you by the ears and tossed you back into the stream." And Ludmila's laughter rang out for a long time.

"You're a funny one!" said Sasha. "And what did you want to say to me today."

Ludmila laughed and did not answer.

"Evidently you were deceiving me," guessed Sasha. "And you promised to show me something, too," he said reproachfully.

"I will! Would you like something to eat?" asked Ludmila.

"I've already had supper," said Sasha. "What a deceiver you are!"

"As though I have to deceive you. Why do you smell so of pomade?" Ludmila suddenly asked.

Sasha blushed.

"I can't stand pomade!" said Lumila with annoyance. "You're made up like a girl!" She passed her hand through his hair, and the hand became oily. She wiped it gently across his cheek. "Please," she said, "don't dare use pomade!"

Sasha was embarrassed. "All right," he said, "I won't. Such strictness. You yourself use perfume!"

"That's perfume, and this is pomade, stupid! You have found some comparison," she said in a convincing voice. "I never use pomade. Why should you glue your hair down! Perfume isn't like that at all. Let me sprinkle you. Would you like it? I'll use lilac—all right?"

"I'd like it," said Sasha smiling. It pleased him to think that he would bring a fragrance home and again surprise Kokovkina.

"Now who gets sprayed?" asked Ludmila looking inquisitively and craftily at Sasha with the bottle of lilac perfume in her hands.

"I get sprayed," repeated Sasha.

"Have you really bayed? You bay like a dog? Now that's something! Bay for me!" * gaily teased Ludmila.

Sasha and Ludmila laughed happily.

"And you aren't afraid that I'll smother you any more?" asked Ludmila. "Do you remember how frightened you were yesterday?"

"I wasn't frightened of anything," interrupted Sasha hotly.

Ludmila laughed and, teasing the boy, began to spray him with the lilac scent. Sasha thanked her and again kissed her hand.

"And please, get your hair cut!" Ludmila said strictly. "What's the good of wearing such locks! Your hairdo would frighten horses."

"All right, I'll cut it off," agreed Sasha. "What terrible strictness. I really have short hair—only half an inch. The inspector has never said anything to me about my hair."

"I love young people with short hair—make a note of that," said Ludmila impressively and threatened him

* *Kto zhelaet* means "who wishes"; *kto zhe laet* means "who's that barking."

with her finger. "I'm not your inspector, I have to be obeyed."

From then on, Ludmila got into the habit of going to Kokovkina's more and more often to see Sasha. She tried—especially in the beginning—to come when Kokovkina was not at home. Sometimes she even relied upon her cunningness and lured the old woman away from the house.

"Akh, you're a coward!" Darya said to her once. "You're afraid of old women. Just go there when she's in and take him out for a walk."

Ludmila heeded her advice and began to go there whenever she felt like it. If she found Kokovkina at home, she would sit with her for a short time and then take Sasha out for a stroll, never keeping him out for any length of time.

Ludmila and Sasha quickly became friends—it was a tender but also a tense friendship. Ludmila herself did not realize that she was awakening the first manifestations—although they were still vague—of desire in Sasha. Sasha often kissed Ludmila's hands and her thin, supple wrists covered with soft, pliant skin. Her winding, bluish veins were visible through the pinkish-yellow cloth of her sleeve, and above that were her long, slender arms, which could be kissed to the very elbow when the ample sleeves were pushed up.

Sasha sometimes did not tell Kokovkina that Ludmila had come. He did not lie—he merely remained silent. It would have been senseless to lie, because the maid could tell on him. But even to be silent about Ludmila's visits was not easy for Sasha, for Ludmila's laughter continued to resound in his ears. He wanted to talk about her, but it would have been awkward to say anything to anyone.

Sasha also soon became friendly with the other sisters. He would kiss all their hands, and soon he even began to call the girls Dashen'ka, Ludmilochka, and Valerochka.

17 : ৡৄৡৄ

Ludmila met Sasha on the street one day and said to him, "Tomorrow is the nameday of the headmaster's oldest daughter—will your landlady be going?"

"I don't know," said Sasha, and at once the joyful hope and, more than that, the desire stirred in his soul that Kokovkina would go so that Ludmila could come and be with him during that time.

In the evening he reminded Kokovkina of the next day's nameday festivity.

"I'd almost forgotten," said Kokovkina. "I shall go —she's such a sweet little girl."

And indeed, when Sasha returned from the gymnasium Kokovkina had gone to the Khripaches'. The thought that he had been able to get Kokovkina out of the house this time pleased Sasha. He was quite convinced that Ludmila would find the time to come.

And so it was—Ludmila did come. She kissed Sasha on the cheek and let him kiss her on the hand. She laughed gaily, and he blushed. A moist, sweet, flower-like aroma hung about Ludmila's clothes—a mixture of rose and iris—the sensuous and voluptuous iris dissolved into the sweet and dreamlike fragrance of roses. Ludmila was carrying a thin box wrapped in fine paper through which a yellowish design was visible. She sat down, placed the box on her knees, and archly looked at Sasha.

"Do you like dates?" she asked.

"Very much," said Sasha with an amused grimace.

"Well then, I shall treat you," said Ludmila with an impressive air. She undid the box and said, "Eat!" She herself took the dates out of the box one by one and inserted them in his mouth, and after each she made him kiss her hand.

"My lips have become sweet," said Sasha.

"There's no harm in that," replied Ludmila gaily. "Kiss—it's good for your health. I don't mind."

"Perhaps it would be better if I gave you all the kisses at once," said Sasha smiling, and he started to reach for a date himself.

"You'll cheat, you'll cheat!" cried Ludmila, speedily closing the box, and she slapped Sasha on the fingers.

"But I'm honest—I won't deceive you," declared Sasha.

"No, no I don't believe you," insisted Ludmila.

"Well, would you like me to kiss you in advance?" proposed Sasha.

"Now we're getting down to business," said Ludmila happily. "Kiss away."

She stretched out her hand to Sasha. Sasha took her long, slender fingers, kissed them once, and, not letting go of her hand, asked with a sly smile, "And you won't deceive me, Ludmilochka?"

"As if I were dishonest!" merrily replied Ludmila. "It's not likely I'll deceive you—you may kiss without doubt."

Sasha bent over her hand and began to kiss it rapidly: he covered the hand evenly with kisses and smacked loudly with his puckered lips. He was pleased that he could kiss her so much. Ludmila was carefully counting the kisses. When she had counted ten, she said, "It's awkward for you to be standing, you should kneel."

"All right then, I'll get more comfortably settled," said Sasha, and he got on his knees and continued to kiss her with fervor.

Sasha loved to eat. It pleased him that Ludmila was treating him to sweets, and he loved her still more tenderly for it.

Ludmila sprinkled Sasha with sugary-smelling perfume. And its odor astonished Sasha—sweet but strange, enveloping, and radiantly misty like a golden but sinful sunrise through a white haze.

"What strange perfume!" said Sasha.

"Try some on your hand," suggested Ludmila, and she gave him an ugly little four-cornered bottle with rounded edges. Sasha looked at it in the light—it was a cheerful, bright yellow liquid. The bottle had a large, multicolored label with a French inscription—it was cyclamen from Piver's. Sasha took hold of the flat glass stopper, pulled it out, and sniffed the perfume. Then he did what Ludmila loved to do—he placed his palm on the mouth of the bottle and quickly turned the bottle over and then back again. He rubbed the drops of cyclamen between his palms and then carefully sniffed his hand. When the spirit had evaporated, the pure aroma remained. Ludmila watched him with excitement and expectation.

"It smells a little like candied bedbug," said Sasha hesitantly.

"No, no, please don't lie," said Ludmila with annoyance. She too put some of the perfume on her hand and smelled it.

"Yes, like bedbug," repeated Sasha.

Ludmila suddenly flared up, and little tears glistened in her eyes. She struck Sasha across the cheek and cried, "Akh, you wicked boy! That was for your bug!"

"That was quite a blow!" said Sasha laughing, and he kissed Ludmila's hand. "Why are you so angry, my darling Ludmilochka! What do you think it smells like?"

Completely bewitched by Ludmila, he was not at all angry at the blow.

"What?" asked Ludmila as she grasped Sasha's ear. "I'll tell you what, but first I'm going to pull your ear."

"Oh, oh, oh, Ludmilochka, darling, I won't do it again!" said Sasha frowning from the pain and bending over.

Ludmila let go of the reddened ear, affectionately drew Sasha to her, and sat him on her knees. "Listen," she said. "Three spirits dwell in cyclamen—the unfortunate flower smells of sweet ambrosia—this is for the worker bees. You probably know that in Russian it is called *dryakva*—cowslip."

"Cowslip," repeated Sasha laughingly. "That's a funny name."

"Don't laugh, you little rogue," said Ludmila. She took him by the other ear and continued, "The sweet ambrosia and the bees buzzing over it—this is the flower's happiness. And besides that it smells of a delicate vanilla, which is not for the bees but for the one they dream of, and this is its desire—the flower and the golden sun overhead. And the third fragrance is of the sweet, tender body for him who loves, and this is its love—the poor flower and the heavy midday sultriness. The bee, the sun, the sultriness—do you understand, my little darling?"

Sasha silently nodded his head. His dark face burned, his long dark eyelashes fluttered. Ludmila dreamily looked far into the distance and, blushing deeply, said, "The tender and sunny cyclamen gives pleasure and induces desires, both sweet and shameful, and stirs up the blood. Do you understand, my little sun, what it is like when things are both sweet and pleasant and painful, and you want to cry? Do you understand? This is what it's like."

She pressed herself to Sasha's lips in a long kiss.

Ludmila stared straight ahead lost in thought. Suddenly a cunning smile flashed across her lips. She gently pushed Sasha away and asked, "Do you like roses?"

Sasha sighed and, closing his eyes, smiled sweetly. "I love them," he whispered quietly.

"Large ones?" asked Ludmila.

"All kinds, large and small," said Sasha quickly, and he stood up, moving from her knees with an agile, boyish motion.

"And do you like flesh-colored roses?" Ludmila asked sweetly, and the sound of her voice wavered from suppressed laughter.

"I love them," Sasha quickly replied.

Ludmila reddened and laughed. "Stupid," she exclaimed, "you like flesh-colored roses, and there's no one to whip them up on you."*

They both laughed and blushed.

Such natural and, therefore, innocent stimulations were for Ludmila the main charm of their relationship. They aroused—and yet they were far from coarse and disgusting attainment.

They began to dispute which of them was stronger. "You may be stronger," said Ludmila, "but what difference does that make? The important thing is agility."

"I'm agile too," put in Sasha.

"You, agile!" cried Ludmila in a teasing voice. They continued to quarrel for a long time, and finally Ludmila proposed, "Well, let's wrestle."

Sasha laughed and said teasingly, "How could you contend with me?"

* *Rozochki* means both "little roses" and "whipping rods."

Ludmila began to tickle him.

"Oh, you!" he cried with a laugh. He wriggled away and grabbed her around the waist.

A tussle began. Ludmila at once saw that Sasha was stronger. Since she could not win by strength, she used her cunning to seize a suitable moment and trip Sasha. He fell, and Ludmila too was drawn down after him. Ludmila, however, nimbly shifted and pinned him to the floor.

"Unfair!" cried Sasha desperately.

Ludmila had her knees on his stomach and was pressing him to the floor with her hands. Sasha strained desperately to get free. Ludmila again began to tickle him. Sasha's ringing laughter mingled with her own laughter which at last forced her to let Sasha go. She fell back on the floor laughing. Sasha jumped to his feet. He was red and quite vexed.

"*Rusalka!*"* he cried.

But the nymph remained on the floor and laughed.

Ludmila sat Sasha down on her knees. Tired from their struggle, they closely and happily looked into one another's eyes and smiled.

"I'm heavy for you," said Sasha. "You'd better let me off before I hurt your knees."

"It's nothing—sit still," said Ludmila tenderly. "You yourself said that you like to cuddle." She stroked his head, and he affectionately pressed himself to her. "You are a handsome one, Sasha," she said.

Sasha blushed and laughed. "The things you make up!" he said.

Thoughts and conversations about beauty as applied

---

* The *rusalka* or water sprite is a female evil spirit who first entices and then drowns or tickles her victims to death. Originally, the term is thought to have been connected with pagan, Dionysian rites.

to him somehow disturbed him—he still had never been curious enough to find out whether he appeared attractive or ugly to people.

Ludmila pinched Sasha's cheek, and Sasha smiled. A red spot appeared on his cheek which looked pretty on him. Ludmila pinched the other cheek too. Sasha did not protest, but taking her hand, he kissed it and said, "That's enough pinching—it hurts me, and you'll hurt your fingers."

"It may be painful, but what a little ladies' man you've become," teased Ludmila.

"I have no more time—I have a lot of homework. Cuddle me a little more for good luck so that I get a five in Greek."

"You're getting rid of me!" said Ludmila. She caught hold of his hand and rolled his sleeve above the elbow.

"What are you trying to do?" asked Sasha in confusion and blushing guiltily.

But Ludmila was lost in admiration of the arm, and she turned it this way and that. "You have such beautiful arms!" she exclaimed loudly and happily, and suddenly she kissed it near the elbow.

Sasha reddened and tried to pull his arm away, but Ludmila held it and kissed it several times more. Sasha became still and cast down his eyes, and his bright half-smiling lips took on a strange expression —under the shade of his dense eyelashes his burning cheeks began to pale.

They said good-bye, and Sasha walked Ludmila to the gate. He would have gone farther, but she told him not to. He stopped by the gate and said, "Come more often, my darling, and bring sweeter honey-cakes."

It was the first time that he had used the familiar

"thou," and it sounded to Ludmila like a sweet caress. She impetuously hugged and kissed Sasha and ran off. Sasha stood there stunned.

Sasha had promised to come. The appointed hour came, however, and no Sasha. Ludmila waited impatiently and walked back and forth in suspense and looked out the window. Whenever she heard steps she would stick her head outside the window. Her sisters teased her. "Oh, you people! Leave me alone," she said angrily and excitedly, and she threw herself fiercely upon them with reproaches because they were laughing at her. By now it was evident that Sasha would not come. Ludmila wept from anger and grief.

"Oy, yoi, yoi—they've got your boy!" Dar'ya teased her.

The sobbing Ludmila spoke softly, in the midst of her grief forgetting to be angry with her sisters for teasing her: "The nasty old hag won't let him—she wants to keep him tucked in the folds of her skirt so that he can study Greek."

"Yes, and he's a lout, too, for not daring to go out," said Dar'ya with coarse sympathy.

"She's gotten tied up with a tiny tot," said Valeriya contemptuously.

But, although both sisters were laughing, they sympathized with Ludmila. They all loved one another fondly but not strongly—it was a superficial, tender love!

"Is it worth-while to grieve and cry over some youngster?" said Dar'ya. "One might say that the devil has bound himself to an infant."

"Who is this devil?" cried Ludmila vehemently, and she blushed crimson all over.

"Why, you are, dearie," Dar'ya calmly replied. "Granted you're young, nevertheless . . ." Darya did not finish, but whistled piercingly.

"Nonsense!" said Ludmila in a strangely ringing voice. A weird and terrible smile illumined her face through her tears like a brightly shining ray at sundown through the last downpour of a sluggish rain.

"Please tell me—what do you see interesting in him?" asked Dar'ya with annoyance.

Ludmila, with this same curious smile, pensively and slowly replied, "He is such a beauty, and there are so many untapped possibilities in him!"

"Well, that's not so special," said Dar'ya with conviction. "All young boys have that."

"Yes, it is special," answered Ludmila angrily. "The others are vile."

"And he is pure?" asked Valeriya, pronouncing "pure" in a slighting way.

"Much you understand!" exclaimed Ludmila, but she at once said quietly and dreamily, "He is innocent."

"I should hope so!" said Dar'ya derisively.

"The best age for boys," said Ludmila, "is fourteen or fifteen. He still cannot do anything, and he does not really understand, but he already has a presentiment of it all. And he doesn't have a disgusting beard."

"How thrilling!" said Valeriya with a contemptuous grimace. She was depressed. It seemed to her that she was small and weak and frail, and she was jealous of her sisters. She envied Dar'ya her gay laugh and even envied Ludmila her weeping.

"You don't understand anything," Ludmila said again. "I don't at all love him in the way you think. It is better to like a young boy than to fall in love with a disgusting mug and its mustache. I love him in an innocent way. I don't want anything from him."

"If you don't want anything, then why do you pester him so?" retorted Dar'ya rudely.

Ludmila blushed, and a guilty expresssion fell painfully on her face. Dar'ya began to feel sorry for Ludmila, so she went up to her, hugged her, and said, "Now don't get upset, we're not speaking maliciously."

Ludmila again began to weep. She pressed against Dar'ya's shoulder and said pitifully, "I know that I have nothing to hope for, but if he cuddled me a little, that would at least be something."

"How depressing!" said Dar'ya with annoyance. She moved away from Ludmila, set her arms on her sides, and sang loudly:

> *Last night I left my precious*
> *And went to bed.*

Valeriya began to laugh loudly and shrilly, and Ludmila's eyes became provocative and merry. She impetuously went off to her room and sprinkled herself with Corylopsis—the sweet, spicy, seductive odor enveloped her with an alluring magnetism.

She went into the street dressed up, excited, and radiating unconcerned temptation. "Perhaps I will meet him," she thought, and she did.

"Well!" she exclaimed happily and reproachfully.

Sasha was both embarrassed and happy. "I didn't have the time," he said in confusion. "I had so much homework, so much to study, that I really didn't have the time."

"You're lying, my darling—but let us go now." Sasha demurred smiling, but it was evident that he was pleased to have Ludmila leading him away. Ludmila took him to her house.

"Look whom I've brought!" she called to her sisters triumphantly, and she led Sasha to her room by the shoulder.

"Just wait until I settle you," she threatened as she bolted the door. "There—no one can help you."

Sasha, his hands in his belt, stood awkwardly in the middle of the room. He felt both pleasant and terrified. The room smelled of some new kind of perfume, festive and sweet, but something in its odor offended and irritated the nerves like contact with gay, nimble little scaly-skinned snakes.

18 : ᢓᢆᢧᢓᢆᢧ

Peredonov was returning from the lodgings of one of the students. Suddenly he was caught in a fine rain, and he began to consider where to drop in so that he would not ruin his new silk umbrella in the rain. Across the street, on a two-story stone home, he saw the sign—Notary Gudaevsky's Office. The Notary's son was a student in the second form of the gymnasium. Peredonov decided to go in. He could kill two birds with one stone by complaining about the student.

He found both the father and the mother at home. They received him with a good deal of fuss—such was the manner in which everything was done here.

Nikolai Mikhailovich Gudaevsky was a man of medium height, stocky, partially bald, black-haired, and with a long beard. His movements were always impulsive and unexpected. He did not walk but, rather, carried himself in short hops like a sparrow. One could never tell by his face or position what he would do the next moment. In the midst of an ordinary business conversation he would suddenly say something that would not only interrupt the conversation but also, by its lack of cause, throw it into confusion. At home or on a visit he would sit and sit, and suddenly he would jump up for no evident reason, stride briskly about the room, make an exclamation, and strike something. On the street he would walk and walk, and suddenly he would stop, squat, or make a lunge forward or do some other gymnastic exercise, and then continue on. In the papers which he drew up or attested, Gudaevsky loved to add ludicrous touches. Instead of writing about Ivan Ivanych Ivanov who lived on Moskovskaya Square in the house of a certain Ermilova, he would, for example, write about Ivan Ivanych Ivanov who lived on the market square in that section where one cannot breathe because of the foul air, etc. Sometimes he even made a note of the number of geese and hens owned by the man whose signature he was witnessing.

Iuliya Petrovna Gudaevskaya, a tall, thin, and dry woman—passionate and terribly sentimental—was strangely similar to her husband in spite of the incongruity of their figures. She had the same abrupt way of moving, quite unlike the movements of other people. She dressed colorfully and youthfully, and long multicolored ribbons with which she loved to adorn her clothing and hairdo in abundance continually fluttered with her quick movements.

Antosha, their slender, active boy, bowed courteously. They seated Peredonov in the living room, and he immediately began to complain about Antosha for being lazy, inattentive, not working in class, for talking and laughing, and for playing pranks during recess. Antosha was surprised—he did not know that he was considered so bad—and he began to defend himself hotly. Both parents became excited.

"Please tell me," exclaimed the father, "of precisely what do these misdeeds consist?"

"Nika, don't defend him," cried the mother. "He shouldn't be naughty."

"Yes, but what has he done?" questioned the father, running about on his short legs so that it looked as if he were gliding.

"He's generally joking, romping, fighting," said Peredonov sullenly. "He is always in mischief."

"I don't fight," cried Antosha plaintively. "Ask whomever you want—I never fight with anyone."

"He doesn't let anyone pass," said Peredonov.

"Very well," said Gudaevsky firmly, "I myself shall go the the gymnasium and find out from the inspector."

"Nika, Nika, why won't you believe him?" cried Iuliya Petrovna. "Do you want Antosha to turn out to be a good-for-nothing? He must be whipped."

"Nonsense! Nonsense!" shouted the father.

"I'll whip him, I'll whip him without fail!" screamed the mother and she grabbed her son by the shoulder and pulled him towards the kitchen. "Come with me, Antosha, darling, and I'll whip you," she cried.

"I won't let you do it!" yelled the father, and he snatched away his son. The mother did not let go, Antosha cried out in despair, and the parents struggled.

"Help me, Ardal'on Borisych," cried Iuliya Petrovna. "Hold this monster while I deal with Antosha."

Peredonov went to her aid, but Gudaevsky tore away his son, strongly shoved his wife away, and, running up to Peredonov, he shouted threateningly, "Don't butt in! When two dogs are having it out, a third had better not get mixed up in it! I'll take care of you!"

Red, disheveled, and sweaty, he brandished his fist in the air. Peredonov withdrew mumbling indistinct words. Iuliya Petrovna ran around her husband and tried to get hold of Antosha, while the father shielded the boy behind him, pulling him to the right and to the left by the arm.

Iuliya Petrovna, her eyes gleaming, screamed, "He'll grow up to be a robber! He'll sit in prison! He'll be sentenced to hard labor!"

"A plague on your tongue!" yelled Gudaevsky. "Shut up, evil fool!"

"You tyrant!" screeched Iuliya Petrovna, and she ran up to her husband, struck him on the back with her fist, and raced headlong out of the living room.

Gudaevsky clenched his fists and ran over to Peredonov. "You came here to cause trouble," he yelled. "Antosha cause trouble? You lie—he never does anything wrong. And if he did, I would know about it without you, and I don't even want to talk with you. You go about the town deceiving fools and whipping boys. You want to get a degree for whipping. But you haven't found that sort here. My dear sir, I ask you to clear out!"

While saying this, he jumped towards Peredonov and trapped him in a corner. Peredonov became frightened and would have been happy to run away, but Gudaevsky in the midst of his excitement did not notice that he was blocking his exit. Antosha seized his father's coat tails from behind and pulled him towards him. His father angrily told him to be quiet and kicked at him. Antosha nimbly jumped out of the way, but he did not let go of his father's coat tails.

"Go way!" exclaimed Gudaevsky. "Behave yourself, Antosha."

"Papa," cried Antosha continuing to pull his father back, "you're preventing Ardal'on Borisych from leaving." Gudaevsky quickly jumped back, and Antosha barely managed to get out of his way.

"Excuse me," said Gudaevsky showing him to the door, "here is the exit—I won't detain you." Peredonov hurriedly walked out of the living room, and Gudaevsky put his fingers to his nose at him and then brought his knee up into the air as though he were kicking his guest out. Antosha snickered.

"Antosha, behave yourself!" Gudaevsky shouted at him. "Tomorrow I am going to the gymnasium, and, if this turns out to be true, I'll hand you over to your mother for punishment."

"I haven't caused any trouble. He's lying," said Antosha tearfully and plaintively.

"Antosha, behave yourself!" cried the father. "You shouldn't say that he is lying—he is mistaken. Only children lie, grownups make mistakes."

Meanwhile Peredonov found the half-dark hallway, took down his coat with some difficulty, and began to put it on. Because of his fear and excitement he could not get his arms into the sleeves, and no one came to help him. Suddenly Iuliya Petrovna ran out from a side door somewhere, her flying ribbons rustling, and excitedly whispered something, waving her arms and jumping up and down on tiptoe. Peredonov did not at first understand her.

"I am so grateful to you," he finally made out. "Such interest on your part is so considerate, so considerate. Most people are so indifferent, but you've put yourself in the position of the poor mother. It is so difficult to raise children, so difficult—you just can't imagine. I have two, and it makes my head go round. My husband is a tyrant. He's a terrible, terrible man, don't you think so? You yourself saw."

"Yes," mumbled Peredonov, "your husband is all that. He shouldn't be that way—I look after them, but he . . ."

"Akh, don't say a word," whispered Iuliya Petrovna, "he is a terrible man. He is driving me to the grave, and he will be glad. He will corrupt my children, my dear Antosha. But I am their mother, and I won't let him. I'll whip the boy in spite of him."

"He won't permit you to do it," said Peredonov, and he motioned with his head in the direction of the rooms.

"When he goes to his club, he won't take Antosha with him! I will be quiet until he goes as though I were in agreement with him, and, just as soon as he goes, I'll whip him, and you can help me. You will help me, won't you?"

Peredonov thought awhile and said, "All right, only how will I know when?"

"I'll send for you, I'll send for you," gaily whispered Iuliya Petrovna. "You wait, and just as soon as he goes to his club, I'll send for you at once."

In the evening Peredonov was brought a note from Gudaevskaya. He read:

> Most Esteemed Ardal'on Borisych!
> My husband has gone to his club, and now I am free from his barbarity until one o'clock tonight. Do your duty and come to me as quickly as you can to take action upon my delinquent son. I realize that we must drive his faults out of him while he's young, or afterwards it will be too late.
>
> With the greatest respect,
> Iuliya Gudaevskaya
> P.S. Please come quickly, otherwise Antosha will have gone to sleep and will have to be awakened.

Peredonov hurriedly dressed, wrapped himself up warmly with a scarf, and set out.

"Where are you going, Ardal'on Borisych, on a night stroll?" asked Varvara.

"On business," gloomily replied Peredonov, hurriedly leaving.

Varvara sadly thought that she would not get much sleep again. It was necessary to force him to marry her more quickly! Then she could sleep at night and during the day—now that would be bliss!

On the street Peredonov was beset by doubts. What if this were a trap? What if it suddenly turned out that Gudaevsky was at home, and he seized him and began to beat him? Wouldn't it be better to go back? "No," he thought, "you should go up to their house—then you'll know what to do."

The night—quiet, chilly, and dark—crept in from all sides and forced him to slow down his steps. Fresh winds came from nearby fields. In the grass by the fences light rustlings and noises arose, and everything around him seemed strange and suspicious—perhaps someone was hiding behind and following him. All objects were strangely and unexpectedly hidden by shadow as if a strange nocturnal life had awakened in them, incomprehensible to man and hostile to him.

Peredonov quietly walked along the streets and mumbled, "You won't get anything out of following me. I'm not doing anything wrong, I'm seeing to my work, brother, and that's that."

Finally he reached the Gudaevsky residence. From the street, light could be seen in only one window— the remaining four were dark. Peredonov went up onto the porch ever so quietly and stood there with his ear to the door and listened—all was quiet. He gently pulled the bronze bell handle—it made a far-off, weak, trembling sound. But, in spite of its weakness, it frightened Peredonov as if all the hostile spirits would be awakened and driven to this door by this sound. Peredonov quickly ran from the porch and pressed himself against the wall, hiding behind a column.

A few short moments passed. Peredonov's heart sank and beat heavily. Then light steps were heard, the sound of a door opening. Iuliya Petrovna, her black, passionate eyes gleaming in the darkness, looked out onto the street.

"Who's there?" she said in a loud whisper.

Peredonov moved away from the wall a little, and, glancing into the narrow opening of the door where it was dark and still, he asked, also in a whisper, "Has Nikolai Mikhailovich left?" and his voice was quivering.

"He's gone, he's gone!" whispered Iuliya Petrovna, happily nodding her head.

Timidly looking around, Peredonov followed her into the dark passageway. "Excuse my not having a light on," whispered Iuliya Petrovna, "but someone might see and gossip."

She walked in front of Peredonov up the stairway to a corridor where a small lamp was hanging, throwing a dim light on the steps above. Iuliya Petrovna laughed quietly and happily, and her ribbons quivered unsteadily from her laughter.

"He has gone," she whispered happily and looked Peredonov up and down with her passionately burning eyes. "I had been afraid that he would stay at home today as he was so upset, but he was unable to do without his whist. I also sent away the servant, so only Liza's nurse is left—otherwise we would be interrupted. You well know what sort of people there are nowadays."

There was a heat about Iuliya Petrovna, and she was all hot and dry like a stick used to stir up a fire. She sometimes grabbed Peredonov's arm, and these brief, dry contacts ran along his whole body like shivers of dry fires. Ever so gently, they walked along the corridor on tiptoe past several closed doors and stopped by the last, the door to the children's room . . .

Peredonov left Iuliya Petrovna at midnight when she was already expecting that her husband would return soon. He walked along the dark street feeling gloomy and sullen. It seemed to him that someone had been standing near the house and now was following him.

"I was going about my job," he mumbled. "It wasn't my fault. She herself wanted it. You won't get me— you've got the wrong man."

When he returned, Varvara was still not asleep. Cards were spread out before her. It occurred to Peredonov that someone could attack him as he came in. Perhaps Varvara herself let in the enemy.

"I'll go to sleep, and you'll work witchcraft on me with the cards. Give me those cards—otherwise you'll bewitch me," said Peredonov, and he snatched away the cards and hid them under his pillow.

Varvara smirked and said, "You're making a fool of yourself. I don't even know how to bewitch with cards—as if I needed to anyway."

Her smirk vexed and terrified him: it meant, he thought, that she could do it without cards. The cat crouched under the bed and its green eyes glistened— she could bewitch him with the cat's fur if she stroked it in the dark and made sparks fly. And there was the gray *nedotykomka* again peeping out from under the dresser—might not Varvara have summoned it out of the night with a quiet whistle like a snore?

Peredonov dreamed a hideous and terrible dream: Pyl'nikov came and stood in the doorway beckoning and smiling. It was as if someone drew Peredonov to him, and Pyl'nikov led him along dark and dirty streets, the cat running alongside, its green pupils shining . . .

19 : ᕿᔌᕿᔌ

The eccentricities in Peredonov's conduct were from day to day disturbing Khripach more and more. He conferred with the school physician about Peredonov's sanity. The doctor answered with a smile that Peredonov was not going out of his mind but was simply behaving stupidly. Complaints were being entered. It began with Adamenko: she sent the headmaster her brother's notebook, which had been given a one for well-done work. During one of the recesses, the headmaster called Peredonov to his office.

"But he really is like a madman," thought Khripach as he observed the traces of disturbance and terror on Peredonov's dull and gloomy face.

"I have a complaint to make against you," said Khripach drily in his rapid way of speaking. "Each time I have to teach a class next to yours, my head literally splits. Such laughter goes on in your class. May I ask you to give lessons with not quite as much humorous content? 'Joking, always joking—how do you stand it?' "*

"It's not my fault," said Peredonov angrily, "they laugh by themselves. One can't always talk about orthography or the satires of Kantemir.† Sometimes you

* The line, slightly misquoted by Khripach, is from Act III, Scene 1 of *Woe from Wit*, an early nineteenth-century play by Aleksander Griboedov. Many of its lines have passed into common usage.

† A. D. Kantemir was an eighteenth century poet who wrote in

say something of your own, and they immediately go into hysterics. They're very spoiled. They should be dealt with."

"It is desirable and even essential that classwork have a serious character," said Khripach drily. "And one more thing," Khripach showed Peredonov two notebooks and said, "here are two notebooks in your subject—both students of the same class, Adamenko and my son. I have compared them, and I must make an inference about your not entirely attentive relation to your work. The last work of Adamenko's has been done exceedingly satisfactorily and has received a one, while the work of my son, done much more poorly, has been given a four. It is evident that you have made a mistake and given one student's grade to another and vice versa. It is true that men do make mistakes, but all the same I will ask you to avoid making similar mistakes. They cause just indignation on the part of the parents and the students themselves."

Peredonov mumbled something indistinct.

Out of spite he viciously began to taunt the small boys in his classes who had been punished because of his complaints within the last few days. He especially picked on Kramarenko, who remained silent and went pale under his deep tan, his eyes glittering.

On this day Kramarenko left the gymnasium but did not hurry home. He stopped by the gate and watched the doorway. When Peredonov came out, Kramarenko followed him at a little distance, waiting till the few other pedestrians were gone.

Peredonov was walking slowly. The gloomy weather depressed him. In the last few days his face had as-

---

syllabic verse, a system which was subsequently abandoned. He is best known for nine satires, modeled after those of the French poet Boileau-Despreaux, which attack ignorance and resistance to progress.

sumed an even duller expression. His glance was either fixed on something far off, or else it wandered strangely. It seemed as if he were continually peering about for something. In his eyes things either were doubled, made no impression, or seemed disjointed.

What was he looking for? Informers. They hid themselves behind objects and whispered and laughed. His enemies had sent a whole army of informers upon Peredonov. Sometimes Peredonov suddenly attempted to spot them, but they always managed to run away just in time as though swallowed up by the earth . . .

Peredonov heard rapid and bold steps behind him on the pavement, and he fearfully looked around. Kramarenko drew even with him and stared at him with burning eyes. He was pale, slender, and malicious-looking, like a small savage about to throw himself on his enemy. This look frightened Peredonov.

"Suppose he bites me?" he thought.

He walked more rapidly, but Kramarenko did not fall behind; he walked more slowly, and Kramarenko lessened his steps. Peredonov halted and said angrily, "What are you up to, you dirty little scoundrel! I'll take you right to your father."

Kramarenko also stopped, but he continued to glower at Peredonov. Now they stood opposite one another on the unsteady slabs of the empty street near a gray fence, indifferent to all living things.

"Villain!" said Kramarenko in a voice all quivering and hissing. He leered and turned to go. He took about three steps, hesitated, and looked back, repeating more loudly, "Villain! Vile creature!" He spat and walked on.

Peredonov sullenly looked after him and also turned homeward. Vague and frightening thoughts were slowly turning over in his mind.

Vershina called to him. She was standing wrapped in

a large black shawl and smoking behind the fence of her garden near the gate. Peredonov did not at once recognize Vershina. Something sinister in her figure threatened him—she was a black witch emitting magic fumes and practicing sorcery. He spat and charmed himself.

Vershina laughed and asked, "What's the matter with you, Ardal'on Borisych?"

Peredonov looked dully at her and finally said, "Ah, it's you! I didn't recognize you at first."

"That's a good sign," said Vershina. "It means I soon will be rich."

This did not please Peredonov—he would much rather have made himself rich. "What makes you think you'll get rich?" he said angrily. "You'll have no more than you have now."

"But I shall win two hundred thousand," said Vershina, smiling crookedly.

"No, I will win the two hundred thousand," argued Peredonov.

"I'll win it in one lottery and you, in another," said Vershina.

"You lie," said Peredonov coarsely. "There wouldn't be two winners at once in one town. I'll win it, I tell you."

Vershina saw that he was angry, and so she stopped arguing. She opened the gate and, motioning to Peredonov, said, "What are we standing here for? Please come in—we have Murin here." Murin's name suggested pleasant things to Peredonov—drinks, *zakuska*. He went in.

In the living room shaded by the trees outside were sitting Marta with a red bow and a kerchief around her neck and gay eyes, Murin, more disheveled than usual and happy about something, and Vitkevich, a grown-up schoolboy who was courting Vershina. He thought that she was in love with him, and consequently, dreamed of quitting the gymnasium, marrying Vershina, and managing her estate.

As Peredonov came in, Murin arose and went towards him with exaggeratedly happy exclamations, which made his expression still more honeyed. His eyes glistened. All of this did not suit his robust figure and his disheveled hair in which some traces of straw could even be seen. "I'm here on business," he said loudly and more huskily. "I have business everywhere, and here these dear ladies indulge me with tea."

"Business indeed!" said Peredonov angrily. "What sort of business do you have! You're not in the government service, but still you get money. Now I have business."

"Still, getting other people's money is business too," retorted Murin with a loud laugh.

Vershina, smiling crookedly, seated Peredonov at the table. The circular table was crowded with glasses and cups of tea, rum, red jam, a silver filigree dish covered with a knitted napkin, and a basket with sweet rolls and homemade almond cookies. A strong smell of rum came from Murin's glass, while Vitkevich had placed a large quantity of jam on a glass plate shaped like a shell. Marta was eating a sweet roll with little bites and obviously enjoying it. Vershina offered tea to Peredonov, but he refused.

"It might be poisoned," he thought. "It's quite easy to poison something—I could drink it and not notice anything because the poison was sweet, and then I would go home and be laid out."

He was also annoyed that Murin had been served jam, but that when he came they had not wanted to bring him a new jar with better jam. They made many other jams besides that kind!

Vershina really was paying special attention to Murin. Seeing that there was little hope of getting Pe-

redonov, she was looking for other possibilities for
Marta. Now she was enticing Murin. Quite unused,
through his pursuit of hard work to obtain profits, to
social relationships, the landowner willingly took the
bait—he liked Marta.

Marta was happy. It was her constant dream that
she would find a beau, get married, and have a good
household and home—in short, a full cup. She looked
at Murin with loving eyes. This forty-year-old, huge
man with a coarse voice and a rather simple expression
on his face, seemed to her in his every movement to
be the ultimate in masculine strength, dashing appearance, handsomeness, and goodness.

Peredonov noticed the loving glances which Marta
and Murin exchanged—he noticed it because he himself expected special attention from Marta. "You're
sitting there beaming just like a prospective bridegroom," he said angrily to Murin.

"That's just because I'm happy that my business has
gone well," said Murin in a happy, excited voice. He
winked at his hostesses, who were both smiling happily.

"Have you found a bride or something? Are they
giving much of a dowry?" asked Peredonov angrily,
screwing up his eyes suspiciously.

"Natal'ya Afanas'evna, God bless her, has agreed to
room my Vaniushka," said Murin as if he had not
heard these questions. "He will live here as if he were
in Christ's bosom, and my mind will be at rest knowing that he won't be spoiled."

"He'll get into trouble with Vladya, and they'll burn
the house down," said Peredonov morosely.

"He wouldn't dare!" declared Murin with conviction. "Don't you worry about that, my dear Natalya
Afanas'evna. He'll be on his best behavior."

In order to end this discussion, Vershina with a wry
smile said, "I would like something tart to eat."

"Would you like some apples and blueberries? I'll get

them," said Marta quickly getting up from her place. "Please, bring some."

Marta ran out of the room. Vershina did not even look at her—she was accustomed to treating Marta's services as a right due her. She was calmly sitting back on the sofa, emitting puffs of blue smoke, and comparing the men who were talking: Peredonov, angry and dull; Murin, gay and lively.

Murin pleased her much more. He at least had a kind face, but Peredonov did not even know how to smile. Murin pleased her in all ways—he was large, stout, attractive, he spoke in a pleasant, low voice, and he was very respectful to her. At times Vershina even thought that she should fix it so that Murin became engaged not to Marta but to herself, but she always ended these speculations by nobly yielding him to Marta.

"Anyone would marry me," she thought, "because I have money, and so I can choose whom I want. I might even take this young man," she thought, and not without pleasure she fixed her glance on the greenish, impudent, but nevertheless attractive face of Vitkevich, who was speaking little and eating much. He was looking at Vershina and smiling impudently.

Marta brought the blueberries and apples in an earthenware dish and began to tell how she had dreamed that night that she was at a wedding as a bridesmaid and ate pineapple and pancakes with honey and found a hundred-ruble note in one pancake. She told how she cried when they took it away from her, and she woke up in tears.

"You should have quietly hidden it so no one would see it," said Peredonov angrily, "and, if you don't even know how to hang on to money in a dream, you'll make some housewife!"

"Well, there's no need to feel sorry about this money," said Vershina. "You can see many things in a dream."

"But I feel simply awful about that money," said Marta ingenuously. "A whole hundred rubles!" Tears welled up in her eyes, and she forced herself to smile in order not to cry.

Murin busily searched in his pocket, exclaiming, "Don't you cry, dear Marta Stanislavovna, we'll fix that right now!" He took a hundred-ruble note from his wallet, placed it on the table before Marta, and slapped his hand into her palm, crying, "Allow me! No one will take this away from you."

Marta was about to be overjoyed, but then she blushed deeply and said with embarrassment, "Akh, Vladimir Ivanovich, I didn't mean it. Really, I can't take it!"

"No, you mustn't offend me," said Murin laughing and not taking away the money. "Let's just say that your dream has come true."

"But how could I? I'm embarrassed. I wouldn't take it for anything," protested Marta, looking with avid eyes at the hundred-ruble note.

"Why protest about what's given you," said Vitkevich with an envious sigh. "Good fortune has fallen right into your hands."

Murin stood in front of Marta and exclaimed in a persuasive voice, "Dear Marta Stanislavovna, believe what I say. Take it, with all my heart, please! And if you don't wish it to be a gift, then accept it for taking care of my Vaniushka. My agreement with Natal'ya Afanas'evna will remain, but this is for you to look after him too."

"But this is so much," said Marta hesitantly.

"It's for the first half year," said Murin, and he bowed to Marta from the waist. "Now don't offend me. Take it and be like an older sister to my Vaniushka."

"Well then, take it Marta," said Vershina, "and thank Vladimir Ivanovich."

Marta, blushing with embarrassment and happiness, took the money. Murin began to thank her ardently.

"Get married at once, it will be cheaper," said Peredonov in a rage. "My, how generous he's become!"

Vitkevich laughed loudly, but the others acted as though they hadn't heard. Vershina was beginning to relate a dream of her own, but Peredonov did not wait to hear the end and got up to say good-bye. Murin invited him to come and visit him in the evening.

"I have to go to Vespers," said Peredonov.

"How is it that you've become so zealous in your church-going, Ardal'on Borisych?" asked Vershina with a quick, cynical laugh.

"I always have been," he replied. "Unlike others, I believe in God. Perhaps I'm the only one in the gymnasium who does. That's why they persecute me. The headmaster is an atheist."

"Let me know when you're free," said Murin.

"I have no time to go visiting," said Peredonov, angrily twisting his hat. But just then he remembered that Murin served good food and drink. "Well, I can visit you on Monday," he said.

Murin went into ecstasies and was about to invite Vershina and Marta, but Peredonov said, "No, don't invite the ladies. If we have a little to drink we might blurt out something that should be censored in their presence."

When Peredonov had gone, Vershina said with a laugh, "Ardal'on Borisych is behaving queerly. He very much wants to be an inspector, and evidently Varvara is leading him by the nose. He's doing all sorts of foolish things."

Vladya, who had hidden himself from Peredonov, came out and said with a malicious smile, "The locksmith's sons have found out from someone that it was Peredonov who told on them."

"They'll smash his windowpanes!" exclaimed Vitkevich with a gleeful laugh.

On the street everything appeared hostile and evil to Peredonov. A ram stood at an intersection and looked dully at Peredonov. This ram was so similar to Volodin that Peredonov became frightened, thinking that perhaps Volodin had turned himself into a sheep in order to follow him.

"How do we know," he thought, "it might be possible—science hasn't discovered how to do it yet, but maybe somebody already knows. Take the French—a learned nation, and yet sorcerers and magicians flourish in their Paris," thought Peredonov, and he became terrified. "This ram might kick me," he thought. The ram bleated in a way which was very much like Volodin's laugh—unpleasant, sharp, and piercing.

Then he encountered the police lieutenant again. Peredonov went up to him and said in a whisper, "You'd best keep an eye on Adamenko. She corresponds with socialists, and she's one herself."

Rubovsky looked at him silently and with surprise. Peredonov walked on a little farther and thought gloomily, "Why is he always turning up? He is following me, and he has put policemen everywhere."

The dirty streets, the sullen sky, the wretched little houses, the shabby, lifeless children—there was an air of anguish, primitive wildness, and unalterable sadness about it all.

"This is an awful town," thought Peredonov, "and the people here are evil and nasty. I must leave here and go to another town as soon as possible, a town where all the teachers will bow down low to me, and where all the students will be afraid and whisper in fear: 'The inspector is coming.' Yes, the authorities have a completely different life in this world."

"Mr. Inspector of the second district of Rubanskaya Province, his excellency, state councilor Peredonov," he mumbled to himself. "Now that's something! They'll know who I am! His highest excellency, the director of the public schools of Rubanskaya Province, honored state councilor, Mr. Peredonov. Hats off! Hand in your resignation! Get out! I'll see to you!"

Peredonov's expression was arrogant—in his meager imagination he had already received his due power.

When Peredonov arrived home and was still taking off his coat, the harsh sounds of Volodin's laughter came to him from the dining room. Peredonov's heart fell.

"He has managed to get here ahead of me," he thought. "Maybe Varvara and he are plotting to trick me. That's why he is laughing—he's happy that Varvara's in league with him."

He went into the dining room feeling spiteful and depressed. The table was already set for dinner. Varvara met Peredonov with a worried look.

"We've had such a time, Ardal'on Borisych!" she exclaimed. "The cat has run away."

"What!" cried Peredonov with an expression of terror on his face. "Why did you let it out?"

"What could I do—sew it's tail to my skirt?" asked Varvara with annoyance.

Volodin snickered. Peredonov thought that perhaps the cat had gone to the police lieutenant to tell everything it knew about him, even where and why he went out at night. It would reveal everything and even meow things that never happened. Trouble! Peredonov sat down in a chair by the table, lowered his head, and, crumpling the edge of the tablecloth, he fell into despondent contemplation.

"Cats always return to their old homes," said Volodin, "because cats get used to a place but not a master. One should swing a cat around when you transfer it to a new home, and don't show it the way, otherwise it will certainly run away."

Peredonov listened and was comforted.

"So you think it's run away to the old house, Pavlusha?" he asked.

"Without a doubt, Ardasha," replied Volodin.

Peredonov stood up and shouted, "Well, let's drink up, Pavlushka!"

Volodin snickered. "That's all right," he said. "It's always all right to have a drink."

"But we must get the cat back from there!" decided Peredonov.

"Some treasure!" replied Varvara with a smirk. "I'll send Klavdiushka after supper."

They sat down to eat. Volodin was in a good mood and he joked and laughed. His laugh sounded to Peredonov like the bleating of that ram on the street.

"And why should he plot evil against me?" thought Peredonov. "What does he need?" And Peredonov thought that perhaps he could get Volodin on his side. "Listen Pavlushka," he said, "if you don't do me any harm, I'll buy you a pound of sugar candy every week, the very best sort—suck them to my health."

Volodin laughed, but then assumed an injured expression and said, "I have not agreed to harm you, Ardal'on Borisych, and I don't need your sugar candy anyway because I don't like them."

Peredonov became depressed.

"Stop playing the fool, Ardal'on Borisych," said Varvara with a smirk. "Why should he harm you?"

"Any fool can do you harm," said Peredonov sadly.

"Volodin stuck out his lips and shook his head in an injured manner. "If that's what you think of me, Ardal'on Borisych," he said, "then I can only say, I thank you humbly. If that's what you think of me, what should I do after this? In what way should I take this?"

"Drink your vodka, Pavlushka, and pour me some," said Peredonov.

"Don't pay any attention to him, Pavel Vasil'evich," Varvara consoled Volodin. "He's only talking—his head doesn't know what his tongue is jabbering."

Volodin said nothing and, maintaining his injured look, began to pour the vodka from the decanter into the glasses.

"How is it you're not afraid to drink vodka he pours, Ardal'on Borisych?" said Varvara with a smirk. "Maybe he's doing something to it—don't you see his lips moving?"

An expression of terror showed on Peredonov's face. He caught hold of the glass which Volodin had filled and dashed the vodka to the floor, screaming, *"Chur menya, chur, chur, chur!* A curse on the curser—may the evil tongue go dry, may the black eye burst. Death to him, *chur-perechur menya."* Then he turned to Volodin with a malicious face, made an offensive gesture, and said, "That's for you. You're clever, but I'm more clever."

Varvara laughed loudly. With a wavering, injured voice, Volodin said, as if he were bleating, "You're the one, Ardal'on Borisych, who knows and pronounces all sorts of magic words, but I have never studied magic. I didn't say a charm over your vodka or anything else, but maybe it's you who've been enchanting my brides away."

"That's likely!" said Peredonov angrily. "I don't need your brides—I can get better ones myself."

"You cast a spell on my eye to make it burst," continued Volodin, "but just watch out that your own glasses don't burst first."

Peredonov grabbed hold of his glasses in fear. "Nonsense!" he growled. "Your tongue is too free."

Varvara looked at Volodin warningly and said angrily, "Don't make malicious remarks, Pavel Vasil'evich. Eat your soup before it gets cold. Eat, you malicious thing!"

She thought that perhaps Ardal'on Borisych had calmed down now. Volodin began to eat his soup. There was a momentary silence, and then Volodin said in an injured voice, "No wonder I dreamed that I was being smeared with honey last night. You were the one smearing me, Ardal'on Borisych."

"You should be smeared, but in another way," said Varvara crossly.

"What for, if I may ask? I haven't done anything," said Volodin.

"Because you have a nasty tongue," explained Varvara. "One shouldn't babble everything that comes into one's head—there's a time for everything."

20 : ಕಾಕಾ

In the evening Peredonov went to his club—he had been asked to play cards. Gudaevsky, the notary, was also there. Peredonov was afraid when he saw him, but Gudaevsky conducted himself civilly, and Peredonov felt more at ease.

They played for a long time and drank a good deal. Late at night, in the barroom, Gudaevsky suddenly bounded up to Peredonov and, without any explanation, struck him on the face several times, smashed his

glasses, and abruptly departed from the club. Peredonov offered no resistance—he pretended to be drunk,
collapsed onto the floor, and began to snore. They
shook him awake and sent him home.

The next day the whole town was talking about this
scuffle.

That evening Varvara had had an opportunity to
steal Peredonov's first forged letter. Grushina demanded that she do this, so that later a difference in
the two forgeries might not be noticed. Peredonov
usually carried this letter with him, but by chance he
had left it at home today. While changing jackets he
had taken it out of his pocket and put it under a textbook on his dresser, where he promptly forgot it. Varvara burned it over a candle at Grushina's.

When, late at night, Peredonov returned and Varvara saw his smashed glasses, he told her that they had
broken by themselves. She believed him and decided
that Volodin's wicked tongue was at fault. Peredonov
himself also felt this way. But on the next day Grushina
described the fight in the club to Varvara at length.

In the morning, when he was getting dressed, Peredonov remembered the letter but could find it no-
where—he was terrified. "Varvara, where is the letter?"
he cried in a wild voice.

Varvara was disconcerted. "What letter?" she asked,
looking at Peredonov with frightened, evil eyes.

"The Princess's!" screamed Peredonov.

Varvara managed to get hold of herself and said with
an insolent leer, "How should I know where it is! You
must have thrown it into the wastebasket, and Klavdiushka burned it. Search your room, if it's still to be
found."

Peredonov went to the gymnasium in a gloomy
mood. He remembered the unpleasant happenings of
the previous day. He thought about Kramarenko: how

had this nasty little boy dared to call him a villain? It meant he was not afraid of Peredonov. Perhaps he knew something about Peredonov? Perhaps he would inform on him.

In class Kramarenko stared at him and smiled, which terrified Peredonov even more.

During the third recess Peredonov was again summoned to see the headmaster. He went, vaguely foreseeing something unpleasant.

Rumors about Peredonov's activities were coming to Khripach from all sides. That morning he had been told about yesterday's goings on in the club. Also, yesterday after classes Volodya Bul'tyakov, who had been punished for several days by his housemother because of Peredonov's complaint, came to see him. Afraid of a second visit with similar consequences, the boy complained to the headmaster.

In a dry, restrained voice Khripach gave Peredonov an account of these rumors—from reliable sources, he added—to the effect that Peredonov visited the students' lodgings, told their parents or guardians inaccurate things about the doings and conduct of their children, and demanded that they be whipped, as a consequence of which serious unpleasantnesses often took place with the parents, as, for example, happened yesterday in the club with the notary Gudaevsky. Peredonov listened with apprehension and hostility. Khripach became silent.

"What of it?" said Peredonov crossly. "He was the one who hit me—is that allowed? He had no right to take a poke at me. He doesn't go to church—he worships a monkey and his son belongs to the same sect. He should be reported—he is a socialist."

Khripach watched Peredonov closely and said severely, "That doesn't concern us, and I am completely at a loss to understand what you mean by your original statement 'he worships a monkey.' In my opinion there is no need to enrich the history of religion with newly formed cults. And concerning the insulting assault upon you, I would advise that you take that to court. The very best thing for you to do would be to leave our gymnasium. This would be the best thing to do, both for you personally and for the gymnasium."

"I am going to be an inspector," retorted Peredonov angrily.

"Until that time," continued Khripach, "you should restrain yourself from such strange actions. I am sure you will agree that such conduct is unbecoming a teacher and injures the respect of the teacher in the eyes of his pupils. You yourself will agree that to go about to homes having boys whipped . . ." Khripach did not finish but merely shrugged his shoulders.

"What do you mean!" retorted Peredonov. "I did it for their own good."

"Please, let us not argue," interrupted Khripach sharply. "I demand of you in the strictest fashion that this not be repeated any more."

Peredonov angrily looked at the headmaster.

That evening they decided to hold a housewarming. They invited all their acquaintances. Peredonov went through all the rooms to see that everything was in order and that there was nothing for which they could report him.

"Well, everything seems all right," he thought. "The forbidden books are not in sight, the icon lamps are lit, the pictures of the tsars are hanging on the wall in the place of honor."

Suddenly Mickiewicz winked at Peredonov from the wall.

"He might cause trouble," thought Peredonov fearfully, and he quickly took down the portrait and hid it in the bathroom, from where he took Pushkin and hung him in its place. "After all, Pushkin was a courtier," he thought as he hung him on the wall in the dining room.

Then he recalled that they would be playing cards during the evening, and he decided to look at the cards. He took an opened pack which had only been used once and began to go through the cards as if searching for something in them. The faces of the royal cards did not please him because of their large eyes.

The last time he had played, it had seemed to him that the cards were smirking like Varvara. Even one of the six of spades had had an insolent appearance and wiggled indecently.

Peredonov gathered together all the cards he had, and with a sharp pair of scissors he punctured the eyes of the royal cards so they would not stare at him. At first he did this with the used cards, but afterwards he also did it to the new ones. As he did all this he kept looking around as if he were afraid he would be detected. Fortunately for him, Varvara was busy in the kitchen, and she did not look into the rooms—she could hardly leave such an abundance of delicacies for Klavdiya to help herself to. When she needed something from one of the rooms, she sent Klavdiya for it. Each time that Klavdiya came in, Peredonov started and hid the scissors in his pocket, pretending that he was playing solitaire.

But while Peredonov was depriving the kings and the queens of the possibility of annoying him with their stares again, an unpleasantness was approaching him from another side. His old hat, which Peredonov had thrown on top of the stove of his former apartment so that he wouldn't wear it, had been found by Ershova. She suspected that the hat had not been left there by chance: her former tenants hated her, and it was very possible, thought Ershova, that they had spitefully put some sort of curse on the hat so that no one would rent the apartment. In fear and anger she took the hat to a gypsy.

The woman looked the hat over, whispered mysteriously and sternly over it, and spat on four sides. "They have done an awful thing to you," she said to Ershova, "but you will pay them back. A powerful witch cast the spell, but I am even cleverer, and I will say a counterspell and take care of his."

And for a long time she continued to mumble things over it, until, when she had received generous compensation from Ershova, she told her to give the hat to a red-haired boy and have him bring it to Peredonov's and give it to the first person he met, and immediately run away without looking back.

It so happened that the first red-haired boy Ershova came across was one of the locksmith's sons who had a grudge against Peredonov for having told about their nighttime mischief. He agreed with pleasure to do the job for five kopecks, and on the way he diligently spat into the hat on his own account. He met Varvara head on in the hallway at Peredonov's, and he thrust the hat into her hands and ran away so quickly that Varvara did not have time to recognize him.

Peredonov had scarcely finished blinding the last knave when Varvara entered the room, surprised and even frightened. "Ardal'on Borisych," she said in a voice trembling from excitement, "look at this!"

Peredonov glanced at it and froze with terror. That very hat which he had tried to get rid of was now in Varvara's hands crumpled, dusty, and with scarcely a trace of its former magnificence. "Where, where did this come from?" he asked gasping with terror.

In a frightened voice Varvara told how she had received this hat from a speedy boy who seemed to have sprung up out of the earth before her and then to have been swallowed up by the earth again. "This could be the work of no one but Ershova," she said. "She put a charm against you on the hat, there's no doubt about it."

Peredonov mumbled something unintelligible, and his teeth chattered with fear. Gloomy fears and forebodings oppressed him. He walked up and down frowning, while the gray *nedotykomka* ran about under chairs and tittered.

The guests came early, bringing many tarts, apples, and pears to the housewarming. Varvara accepted everything happily, saying, merely from courtesy, "Well, what is this? Oh, you shouldn't have gone to the trouble." But if it seemed to her that they had brought something cheap or poor, then she was angry. She was also displeased when two guests brought the same thing.

Without wasting any time, they sat down to cards. They played a form of blackjack at two tables.

"Good lord!" cried Grushina. "My king is blinded!"

"Yes, and my queen has no eyes," said Prepolovenskaya when she examined her cards. "Yes, and the knave too."

The guests began to scrutinize their cards with laughter.

"Now I see why the cards are rough," said Prepolovensky. "They were sticking together on me, and I kept feeling them. What kind of rough backs are these, I thought, and it turns out that it was these holes through them. That's what makes the cards adhere."

Everyone laughed—only Peredonov remained gloomy. "Well, you know my Ardal'on Borisych," said Varvara with a smirk. "He's always playing pranks, always thinking up different jokes."

"But why did you do this?" asked Rutilov with a loud laugh.

"What do they need eyes for?" said Peredonov sullenly. "They don't have to look."

They all laughed, but Peredonov remained sullen and was silent. It seemed to him that the blinded figures were making faces, laughing, and winking at him with gaping holes where their eyes had been.

"Perhaps they've managed to learn to look through their noses," thought Peredonov.

He was unlucky—as almost always—and it seemed to him that an expression of laughter and malice was on the faces of the kings, queens, and knaves. The queen of spades even gritted her teeth, evidently infuriated that she had been blinded. Finally, after a heavy loss, Peredonov grabbed the pack of cards and began to tear them to pieces in a fury. The guests roared.

With her usual smirk Varvara said, "This man of mine is always like this—he drinks and then begins to play pranks."

"You mean because he's drunk?" said Prepolovenskaya bitingly. "Listen to what your cousin thinks of you, Ardal'on Borisych."

Varvara colored and said angrily, "What are you trying to read into my words?" Prepolovenskaya smiled and said nothing. They took a new pack of cards instead of the mutilated ones and continued the game.

Suddenly a crash was heard—the windowpane had been broken, and a stone fell to the floor near the table where Peredonov was sitting. Under the window could be heard quiet talking, laughter, and then the sound of rapidly receding footsteps. Everyone jumped up from his place in alarm; the women—as always—screamed. They picked up the stone and looked at it fearfully, but no one dared go near the window. Instead, they sent Klavdiya out into the street, and only when she reported that the street was empty did they begin to examine the broken windowpane.

Volodin suggested that the stone had been thrown by gymnasium students. The guess seemed likely, and everyone glanced significantly at Peredonov. Peredonov frowned and mumbled something unintelligible. The guests began to talk about how insolent and dissolute boys are.

The guilty ones were, of course, not students but the locksmith's sons.

"The headmaster put the students up to it," declared Peredonov suddenly. "He goes out of his way to pick on me, and he thought up this."

"Quite a prank!" cried Rutilov with a laugh. Everyone laughed.

But Grushina said, "What would you expect from such a venomous man. He'll do anything, but not himself—he stands on the side and puts his sons up to it."

"It makes no difference that they're aristocrats," bleated Volodin in an offended voice. "One can expect anything from them."

Many of the guests thought that he was perhaps right, and they stopped laughing.

"You're unlucky with glass, Ardal'on Borisych," said Rutilov. "First your glasses were broken and now your window." This brought a fresh outbreak of laughter.

"Broken glass means a long life," said Prepolovenskaya with a suppressed smile.

When Peredonov and Varvara were preparing to go to sleep, it seemed to Peredonov that Varvara had something evil on her mind. He took all the knives and forks away from her and hid them under the bed.

"I know you," he said in a slow, dull way. "Just as soon as you marry me, you'll report me to get me out of the way so that you will receive a pension while I'll be serving time in Petropavlovsky prison."

During the night Peredonov became delirious. Nebulous terrible figures walked about noiselessly—kings and knaves swinging their scepters. They whispered and tried to hide from Peredonov and stealthily crept towards him under the pillow. But soon they became bolder and began to walk and run and fly about Peredonov everywhere—on the floor, the bed, the pillows. They whispered and teased Peredonov, stuck out their tongues at him, made terrible faces at him, stretching their mouths hideously. Peredonov saw that they were all small and mischievous and that they would not kill him, but merely mock him, boding evil. But he was terrified, and he muttered chants, fragments of spells he had heard in childhood. Soon he began to curse at them and to drive them away, waving his arms and crying out in a hoarse voice.

Varvara woke up and crossly asked, "What are you shouting about, Ardal'on Borisych? You won't let me get any sleep."

"The queen of spades is always crawling round in a mattress ticking dressing gown," mumbled Peredonov.

Varvara got up, and, grumbling and cursing, she gave Peredonov some sort of drops to quiet him down.

In the local district paper there appeared a short article about how a certain Madame K. whipped the students who boarded in her house—sons of the best district gentry. Notary Gudaevsky indignantly carried this news all over town.

And various other foolish rumors were circulating in the town about the local gymnasium: they talked about a girl who was disguised as a schoolboy, and later the name of Pyl'nikov began to be connected with Ludmila's. His comrades began to tease Sasha about being in love with Ludmila. At first he paid little attention to their jokes, but then from time to time he began to get angry and to defend Ludmila declaring that no such thing had happened.

And because of all this, he began to be ashamed to go to Ludmila's, although it made him want to go even more. Confused, burning feelings of shame and attraction excited him, and vaguely passionate visions filled his imagination.

21 : ૬✺૬✺

On Sunday, when Peredonov and Varvara were having lunch, someone came into the hall. Varvara, as was her habit, went up to the door stealthily and looked out through the crack. She returned just as quietly to the table and whispered, "The postman. We have to give him some vodka—he's brought another letter."

Peredonov silently nodded his head—he wasn't stingy about a glass of vodka.

"Postman, come in!" called Varvara.

The letter carrier entered the room. He dug in his bag and pretended that he was searching for the letter. Varvara poured some vodka into a large glass and cut a piece of pie. The letter carrier looked at what she was doing with longing. Meanwhile Peredonov was trying to think whom the mailman resembled. Finally, he remembered—this was the same red-haired, pimpled knave who had made him lose so much at cards not long ago.

"Maybe he'll trick me again," thought Peredonov sullenly, and he made an insulting gesture to the postman in his pocket.

The red-haired knave gave a letter to Varvara.

"Here you are," he said respectfully. He thanked them for the vodka, drank it down, made a quacking sound, and then grabbed the pie, and left.

Varvara turned the letter over in her hands and, without unsealing it, handed it over to Peredonov. "Well, read it; it seems that it's from the Princess again," she said with her leer. "It would be better if she gave you the job rather than just continuing to write to you."

Peredonov's hands were shaking. He tore open the envelope and quickly read through the letter. Then he jumped from his place, waved the letter about, and shouted, "Hurrah! There are three inspector positions, and I may choose any one I want. Hurrah, Varvara, we've got it!"

He began to dance in circles around the room. With his never-changing red face and his dull eyes, he seemed strangely like a great mechanical dancing doll. Varvara smirked and watched him happily.

"Well now it's all set, Varvara—we'll get married," he cried. He seized Varvara by the shoulders and began to whirl her around the table stamping with his feet. "A Russian dance, Varvara!" he screamed. Varvara set her hands on her hips and struck out into a dance, while Peredonov danced in front of her in a crouch.

Volodin came in and happily bleated, "The future inspector is doing a wild *trepak!*"

"Dance, Pavlushka!" screamed Peredonov.

Klavdiya peeked out from behind the door, and Volodin called to her, laughing and making faces, "Dance, Klavdiushka—you too! Everyone together! We'll entertain the future inspector!" Klavdiya squealed and glided into the dance, moving her shoulders back and forth. Volodin jauntily turned about in front of her—he crouched, he whirled, he jumped forward, he clapped his hands. He was especially dashing when he lifted a knee and clapped his hands beneath it. The floor trembled under their heels. Klavdiya was overjoyed because her partner was such a graceful, young rake.

When they became tired, they sat down at the table, while Klavdiya ran into the kitchen laughing gaily. They drank vodka and beer, smashed bottles and glasses, and roared with laughter. They waved their hands and hugged and kissed each other. Later, Peredonov ran off to the town park with Volodin—Peredonov was anxious to brag about his letter.

They found the usual crowd in the billiard room. Peredonov showed the letter to his friends. It made a great impression. Everyone looked at it credulously. Rutilov grew pale and, mumbling something, spat.

"The postman brought it to me!" exclaimed Peredonov. "I opened it myself, so there can be no trickery about it."

And his friends all looked at him with respect. A letter from a Princess!

From the park Peredonov went straight to Vershina's. He walked rapidly and evenly, swinging his arms in time and mumbling something to himself; it seemed as though there were no expression on his face—it was immutable like that of a wound-up doll, and there was nothing but a devouring fire gleaming lifelessly in his eyes.

The day was extremely clear and hot. Marta was sitting in the summerhouse knitting a sock. Her thoughts were vague and pious. At first she thought about her sins, but then she directed her thoughts to a more pleasant subject and began to contemplate her virtues. Her thoughts began to be shrouded in drowsiness, and the less and less the images were intelligible in words, the more the clarity of their fantasmal features increased. The virtues stood before her like enormous, handsome dolls in white dresses, radiant and fragrant.

They promised her rewards and jingled keys in their hands, while bridal veils fluttered on their heads.

Yet one was strange and unlike the others. She promised nothing, but merely stared reproachfully, and her lips moved with an unuttered threat. It seemed that if she said a word it would be terrifying. Marta guessed that this was her conscience. She was dressed all in black, this strange and terrible visitor, and she had black eyes and black hair. Suddenly she began to talk about something, rapidly and without pause but distinctly. She looked exactly like Vershina. Marta started and replied something to her question, answering almost unconsciously, and then the dream overpowered Marta.

The conscience, or Vershina, sat down opposite her and rapidly and distinctly said something that was incomprehensible, while smoking something exotic. She was quiet, but firm and insistent that everything be as she wished. Marta wanted to look this bothersome visitor straight in the eyes, but somehow she was unable to. The visitor smiled strangely, mumbled something, and her eyes roamed somewhere and stopped on far-off mysterious objects upon which Marta was afraid to look . . .

Loud conversation awakened Marta. Peredonov was standing in the summerhouse greeting Vershina in a loud voice. Marta looked fearfully about. Her heart was pounding, her eyes were barely open, and her thoughts were still wandering. Where was her conscience? Or had it not been there at all? Why shouldn't it be here now?

"You were sound asleep," said Peredonov to her. "You were snoring your head off. Are you studying lumber mills?" *

* *Sosna* means "pine"; *so sna* means "from sleep." *Sonya* is a diminutive form of Sof'ya and also means "sleepyhead."

Marta did not understand his witticism, but smiled, guessing from the smile on Vershina's lips that he had said something that was supposed to be funny.

"You should be called Sof'ya and not Marta," continued Peredonov.

"Why is that?" asked Marta.

"Because you're always sleeping on the sofa."

Peredonov sat down on the sofa next to Marta and said, "I have some news, it's very important."

"Well, if you have some news, share it with us," said Vershina, and Marta at once envied Vershina's great facility with words that enabled her to express the simple question: what sort of news have you got?

"Guess," said Peredonov sullenly and triumphantly.

"How can I guess what news you have," replied Vershina. "Simply tell us, and then we'll know what your news is."

Peredonov was unhappy that they did not want to guess the news. He became silent and sat there awkwardly bent over, staring dully and grimly straight ahead. Vershina smoked and smiled wryly, revealing her dark yellow teeth.

"I know how I can guess your news," she said after she had been silent awhile. "Let me tell your fortune by cards. Marta, bring the cards from the house."

Marta stood up, but Peredonov angrily stopped her. "Sit down and don't bother. I don't wish it. Guess it yourself, and leave me alone. You can't get the answer at my expense. Here, I'll show you something that will make your mouths hang open."

Peredonov promptly drew his wallet out of his pocket, took the letter in its envelope out of it, and showed it to Vershina without letting go of it. "Look," he said, "an envelope. And there's a letter in it." He drew out the letter and read it slowly with a dull expression of malicious satisfaction in his eyes. Vershina was astounded. She had not believed in the Princess to the last, but now she realized that Marta had no more hope with Peredonov.

She smiled crookedly and with annoyance, "Well, that's lucky for you," she said.

Marta, sitting with a surprised and fearful face, smiled in confusion.

"Now who's got the upper hand?" asked Peredonov full of spiteful joy. "You thought that I was a fool, but I have turned out cleverer than you. You spoke about an envelope—well, here's the envelope. No, this matter is on the up and up."

He put his fist down on the table, but he did it neither strongly nor loudly, and his movement and the sound of his words had a weird indifference about them, as though he were a stranger and far removed from what he was doing.

Vershina and Marta exchanged glances in a distasteful and puzzled way.

"What are you looking at each other for?" said Peredonov coarsely. "There's nothing to exchange glances about: now I'm going to marry Varvara of course. Many young ladies have tried to catch me here."

Vershina sent Marta after cigarettes, and Marta happily ran out of the summerhouse. On the sandy paths scattered with fallen leaves, she felt freer and more relaxed. She met barefooted Vladya near the house, and she became even more happy and gay. "He's decided that he's going to marry Varvara," she said happily, lowering her voice, and pulling her brother into the house.

Meanwhile Peredonov, not waiting for Marta, got up to say good-bye. "I have no time," he said. "Getting married's not like tying your shoelaces, you know."

Vershina did not detain him and parted with him coldly. She was terribly vexed: she still had had the faint hope of fixing Marta up with Peredonov and taking Murin herself, but now the last hope had vanished. This was to be a hard, tearful day for Marta!

As Peredonov left Vershina's, he decided he wanted to have a smoke, but he suddenly saw a policeman standing by himself on the corner nibbling sunflower seeds. Peredonov became depressed. "Another spy," he thought. "They're watching me so that they can find fault with me." He did not dare to smoke the cigarette which he had taken out, but went up to the policeman and timidly asked, "Is it all right to smoke here, Mr. Policeman?"

The policeman put his hand to his cap and respectfully inquired, "Why do you wish to know, sir?"

"A cigarette," explained Peredonov. "May one have a little smoke here?"

"There's no law that says you can't," answered the policeman evasively.

"There isn't any?" said Peredonov with sadness in his voice.

"No, there's none, none at all. We haven't been ordered to stop gentlemen from smoking, and, if such a law has been passed, I don't know about it."

"If there isn't one, I still won't start," said Peredonov meekly. "I'm a law-abiding person. I'll even throw the cigarette away. I'm a state councilor, you know."

Peredonov crumpled up the cigarette and threw it to the ground, and, fearing that he had already said too much, he hurried home. The policeman looked after him in perplexity. Finally he decided that the gentleman had had "a wee bit too much," and, comforted by this explanation, he again began calmly to peel his sunflower seeds.

"The street has hunched up," muttered Peredonov. The street was on a not very steep incline and on the other side there was a dip. The arch of the street with a shack at either side was accentuated against the sad, blue, evening sky. This still region of poor life was absorbed in itself and was grieving and tormenting itself terribly. The trees reached their branches over the fences. They dipped down and blocked the way, and their whisper was mocking and threatening. A ram stood at the crosswalk and looked dully at Peredonov.

Suddenly he heard a bleating laugh from around the corner, and Volodin came into view and went up to Peredonov to greet him. Peredonov looked at him sullenly and thought about the sheep that had just been standing there and had suddenly disappeared.

"Of course!" he thought. "It was Volodin turned into a sheep. It's not an accident that he's so similar to a sheep and that you can't tell whether he's laughing or bleating."

These thoughts so occupied him that he completely missed what Volodin said to him in greeting.

"Why are you kicking me, Pavlushka?" said Peredonov dejectedly.

Volodin grinned and answered with a bleat, "I'm not kicking you, Ardal'on Borisych, I'm shaking hands with you. Maybe where you come from they kick with their hands, but where I come from kicking is done with the feet, and even then it's not people but, if I may say so, ponies."

"Maybe you'll butt me then," growled Peredonov.

Volodin took offense and said in a jarring voice, "I haven't grown any horns yet, Ardal'on Borisych, and perhaps you'll grow horns sooner than I will."

"You have a long tongue, and it blabs things it shouldn't," said Peredonov angrily.

"If you think that of me, Ardal'on Borisych," said Volodin quickly, "then I won't say anything."

And his face appeared utterly dejected, his lips sticking way out. Nevertheless, he walked alongside of

Peredonov—he still had not had dinner and he counted on dining at Peredonov's house that day: fortunately, they had invited him in the morning.

Important news awaited Peredonov at home, and, even in the hallway, one could tell that something unusual had happened. A racket of frightened exclamations could be heard in the rooms. Peredonov thought that dinner was still not ready, and, when they saw him coming, they became frightened and were hurrying. He was pleased that they were so afraid of him! But it turned out that there was another cause. Varvara ran out into the entranceway and cried, "They've returned the cat!"

In her fear she did not at once notice Volodin. Her clothing was, as usual, slovenly. She had on a greasy blouse and a dirty, gray skirt and worn-out slippers. Her hair was uncombed and disheveled. "It's that Irishka!" she excitedly told Peredonov. "She's played another trick on us out of spite. A boy ran up again, and he was carrying the cat. He threw it down, and the cat had rattles tied to its tail—that's what the noise is. The cat has gone under the sofa and won't come out."

Peredonov was terrified.

"What can we do?" he asked.

"You're younger, Pavel Vasil'evich," said Varvara, "drag it out from under the sofa."

"We'll get him, we'll get him," said Volodin giggling, and he went into the living room.

Somehow or other they dragged the cat out and took the rattles off its tail. Peredonov found some burrs and began to stick them onto the cat's fur. The cat hissed furiously and ran into the kitchen. Peredonov, tired from struggling with the cat, sat down in his usual pose with his elbows on the arms of the easy chair, his fingers intertwined, his legs crossed, and his face motionless and sullen.

.   .   .

Peredonov took better care of the Princess's second letter than he had of the first. He always carried it with him in his wallet, and he showed it to everyone, assuming a mysterious air as he did. He watched vigilantly to see that no one took his letter away. He would not let anyone hold it, and after each showing he would put it in his wallet, place the wallet in the breast pocket of his jacket, button up the jacket, and cast grave and significant glances at those with whom he was talking.

"Why do you carry it around like that?" Rutilov sometimes asked with a laugh.

"Just in case," said Peredonov morosely. "Who knows—you might filch it from me!"

"I would obviously be sent to Siberia," said Rutilov laughing, and he slapped Peredonov on the shoulder.

But Peredonov was unruffled and retained his pomposity. He had of late generally been acting more important than usual.

"Yes," he often boasted, "I shall be an inspector. You'll be wasting away here, while I'll have two districts under my authority. And then perhaps three. Ho, ho, ho!"

He firmly believed that very shortly he would receive an inspector's position. More than once he said to the schoolteacher, Falastov: "I'll get you out of here, too, brother."

Falastov became very respectful in his attitude towards Peredonov.

22 : 🐦🐦

Peredonov began to go to church often. He would stand in a conspicuous place and cross himself more frequently than was necessary and then stand like a post and stare dully ahead. He imagined that spies were hiding behind the pillars and peeping out trying to make him laugh. But he withstood them.

Laughter sounded in Peredonov's ears—the quiet, smothered laughter, the giggling, and the whispering of the Rutilov girls. At times it reached an extraordinary intensity as if the cunning girls were laughing right into his ears to make him laugh and to disgrace him. But Peredonov withstood them.

Occasionally, the cloudy blue *nedotykomka* appeared in the clouds of incense smoke. Its eyes glittered with fire. Sometimes it moved about in the air with a faint tinkling noise, though never for long; generally, it rolled about at the feet of the worshipers taunting and torturing Peredonov continually. It wanted, of course, to frighten Peredonov so that he would leave church before the end of Mass. But he understood its cunning plan—and he withstood it.

The church service, so dear to so many people not because of the words or the rituals but because of its intrinsic essence, was incomprehensible to Peredonov. Therefore, it frightened him. The swinging of the censers terrified him and seemed like mysterious witchcraft. "Why is he swinging it so much?" he thought.

The garments of the priests seemed to him coarse,

offensively colored rags, and, when he looked at a robed priest, he grew spiteful and wanted to tear away the liturgical vestments and smash the sacred vessels. The church rites and mysteries seemed to him to be evil sorcery intended to subjugate the common people.

"He's crumbled the wafer into the wine," he thought angrily about the priest. "It's cheap wine—they fool the people in order to get more money to conduct their ceremonies."

The secret of the eternal transubstantiation of inert matter into a force breaking the bonds of death was forever screened from him. He was a walking corpse, an absurd blend of disbelief in the living God and His Christ and belief in sorcery!

People began to leave the church. The rural schoolmaster, Machigin, a plain young fellow, was standing near the girls, smiling and chatting animatedly with them. Peredonov thought that it was unfitting for him to behave so freely before a future inspector. Machigin had on a straw hat, but Peredonov recalled that sometime during the summer he had seen him outside of town in a uniform cap with a cockade. Peredonov decided to complain. As it happened, Inspector Bogdanov was standing right there. Peredonov went up to him and said, "Did you know that your Machigin wears a hat with a cockade? He's playing the gentleman."

Bogdanov was alarmed and began to tremble, making his dull Adam's apple quiver. "He has no right! He has no right whatsoever!" he said anxiously, blinking his red eyes.

"He may not have the right, but he wears it," complained Peredonov. "I told you a long time ago that the discipline has to be tightened up, or else every boorish *muzhik* will be wearing a cockade—that's what'll happen!"

Bogdanov, who had been frightened enough by Peredonov before, was now shaking all over. "But how could he dare?" he whined. "I shall speak with him immediately, immediately, and deal with him most strictly." He said good-bye to Peredonov and hurriedly began to trot to his house.

Volodin, walking next to Peredonov, said in a reproachfully bleating voice, "Wearing a cockade. Now I ask you! It's as though he had become an official. How can he do it!"

"You can't wear a cockade either," said Peredonov.

"I can't, and I don't need to," replied Volodin. "Still, sometimes even I put on a cockade—but I know when and where to do it. I go out of town, and then I put it on. I enjoy it, and there's no one to stop me. And it makes the *muzhiks* more respectful when they see it."

"A cockade doesn't suit your snout, Pavlushka," said Peredonov. "And move away from me, you're getting dust on me with your hooves."

Volodin maintained an offended silence but continued to walk beside him.

"The Rutilov wenches have to be reported too," said Peredonov in a preoccupied way. "They only go to church to laugh and talk. They paint themselves, get all dressed up, and then they go to church. And they steal incense and make perfume out of it—that's why they always stink so."

"You don't say!" said Volodin, shaking his head with his stupid eyes protruding.

The shadow of a cloud running quickly along the ground brought a feeling of dread on Peredonov. The gray *nedotykomka* sometimes glimmered in the clouds of dust stirred up by the wind. Whenever the wind moved the grass, it seemed to Peredonov that the gray *nedotykomka* ran along it feeding on it and stuffing itself.

"Why should there be grass in the town?" he thought. "What disorder! They should root it out."

A branch stirred in a tree, and then, gathering itself together and showing black, it cawed and flew away. Peredonov shivered, gave a wild cry, and ran home. Volodin anxiously ran after him with a puzzled expression in his bulging eyes, holding his hat to his head and waving his cane.

That very day Bogdanov summoned Machigin. Before entering the inspector's house, Machigin stood on the street with his back to the sun, took off his hat, and combed his hair with his fingers, watching his shadow as a guide.

Bogdanov immediately fell on Machigin. "What's all this about you, young man, eh? Just what have you been up to, eh?"

"What's wrong?" asked Machigin casually, toying with his straw hat and swinging his left foot.

Because he was intending to lecture him, Bogdanov did not ask him to sit down. "How is it that the likes of you wears a cockade, young man, eh? What made you decide to take the liberty, eh?" he asked putting on an expression of severity. His dull Adam's apple was moving up and down.

Machigin blushed but replied glibly: "And why not —don't I have the right?"

"Do you imagine yourself an official, eh? An official?" asked the excited Bogdanov. "What sort of official are you, eh? A registry clerk, eh?"

"It's a sign of the teacher's calling," said Machigin smartly, and suddenly he smiled sweetly as he recalled how important his job as a teacher was.

"Carry a cane in your hands," advised Bogdanov shaking his head. "A cane is the real sign of a teacher's calling."

"But Sergei Potapych," said Machigin in an injured

voice, "an ordinary cane! Anyone can carry a cane, but a cockade gives one prestige."

"And what do you need prestige for, eh? Prestige for what, for what, eh?" asked Bogdanov attacking the young man. "What sort of prestige do you need, eh? Do you imagine yourself an official!"

"But Sergei Potapych," argued Machigin soberly, "this immediately awakens a great deal of respect in the uneducated peasant class—they've been bowing much lower lately."

Machigin contentedly smoothed down his reddish little mustache.

"No, you can't do it, young man, you simply can't do it," said Bogdanov shaking his head mournfully.

"But Sergei Potapych, a teacher without his cockade is like the British lion without a tail," declared Machigin. "He's only a caricature of what he should be."

"What do you need a tail for, eh? Why do you need a tail, eh?" said Bogdanov excitedly. "Are you intending to go into politics, eh? And do you think it's your business to meddle in politics, eh? No, you'd best take off the cockade, young man, for Heaven's sake. One can't do as one wants, or, God preserve us, there's no telling who might find out about it!"

Machigin shrugged his shoulders and wanted to say something else, but Bogdanov interrupted him—a brilliant thought, in his estimation, had flashed across his mind. "But you came to me without a cockade, eh? Without a cockade? So you yourself must feel that it isn't permissible."

Machigin was taken aback for a moment, but he found what to say this time too: "We village schoolmasters have our privileges in the village, but in the town we are ordinary intelligentsia."

"Now listen, young man," said Bogdanov angrily, "know that this is not allowed, and, if I hear of it again, we shall dismiss you."

. . .

Grushina from time to time gave evening parties for young people from among whom she hoped to catch a husband. For appearance's sake, she also invited married friends.

This evening she was having such a party. The guests arrived early.

On the walls in Grushina's living room there were pictures hanging covered with thick muslin. Actually, there was nothing indecent about them. When Grushina with an arch, immodest smile lifted the muslin drapes, the guests found themselves staring at poorly drawn, naked women.

"Why is this woman so crooked?" asked Peredonov sullenly.

"There's nothing crooked about her," said Grushina, hotly defending the picture, "she's just twisted that way."

"Crooked," repeated Peredonov, "and her eyes are not the same, like yours."

"Well, much you understand!" said the injured Grushina. "These pictures are very good and very expensive. Artists have to paint like that."

Peredonov suddenly burst out laughing: he recalled the advice which he had given Vladya a few days ago.

"What are you neighing about?" asked Grushina.

"Nartanovich, the gymnasium student, is going to set fire to his sister Marfa's dress. I advised him to do it," he explained.

"If he does it, you've found a fool!" replied Grushina.

"Of course he'll do it," said Peredonov with assurance. "Brothers always fight with their sisters. When I was little I always played dirty tricks on my sisters—I beat the little ones up and ruined the clothes of the older ones."

"Not everyone quarrels," said Rutilov. "I, for instance, don't quarrel with my sisters."

"What do you do—kiss them perhaps?" asked Peredonov.

"You are a swine and a scoundrel, Ardal'on Borisych, and I'm going to give you a slap in the face," said Rutilov very calmly.

"Look, I don't like such jokes," replied Peredonov, and he edged away from Rutilov. "Yes," he thought, "he might really do it—there is something very nasty about his face."

"She only has one dress, a black one," he went on, talking about Marta now.

"Vershina will sew her a new one," said Varvara maliciously out of envy. "She'll make her everything for her dowry. She's such a beauty that even horses are frightened," she mumbled quietly and looked spitefully at Murin.

"It's time you got married," said Prepolovenskaya. "What are you waiting for, Ardal'on Borisych?"

The Prepolovenskys could clearly see that after the second letter Peredonov had decided definitely to marry Varvara. They also believed the letter. They began to say that they had always favored Varvara. There was no sense in their quarreling with Peredonov: it was profitable to play cards with him. Besides, there was nothing to be done—Genya would have to wait, and they would have to find a new match for her.

"Of course you should get married," said Prepolovensky. "You'll be doing a good thing, and you'll be pleasing the Princess. It will be pleasant for the Princess that you're getting married, and so you'll be pleasing her and doing a good thing. And that will really be good because, well, um, because you will be doing a good thing and it will be pleasing to the Princess."

"And I say the same thing," said Prepolovenskaya.

But Prepolovensky was unable to stop, and seeing that everyone had turned away from him, he sat down next to a young official and began to tell him the same thing.

"I have decided to get married," said Peredonov, "only Varvara and I don't know how one goes about getting married. One should do something, but I don't know what."

"It really doesn't take a great deal of cunning," said Prepolovenskaya, "and, if you want, my husband and I will arrange everything, and you can sit back and not think about anything."

"Fine," said Peredonov, "I agree. Only everything must be done well and correctly. I don't mind the money."

"Everything will be all right, don't you worry," Prepolovenskaya assured him.

Peredonov continued, listing his specifications: "Others, from stinginess, buy thin, gold-plated silver wedding rings, but I don't want mine to be anything but real gold. And instead of thin wedding bands, I even want to get wedding bracelets—that will be more expensive and impressive."

Everyone laughed.

"You can't use bracelets," said Prepolovenskaya, laughing slightly, "you have to use rings."

"Why can't I?" asked Peredonov with vexation.

"Well, because it's not done."

"And maybe it is done," said Peredonov distrustfully. "I'll have to ask a priest about this, he'll know better."

"Or, better yet, Ardal'on Borisych," advised Rutilov giggling, "order wedding belts."

"No, I don't have enough money for that," replied Peredonov, not noticing the laughter. "I'm not a banker. But recently I dreamed that I was getting married, and I had on a dress coat, and Varvara and I had golden bracelets. And two headmasters were standing behind us, holding wreaths over us and singing alleluias."

"I also had an interesting dream today," announced Volodin, "but I don't know what it was about. It seems that I was on a throne with a golden crown, and there was grass before me, and on the grass were little sheep, lots and lots of little sheep—baaa! baaa! baaa! And the little sheep were walking about and holding their heads like this, and all the time—baaa! baaa! baaa!"

Volodin walked about the room shaking his forehead and, with his lips out, bleating. The guests laughed. Volodin sat down in his place. He looked at everyone blissfully, wrinkled his eyes with pleasure, and laughed in his usual sheeplike, bleating way.

"And then what happened?" asked Grushina, winking at the guests.

"Well, there were lots and lots of sheep, and then I woke up," concluded Volodin.

"A sheep has sheepish dreams," grumbled Peredonov. "Being tsar of the sheep is nothing to brag about."

"Well I had a dream that can't be told in front of the men," said Varvara with her insolent laugh. "I'll tell it when they leave."

"Why isn't that strange, my dearest Varvara Dmitrievna, I had one like that too," replied Grushina, giggling and winking at everyone.

"Tell us," said Rutilov, "we're modest gentlemen like the ladies."

The other men also asked Varvara and Grushina to tell their dreams. But the pair exchanged glances, laughed meaningfully, and did not tell.

They all sat down to play cards. Rutilov declared that Peredonov played very well. Peredonov believed him, although today, as always, he lost. Rutilov was the winner, and because of this he was in a very good humor and spoke with more animation than usual.

The *nedotykomka* teased Peredonov. It hid somewhere near, sometimes showed itself, stuck its head out from behind a table or someone's back, and then hid again. It seemed that it was waiting for something. It was terrifying. The very appearance of the cards terrified Peredonov. There were two queens to a card.

"But where is the third?" thought Peredonov. He dully surveyed the queen of spades and then turned it over—perhaps the third was hiding behind its back.

"Ardal'on Borisych is peeking under his queen's blouse," * said Rutilov.

Everyone laughed.

Meanwhile, to the side, two young policemen sat down to play jokers. They played very rapidly. The winner laughed with joy and made a long nose at the loser, who became angry.

The smell of food arose, and Grushina called her guests to the dining room. They all went in with affected manners, pushing each other. Somehow or other they seated themselves.

"Swallow away, my dears, and fill your bellies right up to your ears," invited Grushina.

"Eat the cake for your hostess's sake!" cried Murin happily. He felt very gay looking at the vodka and thinking about how he had won.

Volodin and the two young policemen were helping themselves more liberally than anyone else—they took the best and most expensive pieces, and they devoured the caviar greedily.

"Our Pavel Vasil'evich is drunk," said Grushina with a forced laugh, "but he can still tell cake from bread."

She had hardly bought caviar for him! Thus, under the pretext of serving the ladies, she took all the best

* *Rubashka* means both "blouse" and "card back."

things away from him. But Volodin was not discouraged and was satisfied with what remained. He had succeeded in eating much of the good food in the beginning, and now it was all the same to him.

Peredonov looked at everyone chewing away, and he imagined that they were laughing at him. Why? For what? He gulped down everything that fell into his hands. He was eating both sloppily and greedily.

After dinner they again played cards. Peredonov, however, soon tired of it, and he threw down his cards, saying, "The hell with you! I have no luck. I'm tired! Varvara, let's go home."

The other guests also got up after him. In the hall Volodin saw that Peredonov had a new cane. He grinned and, turning the stick over in his hands, asked, "Ardasha, why are these fingers rolled into a little fist? What does it signify?"

Peredonov angrily took the stick out of his hands and put the handle with its insulting gesture carved in the dark wood close to Volodin's nose. "This means a fig for you—with butter,"* he said.

Volodin assumed an injured expression. "Excuse me, Ardal'on Borisych," he said. "I eat bread with butter, but I have no desire to eat a fig with butter."

Peredonov without listening to him was carefully wrapping a scarf around his neck and buttoning all the buttons on his coat.

"Why are you bundling up, Ardal'on Borisych?" asked Rutilov with a laugh. "It's warm."

"Good health is worth more than anything," replied Peredonov.

Outside it was quiet—the street was stretched out in the dark and seemed to be snoring gently. It was

* The *kukish* or *shish* (both mean "fig"), a closed fist with the thumb between the first and second fingers, is a strongly insulting gesture.

dark, gloomy, and damp. Ponderous clouds moved across the heavens.

"It has gotten dark, but why?" grumbled Peredonov. But he was not afraid now because he was walking with Varvara and was not alone.

Soon a fine, rapid, prolonged rain began to fall. Everything was still, and only the rain breathlessly babbled something quickly over and over—unclear, tiresome, melancholy phrases.

In nature Peredonov felt reflections of his own anguish and fear in the form of its hostility towards him. He was insensitive to the intrinsic, undefinable life in all nature, that life which alone is the cause of deep, true, and unfailing relations between man and nature. All nature appeared to him permeated with petty human feelings. Blinded by illusions of personality and separate existence, he could not understand the spontaneous Dionysian ecstasies triumphantly calling in nature. He was blind and pitiful—like many of us.

23 : ౙ☙ౙ☙

The Prepolovenskys undertook to make arrangements for the wedding. It was decided to have the wedding in the country about six versts from town: it would be awkward for Varvara to be married in the town as she had lived with him so many years calling herself his relative. They kept the wedding date secret. The Prepolovenskys spread a rumor that the wedding was to be on Friday, but the wedding was really to take place

Wednesday afternoon. This was done to keep the curious in town from coming.

"Don't tell when the wedding is going to be, Ardal'on Borisych, otherwise people will mess things up," Varvara repeatedly told Peredonov.

Peredonov gave the money for the cost of the wedding unwillingly and with insults to Varvara. Sometimes he would bring his cane with the fist carved into an insulting gesture on its head and say to Varvara, "Kiss it, and I'll give you the money. Don't, and I won't." She kissed it.

"What do I care, it won't split my lips," she said.

They did not tell the best men the date of the marriage until the appointed day itself so that they would not gossip. First they asked Rutilov and Volodin to be the best men, and they both readily agreed. Rutilov was expecting some amusing incident, and Volodin was flattered to play such a significant role in such an important moment in the life of such a respected person.

Then Peredonov decided that one best man was not enough for him. "You will have one, Varvara," he said, "but I need two—one is not enough because I am a big man, and it will be difficult to hold the wreath over me." And so Peredonov invited Falastov to be his second best man.

"The hell with him," grumbled Varvara. "There are already two, who needs more?"

"He has gold glasses, and the service will be more impressive with him there," said Peredonov.

On the morning of the wedding day Peredonov, as always, washed himself with warm water in order not to chill himself, and then he rouged himself, explaining, "I'll have to touch myself up every day now, otherwise they'll think I'm getting run down, and they won't make me an inspector."

Varvara disliked letting him use her rouge, but she finally had to yield to him, and Peredonov reddened his cheeks. "Veriga himself puts on make-up to appear younger," he mumbled, "so I can't get married with white cheeks."

Next, he locked himself in the bedroom. He had decided to make a mark on himself so that Volodin could not change places with him. On his chest, his belly, his elbows, and on various other places, he inked the letter "P."

"I ought to mark Volodin too, but how can I do it?" thought Peredonov ruefully. "He'll see it and rub it off."

Then it came into his head that it would not be a bad idea to put on a corset, or else they would take him for an old man if he happened to bend over. He demanded a corset from Varvara. But Varvara's corsets turned out to be too small for him—he couldn't get one of them laced up.

"I ought to have bought one earlier," he grumbled. "No one ever thinks of anything."

"Whoever heard of a man wearing a corset," retorted Varvara. "No one wears one."

"Veriga does," said Peredonov.

"But Veriga's an old man, while you, Ardal'on Borisych, are, thank God, in the prime of life."

Peredonov smiled with self-satisfaction, looked into the mirror, and said, "Yes, and I'll live for another hundred and fifty years."

The cat sneezed under the bed. "Well, the cat sneezed," said Varvara grinning, "so that means you're right."

But Peredonov suddenly frowned. The cat was by now frightening to him, and its sneezing seemed to him to be evil cunning. "It'll sneeze something it shouldn't," he thought, and he crawled under the bed and began to chase the cat. The cat mewed wildly, pressed itself against the wall, and suddenly, with a loud and piercing screech, it darted through Peredonov's hands and bounded out of the room.

"Dutch devil!" Peredonov angrily swore after it.

"It is a devil," agreed Varvara. "A completely wild cat—you can't even stroke it, just as though there were a devil in it."

The Prepolovenskys sent for the best men early in the morning. Shortly before ten they all gathered at Peredonov's.

Grushina and Sof'ya and her husband came. Vodka and *zakuska* were served. Peredonov ate little—he was sadly thinking how he could differentiate himself still more from Volodin.

"His hair is as curly as a sheep's," he thought spitefully, and he suddenly decided that he would have his hair done in a special way. He got up from the table and said, "You eat and drink, I'm not stingy, but I'm going to a hairdresser and have a Spanish hairdo."

"What does a Spanish hairdo look like?" asked Rutilov.

"You'll see."

When Peredonov left to have his hair cut, Varvara said, "He's always thinking up different things. He always imagines he sees devils. He should guzzle less brandy, the damned drunkard!"

"You'll get married, Ardal'on Borisych will receive his position, and then he'll calm down," said Prepolovenskaya with a cunning smile.

Grushina giggled. The secrecy of this marriage amused her, and she had had an urge to arrange something nasty in a way so that she wouldn't be involved. The evening before she had confidentially whispered the hour and place of the wedding to several of her friends. Early that morning she summoned the locksmith's younger son to her house, gave him five kopecks, and instructed him to wait for the newlyweds to pass by outside of town towards evening and to throw paper and litter into their carriage. The locksmith's boy gladly agreed and took an oath not to betray her.

"But you betrayed Cherepnin as soon as they whipped you," Grushina reminded him.

"We were fools," said the boy, "but now they can hang us and we won't tell." And in confirmation of his vow he ate a handful of dirt, for which Grushina gave him three extra kopecks.

At the barber's Peredonov demanded the owner himself. The owner, a young man who had graduated from public school not long ago and who read books from the district library, was finishing cutting the hair of a landowner whom Peredonov did not know. He soon was done and went up to Peredonov.

"Let him leave first," said Peredonov angrily. The landowner paid and left. Peredonov sat down before the mirror. "I want my hair cut and arranged," he said. "I have something very special and important to do today, so give me a Spanish hairdo."

A small schoolboy standing by the door snorted with amusement. The owner looked at him sternly. He had never had to give a Spanish hairdo, and he did not know what one was like or even if there was such a style. But if the gentleman ordered it, then, one had to assume, he knew what he wanted. The young barber did not wish to display his ignorance.

"It would be impossible to give one to your type of hair, sir," he said respectfully.

"And why not?" asked Peredonov offended.

"Your hair is poorly nourished," explained the hairdresser.

"What would you like me to do, pour beer over it?" growled Peredonov.

"Good gracious, why beer, sir?" asked the barber smiling affably. "Just consider that, since your head already shows through somewhat, there won't be enough left for a Spanish hairdo after it's cut."

Peredonov felt overwhelmed at the impossibility of having a Spanish hairdo. "Well, cut it as you wish," he said sadly.

"They obviously bribed this barber not to cut my hair in an elegant fashion," he thought. He shouldn't have said anything at home. Evidently, while Peredonov was walking gravely and sedately along the streets, Volodin had run like a sheep along side streets and plotted with the barber.

"Would you like me to wet your hair?" asked the barber when he had finished cutting it.

"Sprinkle me with mignonette, and a lot of it," demanded Peredonov. "You can at least make up for the other somewhat with a lot of mignonette."

"I'm sorry, but we don't carry mignonette," said the barber in confusion. "Would you like some camphor liniment?"

"You can't do anything you ought to," said Peredonov woefully. "Just sprinkle me with what you have."

He returned home in a foul mood. It was a windy day. The gates were banging and yawning and laughing in the wind. Peredonov watched them with anxiety. How could he go to get married now? But everything had been all arranged.

There were three rented carriages—it was necessary to get seated and go before the vehicles attracted attention and onlookers gathered and drove after them to watch the wedding. They divided up and left: Peredonov with Varvara, the Prepolovenskys with Rutilov, and Grushina with the other two best men.

A cloud of dust was raised in the square, and Peredonov heard the sound of axes falling. Barely visible through the dust, a wooden wall loomed and grew in size. They were tearing down a fortress. Fierce-looking, morose *muzhiks* glimmered in their red blouses.

The carriages rushed past, and the terrible vision wavered and disappeared. Peredonov glanced back in horror, but he could see nothing, and he decided not to say anything to anyone about his vision.

Sadness tormented Peredonov the whole way. Everything looked hostilely at him, and the air was seething with threatening signs. The heavens frowned. The wind blew straight towards them and was moaning about something. The trees did not wish to give shade —they kept it to themselves. And the dust rose up in the form of a long, semi-transparent, gray serpent. The sun for some reason was hidden behind the clouds— was it spying on him?

The road had many dips. Unexpected bushes, groves, and fields rose from behind bluffs; streams ran under hollow-sounding, arched, wooden bridges.

"An eyebird flew by," said Peredonov sullenly, staring into the misty, white reaches of the sky. "One eye and two wings—nothing more."

Varvara smirked—she thought that Peredonov had been drunk since morning. But she did not argue with him. "If I do," she thought, "he might get angry and call off the wedding."

In the church behind a column in a corner were hiding all four of the Rutilov sisters. Peredonov did not see them at first, but afterwards during the actual ceremony, when they came out of their ambush and moved forward, he saw them and was frightened. They did not, however, do anything wrong such as—this was what he feared at first—drive Varvara away and demand that he take one of them. They merely laughed continually. And their laughter, in the beginning quiet, resounded louder and louder and more evilly in his ears like the laughter of indomitable furies.

There were almost no outsiders in the church, only two or three old people who had come from somewhere, and this was fortunate, for Peredonov conducted himself foolishly and strangely. He yawned, grumbled, jostled Varvara, and complained about the smell of incense, wax, and *muzhiks*.

"Your sisters are always laughing," he grumbled, turning to Rutilov. "They're piercing my liver with their laughter."

Besides that, the *nedotykomka* was harassing him. It was dirty and dusty, and it was hiding under the priest's chasuble.

The church ceremonies seemed ridiculous to both Varvara and Grushina, and they giggled incessantly. The words about how a wife must cling to her husband especially amused them. Rutilov also giggled—he considered it his duty at any time and in any place to amuse the ladies. Volodin, however, conducted himself sedately and crossed himself, preserving an expression of profound contemplation upon his face. The church ceremonies meant nothing to him except that they were custom and ought to be carried out. The fulfillment of these ceremonies gave him a certain internal satisfaction: he went to church on holidays and prayed—and was forgiven. Then he sinned, repented —and was again forgiven. It was nice and convenient —all the more so because outside of church it was not necessary to think about all this church business, and consequently he guided himself by completely different, worldly rules.

The wedding had just finished, and they had not yet left the church, when suddenly something unexpected happened. A drunken crowd tumbled noisily into the church—Murin and his friends.

Murin, disheveled and dull as always, embraced Peredonov and cried, "You can't hide from us, brother! You kept it from us, you tricky fellow, but you can't make such friends angry by throwing water on us."

Exclamations were heard all around.

"Scoundrel, you didn't invite us!"

"But we're here anyway!"

"Yes, we found out anyway!"

Again the newcomers embraced and congratulated Peredonov.

"We strayed off a ways to have a drink," said Murin, "otherwise we would have given you the satisfaction of our presence from the beginning."

Peredonov glowered and did not reply to the congratulations. He was tormented by fear and anger. "They follow me everywhere," he thought sadly.

"You should have crossed your foreheads," he said angrily, "unless, perhaps, you are wishing me evil."

The guests crossed themselves, laughed, and swore blasphemously, especially the young officials. The deacon reproachfully quieted them down.

Among the guests there was one young man with a red mustache whom Peredonov did not even know. He was remarkably similar to the cat. Could they have turned his cat into a man? It was no accident that this man was continually sniffing—he had not forgotten his cat habits.

"Who told you?" Varvara angrily asked the new guests.

"Some good people, our young bride, but we have forgotten who," replied Murin.

Grushina turned around and winked. The new guests laughed but did not give her away.

"No matter what you say, Ardal'on Borisych," said Murin, "we are going to your house, and you must give us champagne—don't be miserly. You thought you could do it on the sly, but you can't make such friends angry by throwing water on us."

When the Peredonovs returned from the wedding, the sun had gone down, and the sky was all fiery and golden. But this did not please Peredonov. "They've scattered pieces of gold in the sky, and it's already falling off. Where did you ever see such waste!" he grumbled.

The locksmith's boys met them outside of town with a crowd of other street urchins. They ran alongside the carriage and hooted. Peredonov trembled with fear. Varvara swore and spat on the boys and made insulting gestures at them. The guests and the attendants laughed heartily.

When they arrived home, the whole band tumbled into Peredonov's house, screaming and roaring and whistling. They drank champagne and then started on the vodka and sat down to play cards. They caroused all night. Varvara got drunk and danced triumphantly. Peredonov also rejoiced—his place had not been taken, after all. The guests, as always, treated Varvara cynically and disrespectfully, but this seemed only natural to her.

Little changed in the daily life of the Peredonovs after the wedding, except that Varvara's attitude towards her husband became more assured and confident. It seemed as if she was less timid before her husband, although, through deep-rooted habit, she was still rather afraid of him. Peredonov, also through habit, shouted at her as before and sometimes even beat her. But even he sensed the great assurance that came over her in her new position, and this made him feel depressed. It seemed to him that, if she was not as frightened of him as before, it had to be because she had decided to carry out her criminal plan to get rid of him and substitute Volodin in his place. "I have to be on my guard," he thought.

Varvara was triumphant. She and her husband paid calls on the women in town, even those whom they barely knew. On these visits she displayed laughable pride and clumsiness. She was received everywhere, although not without surprise in many homes. Well in advance, Varvara had given the best local milliner an order for a hat from the capital for these visits. The large, colorful flowers set in abundance on the hat delighted Varvara.

The Peredonovs began their visits with the headmaster's wife, and then they went to see the wife of the marshal of the nobility.

On the day when the Peredonovs were preparing to make their calls—which the Rutilovs, of course, knew of beforehand—the sisters, curious to see how Varvara would conduct herself there, went to visit Varvara Nikolaevna Khripach. Soon the Peredonovs also arrived. Varvara curtsied to the headmaster's wife and, in a voice more jarring than usual, said, "Here we are. I beg you to be kind and gracious to us."

"I am very happy to see you," replied the headmaster's wife with effort, and she seated Varvara on the divan.

Varvara sat down with evident satisfaction in the place offered her, spread out her rustling green dress, and, attempting to conceal her embarrassment with undue familiarity, said, "I was a mamzell before, but now I've become a madam. We're namesakes—I'm Varvara, and you're Varvara—but we've never visited each other. While I was a mamzell I always sat at home —but why should I always sit behind the stove? Now Ardal'on Borisych and I will live openly. You are always welcome to visit us, and we will visit you—mooseyour to mooseyour, madam to madam."

"But it seems that you won't be living here long," said the headmaster's wife. "I have heard that your husband is going to be transferred."

"Yes, soon the paper will arrive, and we will go," replied Varvara. "But until the paper comes, we have to live here and make appearances."

Varvara actually did have hopes for the inspector's position. After the wedding she wrote the Princess a letter, but as yet she had received no answer. She decided to write again at New Year's time.

"And we thought that you were going to marry the Pyl'nikova girl, Ardal'on Borisych," said Ludmila.

"Why should I marry just anyone," said Peredonov. "I needed patronage."

"But what happened between you and Mademoiselle Pyl'nikova?" teased Ludmila. "You were courting her, weren't you? Did she refuse you?"

"I'll unmask her yet," grumbled Peredonov sullenly.

"This is an *idée fixe* with Ardal'on Borisych," said the headmaster with his dry laugh.

24 : ॐॐ

Peredonov's cat ran wild, hissed, and did not come when it was called—it had gotten completely out of hand. Peredonov was terrified of it. Sometimes Peredonov mumbled his magic chants to protect himself from it. "Will it do any good?" he thought. "The cat has powerful electricity in its fur, that's what the trouble is."

Once he thought: "The cat's fur should be trimmed." No sooner said than done. Varvara was not at home. Having slipped a bottle of cherry brandy into her pocket —there was no one to prevent it now—she had gone to Grushina's. Peredonov tied the cat to a cord, made a collar out of a handkerchief—and led the cat to the barber's. The cat mewed wildly, first dashing about and then refusing to move. Sometimes, in desperation, it hurled itself at Peredonov, but Peredonov would beat it off with his cane. A crowd of boys ran behind him, hooting and laughing. People walking by stopped, and people looked out of their windows at the racket. Peredonov was not at all disturbed as he sullenly pulled the cat along on the cord.

When he arrived, he said to the barber, "I would like my cat trimmed smooth, sir."

Boys were crowded around the door on the outside, laughing and making faces. The barber took offense and blushed. "Excuse me, sir," he said in a slightly trembling voice, "we don't do that sort of work. And I have never even seen any shaven cats—this must be the latest fashion that hasn't reached us yet."

Peredonov listened to him in dull perplexity. "Just admit that you don't know how to do it, charlatan," he shouted. And he left, dragging the furiously howling cat.

On the way home he thought sadly that everyone, everywhere was always laughing at him—no one wanted to help him. Anguish gripped his heart.

Peredonov went with Volodin and Rutilov to the park to play billiards.

"You can't play today, gentlemen," the scorekeeper told them with embarrassment.

"Why is that?" asked Peredonov angrily. "We can't play indeed!"

"Forgive me, but there are no balls," said the score-keeper.

"The booby mislaid them," cried the bartender loudly from behind the partition.

The scorekeeper shuddered and suddenly his reddened ears twitched like a hare's. "They were stolen," he whispered.

"What! Who stole them?" cried Peredonov fearfully.

"We don't know," continued the scorekeeper. "Everything was all right, and suddenly I looked—no balls."

Rutilov tittered and exclaimed, "This is really something."

Volodin assumed an offended expression and scolded the scorekeeper: "If you allow someone to steal the balls or if you were in another place and the balls were taken, then you should quickly get new balls so that we can play with them. We came here wanting to play, but, if there are no balls, how can we play?"

"Stop whining, Pavlushka," said Peredonov. "It's bad enough without you. Find the balls, scorekeeper, because we simply must play, but meanwhile bring us a couple of beers."

They started to drink the beer, but it was boring. The balls positively could not be found. They cursed among themselves and swore at the scorekeeper. He himself felt at fault and so was silent.

In this theft Peredonov saw a new enemy trick. "Why?" he thought with anxiety, unable to understand it. He walked into the park, sat down on a bench near the pond—he had never sat there before—and dully stared at the greenish water. Volodin, sharing his sadness, sat next to him and also looked at the pond with his sheep-like eyes. "Why is there such a dirty mirror here, Pavlushka?" asked Peredonov, and he poked his cane in the direction of the pond.

Volodin grinned and replied, "That's not a mirror, Ardasha, that's a pond. There's no breeze now, so the trees are reflected in it as in a mirror."

Peredonov lifted his eyes. A fence on the other side of the pond separated the park from the street. "And why is the cat on the fence?"

Volodin looked in that direction. "He was, but he's gone now," he said giggling.

There actually had been no cat—it was Peredonov's

imagination: a cat with great, green eyes, his cunning, tireless enemy.

Peredonov again began to think about the balls. Who needed them? Could the *nedotykomka* have devoured them? "I haven't seen it today," thought Peredonov. "Perhaps it gorged itself and has gone to sleep somewhere now."

Peredonov despondently started to trudge slowly home.

The sun was fading in the west. A wandering cloud hovering in the sky crept up—clouds have a stealthy tread—and spied on him. A mysterious smile gleamed on its dark edges. Over the stream which flowed between the park and the town, shadows of houses and bushes wavered and whispered as if they were seeking someone.

And on land, in this dark and eternally hostile town, all the people were evil and nasty. Everything was blended into a general antagonism towards Peredonov. Dogs laughed at him, people barked at him.

The town women began to return Varvara's visits. Some of them rushed there with gleeful curiosity on the second or third day to see what Varvara's home was like. Others waited a week or more, and some, Vershina, for example, did not come at all.

The Peredonovs waited for return visits every day with anxious impatience and kept count of those who still had not come. They awaited the headmaster and his wife especially impatiently. They waited and became excessively excited—but the Khripaches did not come.

A week passed. Still no Khripaches. Varvara began to be angry and to curse at them. The waiting plunged Peredonov into a deep state of depression. His eyes became completely vacant—it was as though they were dead, and sometimes it did seem that these were the eyes of a dead man. Ridiculous fears were tormenting him. Without any evident reason he suddenly became afraid of this or that object. Somehow the thought that they would cut his throat came into his head and tormented him for several days. He feared everything sharp and hid the knives and forks.

"Perhaps," he thought, "they have been affected and whispered over. I might slit myself on a knife."

"Why should we use knives?" he asked Varvara. "The Chinese eat with little sticks."

Because of this they did not cook meat for a whole week but contented themselves with cabbage soup and porridge.

Varvara, avenging herself on Peredonov for her suffering before the marriage, sometimes agreed with him and strengthened his conviction that his whims were fact. She would tell him that he had many enemies, and, indeed, why shouldn't he be envied? More than once she teased him and said that they had surely already reported him and brought his name before the authorities and even before the Princess. It pleased her that he was visibly frightened.

It seemed clear to Peredonov that the Princess was displeased with him. Otherwise, why didn't she send him an icon or a cake for his wedding? "I must do her some kindness," he thought, "but what? Should I lie? Slander someone? Start a scandalous rumor? Report someone?" All women—so he reasoned—love gossip, and so he would invent an amusing and spicy story about Varvara and send it to the Princess. She would laugh and give him the position.

But Peredonov did not dare to write such a letter— he was afraid to write to the Princess herself. Later, he forgot all about this undertaking.

Peredonov entertained his ordinary guests with vodka and the cheapest port, but for the headmaster he bought a three-ruble bottle of madeira. Peredonov considered this wine extremely expensive, and he kept it in his bedroom. He only showed it to his other guests, saying, "For the headmaster."

One time when Rutilov and Volodin were sitting at Peredonov's he showed them the madeira.

"Why look at the outside—that isn't delicious!" said Rutilov giggling. "Treat us to some of your expensive madeira."

"How could you!" exclaimed Peredonov angrily. "What would I give the headmaster?"

"The headmaster can have a glass of vodka," said Rutilov.

"A headmaster can't drink vodka, a headmaster is supposed to drink madeira," said Peredonov with conviction.

"But what if he likes vodka?" insisted Rutilov.

"Such a high official can't like vodka," said Peredonov confidently.

"Give us some anyway," persisted Rutilov.

But Peredonov hurriedly took the bottle away, and he could be heard locking the cupboard in which he kept the wine. When he returned to his guests, in order to change the subject, he began to talk about the Princess.

"Some Princess!" he said morosely. "She used to sell rotten apples in the market place, but she seduced the Prince."

Rutilov broke out laughing and exclaimed, "Since when do princes walk about in markets?"

"Well, she knew how to lure him in," said Peredonov.

"You're making it up, Ardal'on Borisych," argued Rutilov. "The Princess is a noblewoman. You're throwing fairy tales in our faces."

Peredonov looked at him angrily and thought, "He's defending her, so obviously he's on the side of the Princess. Even though she lives far away, the Princess has clearly bewitched him."

Meanwhile, the *nedotykomka* rushed about, laughing

noiselessly and shaking with merriment. It reminded Peredonov of various horrible matters. He fearfully looked around and whispered, "In each town there is a secret plain-clothes policeman. He wears ordinary clothes —sometimes he works in the civil service, sometimes he's a merchant, or sometimes he does something else. But at night, when everyone is asleep, he puts on his blue uniform and suddenly becomes a police officer."

"But why the uniform?" inquired Volodin matter-of-factly.

"One can't go before the authorities without a uniform—they would whip you," explained Peredonov.

Volodin snickered. Peredonov bent closer to him and whispered, "Sometimes he even becomes a werewolf. You think that it's only a cat, but you're wrong! It's a policeman running about. No one hides from a cat, and he eavesdrops on everything."

Finally, after about a week and a half, the headmaster's wife returned the visit to Varvara. She arrived with her husband on a weekday at four o'clock, well attired, attractive, and smelling of sweet violet. The Peredonovs were caught completely off guard—they had expected the Khripaches to come on a Sunday and earlier in the day. They were thrown into a flurry. Varvara was in the kitchen, half-dressed and dirty. She rushed to get dressed, while Peredonov, who looked as though he had just been awakened, occupied the guests.

"Varvara will be right here," he mumbled. "She's getting dressed. We have a new servant who doesn't know how we do things—an utter fool."

Soon Varvara came out haphazardly dressed and with a red, frightened face. She thrust a dirty, clammy hand at her guests, and in a voice trembling from excitement she said, "I'm sorry that I made you wait. We didn't know that you paid visits on weekdays."

"I seldom go out on Sunday," said Madam Khripach. "There are drunkards in the streets. We let the servant have this day off."

The conversation somehow got under way, and the kindness of the headmaster's wife cheered Varvara up a little. She treated Varvara somewhat disdainfully but kindly—as one treats a repentant sinner to whom one should be nice, but whose contact is still unpleasant. She gave several hints to Varvara, as if in passing, about clothes and furniture.

Varvara was trying to please the headmaster's wife, but the fearful trembling of her red hands and chapped lips did not stop. This embarrassed Madam Khripach, and, although she attempted to be more gracious, an involuntary feeling of repulsion overcame her. Her every word gave Varvara to understand that there could not be a close relationship between them. But, because she did this in such a friendly way, Varvara did not understand and imagined that she and the headmaster's wife were going to be great friends.

Khripach had the look of a man out of his element, although he skillfully and manfully concealed the fact. He refused the madeira—he was not accustomed to drinking wine at this hour. He talked about local happenings and about the proposed changes in the structure of the district court. But it was quite noticeable that he and Peredonov moved in different circles of local society.

They did not stay long—they came and went. Varvara was happy when they left. As she undressed again, she said to Peredonov with relief, "Well, thank God they've gone. I couldn't think of a thing to say to them. That always happens with people you don't know very well— you don't know how to approach them."

Suddenly she remembered that the Khripaches had not invited them to visit them when they were saying good-bye. At first this disturbed her, but then she rationalized, "They'll send a card with a note about when to come. These people have their own time for everything. I suppose I should begin to jabber French now, but I don't even know how to swear in French." *

On the way home the headmaster's wife said to her husband, "She is pitiful and hopelessly low—it would be impossible to be on any sort of equal relationship with her. She has nothing that corresponds to her position."

"She completely corresponds to her husband," replied Khripach. "I am waiting impatiently for that time when they take him from us.

After Varvara's wedding she began to drink with abandon, most often with Grushina. Once, when she was tipsy and Prepolovenskaya was visiting her, Varvara let something slip out about the letter. She did not tell everything, but she hinted clearly enough. That was enough for the clever Sof'ya, and it suddenly became clear to her. "How could I not have guessed it at once!" she mentally reproached herself. She told Vershina about the forged letters confidentially—and from her it spread around the whole town.

Whenever Prepolovenskaya saw Peredonov, she was unable to keep from laughing at his gullibility. "You are really very simple, Ardal'on Borisych," she said.

"I am not at all simple," he replied. "I am a university graduate."

"You may be a graduate, but anyone who wants to can fool you."

"I myself fool everyone," argued Peredonov.

Prepolovenskaya would smile cunningly and go off.

* The meaning here is obscure and depends upon regional usage. I have translated *a to ya po-frantsuzski ni be, ni me* as a Russian version of the French *ne parler que par b ou par f*—"never to speak without swearing." More simply, it may merely indicate lack of ability to communicate.

"Why did she say that?" Peredonov dully tried to figure out. "Out of spite!" he thought. "Everyone's my enemy." And he made a rude gesture after her. "She can't do anything to me," he thought, consoling himself, but fear tormented him.

These hints of Prepolovenskaya's were not very substantial. She did not wish to tell him the whole truth in plain words. Why quarrel with Varvara? From time to time she sent Peredonov anonymous letters in which the hints were clearer, but Peredonov misinterpreted them.

Once Sof'ya wrote him: "Search and see if the Princess who wrote you the letters doesn't live here."

But Peredonov thought that the Princess had really come here to spy on him. "Obviously," he thought, "she has fallen madly in love with me and wants to take me away from Varvara."

These letters both terrified and angered Peredonov.

"Where is the Princess?" he would ask Varvara. "They say that she has come here."

Varvara, taking revenge for former times, tormented him with hints, taunts, and with tortuous, malignant round-about statements. With a nasty smirk, she spoke in a false tone, as people speak when they are deliberately lying with no desire to be believed: "How should I know where the Princess is living now!"

"You're lying, you do know!" said Peredonov in terror.

He did not know which to believe—the words she spoke, or the lie that was revealed in the sound of her voice—and, as with everything which he could not understand, this made him feel terrified.

"What do you want from me!" retorted Varvara. "Maybe she left Peter and went somewhere—she doesn't have to ask my permission, you know."

"But couldn't she really have, perhaps, come here?" asked Peredonov timidly.

"It could be," said Varvara in a teasing voice. "She has fallen madly in love with you and has come here to feast her eyes on you."

"You lie!" screamed Peredonov. "Do you think she's really fallen madly in love with me?"

Varvara laughed maliciously.

From this time on, Peredonov began to watch attentively to see if he could spot the Princess anywhere. Sometimes it seemed to him that she was peeking in a window or a door, eavesdropping and whispering with Varvara.

Time passed, but day after day the awaited paper which would make him an inspector still did not come, and there was no private information about the position. Peredonov did not dare to inquire of the Princess herself—Varvara continually frightened him with the fact that she belonged to the nobility. Moreover, he imagined that, if he undertook to write her himself, very unpleasant consequences could result. He did not know precisely what they would do to him if the Princess complained, but that made it all the more terrifying.

"You know what aristocrats are like, don't you?" said Varvara. "Just wait, and they'll do what should be done. But if you remind them, they will be offended, and it'll be the worse for you. They're really touchy! They're proud and love to be taken on their word."

And Peredonov still believed her, and he began to be angry at the Princess. Sometimes he even thought that the Princess would report him in order to get out of her promises. Or she would report him because she was angry that he had married Varvara, when she herself was in love with him. For that reason he thought that she had surrounded him with spies who followed him everywhere and surrounded him so that he had no air, no light. She was not a noblewoman for nothing. She could do anything she wanted to.

In his anger Peredonov made up absurd stories about the Princess. He told Rutilov and Volodin too that he had formerly been her lover and that she had paid him large sums of money. "But I drank it all away. Why should I give a damn! She even promised me a pension for the rest of my life, but she has deceived me."

"And would you have taken it?" asked Rutilov giggling.

Peredonov did not understand the question and was silent, but Volodin answered for him with assurance and conviction: "Why not take it, since she's rich. She was pleased to have her fun, so she must pay for it."

"It would have been all right if she had at least been a beauty!" said Peredonov sadly. "But she's pock-marked and snub-nosed. It was only because she paid well, otherwise I wouldn't even have wanted to spit on her, the she-devil. She has to fulfill my request."

"You're lying, Ardal'on Borisych," said Rutilov.

"Well then, I'm lying. But do you suppose she paid me all that money for nothing? She's jealous of Varvara, and that's why she's taking so long to give me the position."

Peredonov did not experience shame when he pretended that the Princess had paid him. Volodin was a credulous listener and did not notice the absurdities and contradictions in Peredonov's stories. Rutilov took exception to the stories, although he still thought that there is no smoke without fire and that there had been something between Peredonov and the Princess.

"She's as old as the hills," * said Peredonov matter-of-factly and with conviction, "only see that you don't blab about it—nothing good would come of it if it reaches her. She smears herself up and takes things in her veins

* "Older than the priest's dog"—a reference to a humorous folk-song.

to make herself look as young as a little piglet. You can't tell that she's old, but she is already a hundred years old."

Volodin shook his head and smacked his lips. He believed it all.

It happened that, on the day following such a conversation, Peredonov happened to read Krylov's fable "The Liar" * in one class. For several days afterward he was afraid to go across the town bridge and took the ferry across instead, lest the bridge perhaps throw him off.

"I told the truth about the Princess," he explained to Volodin, "only the bridge might suddenly not believe me and toss me to the devil."

25 : ६❧६❧

Rumors about the forged letters spread around the town, and talk about this occupied and delighted the townsfolk. They almost all praised Varvara and were glad that Peredonov had been duped. And everyone who had seen the letters imagined in his head that he had guessed the truth at once.

The malicious glee was especially great in Vershina's house because Marta, although she had now married

---

* "The Liar" by Ivan Krylov, Russia's foremost fabler, is about a traveler who boasts of the grand sights he has seen abroad. His listener tells him that their town too has a natural wonder, a bridge which tosses all liars into the water. The boaster hedges and finally suggests that they ford the stream.

Murin, had all the same been rejected by Peredonov. Vershina had wanted to take Murin for herself, but she had had to give him up to Marta. Vladya had considerable reasons of his own to hate Peredonov and to rejoice at his misfortune. Although he was vexed that Peredonov would still remain at the gymnasium, his happiness that Peredonov had been taken in outweighed that annoyance. Moreover, for the last few days there had been a persistent rumor among the students that the headmaster had reported to the superintendent of education in the district that Peredonov had gone out of his mind. They also said that he would be examined and then taken out of the gymnasium.

When acquaintances encountered Varvara, they began to talk more or less bluntly with coarse jokes and insolent winks about the trick she had played. She would smirk boldly, and, although she did not confirm it, she did not argue either.

Some people hinted to Grushina that they knew about her part in the prank. She became frightened and went to reproach Varvara for having blabbed.

"Don't be foolish," Varvara said to her with a smirk, "I didn't even think of telling anyone."

"Then how did everyone find out?" asked Grushina vehemently. "I certainly didn't tell anybody. I'm not that much of a fool."

"I didn't tell anyone either," declared Varvara arrogantly.

"Give me back the letter," demanded Grushina, "otherwise he'll examine it more closely and find out from the handwriting that it's a forgery."

"Well, let him find out!" said Varvara with annoyance. "I'd like to see the fool's face."

Grushina's different-sized eyes shone, and she cried out: "It's all right for you to talk, you've received what you wanted, but because of you they'll put me in prison!

You can do as you please, but give the letter back to me. They might even unmarry you."

"Now really! Stop that!" replied Varvara with her arms set brazenly on her hips. "They might announce it in the square, but they can't undo the marriage."

"I'm serious!" exclaimed Grushina. "There's no such law that says you can be married by deceit. If Ardal'on Borisych takes the whole business to the authorities and it goes to the senate, they could annul the marriage."

Varvara became frightened. "Don't get in a huff, I'll get the letter for you," she said. "There's nothing to be afraid of, I won't betray you. Do you think I would be such a beast? I have a soul too!"

"Some soul!" said Grushina rudely. "Man and dog have nothing but their breath. There is no soul. First you live, then you're gone."

Although it would be difficult, Varvara decided to steal the letter. Grushina urged her to hurry. There was one hope—to get the letter from Peredonov when he was drunk. And he drank often. Occasionally he even appeared at the gymnasium slightly high and said things so shameless that they aroused repulsion in even the worst of the boys.

Once Peredonov returned from playing billiards drunker than usual—they had been celebrating over the new balls. But he still did not part from his wallet: he got undressed somehow and thrust it under his pillow.

He slept restlessly but heavily. He was delirious, and his ravings were about something terrible and hideous. They brought a sinister fear upon Varvara.

"Well, it's nothing," she assured herself, "if only he doesn't wake up."

She shook him and tried to wake him up—he mumbled something and swore loudly, but he did not wake up. Varvara lit a candle and placed it so that the light did not fall into Peredonov's eyes. Rigid with fear, she got out of bed and cautiously inched her hand under the pillow towards Peredonov. The wallet lay close, but for a long time it eluded her fingers. The candle burned dimly. Its flame wavered. Timid shadows licked at the walls and the bed—evil little demons darting to and fro. The air was stuffy and motionless. The smell of vodka permeated everything, and his snoring and drunken delirium filled the entire bedroom. The whole room was the incarnation of a nightmare.

With trembling fingers, Varvara drew out the letter and pushed the wallet back into its former place.

In the morning Peredonov searched for the letter. When he could not find it, he became frightened and shouted, "Where is the letter, Varya?"

Varvara, concealing her terrible fear, said, "How should I know, Ardal'on Borisych? You show it to everyone, so it must be that you dropped it somewhere. Or they may have stolen it from you. You have a good many friends and acquaintances with whom you carouse at night."

Peredonov thought that his enemies, especially Volodin, had stolen the letter. Volodin was holding the letter, and afterwards he would get all the papers in his clutches and receive the appointment and become an inspector, while Peredonov would be left an embittered tramp.

Peredonov resolved to protect himself. Each day he composed a denunciation of his enemies: Vershina, the Rutilovs, Volodin, and his colleagues who, it seemed to him, were aspiring for the very same position. In the evenings he took these denunciations to Rubovsky.

The police lieutenant lived in a prominent place on the square near the gymnasium. Many people watched from their windows each time Peredonov entered the police lieutenant's gates. But Peredonov thought that no one would think anything of it. Still, he intentionally brought the denunciations in the evenings and used the back door through the kitchen. He always held the paper under his coat flap. It was evident at once that he was holding something. If he had to take out his hand to greet someone, he held the paper under his coat with his left hand and thought that no one could suspect anything. If the people he met asked him where he was going, he lied to them extraordinarily unskillfully—although he himself was satisfied with his own improbable fabrications.

"They're all traitors," he explained to Rubovsky. "They pretend to be friends so they can deceive you even more. But they don't realize that I know things about all of them for which even Siberia would be too soft for them."

Rubovsky listened to him in silence. The first denunciation, obviously absurd, he forwarded to the headmaster, as he also did with several others. He kept some in case he should need them. The headmaster wrote to the superintendent of education that Peredonov was displaying clear signs of mental disease.

At home Peredonov continually heard unceasing, annoying, and mocking rustling noises. "Someone is always walking around here on tiptoes," he said to Varvara dejectedly. "There are so many spies in our house that they bump into each other. You aren't taking care of me, Var'ka."

Varvara did not understand what Peredonov's ravings meant. Sometimes she taunted him, at other times she felt afraid. "Your eyes see all sorts of things when you're drunk," she said maliciously and fearfully.

The door into the hall seemed especially suspicious to Peredonov—it would not close tightly. The crevice between the door and the doorpost hinted at something hiding outside. Wasn't that a knave spying in? Someone's keen and evil eye was glittering there.

The cat, with its large, green eyes, followed Peredonov everywhere. Sometimes it winked, sometimes it yowled fearfully. It was obvious that the cat wanted to catch Peredonov at something but could not and, therefore, was angry. Peredonov spat to protect himself from it, but the cat did not go away.

The *nedotykomka* ran under the chairs and in the corners, screeching all the while. It was dirty, stinking, repulsive, and terrifying. Quite clearly, it was hostile to Peredonov and had come especially for him, never having existed anywhere before. It had been created and then bewitched. Thus, the enchanted many-shaped creature lived and reduced him to fear and torment—it followed him, deceived him, laughed at him, now rolling along the floor, now pretending to be a rag, a ribbon, a branch, a flag, a cloud, a dog, a column of dust in the street. Everywhere it crawled and ran after Peredonov. It wearied and exhausted him with its vacillating dance. If only someone would save him by saying some sort of magic word or by a fierce backhand swipe at it. But he had no friends here. No one would come to save him, and he had to use his own wits or the malicious creature would bury him.

Peredonov thought of a plan—he smeared the whole floor with glue so that the *nedotykomka* would stick to it. The bottoms of shoes and the hems of Varvara's dresses stuck to the floor, but the *nedotykomka* rolled about freely and laughed shrilly. Varvara swore angrily.

The fixed notion that he was being persecuted obsessed and terrified Peredonov. He was becoming more and more immersed in a world of wild fantasies, and this was reflected in his face, which became a motionless mask of terror.

Peredonov now stopped going to play billiards in the

evenings. After dinner he locked himself in his bed-room, blockaded the door with various objects—a chair upon a table—and, having carefully surrounded himself with crosses and charms, sat down to write denunciations about anyone who came into his mind, not only about people, but also about the playing-card queens. He would write one and immediately bring it to the police lieutenant. And so he passed each evening.

The playing-card figures would walk all around in front of Peredonov's eyes as though they were alive—kings, queens, knaves. Even the insignificant cards walked about—these were people with shiny buttons, schoolboys and policemen. The ace was stout and had a protruding stomach—in fact, it was almost nothing but stomach. Sometimes the cards turned into people he knew. The living people were mingled with these strange phantasms.

Peredonov was convinced that a knave was standing outside the door, waiting, and that this knave had some sort of strength and power, similar to a policeman's, and could take him away to some sort of terrible police station. And under the table sat the *nedotykomka*. Peredonov was afraid to look either under the table or behind the door.

The fidgeting, little-boyish eights teased Peredonov—these were werewolf-students. They lifted their legs in a strange, lifeless motion which made the legs resemble compass arms except that they were shaggy and hooved. Instead of tails they had grown whipping rods, and the boyish figures waved them with a swish, yelping at each stroke. The *nedotykomka* grunted from under the table, laughing at the antics of these eights. Peredonov angrily thought that the *nedotykomka* would not dare behave this way in the home of some important official. "It certainly wouldn't be allowed," he thought with envy. "The servants would drive it away with mops."

At last Peredonov could no longer endure its evil, nasty, yelping laughter. He brought an axe from the kitchen and demolished the table under which the *nedotykomka* was hiding. The *nedotykomka* squeaked sorrowfully and angrily, rushed out from under the table, and rolled away. Peredonov shivered. "It'll bite me," he thought, and he screamed in terror and sat down. But the *nedotykomka* hid itself quietly. Not for long . . .

Sometimes Peredonov took the cards and with a ferocious expression he chopped off the heads of the playing-card figures with a penknife. Especially the queens. As he beheaded the kings, he glanced around so that he would not be seen and charged with a political crime. But even these reprisals did not help for long. Guests were always arriving, cards were continually being purchased for them, and the evil spies would settle down again in the new cards.

Peredonov had already begun to consider himself a secret criminal. He imagined that he had been under police observation even from his student days, and that was why he thought he was being followed. This both terrified and flattered him.

A breeze stirred the wallpaper, making it rustle with a soft, evil sound. Very slight shadows flashed across its multicolored design. "A spy is hiding behind the wallpaper," thought Peredonov in anguish. "Wicked people! It's not an accident that they put the wallpaper on so unevenly and so badly that a clever, flat, and patient villain could creep behind it and hide himself. There have been cases like that before."

Vague recollections stirred in his head. Someone had hidden behind wallpaper, and someone had been stabbed with either a dagger or an awl.* Peredonov bought an awl. When he returned home, the wallpaper

* Hamlet's murder of Polonius? Some readers will already have noticed the delightful little Lear parody in Chapter IV.

was moving unevenly and disturbingly—perhaps the spy sensed the danger and was trying to crawl somewhere farther away. A shadow dashed about and leaped to the ceiling from where it twisted and threatened.

Peredonov seethed with anger. He impulsively struck at the wallpaper with his awl. A shudder ran along the wall. Peredonov howled victoriously and began to dance, waving the awl. Varvara came in.

"Why are you dancing alone, Ardal'on Borisych?" she asked with her perpetual stupid and insolent leer.

"I have killed a bug," explained Peredonov sullenly.

His eyes glimmered in wild exultation. Only one thing was wrong: it smelled awful. The pierced spy was decomposing and stinking behind the wallpaper. Triumph and terror moved Peredonov—he had killed an enemy! With this murder his heart was now capable of anything. It was not a real murder, but for Peredonov it was a very real one. His mad terror had forged the preparedness for a criminal act in him. Now, a dark unconscious premonition of future murder hiding in the lower depths of his spiritual life, a tormenting drive to murder, a state of primitive fury oppressed his depraved will. This desire—still alive many generations after the ancient Cain—found satisfaction in breaking and ruining things, in chopping with an axe, in slicing with a knife, in cutting down trees in the garden so that a spy could not look out from behind them. And that ancient demon, the spirit of eternal disorder and aged chaos, rejoiced in the destruction of things, while the wild eyes of the madman reflected terror similar to that of horrible death agonies.

And the same illusions kept on repeating themselves and tormenting him. Varvara, amusing herself at Peredonov's expense, sometimes would sneak up to one of the doors of the room where Peredonov was sitting and from there talk in strange voices. He would become terrified, carefully approach to catch the enemy, and find Varvara.

"Why were you whispering here?" he would ask sullenly.

"You're just imagining it, Ardal'on Borisych," replied Varvara with a leer.

"Not everything is imagination, there's also truth in the world," mumbled Peredonov sadly.

Yes, even Peredonov strove towards truth according to the general law of every conscious being, and this striving tormented him. He himself did not realize that, like all people, he also was striving for truth, and, therefore, he was tormented by anxiety. He was unable to discover truths for himself, and he became entangled and was perishing.

Now acquaintances began to tease Peredonov about the trick that had been played on him. With the usual callousness towards the weak found in our town, they spoke about this deceit in front of him.

"Why haven't you stepped into your inspector's position yet, Ardal'on Borisych?" asked Prepolovenskaya with a cunning smile.

"We'll get the paper and the position," replied Varvara for him with restrained anger.

These questions depressed Peredonov.

"How can I live, if they don't give me the position?" he thought.

He continually devised new plans to protect himself from his enemies. He took the ax out of the kitchen and hid it under the bed. He bought a Swedish penknife and always carried it in his pocket. He was constantly sullen. At night he set traps around the house and even in the rooms, and he checked them the next morning. These traps were, of course, constructed so that they could not catch anything—they pinched, but they did not hold and one could get out of them. Peredonov had neither technical knowledge nor cleverness. Seeing each morning that no one had been caught, Peredonov thought that his enemies had spoiled the traps. This frightened him still more.

Peredonov paid special attention to Volodin. Occasionally he went to Volodin's house when he knew that no one was at home and rummaged to see if there were any of his own papers there.

Peredonov began to suspect that the Princess wanted him to love her again. The old woman was repulsive to him. "She's a hundred and fifty years old," he thought, "but she also has great power." And his repulsion was mingled with desire. Peredonov imagined her as barely warm and smelling like a corpse, and he was held motionless in wild ecstasy.

"Perhaps I could meet with her, and she would show me favor. Why not write her a letter?" And, on this occasion, Peredonov, without stopping to think long, composed a letter to the Princess.

"I love you," he wrote, "because you are cold and distant. Varvara sweats, and it is uncomfortable to sleep with her. She's like an oven. I want to have a cold and distant lover. Come to me and fulfill my need."

He wrote and mailed it, but then he regretted what he had done. "What if something comes of it? Perhaps I ought not to have written," he thought. "I ought to have waited until the Princess herself came."

This letter was an accident as was so much that Peredonov did. He moved like a corpse motivated by external forces, which, however, had no desire to bother themselves about him for long: one played with him and then tossed him to another.

Soon the *nedotykomka* appeared again—for a long time it rolled around Peredonov as though it were on the end of a lasso and kept teasing him. It was now noiseless and laughed only by shaking its entire body. But it blazed with dim, golden sparks, evil and shameless—it menaced and glowed with an insufferable air of triumph. The cat also threatened Peredonov; its eyes glittered, and it mewed insolently and ominously.

"Why should they be rejoicing?" thought Peredonov sadly, and suddenly he understood that the end was approaching, that the Princess was already here, near, very near—perhaps in this pack of cards.

Yes, undoubtedly she was either the queen of spades or the queen of hearts. Perhaps she was hiding in another deck or behind other cards—he was unsure what she looked like. The misfortune was that Peredonov had never seen her. He could ask Varvara, but it was not worth it—she would lie.

Finally, it occurred to Peredonov that he should burn the whole deck. Let them all burn. If they had crept into the cards to do him harm, then they themselves were to blame.

Peredonov seized a moment when Varvara was not there and the stove in the hall was burning—he tossed the cards, the whole pack, into the stove.

With a crackle, mysterious pale red blossoms of flame unfolded and burned, black about the edges. Peredonov watched the flaming blossoms in terror.

The cards warped and twisted and moved as though they wished to jump out of the stove. Peredonov grabbed the poker and thrashed them about. He was surrounded on all sides by minute bright sparks—and suddenly, in a bright and evil flurry of sparks, the Princess arose from the fire. She was a small ash-gray woman, covered with fading sparks: she wailed piercingly in a thin voice, hissed, and spat on the fire.

Peredonov jumped backwards and shrieked in terror. Gloom took hold of him. It tickled him and laughed at him with cooing voices.

26 : ❧❧

Sasha was enchanted with Ludmila, but something prevented him from speaking about her with Kokovkina. It was as though he were ashamed. And he began sometimes to fear her arrivals. His heart stopped beating, and involuntarily his brows knit when he saw her rose-yellow hat flash quickly under his window. But all the same he awaited her with anxiety and impatience, and he felt depressed if she did not come for a long time. Contradictory feelings mingled in his soul, dark and nebulous feelings. They were perverse because they were premature, and they were sweet because they were perverse.

Ludmila had not come yesterday or today. Sasha had grown weary with expectation and had already given up hope, when suddenly she came. He beamed and rushed to kiss her hands.

"Well, where did you disappear to?" he grumbled at her. "I haven't seen you for forty-eight hours."

She laughed and was happy. The sweet, languid, and honeyed odor of Japanese perfume wafted from her, seeming to stream from her light brown locks.

Ludmila and Sasha went for a stroll beyond the town. They had invited Kokovkina, but she did not come.

"Why should an old woman like me go for a stroll!" she said. "I would only get under foot. Go by yourselves."

"But we'll get into mischief," laughed Ludmila.

. . .

The warm, heavy, still air caressed them and recalled irrevocable things. The sun was shining dully and crimson in the pale, tired sky as though something were wrong with it. Dry leaves lay peacefully on the warm earth, dead.

Ludmila and Sasha walked down into a ravine. It was cold, refreshing, and almost damp there. A tender autumnal weariness reigned between its shady slopes.

Ludmila walked in front. She raised her skirt revealing her little shoes and flesh-colored stockings. Sasha, looking down in order not to stumble over roots, saw the stockings. It seemed to him that she had put on her shoes without stockings. A shameful and passionate feeling was aroused in him. He reddened. His head went round. "If I could fall down at her feet as if by accident," he dreamed, "and snatch off her shoe and kiss her lovely foot."

Ludmila seemed to sense Sasha's passionate glance, his restless desire. Laughing, she turned to Sasha and asked, "Are you looking at my stockings?"

"No, I was just . . ." mumbled Sasha in confusion.

"Akh, what stockings I have," said Ludmila laughing and not listening to him. "They're simply terrible! One would think that I had put my shoes on my bare feet —they're perfectly flesh-colored. Don't you think they're terribly ridiculous stockings?" She turned her face to Sasha and lifted up the hem of her dress. "Aren't they foolish?" she asked.

"No, they're beautiful," said Sasha, red with embarrassment.

Ludmila raised her eyebrows in feigned surprise and exclaimed, "And just what, if you please, do you know about beauty!"

Ludmila laughed and walked farther on. Sasha, burning with embarrassment, awkwardly walked behind, frequently stumbling. They made their way through the ravine and sat down on a birch trunk which had been blown over by the wind.

"I have so much sand in my shoes that I can't go on," said Ludmila. She took off her shoes, shook out the sand, and glanced archly at Sasha.

"Is my foot pretty?" she asked.

Sasha blushed even more and was at a loss as to what to say. Ludmila drew off her stockings.

"Is it a lily-white little foot?" she asked again, smiling strangely and cunningly. "Kiss my knees!" she said strictly, and an expression of triumphant cruelty lay on her face.

Sasha nimbly dropped to his knees and kissed Ludmila's legs.

"It's nicer without stockings," said Ludmila placing the stockings in her pocket and putting on her shoes.

And her face again became peaceful and gay as if Sasha had not just been kneeling before her and kissing her naked feet.

"Won't you get chilled, dear?" asked Sasha, and his voice sounded tender and quavering.

Ludmila laughed. "Of course not—I'm used to it. I'm not such a mollycoddle."

Once Ludmila came to Kokovkina's early in the evening and called Sasha: "Come to my house and help me hang a new shelf."

Sasha loved to hammer nails, and once he had promised Ludmila to help her arrange the furniture in her room. And now he agreed to go, happy that there was an innocent pretext to accompany Ludmila to her house. And the innocent, bitter odor of extract of muguet drifted from Ludmila's green dress and soothed him.

Ludmila changed her clothes for work behind a screen and came out to Sasha in a short, dressy outfit with short sleeves. She had on the sweet, languid, and honeyed Japanese perfume.

"My, how dressed up you are!" said Sasha.

"Yes, I am dressed up," said Ludmila. "Look, my feet are bare," she said slowly in a timid and seductive manner.

Sasha shrugged his shoulders and said, "You're always dressed up. Well, let's start hammering. Have you got any nails?" he asked with a preoccupied air.

"Wait a little," replied Ludmila. "Sit with me awhile. You act as though you had come on business and find it boring to talk with me."

Sasha blushed and said tenderly, "Dear Ludmilochka, I'd like to sit with you as long as you want and until you drive me out, but the problem is that I have my lessons to study."

Ludmila sighed gently and slowly said, "You are growing more handsome, Sasha."

Sasha reddened, laughed, and stuck out the end of his tongue curled into a little pipe.

"You must think that I'm a girl, the way you talk," he said.

"You have a handsome face, but what about your body. Show it to me at least to the waist," requested Ludmila, caressing Sasha with her arm around his shoulder.

"What a thing to think of!" said Sasha both embarrassed and annoyed.

"And what's wrong with it?" asked Ludmila in a careless tone. "What do you have to hide!"

"Someone might come in," said Sasha.

"Who would come in?" said Ludmila in the same light and careless way. "We can lock the door, and then no one will come in."

Ludmila swiftly went up to the door and bolted it. Sasha sensed that Ludmila was in earnest.

"We shouldn't do it, Ludmilochka," he said, blushing

all over and with little beads of perspiration on his forehead.

"And why not, stupid?" asked Ludmila in a persuasive voice.

She drew Sasha to her and began to unbutton his blouse. Sasha drew back and caught hold of her wrists. His face looked both frightened and ashamed. These feelings seemed to cause him to weaken. Ludmila knitted her brows and began to undress him with determination. She took off his belt and somehow pulled out his blouse. Sasha resisted with more and more desperation. They tussled with each other, and, circling around the room, they collided with tables and chairs. The honeyed odor coming from Ludmila intoxicated Sasha and weakened him.

With a quick shove on the chest Ludmila pushed Sasha down onto the sofa. A button popped off the shirt which she was pulling at. Ludmila quickly bared Sasha's shoulder and began to pull his arm out of the sleeve. While he was resisting, Sasha accidentally struck Ludmila across the cheek with his palm. He had not wanted to hit her, of course, but the blow fell hard and loud on Ludmila's cheek. Ludmila shivered and staggered back, and blushed a blood red, but she did not let go of Sasha's arm.

"You're an evil boy to fight!" she cried in a panting voice.

Sasha was terribly embarrassed. He dropped his arms and looked guiltily at the imprint of white stripes made by his fingers on Ludmila's left cheek. Ludmila made use of his confusion. She quickly pulled his shirt off both shoulders and down to his elbows. Sasha recovered himself and tore away from her, but that only made things worse—Ludmila nimbly pulled the sleeves from his arms, and the shirt dropped to his waist. Sasha felt cold, and a new onset of strong and merciless shame made his head whirl. Now Sasha was bare to the waist. Ludmila held him tightly by the arm and patted his naked back with her quivering hand while looking into his downcast, strangely glimmering eyes under their blue-black eyelashes.

And suddenly these eyelashes quivered, his face was contorted by a pitiful childish grimace, and he began to sob.

"Bad girl!" he cried in a sobbing voice. "Let me go!"

"The little boy is crying!" said Ludmila, angry and disturbed, and she shoved him away.

Sasha turned away and wiped his tears away with his palms. He was ashamed that he had cried and he tried to hold back his tears. Ludmila looked avidly at his bare back.

"There is so much pleasure in the world!" she thought "People hide so much beauty from themselves—why?"

Sasha, cowering with embarrassment because of his bare shoulders, tried to put on his shirt, but it only became tangled in his shaking arms, and he was unable to get his arms into the sleeves. Sasha grabbed for his blouse—let the shirt remain as it is for the time.

"Oh, so you're afraid of losing what's yours. I won't steal it!" said Ludmila in an angry voice ringing with tears. She abruptly threw his belt to him and turned towards the window. Why should she want him, wrapped up in his gray blouse—horrid, unnatural boy.

Sasha quickly put on his blouse, straightened up his shirt a bit, and looked at Ludmila timidly, indecisively, and ashamedly. He saw that she was rubbing her cheeks with her hands, and he timidly went up to her and looked in her face. The tears flowing down her cheeks suddenly filled him with tender pity for her, and he was no longer ashamed or angry.

"Why are you crying, dear Ludmilochka?" he asked quietly. Suddenly he reddened as he remembered his blow. "Forgive me," he said timidly. "I struck you, but it wasn't on purpose."

"Are you afraid you'll melt away if you sit with bare shoulders, stupid boy?" said Ludmila reproachfully. "Or are you afraid you'll get sunburn? Maybe your beauty and your innocence will be taken away from you."

"But why did you want me to do it, Ludmilochka?" asked Sasha with an embarrassed expression.

"Why?" said Ludmila with passion. "I love beauty. I am a pagan, a sinner. I ought to have been born in ancient Athens. I love flowers, perfumes, bright clothes, the naked body. They say there is a soul. I don't know, I haven't seen it. But why do I need one? Let me die completely like a water nymph, let me melt away like a cloud under the sun. I love the body, strong, agile, naked, and capable of enjoyment."

"And also capable of suffering," said Sasha softly.

"Yes, it is also good to suffer," whispered Ludmila passionately. "There is sweetness in pain too, if you can feel the body and see its bareness and its beauty."

"But isn't it shameful to go without clothes?" said Sasha timidly.

Ludmila suddenly threw herself down before him on her knees. Breathlessly, she kissed his hands and whispered, "My darling, my idol, my godlike boy—for a minute, just for one minute let me admire your wonderful shoulders."

Sasha sighed. He lowered his eyes, blushed, and awkwardly took off his blouse. Ludmila embraced him with hot hands and covered his shoulders, trembling from shame, with kisses.

"Look how obedient I am!" said Sasha with a forced smile, trying to cover up his embarrassment with a jest.

Ludmila was rapidly kissing Sasha's arms from the shoulders to the fingers, and Sasha, excited and immersed in passionate, terrible dreams, did not take them away. Ludmila's kisses were warm with adoration, and it was as though it were not a lad, but a boy-god her burning lips were kissing in a thrilling and mysterious worship of the blossoming Flesh.

Meanwhile, Dar'ya and Valeriya were standing behind the door taking turns looking through the keyhole. They pushed each other impatiently, and they were numb with passionate and burning excitement.

"I have to get dressed now," said Sasha finally.

Ludmila sighed, and, with the same reverent expression in her eyes, she helped him on with his shirt and blouse, fussing over him respectfully and carefully.

"So you are a pagan?" asked Sasha skeptically.

Ludmila laughed gaily. "And you?" she asked.

"What do you mean!" replied Sasha with conviction. "I know the whole catechism by heart."

Ludmila broke into laughter. Sasha, looking at her, smiled and asked, "If you are a pagan, why do you go to church?"

Ludmila stopped laughing and became pensive. "Well," she said, "one must pray all the same. One must pray and weep and light candles and pray for the dead. And I love it all—the candles, the icon lamps, the incense, the chasubles, the singing—if the singers are good—and the icons with their settings and ribbons. Yes, all of that is beautiful. And I also love . . . Him . . . you know: the Crucified . . ."

Ludmila spoke these last words very quietly, almost in a whisper, and she blushed guiltily and lowered her eyes.

"I dream of Him sometimes, you know—He is on the cross, and there are little droplets of blood on His body."

From that time on, Ludmila took Sasha to her room many times and unbuttoned his blouse. At first he was mortified to tears, but he soon became accustomed to it and even watched calmly and casually as Ludmila took off his shirt, baring his shoulders, and caressed his back with resounding kisses. At last, he himself would take off his clothes.

It was pleasing to Ludmila to hold him half-naked on her knees and to embrace and kiss him.

Sasha was alone at home. He recalled Ludmila's sultry glances at his naked shoulders.

"What does she want?" he thought, and suddenly he blushed furiously, and his heart pounded in his chest. A wild ecstasy possessed him. He upset his chair, did several somersaults, threw himself on the floor, bounded on the furniture—he hurled himself from corner to corner with a thousand absurd movements, and his gay, clear laughter resounded throughout the house.

Kokovkina, returning home at this moment, heard the unusual commotion, and went into Sasha's room. She stood in the doorway shaking her head in perplexity.

"Are you possessed or something, Sashen'ka!" she said. "It would be all right if you were with comrades, but you're by yourself. For shame, young man—you're not a little boy."

Sasha stood there, and in his embarrassment he didn't know what to do with his heavy, awkward hands. His whole body still trembled with excitement.

Once Kokovkina came home to find Ludmila giving Sasha sweets.

"You're spoiling him," said Kokovkina affectionately. "This one of mine loves sweets."

"Yes, but he calls me a bad girl," complained Ludmila.

"Oh, Sashen'ka, how could you!" said Kokovkina in gentle reproach. "What did you say that for?"

"Well, she was pestering me," stammered Sasha. He glanced angrily at Ludmila and blushed crimson.

Ludmila laughed loudly.

"Gossip," whispered Sasha to her.

"How can you be so rude, Sashen'ka!" said Kokovkina. "One mustn't be rude!"

Sasha glanced at Ludmila, smiling, and whispered
softly, "Well, I won't do it any more."

Now, each time that Sasha came, Ludmila locked
herself in with him, took off his clothes, and dressed
him up in different costumes. Their sweet shame was
covered up with laughter and jokes. Sometimes Ludmila
tied Sasha up in a corset and put her own dress on him.

In the low-cut dress, Sasha's bare arms, full and deli-
cately rounded, and his curved shoulders seemed very
beautiful. His skin was yellowish, but of a rarely seen
uniformity and softness. Ludmila's skirt, shoes, and
stockings, it turned out, all fitted Sasha, and they all
looked well on him. Completely dressed in women's
clothing, Sasha obediently sat and waved a fan. Dressed
in this way, he really was like a young girl, and he attempted to behave like a girl. Only one thing was incongruous—Sasha's short-cut hair. But Ludmila did not
want to put a wig on him or attach some hair to Sasha's
head because it seemed repulsive to her.

Ludmila taught Sasha how to curtsy. In the beginning he did it awkwardly and bashfully, but he had
grace in spite of his comical boyish awkwardness. Blushing and laughing, he mastered the curtsy and flirted
wildly.

Sometimes Ludmila seized his bare, slender arms and
kissed them. Sasha did not resist, and he laughed as he
looked at Ludmila. Sometimes he himself put his hands
to her lips and said, "Kiss!"

But most of all they both liked the strange costumes
which Ludmila herself had sewn: a fisherboy's costume
with bare legs, the tunic of a bare-legged Athenian boy.

Ludmila would dress him up and admire him, but then she herself would go pale and become depressed.

Sasha was sitting on Ludmila's bed, fingering the folds of his tunic, and swinging his bare legs. Ludmila stood before him looking at him with an expression of happiness and bewilderment.

"Aren't you a stupid one!" said Sasha.

"There is so much happiness in my stupidity," whispered the pale Ludmila. She was weeping and kissing his hands.

"Why do you weep?" asked Sasha with a carefree smile.

"My heart is stung with joy. My breast is pierced with the seven swords of happiness—how could I not cry."

"You are a little fool, really a little goose!" said Sasha laughing.

"And you are wise!" said Ludmila with sudden irritation as she sighed and wiped her eyes. "Listen, my stupid," she said in a quiet, persuasive voice, "there is happiness and wisdom only in madness."

"Oh sure!" said Sasha skeptically.

"You must forget and forget, and then you will understand everything," whispered Ludmila. "Do you suppose that wise men think?"

"What other way is there?"

"They simply know. It is given to them at once: they have only to look and everything is at once revealed to them . . ."

Quietly the autumn evening lingered. Occasionally a barely audible murmur sounded on the other side of the window when a breeze in the air rocked the branches of the trees. Sasha and Ludmila were alone. Ludmila was dressing him as the bare-legged fisherboy —it was a blue costume made from fine linen. She had placed him on a low couch, and she was sitting on the floor by his bare legs. She was herself barefooted and had on only a chemise. She sprinkled Sasha's clothes and body with perfume—it had a heavy, verdant, and delicate odor like the still air of a strangely blossoming valley locked between mountains.

Large, lustrous beads glittered on Ludmila's neck, golden, figured bracelets tinkled on her arms. Her body smelled of iris—it was a sultry, sensual, provoking odor, inducing somnolence and laziness, permeated with the vapor of still water. She sighed and was in torment as she looked at his smooth face, his blue-black eyelashes, and his midnight eyes. She placed her head on his bare knees, and her bright locks caressed his smooth skin. She kissed Sasha's body, and her head whirled from the strange and powerful aroma mingling with the scent of young flesh.

Sasha lay there and smiled a quiet, changing smile. A vague desire was born in him, and it sweetly tormented him. And when Ludmila kissed his knees and feet, the tender kisses aroused weary, almost dream-like thoughts. He wanted to do something to her, painful or pleasant, tender or shameful—but what? To kiss her legs? Or to beat her long and hard with long, supple twigs? But why—to make her laugh with happiness or cry from pain? Perhaps she desired both—but that was not enough. What did she want? Here they were, both half-naked, and their freed flesh brought forth both desire and restraining shame—just what was this mysterious power of the flesh? And how could he sweetly sacrifice his blood and his body to her desire and to his shame?

Ludmila languished and stirred about at his feet, growing pale with impossible desires, now passionate, now cold.

"Am I not beautiful!" she whispered passionately. "Do I not have burning eyes! Do I not have luxuriant hair! Oh caress me! Stroke me! Tear off my bracelets, pull off my necklace!"

Sasha was terrified, and his impossible desires tormented him agonizingly.

27 : ક્ક*ક*ક્ક*

Peredonov awoke early in the morning. Someone was looking at him with huge, dull, four-cornered eyes. Was it not Pyl'nikov? Peredonov went up to the window and the malevolent apparition disappeared.

Everything was bewitched and possessed. The wild *nedotykomka* screeched, and both people and beasts looked evilly and angrily at Peredonov. All were hostile to him—he was one against all.

At the gymnasium during his lessons, Peredonov said malicious things about his fellow teachers, the headmaster, parents, and the students. The students listened with astonishment. Some, boors by nature, curried favor with Peredonov and agreed with him. Others remained sullenly silent or hotly defended their parents when Peredonov attacked them. Peredonov looked on these students gloomily and fearfully, and, mumbling something, avoided them.

In some of his classes, Peredonov amused the students with ridiculous comments. Once they were reading Pushkin's lines:

> *Dawn comes up, in haze and wet,*
> *On fields of corn, quiet yet.*

Then, his hungry mate in sway,
*The wolf sets out upon his way.**

"Let us pause here," said Peredonov. "This has to be really understood. There is an allegory concealed here. Wolves travel in pairs: a wolf and his hungry mate. The wolf is well-fed, but she's hungry. The wife always must eat after the husband. The wife must be subordinate to the husband in all things."

Pyl'nikov was in a good mood. He smiled and looked at Peredonov with his deceptively clear, fathomless black eyes. Sasha's face tormented and enticed Peredonov. The damn boy was bewitching him with his insidious smile.

But was he really a boy? Or, perhaps, there were two of them—brother and sister—but you can't tell the difference. Or he might even know how to change himself from a boy to a girl. It was not for nothing that he was always so clean—when he transformed himself, he splashed himself with various magic waters—otherwise he couldn't transform himself. He was always smelling of perfumes.

"What have you scented yourself with Ply'nikov?" asked Peredonov. "Stinkweed?"

The boys laughed. Sasha turned red at the insult but was silent.

Peredonov could not understand the honest desire to please, not to be repulsive. He considered any such manifestation, even on the part of a boy, to be a plot against himself. If someone dressed neatly, it meant that he was trying to gain Peredonov's favor. What other reason could there be for dressing up? Neatness and cleanliness were repulsive to Peredonov. Perfumes smelled awful to him: he preferred the odor of a manured field, which he considered beneficial to the health, to any perfumes. To be neatly dressed, to be clean, to

* The passage is from *Evgeny Onegin*, Chapter IV, Stanza XLI.

wash—all this required time and work, and the thought of work depressed Peredonov and made him fearful. It would be good if there were nothing to do but eat, drink, and sleep—nothing more!

Sasha's schoolmates teased him about scenting himself with "stinkweed" and also about Ludmila's being in love with him. He flushed and retorted hotly that it was not true: she was not in love with him, and all this was Peredonov's invention, because he had courted Ludmilochka, and Ludmilochka had turned up her nose at him . . . this was why he was angry and was spreading bad rumors about her. His comrades believed him—they knew Peredonov well—but they did not stop teasing him: it is so pleasant to tease someone.

Peredonov persistently told everyone about Pyl'nikov's depravity. "He's fallen in with Ludmila," he said. "They kiss so diligently that she has given birth to one mistake and is carrying another now."

In the town they began to talk about Ludmila's love for the gymnasium student with much exaggeration and many stupid, obscene details. But there were few who believed it—Peredonov had over spiced his tale. Nevertheless, vicious people—and there are many such in our town—asked Ludmila: "What made you fall in love with a boy? It's an insult to our men-about-town."

Ludmila laughed and said, "Nonsense!"

The townsfolk watched Sasha with obscene curiosity. General Poluyanov's widow, a rich woman of the merchant class, made inquiries about his age and discovered that he was still too small, but that in about two years one might take up the question of his development.

Sasha began sometimes to reproach Ludmila because they were teasing him on account of her. It sometimes even happened that he shoved her because she laughed so loudly about it.

In order to put an end to the stupid gossip and to

get Ludmila out of an unpleasant situation, all the Rutilovs, their numerous friends, and their close and distant relatives acted zealously againt Peredonov and declared that all these stories were the fantasies of a madman. Peredonov's wild acts caused many to accept this explanation.

At the same time, denunciations of Peredonov showered down upon the superintendent of the school district, and from district headquarters they sent an inquiry to the headmaster. Khripach referred them to his previous reports, adding that the continued presence of Peredonov in the gymnasium constituted a positive danger inasmuch as his mental aberration was progressing noticeably.

Peredonov was now completely in the power of his wild delusions. He was shut off from the world by ghosts. His mad, dull eyes wandered and would not come to rest on objects, as if he wished to look beyond them to the other side of the objective world, and he was seeking some sort of peepholes.

When he was alone, he would talk to himself and shout senseless threats to someone: "I'll kill you! I'll slice you to pieces! I'll caulk you up!"

Varvara would listen and sneer. "Kick up the devil!" she thought maliciously. It seemed to her that this was only his rage because he had guessed that he had been deceived and was angry. He wouldn't go out of his mind—a fool has no mind to go out of—and even if he did, what of it: madness keeps the stupid happy!

"You know, Ardal'on Borisych," said Khripach once, "you have a very unhealthy appearance."

"I have a headache," said Peredonov sullenly.

"Do you know, my esteemed sir," continued the headmaster in a guarded way, "I would advise you not to come to the gymnasium at present. It would be better for you to attend to your nerves which, evidently, are rather unstrung."

"Not go to the gymnasium! Of course," thought Peredonov, "that's the best thing to do. Why didn't I think of it earlier! I'll say I'm sick and sit at home and see what happens."

"Yes, yes," he told Khripach happily, "I won't come —I'm sick."

At the same time, the headmaster once again wrote to the district headquarters and from day to day was waiting for the appointment of physicians for an examination. But the officials did not hurry. That was because they were officials.

Peredonov did not go to the gymnasium. He too was awaiting something. In the last few days he clung continually to Volodin. It was terrible to let him out of his sight—he could do much harm. As soon as he woke up in the morning, Peredonov thought of Volodin with dread: where was he now? what was he doing? Sometimes he fancied that he saw Volodin: clouds floated across the sky like a flock of sheep, and among them ran Volodin with a bowler on his head, bleating with laughter. At other times it was in the smoke coming out of chimneys that he appeared, making horrible faces and prancing in the air.

Volodin thought and told everyone with great pride that Peredonov liked him very much and simply couldn't live without him.

"Varvara tricked him," said Volodin, "but he sees that I alone am his faithful friend, and so he'll stick to me."

Peredonov would leave his house to search for Volodin and find him coming towards him in his bowler with a cane, skipping gaily, and happily bleating with laughter.

"Why do you always wear a bowler?" Peredonov once asked him.

"And why shouldn't I wear a bowler, Ardal'on Boris-ych?" gaily and assuredly replied Volodin. "It's modest and it looks well on me. I'm not permitted to wear an official cap with a cockade, and, as for a stovepipe —let the aristocrats have that custom, it doesn't suit us."

"You'll stew yourself with that pot on your head,"* said Peredonov morosely.

Volodin snickered.

They walked to Peredonov's house.

"There's so much walking to do," said Peredonov angrily.

"It's good to keep moving, Ardal'on Borisych," said Volodin with conviction. "You work, you take a stroll, you eat, and you're healthy."

"Oh sure," said Peredonov. "Do you think that in two or three hundred years people will work?"

"What else? If you don't work, you don't get bread to eat. They give bread for money, and you've got to work for money."

"I don't want bread."

"And there wouldn't be any rolls or tarts," said Volodin with a giggle. "No one would have money to buy vodka and there would be nothing to make liquor out of."

"No, people won't have to work themselves," said Peredonov, "machines will do everything. Just turn a crank like an *ariston*, and it's ready . . . but it'll be boring to turn for a long time."

Volodin became lost in thought, bowed his head, protruded his lips, and said, pensively, "Yes, that will be very good. Only we won't be here then."

Peredonov looked at him spitefully and grumbled, "You won't be here, but I shall live until then." †

* *Kotelok* means both "pot" and "bowler."
† This scene is a tongue-in-cheek reference to the philosophy, generally associated with Chekhov, in which the futility of present

"God grant that you live two hundred years and then crawl on all fours for three hundred," said Volodin gaily.

Peredonov had already given up saying charms—let come what would. He would be victorious over everyone. It was necessary only to keep both eyes open and not to yield.

At home, sitting in the dining room drinking with Volodin, Peredonov told him about the Princess. The Princess, in Peredonov's imagination, was growing more decrepit and becoming more terrible day by day: yellow, wrinkled, bent over, tusked, evil, she incessantly appeared before Peredonov.

"She's two hundred years old," said Peredonov, and he stared strangely and sadly straight ahead. "She wants me to cat around with her again, and until then she doesn't want to give me a job."

"She doesn't want much!" said Volodin shaking his head. "What a hag!"

Peredonov was delirious about murder.

"I have one hidden there behind the wallpaper, and I'm going to kill another one under the floor," he said to Volodin, fiercely knitting his brows.

But Volodin was not frightened and snickered.

"Do you catch the stench behind the wallpaper?" asked Peredonov.

"No, I don't catch anything," said Volodin, giggling and making faces.

"Your nose is stuffed," said Peredonov. "It's not for nothing that your nose is so red. It's rotting there behind the wallpaper."

"A bug!" exclaimed Varvara, and she broke into

---

life is justified by faith in the eventual establishment of a happy and free world. Cf. the conclusion of Chekhov's 1901 play, *Uncle Vanya*.

laughter. Peredonov looked on with a dull air of importance.

Peredonov was becoming more and more engulfed in his insanity. He now began to write denunciations against the playing-card figures, the *nedotykomka*, and the ram, saying that the ram was an impostor pretending to be Volodin and trying to receive a high position, but that it was simply a ram, and against the forest destroyers who were cutting down all the birches so that there was no wood for steam baths and it was difficult to bring up children—they left only the aspens, and what good was aspen?

Meeting schoolboys on the street, Peredonov terrified the younger ones and amused the older ones with the shameless and nonsensical things he said. The older boys walked after him in a crowd, but they scattered when they saw one of their other teachers. The younger boys kept away from him of their own accord.

Charms and magic presented themselves to Peredonov in everything. Hallucinations terrified him, forcing mad wails and squeals from his chest. The *nedotykomka* appeared before him, now bloody, now flaming, groaning and shrieking, and its shrieking gave Peredonov an unendurable, splitting headache. The cat grew to terrible dimensions, stamped about in boots, and pretended to be a grown man with a long, red mustache.

28 : ঠ৶ঠ৶

Sasha left after dinner and had not returned at the appointed time, seven o'clock—Kokovkina was worried: God save him from meeting one of his teachers on the street at this forbidden hour. They would punish him, and it would be awkward for her too. She always had well-behaved boys, who did not run about at nights, at her house. Kokovkina went to look for Sasha. Obviously he must be at the Rutilovs.

Sad to say, Ludmila had forgotten to bolt the door that day. Kokovkina came in, and what did she see? Sasha was standing before the mirror in a woman's dress, waving a fan. Ludmila was laughing and fixing the ribbons on his brightly colored belt.

"Dear God!" exclaimed Kokovkina in terror. "What is this! I was worried and went to look for him, and here he is putting on a comedy. It's shameful for you to be in a woman's skirt! And you too—aren't you ashamed, Ludmila Platonovna!"

In the first minute Ludmila was taken aback by the surprise, but she quickly recovered. With a gay laugh she embraced Kokovkina, seated her in a chair, and made up a story for her: "We want to put on a show at home—I am going to be a boy, and he will be a girl. It will be terribly amusing."

Sasha stood there, all red and frightened, with tears in his eyes.

"If that isn't stupid!" said Kokovkina angrily. "He

has to study his lessons and not appear in shows. What a thing to have thought of! Dress yourself at once, Aleksandr, and march home with me."

Ludmila laughed loudly and gaily and kissed Kokovkina. The old woman thought that the gay young lady behaved like a child and that Sasha gladly carried out her whims through stupidity. Ludmila's merry laughter showed this to be nothing but a childish prank for which only a good lecture was required. Although she grumbled and assumed an angry expression, her heart had already calmed down.

Sasha quickly changed behind the screen where Ludmila's bed stood. Kokovkina led him away and scolded him all the way home. Sasha, ashamed and frightened, did not even try to justify himself. "And what will happen to me at home?" he fearfully thought.

And at home Kokovkina acted strictly with him for the first time and ordered him to get down on his knees. But Sasha had been in that position for only a few minutes when, softened by his guilty face and silent tears, she let him up.

"What a dandy," she grumbled. "One can smell your perfumes a verst away!"

Sasha bowed gracefully and kissed her hand, and the grace of the punished boy touched her even more.

But meanwhile a storm was gathering over Sasha. Varvara and Grushina composed and sent to Khripach an anonymous letter saying that the schoolboy Pyl'nikov had been enticed by the Rutilov girl and that he spent whole evenings at her house, where he gave himself over to debauchery. Khripach recalled a certain recent conversation. One evening a few days ago at the home of the marshal of the nobility someone had thrown out a vague remark, which no one had picked up, about a young girl who was in love with a juvenile. The conversation had immediately shifted to other subjects—in

Khripach's presence, according to the unwritten law of those accustomed to move among good society, this was considered an extremely awkward topic for conversation, and so they made the appearance that such conversation was improper in the presence of ladies and that the subject was trivial and not likely true. Khripach, of course, had observed all of this, but he was not uncultured enough to have asked anyone about it. He was firmly convinced that he would know all about it soon and that, one way or another, he learned all the news in proper time. And here was this letter with the expected news.

Khripach did not for a moment believe that Pyl'nikov had been corrupted or that his acquaintance with Ludmila had any improper aspects to it. "This," he thought, "is that same stupid invention of Peredonov's, nourished by the envy and spite of Grushina. Still," he thought, "this letter shows that undesirable rumors are going about which might reflect upon the virtue of the gymnasium entrusted to me. Therefore, suitable steps should be taken."

The first thing that Khripach did was to invite Kokovkina in to see him in order to discuss with her those circumstances which might have given rise to the undesirable talk.

Kokovkina already knew what the trouble was—they had informed her of it even more forcefully than the headmaster. Grushina had waited for her on the street, engaged her in a conversation, and said, finally, that Ludmila had already seduced Sasha. Kokovkina was dumfounded. At home she showered reproaches upon Sasha. She was all the more annoyed because this had happened before her eyes, and Sasha had gone to the Rutilovs' with her knowledge.

Sasha pretended that he did not understand anything and asked, "But what did I do wrong?"

Kokovkina became confused.

"What did you do wrong? And you yourself don't know? Didn't I find you in a skirt recently? Are you so shameless that you've forgotten that?"

"But what was especially wrong with that? And didn't you punish me for it? And it wasn't as if I had on a stolen skirt!"

"Look how he talks, if you please!" said Kokovkina at a loss. "I punished you, but evidently not well enough."

"Well, punish me more," said Sasha stubbornly with the air of an unjustly injured person. "You yourself forgave me, but now it isn't enough. And I didn't ask you to forgive me—I would have stayed on my knees all evening. Besides, what good is all this scolding!"

"Why they're talking about you and your Ludmilochka all over town, young man," said Kokovkina.

"And what are they saying?" asked Sasha with innocent curiosity in his voice.

Kokovkina again became confused.

"It's clear enough what they're saying! You yourself know what they might say about you. They're not saying much that's good. You're up to no good with your Ludmilochka, that's what they're saying."

"Well, I won't do it again," promised Sasha as calmly as if the conversation concerned a game of tag.

He assumed an innocent appearance, but his conscience was disturbed. He questioned Kokovkina as to what they were saying, and he was afraid that he would hear rude things. What could they be saying about them? The windows of Ludmilochka's bedroom faced the garden and were not visible from the street, and, anyway, Ludmilochka always lowered the curtains. And even if someone looked in, what could they say about it. Something vexing and insulting? Or might they simply be saying that he often went there?

And then, on the next day, Kokovkina received

the invitation to visit the headmaster. It completely un-
nerved the old woman. She did not even say anything
to Sasha but got herself ready quietly and left at the
appointed hour. Khripach courteously and gently informed her about the letter which he had received. She
began to cry.

"Calm yourself," said Khripach. "We don't blame
you. We know you well. Of course, you'll have to keep
track of him more carefully. But now tell me just what
really has happened."

Kokovkina arrived home from the headmaster's with
fresh reproaches for Sasha.

"I am going to write your aunt," she said, weeping.

"I'm not guilty of anything," said Sasha. "Let my
aunt come, I'm not afraid." And he too wept.

On the next day Khripach called Sasha in and asked
him drily and sternly: "I wish to know what sort of
acquaintances you have in the town."

Sasha looked at the headmaster with deceptively innocent and calm eyes. "What sort of acquaintances?"
he said. "Olga Vasil'evna can tell you—I only go to my
comrades', yes, and also to the Rutilovs'."

"Yes, precisely," Khripach continued his interroga-
tion. "And what do you do at the Rutilovs'?"

"Nothing special," said Sasha with the same innocent
expression. "Mainly, we read. The Rutilov girls love
poetry very much. And I am always home by seven
o'clock."

"Well, perhaps, not always?" asked Khripach, fixing
a glance, which he tried to make piercing, on Sasha.

"Yes, once I was late," said Sasha with the calm
frankness of an innocent boy. "But Olga Vasil'evna
gave it to me, and I haven't been late since then."

Khripach was silent. Sasha's calm replies disconcerted
him. In any case, it was necessary to give him a reprimand and a lecture, but how and for what? It had to be

done so that no nasty thoughts (which—so Khripach believed—he had not had before) were planted in the boy's mind and so that he did not offend the boy, but, at the same time, so that any unpleasantnesses which might arise because of this relationship in the future were eliminated. Khripach considered that the pedagogue's job was a difficult and responsible one, especially if one had the honor to be the head of an educational institution. Yes, the task of a pedagogue was a difficult and responsible one! This banal cliché gave wings to Khripach's sluggish thoughts. He began to speak rapidly, distinctly, and boringly. Sasha caught only portions of what he said.

". . . your first obligation as a student is to study . . . you must not be attracted by society, no matter how pleasant and irreproachable it is . . . in any event it must be said that the company of boys of your own age is much more suitable for you . . . it is necessary to uphold both your own reputation and that of your school . . . finally, I will tell you bluntly, that I have some basis to suppose that your relations with the young ladies have a degree of freedom unpermissible at your age and not in accordance with socially acceptable rules of conduct."

Sasha began to cry. It upset him that they should talk and think about dear Ludmilochka as though she were a person with whom one could behave loosely and improperly.

"On my word of honor, there was nothing bad—we only read, strolled, played, well, sometimes we ran—but there was nothing more."

Khripach slapped him on the shoulder and said, in a voice which attempted to be hearty but remained dry, "Listen, Pyl'nikov . . ."

(Why should he not sometimes call this boy Sasha? Was it because there had been as yet no bulletin from the ministry on the subject, and so it was not yet correct?)

"I believe you when you say that there was nothing wrong, but, nevertheless, you had better put an end to these frequent visits. Believe me, it will be much better this way. This is being said to you not only by your teacher and authority, but also by your friend."

Sasha had no choice but to bow, thank him, and then obey. And so Sasha began to go to Ludmila's only on very short visits of five and ten minutes—but still, he tried to go every day. It was annoying to have to see her on such short visits, and Sasha took out his vexation on Ludmila herself. He frequently called her Ludmilka, little fool, or stupid ass, and shoved her. But Ludmila only laughed at it all.

A rumor was going around town that the actors of the local theater were going to give a masquerade ball in the community hall with prizes for the best man's and the best woman's costumes. Exaggerated reports circulated concerning the prizes. It was said that the woman would receive a cow, and the man, a bicycle. These rumors excited the townspeople. Everyone wanted to win because the prizes were so substantial. People were hurriedly sewing costumes. No expense was spared. They hid their costume creations even from their closest friends so that their brilliant ideas would not be stolen.

When the printed announcement of the masquerade appeared—huge placards which were pasted on fences and sent to the prominent citizens—it turned out that the prizes were not a cow and a bicycle at all, but only a fan for the woman and an album for the man. This angered and disillusioned all those who had been preparing for the masquerade. They began to grumble.

"It was a waste of money!" they said.

"The prizes are simply a joke."

"They should have declared what the prizes were at once."

"It's only among us that the public can be treated in this manner."

Nevertheless, preparations continued—no matter what the prize, there was the honor of winning it.

The prize did not interest Dar'ya or Ludmila either at first or afterwards. Much they needed a cow! And a fan—there was a wonder indeed! Besides, who would award the prizes? Some taste these judges have! But both sisters were attracted by Ludmila's idea of sending Sasha to the masquerade in a woman's dress—thus deceiving the whole town—and fixing it so that they gave the prize to him. Valeriya also made it seem that she was in agreement. She was annoyed like a weak and envious child: he was Ludmila's little friend, and he didn't come to see her. Still, she didn't want to quarrel with her two older sisters.

"He won't dare," she said with a contemptuous smile.

"Well," said Dar'ya resolutely, "we'll make it so that no one will recognize him."

And when the sisters told Sasha about their plan, and Ludmilochka said to him, "We'll dress you up as a Japanese." Sasha jumped up and squealed with joy. Let come what would—and especially if no one was to know! Agree—how could he not agree? Why it would be great fun to fool everyone!

They at once decided that Sasha should be dressed as a geisha. The sisters kept their idea a very strict secret—they didn't even tell Larisa or their brother. Ludmila made the geisha costume herself from the design on the label of one of her perfume bottles. It was a long and wide dress of yellow silk on red satin, with a bright pattern—large flowers of a whimsical design—sewn on the dress. The girls also made the fan themselves from thin Japanese paper with designs and thin bamboo sticks. They made his umbrella of fine, rose-colored silk, and it even had a bamboo handle. They got rose-colored stockings for his feet and wooden sandals with little crosspieces under them. And Ludmila, the master, painted the mask for the geisha: it was a yellow but sweet, thin face with a slight, fixed smile, obliquely cut eyes, and a small, thin mouth. It was only the wig that they had to order from Petersburg—it was black with smooth, already arranged hair.

Time was necessary to fit the costume, but Sasha could only drop in for short visits, and then not every day. Still, they found the time. Sasha would slip out through the window at night when Kokovkina was already asleep. Everything went well.

Varvara was also preparing for the masquerade. She bought a mask with a stupid expression, and she had no problem about her costume—she dressed as a cook. She hung a ladle from her waist and put a white cook's cap on her head. Her arms were bare above her elbows, and she rouged them heavily—a cook straight from the kitchen stove—and the costume was ready. If they gave her the prize, all to the good, and if they didn't give it to her, she could manage without it.

Grushina decided to go as Diana. Varvara laughed and asked, "And will you wear a collar?"

"Why should I wear a collar?" asked Grushina with surprise.

"Well, you said you're going to dress as Dianka, the dog," explained Varvara.

"What you won't think of!" replied Grushina with a laugh. "Not Dianka, but Diana the goddess."

Varvara and Grushina both dressed for the masquerade at Grushina's. Grushina's costume was exceedingly scanty: bare arms and shoulders, bare back, bare chest, legs bare to the knees, light slippers on her feet, and a light costume of white linen with a red border hung directly upon her bare body—it was a short dress, but it was wide and had many folds.

"It's sort of bare," said Varvara with a leer.

"It'll attract the fellows," replied Grushina with a vulgar wink.

"But why do you have so many folds?" asked Varvara.

"I can fill them with candies for my little devils," explained Grushina.

All of Grushina's boldly revealed body was, in spite of it all, beautiful—but what contradictions! She had flea bites on her skin, her manners were coarse, and her talk was insufferably banal. Another example of profaned bodily beauty.

Peredonov thought that the masquerade had been planned on purpose as some sort of a trap for him. Nevertheless, he went there—not in a costume, but in an ordinary jacket. He wanted to see for himself what evil plots had been devised.

The thought of the masquerade had kept Sasha in high spirits for several days. But then doubts began to bother him. How could he get away from home? And especially now after these unpleasantnesses. If they were to find out about it in the gymnasium, it would be a catastrophe, and he would certainly be expelled at once.

Recently the proctor—a young man so liberal that he was unable to call a cat Vas'ka, but called it, the cat, Vasily—had made a very significant remark to Sasha as he handed out the marks: "Look here, Pyl'nikov, you must spend more time on your work."

"But I haven't gotten any twos," replied Sasha carelessly, but his heart fell: what would he say next? No, nothing, he just grumbled and looked at him sternly.

On the day of the masquerade it seemed to Sasha that he would not have the nerve to go. He was afraid. But the costume was ready at the Rutilovs'—should that all be for nothing? And all the dreams and the work—should that be for nothing? Ludmilochka would cry. No, he had to go.

His habit of reticence, recently acquired in the last few weeks, helped Sasha hide his excitement from Kokovkina. Fortunately, the old woman went to bed early. Sasha too went to bed early, and to avoid suspicion he placed clothing on a chair by the door and put his boots outside of the door.

There remained only the departure—the most difficult part. He would take the same path, through the window, that he had used earlier when he had gone for his fittings. Sasha put on a light summer blouse—it was hanging in the closet in his room—and light bedroom slippers, and he cautiously climbed out of the window to the street, having chosen a moment when no footsteps or voices could be heard nearby. There was a fine drizzle, and it was muddy, cold, and dark. But it continually seemed to Sasha that he would be recognized. He took off his cap and his slippers and tossed them back into his bedroom. Then he turned up his trousers and ran, hopping with his bare feet along the slippery and rickety pavement. His face was poorly visible in the darkness, especially since he was running, and anyone who had encountered him would have thought he was a peasant lad sent on an errand to the store.

Valeriya and Ludmila had made unoriginal but artistic costumes for themselves: Ludmila dressed as a gypsy; Valeriya, as a Spaniard. Ludmila had on bright rags of silk and velvet, and the slender and frail Valeriya had on black silk and lace. In her hand she carried a black lace fan. Dar'ya had not made herself a new costume—she still had her last year's costume, a Turkish woman. She put it on and said with assurance, "It's not worth-while to think up another one!"

When Sasha arrived, all three sisters began to dress him. The wig disturbed Sasha more than anything.

"What if it falls off!" he kept repeating fearfully.

Finally, they fastened the wig down with ribbons tied under his chin.

29 : ৡ৽ৡ৽

The masquerade was held in the community hall, a two-story stone building resembling a barracks and painted bright red, which stood on the marketplace square. The masquerade had been arranged by Gromov-Chistopol'sky, an actor and the manager of the local theater.

At the entrance, covered by a calico awning, small glass lamps were burning. A crowd in the street met those who were arriving at the masquerade by carriage and on foot with critical comments, for the most part unfavorable, especially since in the street the guests' costumes were almost not visible under their overcoats—making the crowd judge them chiefly by instinct. The policemen kept order in the street with sufficient zeal—the chief of police and the police inspector were in the hall as guests.

Upon entering, each guest received two tickets: one was a pink one for the best woman's costume and the other was a green one for the man's. They were to be handed over to the deserving ones.

"May we keep them ourselves?" inquired some people.

At first the ticket usher asked them in perplexity, "Why for yourself?"

"But suppose, in my opinion, my costume is best," the guest would reply.

Later the usher ceased to be surprised at such questions and said with a satirical smile (he was a young man with a sense of humor): "Do as you wish. You may keep both for yourself."

Inside it was rather dirty, and from the very beginning a significant portion of the crowd seemed to be drunk. Crooked chandeliers were burning in the crowded rooms with their sooty walls and ceilings—they were huge and heavy and seemed to be consuming much of the air. The faded curtains by the doors had an appearance such that it was unpleasant to brush up against them. Crowds collected here and there, and exclamations and laughter were heard—this was due to certain costumes which attracted the general attention.

The notary, Gudaevsky, came as an American Indian. He had cocks' feathers in his hair, a copper-red mask with foolish green designs on it, a leather jacket, a checked plaid blanket across his shoulder, and high leather boots with green tassels. He waved his arms, jumped about, and walked with an athletic stride, lifting up his bare knees exaggeratedly. His wife was dressed as an ear of corn. She had on a bright dress of green and yellow patches, and ears of corn stuck out from her on all sides. They brushed and struck against everyone. People harassed and plucked at her. "I'll scratch," she screeched angrily. Everyone around her laughed.

"Where did she collect so many ears of corn?" someone asked.

"She stored it up in the summer," they answered him. "Every day she went to the fields to steal some."

Several officials without mustaches who were enamored of Gudaevskaya and had, therefore, been told by her in advance what she would be wearing, accompanied her. They were collecting tickets for her—rudely and almost by force. They simply snatched them away from some who were not especially bold.

There were also other costumed women earnestly collecting tickets through their cavaliers. Some simply looked avidly at the tickets which had not been surrendered and asked for them. They received insults.

A down-hearted woman dressed as Night in a blue costume with a glass star and a paper moon on her forehead timidly said to Murin, "Give me your ticket."

"What for?" replied Murin rudely. "Give my ticket to you! I don't care for your snout!"

Night grumbled something angrily and moved away. She only wanted to get two or three tickets so that she could show them at home and prove that she had gotten some too. Modest dreams are futile.

The schoolteacher, Skobochkina, was dressed as a bear, that is, she had simply thrown a bearskin over her shoulders and placed a bear's head on her own, like a helmet, above the ordinary half-mask. This was quite awful, but all in all it suited her robust frame and loud voice. The she-bear walked with heavy steps and roared out so that the flames in the chandeliers trembled. Many people liked the she-bear. She collected more than a few tickets. But she had not found a clever male helper like many others had. The tradesmen gave her things to drink: they felt at ease with her ability to display bearish manners. People in the crowd cried out, "Look over there, the she-bear is guzzling vodka!"

Skobochkina had been unable to resist the vodka. It seemed to her that a bear ought to drink vodka if it was given to her. She soon became drunk, and later more than half of her tickets were craftily stolen by Dar'ya and Ludmila and given to Sasha.

A certain gentleman dressed as an ancient German stood out because of his posture and fine physique. He pleased many because of his robustness and because his powerful arms with exceedingly well-developed muscles were visible. Women, particularly, walked after him, and a whisper of admiration and flattery could be heard around him. The ancient German was recognized as the actor, Bengal'sky. Bengal'sky was well liked in our town, and for that reason many people gave him their tickets. They reasoned thusly: "If I'm not going to receive the prize, then better let an actor (or actress) get it. If one of our people gets it, he'll weary us with boasting."

Grushina's costume also was a success—a scandalous success. Men walked after her in a large crowd, laughing and making immodest observations. Women turned away in embarrassment. Finally, the chief of police walked up to Grushina and, sweetly licking his lips, said, "You must cover yourself, madam."

"But why? There's nothing improper to be seen about me," replied Grushina glibly.

"The ladies are taking offense, madam," said Min'-chukov.

"I'd like to spit on your ladies!" exclaimed Grushina.

"You should at least, madam," requested Min'chuk-ov, "place a handkerchief in your bosom, yes, and try to cover your back."

"But what if my handkerchief is snotty?" retorted Grushina with a vulgar laugh.

But Min'chukov insisted: "As you wish, madam, but if you do not cover yourself up a little, you will have to leave."

Cursing and grumbling, Grushina went off to the bathroom and there, with the help of a servant, she re-arranged the folds of her dress onto her chest and back. Although she had a more modest appearance when she returned to the hall, she still vigorously con-tinued to seek supporters and flirted brazenly with all the men. And when their attention was diverted elsewhere, she went into the buffet to steal sweets. Soon she re-turned to the hall and showed Volodin two peaches.

"I requisitioned them myself," she said, smirking and she at once hid the peaches in the folds of her costume.

Volodin grinned happily. "Well!" he said. "If that's the case, I'll go too."

Soon Grushina had had too much to drink and was behaving wildly. She shouted, waved her arms, and spat. "The gay Madam Dianka!" they said about her.

Such was the masquerade to which the capricious girls had attracted an imprudent schoolboy. The three sisters and Sasha came rather late in two cabs—they were late because of him. Their entrance into the hall was noticed. The geisha especially pleased many people. A rumor spread that the geisha was Kashtanova, an actress very popular with the male portion of local society. Therefore, they gave Sasha many tickets. Kashtanova was not at the masquerade at all—her small son had fallen dangerously ill the day before.

Sasha, intoxicated by his new position, flirted wildly. The more they thrust their tickets into the little geisha's hand, the more gaily and provocatively sparkled the eyes of the coquettish Japanese girl through the narrow slits in the mask. The geisha curtsied, lifted her small fingers, tittered in an intimate tone, waved her fan, tapped now one man and now another on the shoulder with it, then closed the fan, and frequently opened her rose parasol. These guileless acts were sufficient for the majority of those who admired the actress Kashtanova.

"My ticket I surrender to the fairest of her gender," said Tishkov, and he gave his ticket to the geisha with a dashing bow. He has already had a good deal to drink, and his face was red; his immobile, smiling face and his clumsy figure made him resemble a doll. He was constantly rhyming.

Valeriya watched Sasha's success and was jealous and vexed: she herself wanted the attention so her costume and her fine, slender figure would please the crowd, and they would give her the prize. But she immediately recalled with irritation that this was not possible because all three sisters had agreed to collect tickets only for the geisha and even to give any they themselves might receive to their Japanese girl.

There was dancing in the hall. Volodin, who had quickly become tipsy, soon began to dance the *trepak* in a crouch, kicking his legs up into the air. The police stopped him.

"Well, if I can't, then I won't," he said obediently and gaily.

But two other men who had followed his example did not wish to stop. "By what law? We paid our fifty kopecks!" they exclaimed and were led out. Volodin accompanied them, grimacing, grinning, and skipping.

The Rutilov girls hastened to search out Peredonov in order to scoff at him. He was sitting alone by a window, watching the crowd with wandering eyes. All people and objects seemed meaningless and absurd, but equally hostile to him. Ludmila, the gypsy, went up to him and said in an affected, throaty voice, "Let me tell your fortune, my good *barin*."

"Go to hell!" shouted Peredonov. The sudden appearance of the gypsy had frightened him.

"Good *barin*, my shining *barin*, give me your hand. I see by your face that you will be rich, a high-ranking official," said Ludmila persuasively, and she took Peredonov's hand.

"Well, take care that you give me a good fortune," grumbled Peredonov.

"Aiii, my most extraordinary *barin*," said Ludmila, "you have many enemies, they will inform on you, you will weep, you will die under a fence."

"You're a witch!" shouted Peredonov, he snatched his hand away.

Ludmila swiftly vanished into the crowd, and Valeriya came in her place. She sat down next to Peredonov and whispered tenderly,

I'm a Spaniard of beauty true
And I love such men as you
But, alas, your wife's a cur,
O most charming, gentle sir.

"You're lying, fool," growled Peredonov.
Valeriya continued, whispering:

Sweeter than night, hotter than day
Is my sultry Seville embrace.
Spit in that stupid Varvara's face—
Your wife's not worth you in any way.
For you're a treasure, Ardal'on
Why you're as wise as Solomon.

"That's true, what you say," said Peredonov. "but how can I spit in her face? She would complain to the Princess, and they wouldn't give me the position."

"And why do you need a position? You're good even without a position," said Valeriya.

"Yes, but how can I live if they don't give me the position?" said Peredonov sadly.

Dar'ya thrust a letter with a rose seal into Volodin's hand. Volodin opened the letter, bleating happily, and read it through proudly but with some confusion. The note was short and clear:

"Meet me tomorrow, dearest, at eleven o'clock at night by the Military Bathhouse.
Your unknown Zh."

Volodin believed the letter, but the question was: was it worth-while to go? And who was this Zh? A Zhenya perhaps? Or could it be that her last name began with the letters Zh?

Volodin showed the letter to Rutilov.

"Go, of course, go!" encouraged Rutilov. "See what will come of it. Perhaps it's a rich young girl who has fallen in love with you, but her parents are interfering, and she wishes to explain to you in this way."

But Volodin thought and thought and still could not decide whether it was worth-while to go. "They're always hanging on my neck, but I don't like such loosely-behaved girls," he said importantly.

He was afraid that he would get beaten up—the Military Bathhouse was located in a lonely place on the edge of town.

When the dense, noisy, festively gay mob was already crowded into all the rooms, noise, laughter, and approving cries were heard by the entrance door. Everyone pressed in that direction. They informed one another that a terribly original mask had come in. A tall, thin man in a patched, soiled dressing gown with a shower broom under his arm and a pail in his hand made his way through the crowd. He had on a cardboard mask— a stupid face with a narrow beard and side whiskers, and on his head was a cap with a round, official cockade. He kept repeating in an astonished voice, "They told me there was to be a gathering and not to wear my clothes, but I don't see anyone bathing here." * And he dejectedly swung a pail. The crowd walked after him, ahing and sincerely admiring his clever idea.

"He'll surely get the prize," said Volodin enviously.

Like many, he was thoughtlessly and automatically envious—but, since he himself did not have on a costume, what reason had he to be envious? Machigin, however, was unusually pleased: the cockade especially delighted him. He laughed happily, clapped his hands, and said to those he knew and didn't know, "A fine criticism! Those civil servies act very important—they

* A secondary meaning of the Russian word *maskarad* is "bath."

love to wear their cockades and dresscoats. Well, there's a criticism for them—very clever."

When it became hot, the official in the bathrobe began to wave his shower broom exclaiming, "Phew, this is some steambath!" The people standing around him laughed gaily and tossed their tickets into his pail.

Peredonov watched the shower broom waving in the crowd. It seemed to him to be the *nedotykomka*. "The beast has turned green," he thought in terror.

30 : ई़३ई़३

Finally, the counting of the tickets which had been received for the costumes began. There was a committee of the club stewards. The expectant, costumed crowd collected by the doors to the judging room. Within a short time it became tediously quiet in the club. The music stopped. The guests grew silent. Peredonov became terrified. But soon conversations began in the crowd, and there was an impatient murmur and noise. Someone declared that both prizes would go to actors. "You'll see," the person's annoyed, hissing voice could be heard, and many believed this.

The crowd was excited. Those who had received few tickets were angry about this. Those who had received many were excited by the expectation of a possible injustice.

Suddenly a delicate and penetrating little bell rang. The judges—Veriga, Avinovitsky, Kirillov, and other club officials—came out. A flurry of excitement ran through the hall, and suddenly everyone became quiet. Avinovitsky spoke out in a resounding voice that carried through the entire hall, "The prize for the best male costume, an album, awarded according to the largest number of tickets received, goes to the gentleman dressed as an ancient German."

Avinovitsky raised the album high and angrily looked at the crowded mass of guests. The sturdy German began to make his way through the crowd. Everyone glanced hostilely at him. They did not even make way for him.

"Don't shove, please!" cried Night—the dejected woman in the blue costume with a glass star and a paper moon on her forehead—in a tearful voice.

"They gave him the prize, and so he imagines that the women must prostrate themselves before him," was heard an angrily hissing voice in the crowd.

"But you won't let me pass," replied the German with restrained anger.

Finally, he somehow made his way to the judges and took the album from Veriga's hands. The orchestra played a flourish, but the sound of the music was lost in the disorderly noise. Curses poured forth. They surrounded the German, tugged at him, and cried, "Take off your mask."

The German was silent. It would not have been difficult for him to fight his way through the crowd, but he evidently was reluctant to exert his full strength. Gudaevsky grabbed for the album, and at the same time someone quickly tore the mask off the German.

"It is an actor!" the crowd exclaimed. Their suppositions proved to be correct: it was the actor, Bengal'-sky.

"Well, so I'm an actor—what of it!" he angrily exclaimed. "You yourselves gave me the tickets!"

Angry cries sounded in reply.

"One could slip in extras."

"You had some tickets printed."

"There were more tickets handed in than there are people here."

"He brought half a hundred tickets in his pocket."

Bengal'sky turned crimson and shouted, "It's foul to talk that way. You can prove it if you like—count the number of guests."

Meanwhile Veriga said to those nearest him, "Calm down, gentlemen, there has been no deceit, I can attest to that. The number of tickets has been checked against the number of those entering."

Somehow the stewards with the help of the few sensible guests quieted down the crowd. Besides, everyone was curious to see who would get the fan.

"Gentlemen," announced Veriga, "the largest number of tickets for a woman's costume was received by the lady dressed in the geisha costume, and she has been awarded the prize—a fan. Will the geisha please come forward—the fan is yours. Gentlemen, I request you most respectfully to be so kind as to make room for the geisha."

The orchestra played a second flourish. The frightened geisha would have been happy to run away, but they shoved, pushed, and led her forward. Veriga with a friendly smile handed her the fan. The motley-colored costumes flashed before Sasha's eyes, which were blurred with fear and confusion. It was necessary to say thank you, he thought—the habitual politeness of a well raised boy expressing itself. The geisha curtsied, said something unclear, giggled, raised her fingers—and again a loud uproar of curses and whistles was heard in the hall. Everyone surged towards the geisha.

"Curtsy, you little beast, curtsy!" shouted the savage and disheveled ear of corn.

The geisha rushed to the doors, but they would not let her out. Angry cries were heard in the excited crowd around her:

"Make her take off her mask!"

"Off with the mask!"

"Catch her! Hold her!"

"Tear it off her!"

"Take away her fan!"

"Do you know who got the prize?" shouted the ear of corn. "The actress Kashtanova. She stole someone else's husband, but they gave her the prize! They don't give it to honorable women, but they give it to that slut!"

And she threw herself towards the geisha screaming piercingly and clenching her bony fists. Others came after her, mostly her cavaliers. The geisha fought back desperately. A wild brawl began. They smashed the fan, tore it up, threw it on the floor, and trampled it. The crowd with the geisha at its center tossed violently about the hall, sweeping onlookers from their feet. Neither the Rutilovs nor the stewards could get through to the geisha. The geisha, strong and alert, was screaming piercingly and scratching and biting. She firmly held her mask on, now with her right hand, now with her left.

"We must beat them all!" screamed an angry woman.

The drunken Grushina, hiding behind others, urged on Volodin and her other acquaintances. "Pinch her, pinch the slut!" she screamed.

Machigin, holding his nose, which was dripping blood, jumped away from the crowd and complained, "She hit me right on the nose with her fist."

A particularly ferocious young man caught the geisha's sleeve in his teeth and ripped half of it off.

"Save me!" cried the geisha.

Others also began to rip away her costume, and her body was revealed in places. Dar'ya and Ludmila pushed desperately trying to break through to the geisha, but in vain. Volodin plucked at the geisha with such enthusiasm and squealed and so carried on that he actually interfered with others less drunk than he and more vicious: he was acting not from meanness but from enjoyment, imagining that a very amusing game was going on. He completely ripped one sleeve from the geisha's dress and tied it around his head.

"This will come in handy!" he cried shrilly, grimacing and laughing loudly. Moving away from the throng, where it seemed too crowded to him, he continued to make a fool of himself in the uncrowded space and danced over the pieces of the fan with wild squeals. There was no one to stop him.

Peredonov looked at him in terror and thought, "He's dancing—he is happy about something. That's how he'll dance on my grave."

Finally, the geisha tore away—the men could not withstand the onslaught of her quick fists and sharp teeth. The geisha dashed from the hall. In the corridor the ear of corn again rushed upon the Japanese and grabbed her by the dress. The geisha was about to tear away, but they were already surrounding her again. The scuffle resumed.

"By the ears, they have her by the ears," someone called. One woman had seized the geisha by the ear and was pulling it, emitting loud triumphant cries. The geisha squealed and somehow broke away, after she had struck the malevolent little woman with her fist.

Finally, Bengal'sky, who in the meantime had managed to change into his ordinary clothes, fought his way through the crowd to the geisha. He took the trembling Japanese in his arms and, shielding her with his huge body and arms as much as he could, he quickly carried her away, nimbly moving the crowd away with his elbows and legs.

"Villain! Scoundrel!" they shouted in the crowd. They pulled at Bengal'sky and punched him in the back.

"I shall not allow you to tear the mask from this woman," he shouted. "Do what you will, I shall not allow it."

In this way he carried the geisha the entire length of the hall, which ended with a small door leading into the dining room. Here Veriga managed to restrain the crowd for a short time. With a firm martial air he stood before the door, blocking it with his body, and said, "You will not go any farther, gentlemen."

Gudaevskaya, rustling with the disorderly remnants of her ears of corn, flew at Veriga, shaking her fists at him and screaming piercingly, "Go away! Let us through!"

But the cold exterior of the general's face and his determined gray eyes deterred her from doing anything. "You might at least have given her a slap in the face instead of gaping, you boob!" she screamed at her husband in helpless fury.

"I couldn't get at her," said the Indian in defense, wildly waving his arms. "Pavlushka was under foot."

"What were you so polite for?" screamed Gudaevskaya. "You should have given it to Pavlushka in the teeth and her in the ear."

The crowd pressed against Veriga. Street language was heard all around. Veriga stood calmly in front of the door and urged those nearest him to put an end to the outrage. A kitchen boy partly opened the door behind Veriga and whispered, "They've gone, your excellency."

Veriga withdrew, and the crowd tore into the dining room and then into the kitchen looking for the geisha, but they could not find her.

Bengal'sky carried the geisha at a run through the dining room into the kitchen. She lay peacefully in his arms and said nothing. It seemed to Bengal'sky that he could hear the strong beating of her heart. On her tightly clutching bare arms he noticed several scratches and near her elbow was the bluish-yellow stain of a bruise. In an excited voice, Bengal'sky said to the help crowding around in the kitchen, "Step lively! A coat, a dressing gown, a sheet, something—I must save this lady."

Someone's coat was thrown over Sasha's shoulders, and Bengal'sky wrapped up the Japanese somewhat. Going along a narrow stairway barely illuminated by smoky kerosene lamps, he carried her outside and through a gate into a side street.

"Take off your mask, they'll be more likely to recognize you in it. It's dark now, so it doesn't matter. I won't tell anyone," he said in a rather disorganized way.

He was curious. He knew for certain that it was not Kashtanova—but then who was it? The Japanese obeyed. Bengal'sky saw an unknown, smooth face on which fear was turning into joy at the eluded danger. Mirthful, even gay eyes were fixed on the actor's face.

"How can I thank you!" said the geisha in a clear voice. "I don't know what would have happened to me if you hadn't pulled me out."

"The girl's no coward—an interesting little lady!" thought the actor. "But who is she?" Evidently she was a new arrival: Bengal'sky knew the local ladies.

"I must take you home at once," he said quietly to Sasha. "Tell me your address, and I'll hail a cab."

The face of the Japanese again grew dark with fear.

"You mustn't, you mustn't!" she whispered. "Leave me here, and I will go alone."

"Now how can you go home in this mud in your wooden sandals—you need a cab," said the actor persuasively.

"No, I'll go by myself. For God's sake, let me down," implored the geisha.

"On my word of honor—I'll tell no one," said Bengal'sky persuasively. "I can't leave you here, you'll catch cold. And tell me quickly—they could even catch you here. You yourself have seen that these people are complete beasts. They are capable of anything."

The geisha trembled. Quick tears suddenly rolled from her eyes. "They are terribly, terribly evil people!" she said sobbing. "Take me to the Rutilovs', I'll spend the night with them."

Bengal'sky hailed a cab. They sat down and drove off. The actor stared at the geisha's smooth face. It seemed strange to him. The geisha turned away. A vague thought flashed through his mind. He recalled the stories in town about the Rutilovs, about Ludmila and her gymnasium student.

"You, you're a boy!" he said in a whisper so that the cabman would not hear.

"For God's sake," implored Sasha, pale with terror, and his smooth hands reached out from under the coat wrapped around him towards Bengal'sky in a sign of entreaty.

Bengal'sky laughed gently and said very quietly, "Don't worry, I won't tell anyone. My job is to get you home, and I know nothing else. You certainly are daring. And won't they find you out at home?"

"If you don't say anything, no one will know," said Sasha in a softly imploring voice.

"Rely on me, your secret's as safe as though it were in a tomb," replied the actor. "I was a boy myself and used to play tricks."

The scandal in the club had already begun to quiet down, but the evening was crowned with a new calamity. While they were tormenting the geisha in the hall, the flaming *nedotykomka*, leaping along the chandeliers, laughed and insisted that Peredonov must strike a match and loose it, the flaming but confined *nedotykomka*, upon these dull, dirty walls; and then, when it had satisfied itself with the annihilation in flames of this building, where such strange and incomprehensible things were happening, it would leave Peredonov in peace. Peredonov was unable to resist its insistent command. He entered a small sitting room which adjoined the dancing hall—there was no one in it. Peredonov looked around, struck a match, placed it beneath a window curtain near the floor, and waited until the curtains caught fire. The fiery *nedotykomka* crept along the curtain like a lively little snake, squealing softly and happily. Peredonov left the sitting room and closed the door behind him. No one had noticed the incendiary.

The blaze was seen from the street only when the whole room was in flames. The fire spread quickly. The people were saved, but the building burned down.

On the following day they talked of nothing else in the town but the scandal with the geisha and the blaze. Bengal'sky kept his word and didn't tell anyone that the geisha was a disguised boy.

Sasha had changed at the Rutilovs' that night, and, having turned again into a simple, barefoot boy, had run home, climbed in the window, and gone quietly to sleep. In a town seething with gossip, in a town where everyone knows everything about everyone, Sasha's nocturnal adventure, nevertheless, remained a secret. For a long time, but not, of course, forever.*

31 :

Ekaterina Ivanovna Pyl'nikova, Sasha's aunt and guardian, received two letters at the same time about Sasha —one from the headmaster and one from Kokovkina.

* Bengal'sky appears again briefly in *Sweeter than Poison*. Grushina also appears in this novel.

These letters greatly disturbed her. She cast aside all her affairs and hurriedly set out from the country to our town along the muddy autumn roads. Sasha welcomed his aunt with glee—he loved her. The aunt had been planning strict punishment for him, but he threw himself around her neck so happily and so covered her hands with kisses that she was unable to use a strict tone with him at first.

"Dearest auntie, how good you are to have come!" said Sasha, and he gazed happily at her full, rosy face with its kind dimples on the cheeks and its serious, hazel eyes.

"Postpone your rejoicing until I take you in hand," said the aunt in an irresolute voice.

"I don't mind," said Sasha calmly. "Take me in hand if there is any cause for it, but all the same you have made me terribly happy."

"Terribly!" repeated his aunt in a displeased voice. "And I have found out some terrible things about you."

Sasha lifted his eyebrows and looked at his aunt with innocent, uncomprehending eyes.

"There is one teacher, Peredonov," he complained, "who imagines that I am a girl and has been bothering me. And then the headmaster lectured me because I had become acquainted with the Rutilov girls. As though I went there to steal things. What business is it of theirs?"

"He is the same child he was before," thought his aunt in perplexity. "Or has he already been so corrupted that he can even deceive me with his face?"

She shut herself up with Kokovkina and talked with her for a long time. She came out saddened. Then she went to see the headmaster. She returned completely downcast. His aunt's strong reproaches showered down upon Sasha. Sasha wept but fiercely maintained that it was all gossip and that he never allowed himself any liberties with the young ladies. His aunt did not believe him. She scolded and scolded, wept, and threatened to give Sasha a severe whipping that very day as soon as she had seen these girls. Sasha sobbed and continued to maintain that nothing bad had happened and that it was all terribly exaggerated and made up.

The angry, tearful aunt set out to the Rutilovs'.

As she waited in the Rutilov sitting room, Ekaterina Ivanovna was very excited. She wanted to heap the most terrible reproaches upon the sisters at once, and she had the nasty, reproachful words all ready—but their quiet, attractive sitting room gave her, against her will, peaceful thoughts and soothed her vexation. The unfinished embroidery left here, the keepsakes, the engravings on the walls, the carefully arranged plants by the windows, the complete absence of dust, and especially that certain domestic atmosphere—all this was not at all what one finds in disreputable houses. Rather, there was what is always valued by housekeepers—could one really in these surroundings imagine the corruption of her modest boy by the gay, young mistresses of this sitting room? All those things which she had read and heard about Sasha seemed to her terribly absurd, and, on the other hand, Sasha's explanations to her about what he did with the Rutilov girls seemed logical: they read, talked, joked, laughed, played . . . they had wanted to stage a play at home but Olga Vasil'evna wouldn't permit him to be in it.

The three sisters felt ill at ease. They still did not know whether Sasha's disguise had remained a secret. But there were three of them, and they all consoled each other. This gave them greater courage. All three were gathered in Ludmila's room conferring in a whisper.

"We have to go to her," said Valeriya. "She's waiting, and it's rude."

"So what—let her cool off a little," replied Dar'ya carelessly, "otherwise she'll fall upon us very angrily."

All the sisters scented themselves with sweet-smelling clematis—they came out calm, gay, attractive, and well-dressed as always. They filled the sitting room with their pleasant and gay chatter. Ekaterina Ivanovna was at once enchanted by their sweet, charming appearance.

"What corrupters they have found!" she thought with annoyance about the gymnasium pedagogues. But then she thought that perhaps they were putting on a modest appearance, and she decided not to submit to their charms.

"Forgive me, young ladies, but I have something serious to discuss with you," she said trying to give her voice a businesslike dryness.

The sisters seated her and chattered merrily.

"Which one of you? . . ." Ekaterina Ivanovna began irresolutely.

Ludmila talked happily and gave the appearance that she was a courteous hostess trying to help her visitor out of a difficult position: "It was I who spent the most time with your nephew. It happens that we have similar views and tastes about many things."

"Your nephew is a very sweet boy," said Dar'ya as if assured that her praise would make their guest happy.

"Yes, he really is sweet, and so entertaining," said Ludmila.

Ekaterina Ivanovna felt more and more awkward. She suddenly realized that she had no reasonable grounds for her complaints, and because of this she was angry with herself. Ludmila's last words gave her an opportunity to express her annoyance.

"He may be an entertainment to you, but to him . . ." she said angrily.

But Dar'ya interrupted her and said in a sympathetic voice, "Akh! Now we see that those stupid Peredonovian fantasies have reached you. But do you know—he is an utter madman. His headmaster does not allow him in the gymnasium. They are only waiting for a psychiatrist to examine him and then they'll throw him out of the gymnasium."

"But pardon me," interrupted Ekaterina Ivanovna in her turn, growing all the more irritated. "It is my nephew and not this teacher who interests me. I have heard that you—forgive me, please—are debauching him." But when she had heatedly hurled this harsh word at the sisters, Ekaterina Ivanovna at once felt that she had gone too far.

The sisters exchanged glances with such well-feigned perplexity and embarrassment that not only Ekaterina Ivanovna would have been fooled. They blushed and exclaimed all at once:

"How charming!"

"Terrible!"

"This is something new!"

"My dear madam," said Dar'ya coldly, "you are not very selective in your choice of words. Before you say coarse things, you should find out if they are warranted."

"Akh, it is so understandable!" said Ludmila with the air of an injured but forgiving and charming girl. "After all, he's not a stranger to you. Naturally, who would not be disturbed by all these stupid rumors. We, too, were sorry for him, and so we were kind to him. But in our town everything is at once made into a crime. You have no idea what terrible, terrible, terrible people there are here!"

"Terrible people!" repeated Valeriya quietly in a clear, delicate voice, and she trembled all over as though she had touched something unclean.

"But you ask him yourself," said Dar'ya. "You look at him—why, he's still a mere child. Perhaps, you have grown accustomed to his simplicity, but it is quite clear to an outsider that he is an absolutely innocent boy."

The sisters lied so convincingly and calmly that one could not help but believe them. And besides, a lie is often more credible than the truth. Almost always. The truth itself, of course, is incredible.

"Of course, it is true that he comes here too often," said Dar'ya, "but we will not allow him in the door any more if you wish."

"And I myself am going to see Khripach today," said Ludmila. "What has he thought up? Can he really believe such stupid nonsense?"

"No, it seems that he doesn't believe it himself," confessed Ekaterina Ivanovna. "He merely says that various bad rumors are circulating."

"There, you see!" exclaimed Ludmila happily. "Naturally he doesn't believe it himself. Then why all this fuss?"

Ludmila had taken Ekaterina Ivanovna in with her happy voice. "And what has really happened?" she thought. "Even the headmaster says that he doesn't believe any of it."

For a long time the sisters continued to chatter in rivalry with each other in convincing Ekaterina Ivanovna of the complete innocence of their relations with Sasha. To reassure her completely they were on the verge of telling her in great detail just exactly what they did with Sasha and when, but they quickly dropped this intention: they were all such innocent, simple things that one just could not remember them. And Ekaterina Ivanovna finally was completely convinced that her Sasha and the charming Rutilov girls were the innocent victims of stupid gossip.

As she was leaving, Ekaterina Ivanovna warmly kissed the sisters and told them, "You are charming, simple girls. At first I thought that you were—forgive the unseemly word—wantons."

The sisters laughed gaily.

"No," said Ludmila, "we are merely happy girls with sharp tongues, and that is why some of the local geese don't like us."

When she returned from the Rutilovs', his aunt did not say anything to Sasha. He, however, felt thoroughly frightened and ashamed, and he watched her carefully and attentively. The aunt went to Kokovkina. They spoke for a long time. Finally the aunt decided, "I am going to see the headmaster again."

On the same day Ludmila set out to see Khripach. She remained in the sitting room with Varvara Niko-laevna for a while and then explained that she had come to see Nikolai Vlas'evich on business.

A lively conversation took place in Khripach's study, not because either of them had much to say to one an-other, but because they both liked to talk. Their rapid speeches poured forth upon each other: Khripach with his dry, pompous, rapid manner of speaking, and Lud-mila with her soft, resonant babbling. Fluently and with the undeniable persuasiveness of falsehood, she poured forth on Khripach a half-false account of her relationship with Sasha Pyl'nikov. Her main motive was, of course, sympathy for the boy who was suffering from such base suspicion as well as a desire to replace the boy's missing family. And also, he was such a fine, gay, and unaffected boy. Ludmila even wept, and, in a wonderfully beautiful way, little tears rolled quickly down her rosy cheeks to her embarrassed, smiling lips.

"It is true that I have grown to love him—like a brother. He is fine and good. He so wants affection. He kissed my hands."

"This is, of course, very admirable on your part," said the slightly embarrassed Khripach, "and it does honor to your feelings. But you have needlessly taken offense at the simple fact that I considered it my duty to inform the boy's relatives of the rumors that had reached me."

Ludmila, not listening to him, ran on, and her voice assumed the tone of a gentle rebuke:

"What is there wrong, tell me please, in our taking the part of a boy beset by your coarse, mad Peredonov? And when will they take him out of our town? Why can't you see yourself that your Pyl'nikov is still nothing but a child—really, a mere child!"

She clasped her small, pretty hands together, rattled her golden bracelet, and laughed softly as though she were crying. She took out her handkerchief to wipe away her tears and a sweet aroma wafted towards Khripach. Khripach suddenly wanted to tell her that she was "as delightful as a heavenly angel" and that this paltry incident "was not worth one moment of her sweet sorrow." * But he restrained himself.

Ludmila's soft, quick whisper went on and on and dissolved into smoke the chimerical structure of Peredonov's lie. One had only to compare the mad, coarse, dirty Peredonov with the gay, delightful, well-dressed, sweet-smelling Ludmilochka. It was all the same to Khripach whether Ludmila was telling the complete truth or fibbing because he felt that not to believe Ludmilochka and to argue with her and begin some sort of an investigation or even to punish Pyl'nikov would inevitably mean an inquiry and a scandal in the whole school district. Moreover, this matter was connected with Peredonov who was, of course, obviously abnormal.

Thus, Khripach, smiling good-naturedly, said to Ludmila, "I am very sorry that this has bothered you so. Not for one minute did I allow myself to have any untoward thoughts concerning your relations with Pyl'nikov. I value the kind and noble intentions which inspired your actions very highly, and not for one minute could I look upon the rumors circulating in the

---

* These lines are from Lermontov's verse tale, *Demon*.

town and reaching me as anything, but stupid and in-
sane gossip, deeply disturbing to me. I was obligated
to inform Madam Pyl'nikova inasmuch as even more
distorted rumors might have reached her—but I did
not wish to upset you, and I did not think that Madam
Pyl'nikova would turn to you with reproaches."

"We have had a peaceful explanation with Madam
Pyl'nikova," said Ludmila cheerfully, "but you must
not punish Sasha on account of us. If our house
is really so dangerous for students, then we shall not
let him in, if you wish it."

"You have been very kind to him," said Khripach
in an indefinite way. "We cannot say anything about
his visiting his acquaintances in his free time, if his
aunt permits it. We do not wish to turn the students'
lodgings into some sort of prison—far from it. Nevertheless, until the Peredonov matter is settled, it would
be better if Pyl'nikov remained more or less at home."

Sasha's and the Rutilovs' lie soon was finally confirmed by a terrible event which took place at the Peredonov house. It definitely convinced the townsfolk
that all the rumors about Sasha and the Rutilov girls
had been the ravings of a madman.

32 : ༄‿༄‿

It was a cold, bleak day. Peredonov was returning from
Volodin's. He was tormented with grief. Vershina enticed Peredonov into her garden. He submitted again

to her sorceress's call. The two walked towards the summerhouse along the wet paths covered by broad, dark, decaying leaves. The summerhouse smelled unpleasantly damp. From behind the bare trees could be seen the house with its closed windows.

"I wish to tell you the truth," mumbled Vershina, quickly glancing at Peredonov and then turning away her dark eyes. She was wrapped in a black jacket, and she had a black kerchief tied around her head. Her lips, blue from cold and holding a black cigarette holder, emitted thick clouds of black smoke.

"I'll spit on your truth. Nothing would please me more than to spit on it," replied Peredonov.

Vershina smiled crookedly and retorted, "You don't say! I feel terribly sorry for you—you've been deceived." Gleeful malevolence could be heard in her voice. The spiteful words poured from her tongue. "You were hoping to receive patronage, but you acted too trustfully," she said. "They fooled you, and you swallowed it easily. It's very easy for anyone to write a letter. You should have known with whom you were dealing. Your spouse is an unscrupulous person."

Peredonov understood Vershina's mumbled speech with difficulty, and her meaning scarcely managed to come to him through all her circumlocutions. Vershina was afraid to speak loudly and clearly—if she did, someone might overhear and tell Varvara, and, as Varvara would not hesitate to make a scandal, unpleasantness might be the result. Also, if she spoke clearly, Peredonov himself would get angry and, perhaps, even beat her. It was better to hint and let him guess for himself. But Peredonov did not guess. People had told him to his face before that he had been duped, but he was utterly unable to comprehend that the letters had been forged and thought only that the Princess herself was deceiving him and leading him by the nose.

Finally Vershina said bluntly, "So you think that

the Princess sent those letters? Well the whole town already knows that Grushina forged them at your wife's request—the Princess had nothing to do with it. Everyone knows, ask whomever you want. They're all gossiping about it. And afterwards, Varvara Dmitrievna filched the letters from you and burned them so that there would be no traces."

Heavy, dark thoughts tossed about in Peredonov's brain. He understood only one thing: he had been deceived. But that the Princess had nothing to do with it—no, she did. Otherwise, why did she appear alive out of the fire?

"You lie about the Princess," he said. "I burned her, but I didn't finish the job—she spat at me."

Suddenly a horrible rage took possession of Peredonov. Deceived! He struck the table savagely with his fist, and, without saying good-bye to Vershina, he dashed away and rushed home. Vershina joyfully watched him go, and black clouds of smoke floated from her dark mouth and diffused and swirled away in the wind.

Rage consumed Peredonov. But when he saw Varvara, an agonizing fear possessed him, and he was unable to say a word.

The next morning, Peredonov got a small garden knife in a leather case and carefully put it into his pocket. He spent the entire morning until lunchtime at Volodin's, watching him work and making stupid comments. Volodin was always glad whenever Peredonov spent time with him, and Peredonov's stupid remarks seemed witty to him.

All day the *nedotykomka* bustled around Peredonov. It would not let him nap after dinner. It completely wore him out. When towards evening he was almost asleep, he was awakened by a frolicsome, snub-nosed, hideous peasant woman who had come from somewhere unknown to him. She approached his bed and muttered, "The *kvas* must be fermented, the tarts must be taken out, the roast must be cooked." Her cheeks were dark, but her teeth glittered.

"Go to hell!" screamed Peredonov.

The snub-nosed woman disappeared as though she had never existed.

It was evening. A melancholy wind whistled in the chimney. A slow, quiet rain sounded steadily against the windows. Outside the windows it was totally dark. Volodin was at the Peredonovs'—Peredonov had invited him for tea that morning.

"Let no one in. Understand, Klavdiushka?" shouted Peredonov.

Varvara sneered.

"All sorts of crones are playing around here," muttered Peredonov. "We must keep a careful lookout. One of them got into my bedroom and wanted to be hired as a cook. But what do I need a snub-nosed cook for?"

Volodin laughed in his bleating way and said, "Peasant women may walk in the street, but they have nothing to do with us, and we won't let them come to our table."

All three sat down at the table and began to drink vodka and snack on tarts. They drank more than they ate. Peredonov was in a dismal mood. Already everything was a meaningless, chaotic, unpredictable nightmare for him. His head ached terribly. One picture constantly repeated itself—Volodin was his enemy. One thought continually pounded at him—he must kill Pavlushka before it was too late. Then all their malevolent cunning would be revealed. Meanwhile Volodin was quickly becoming drunk and was talking nonsense, to the amusement of Varvara.

Peredonov was uneasy. "Someone is coming," he muttered. "Let no one in. Tell them that I have gone to pray at the Cockroach Monastery."

He was afraid that visitors would interfere. Volodin and Varvara were amused—they thought that he was only drunk. They winked at one another and walked out separately. They knocked on the door, and asked in altered voices, "Is General Peredonov at home?"

"A diamond medal for General Peredonov."

But Peredonov had no use for a medal today. "Don't let them come in!" he screamed. "Chase them away. Let them bring it in the morning. Now is not the time."

"No," he thought, "I must conserve my strength today. Today will reveal everything, but meanwhile my enemies are ready to send everything and anything against me in order to make sure they destroy me."

"Well, we drove them away. They'll bring it tomorrow morning," said Volodin as he again sat down behind the table.

Peredonov fixed his dull eyes on him and asked, "Are you my friend or my enemy?"

"Friend, friend, Ardasha!" replied Volodin.

"Even a true friend's a cockroach in the end," said Varvara.

"Not a cockroach, but a ram," corrected Peredonov. "Well, let's drink together, Pavlusha, just the two of us. And you drink too, Varvara—we'll drink together, the two of us."

Volodin snickered. "If Varvara drinks with us, then it'll come out three, not two."

"Two," repeated Peredonov sullenly.

"A husband and wife make one devil," said Varvara, and she laughed loudly.

Until the very last moment Volodin did not suspect that Peredonov wished to cut his throat. He bleated, cavorted, said stupid things, and amused Varvara. But Peredonov throught about his knife all evening. When Volodin or Varvara approached him on the side where he had the knife hidden, Peredonov would scream fiercely to make them go away. Sometimes he pointed to his pocket and said, "I have a joke here, Pavlushka, that will make you quack."

Varvara and Volodin laughed.

"I'm always able to quack, Ardasha," said Volodin. "Quack, quaack. It's really very simple."

Red and drunk from the vodka, Volodin quacked and protruded his lips. He was becoming more and more insolent towards Peredonov.

"They made a fool of you, Ardasha," he said with contemptuous pity.

"I'll fool you!" shouted Peredonov wildly.

Volodin appeared terrible and ominous to him. He had to defend himself. Peredonov quickly drew out the knife, threw himself upon Volodin, and sliced his throat. The blood spurted forth in a stream.

Peredonov was frightened. The knife dropped out of his hands. Volodin was bleating steadily and attempting to reach his throat with his hands. It was evident that he was mortally frightened and that he was growing weaker. His hands were not going to reach his throat. Suddenly he grew deathly pale and toppled onto Peredonov. There was an intermittent squeal as though he were choking, and then—quiet.

Peredonov shrieked in terror, and then Varvara shrieked too. Peredonov pushed Volodin away. He fell to the floor with a thud. He groaned, moved his feet, and was soon dead. His open eyes stared glassily straight up. The cat came out of the adjoining room, sniffed the blood, and mewed evilly. Varvara stood as though she were mesmerized. Klavdiya rushed in because of the noise.

"Ooooh!" she wailed. "They've cut his throat."

Varvara came to her senses and with a scream ran out of the dining room with Klavdiya.

News of what had happened spread quickly. Neighbors gathered in the street and the yard. Bolder ones entered the house, but for a long time they did not dare go into the dining room. They peered in and whispered. Peredonov was looking at the corpse with his demented eyes. He heard the whispers behind the door. . . . A dull sadness tormented him. He had no thoughts.

Finally they grew bolder and went in—Peredonov was sitting with his head hanging, mumbling something incoherent and meaningless.

Notes

1. The Russian title of the novel, *Melky bes*, is not easily rendered in English. The adjective *melky* is both qualitative (petty) and quantitative (divided into minute portions). One alternative translation, therefore, could be *A Very Common Demon* with "common" understood in its double sense. Also, the Russian language is far richer in demonology than ours. *Bes*, an evil spirit of comparatively low standing, may be derived from the Latin *bestia*. In any case, the word *bes* acquired a marked satirical connotation during the reign of Peter the Great when European standards of dress were forcibly introduced among the upper classes. A person dressed in this strange, "un-Russian" manner was often called a *bes*. Thus the *bes* is frequently a rather human sort of devil. Pushkin's use of *melky bes* in *Evgeny Onegin* (VII, 26): "Oh, how he flattered Tanya/ He showered praise like a petty demon" and Gogol's phrase, "to drive up like a petty demon," help to convey the sense of Sologub's title. Another, freer translation of it might be *An Unclean Spirit*.

2. The quotation at the front of the novel is taken from the following poem:

> *I wished to burn her, the wicked witch*
> *But she called forth evil words—*
> *I saw her, again living,*
> *Her head all in flame and sparks.*
>
> *And saying: I did not burn—*
> *The fire renewed my charms.*
> *I take my body, nourished by the flames,*
> *Away from the blaze to my sorcery.*

And as I go, the flame grows dim
In the folds of my magic garments.
Fool! You'll not find your hopes
In my mysteries.—

Sologub wrote the poem on June 12, 1902, presumably upon the completion of the novel.

3. THE AUTHOR'S INTRODUCTION TO THE SECOND EDITION

My novel, *The Petty Demon*, was begun in 1892 and was finished in 1902. It was published for the first time in the periodical, *Voprosy zhizni*, for 1905 (Numbers 6-11), but without the final chapters. In its complete form the novel appeared for the first time in the *Shipovnik* edition in March, 1907.

In the printed and verbal opinions which I came to hear, I have observed two contrary opinions:

One group thinks that the author, being a very depraved man, desired to paint his own portrait and has portrayed himself in the character of the schoolteacher, Peredonov. Because of his sincerity, the author did not wish to justify or romanticize himself in any way, and that is why he has smeared his image with the darkest colors. He performed this strange undertaking to ascend a kind of Calvary and there to suffer for some reason. The result was an interesting and harmless novel.

Interesting, because it shows what sort of people there are in the world. Harmless, because the reader can say, "This was not written about me."

Others, not so unkind to the author, think that the image of Peredonovism in the novel is a rather widespread phenomenon.

Some even think that each of us, who has carefully examined himself, will discover in him unquestionable streaks of Peredonov.

Of these two opinions, I show preference to that one which is the more pleasing to me, namely the latter. I was not compelled to imagine or make up a story from within myself. Each episode in my novel, whether moral or psychological, was created from very careful observations, and I had sufficient "models" for my novel around me. And if my work on the novel has been particularly drawn out, it was only to elevate to the deliberate that which occurred by chance, so that the austere Ananke should reign upon the throne of Aisa, the scatterer of tales.

It's true that people love to be loved. It is pleasing to them when the sides of their character which are the noblest and most lofty are shown. And even in villains they want to see glimpses of good—"God's spark"—as they said in olden times. That is why they find it hard to believe when there is placed before them a picture which is true, accurate, somber, evil. They wish to say, "He has written this about himself."

No, my dear contemporaries, it is of you that I have written my novel about the petty demon and its frightening *nedotykomka*, about Ardal'on and Varvara Peredonov, Pavel Volodin, Dar'ya, Ludmila, and Valeriya Rutilova, Aleksandr Pyl'nikov, and the rest. It is of you.

This novel is a mirror which has been skillfully constructed. I have been working on it diligently, polishing it for a long time.

The surface of my mirror is level and clean. It was continually measured and carefully checked—it does not have a single imperfection.

The ugly and the beautiful are reflected in it with exactly the same accuracy. (Jan., 1908)

4. INTRODUCTION TO THE FIFTH EDITION

It once seemed to me that Peredonov's career was finished and that he would not leave the psychiatric hospital where they placed him after he had cut Volodin's throat. But very recently rumors have reached me to the effect that Peredonov's mental illness proved to be only temporary and that after a short time he was released. Rumors, of course, cannot be depended upon. I mention them only because in our times even the improbable occurs. I even read in one newspaper that I am preparing to write a sequel to *The Petty Demon* (*Sologub is referring to an interview which appeared in the "Birzhevye vedomosti," Oct. 16, 1908—A.F.*)

I have heard that Varvara has apparently succeeded in convincing someone that Peredonov had cause to act as he did, that Volodin had on several occasions said objectionable things and betrayed shocking intentions—and that, prior to his death, he had said something incredibly shocking which led to the fatal mishap. With this story, I am told, Varvara gained the interest of Princess Volchanskaya, who, although she had previously neglected to put in a word for Peredonov, now took an active interest in his fate.

My information as to what became of Peredonov after his release from the hospital is uncertain and contradictory. Some have told me that Peredonov entered the police department, as Skuchaev had advised, and was a councilor in a provincial district. Supposedly he distinguished himself in some way or other in this job and has a good career before him.

From others, however, I have heard that it is not Ardal'on Borisych but another Peredonov, a relative of ours, who is in the police department. Ardal'on Borisych himself did not succeed in entering the service, or perhaps he did not want to. He has, they say, become a literary critic. His articles reveal those same qualities by which he distinguished himself previously.

This rumor strikes me as being even more unlikely than the first.

At any rate, if I succeed in receiving definite information concerning Peredonov's present activity, I shall relate it in full detail. (1909)

5. DIALOGUE (TO THE SEVENTH EDITION)

'My soul, why are you so dismayed?'

'Because of the hostility which surrounds the name of the author of *The Petty Demon*. Many people who disagree in everything else concur in this.'

'Accept the malice and the abuse quietly.'

'But is not our labor worthy of gratitude? Why all this hostility?'

'The hostility resembles fear. You jar the conscience too strongly. You are too frank.'

'But is there not benefit in my truthfulness?'

'You are seeking compliments! But this is not Paris!'

'Oh yes, this is not Paris!'

'You, my soul, are a true Parisienne, a child of European civilization. You have worn a fancy dress and light sandals to a place where they wear peasant blouses and greased boots. Don't be surprised then if a greased boot sometimes steps rudely on your tender foot. Its owner is an honest chap.'

'But how morose, how coarse he is!' (May, 1913)

6. In Sologub's trilogy, *The Created Legend,* we are to meet Peredonov once more. He is the same Peredonov, but he has actually received patronage and is the vice-governor of the province, a job for which he seems eminently well suited. There is even a rumor that he will soon be made a governor. Only the first part of the trilogy has been translated in English (see Introduction). My article, *"The Created Legend: Sologub's Symbolic Universe"* (*Slavic and East European Journal,* Winter, 1961), contains a précis of the complete work.

FYODOR SOLOGUB *was the pen name of Fyodor Kuz'mich Teternikov. He was born in 1863 in St. Petersburg. His father, a tailor, died four years later, and his mother became a domestic servant. The family for which she worked had broad intellectual tastes and took an interest in her precocious child, eventually helping to send him to a St. Petersburg teachers' college. He began to teach and to contribute to the support of his mother and sister when he was only nineteen. In 1899 he was promoted to the post of school inspector. By this time his work was appearing in well known literary periodicals. But only with the publication of* The Petty Demon *was Sologub finally able to retire from teaching and devote himself entirely to literature. Together with Dmitri Merezhkovsky, Zinaida Gippius, Konstantin Bal'mont, Nikolai Minsky, and Valery Briusov, he was a member of the so-called first generation of the Russian symbolist movement. After the 1917 revolution, Sologub, who vehemently opposed the Bolsheviks, was unable to obtain a visa to leave the country. In 1921 his wife, despairing in the futility of their situation, committed suicide. Although by now he could no longer publish at all, Sologub still continued to write, and, after his death in December, 1927, friends managed to have his papers deposited in the* Pushkinsky dom, *a literary archive in Leningrad. Little is known about this material.*

ANDREW FIELD, *the translator of this edition was born in New Jersey in 1938. He attended Columbia College and Columbia University from which he received his M.A. degree. He is presently in the Russian Literature Department at Harvard University, and has translated works by Soviet authors including those of Leonov, Zhdanov and Chukovsky.*

MIDLAND BOOKS